2

COWL

Also by Neal Asher

The Parasite
Runcible Tales
The Engineer
Mindgames: Fool's Mate
Gridlinked
The Skinner
The Line of Polity

COWL

Neal Asher

TOR

First published 2004 by Tor
an imprint of Pan Macmillan Ltd
Pan Macmillan, 20 New Wharf Road, London N1 9RR
Basingstoke and Oxford
Associated companies throughout the world
www.panmacmillan.com
www.toruk.com

ISBN 1 4050 0137 2 (HB)
ISBN 1 4050 4805 0 (TPB)

1 3 5 7 9 8 6 4 2

A CIP catalogue record for this book is available from
the British Library.

Typeset by SetSystems Ltd, Saffron Walden, Essex
Printed and bound in Great Britain by
Mackays of Chatham plc, Chatham, Kent

In memoriam
Alan Henry Wood
1941–2003

Acknowledgements

As ever, my thanks to Caroline for her support and for being there, to my parents as first readers and critics, and to Peter Lavery for that scary pencil and all those fish-and-chip suppers. Also thanks to all the usual suspects at Macmillan including in no particular order: Stefanie Bierwerth, Dusty Miller, James Hollywell and Steve Rawlings, Jason Cooper, Chantal Noel, Vivienne Nelson, Rebecca Saunders, Liz Cowen, and many others. And further thanks to John Jarrold for castinbg a judicious eye over the typescript

1

Engineer Goron:
From what I have learnt from the two survivors, we have to find another way to attack Cowl. The first of the group took with them a fusion and displacement generator to punch through into interspace to provide an energy tap. This was so subsequent travellers could arrive accurately at the same location – the inaccuracy of time travel increasing proportionally to the temporal distance from a suitable energy source. In this they succeeded. But being able to transport only a few personnel and small amounts of equipment on each trip, it still took them too long to establish a base. The preterhuman detected the tap and sent his pet – now grown into something titanic. It killed them on Earth and in interspace as they fled. Ate them alive.

A storm was opening white-hot cracks in the basalt sky and soon the rain would be etching all exposed metal. Polly knew she should get undercover, as such acidic downpours made all but synthetic clothing degrade to the strength of wet blotting paper, caused hair to fall out and laid rashes across a person's scalp. After grinding out her cigarette, she pulled her rain film from its cigar-sized cartridge and suddenly felt a loneliness the vodka had failed to dispel. It was at times like this that she most missed Marjae: they would have headed back to the flat to split a block of Moroccan, drink coffee and jaw away the evening before setting out for the night trade.

When Polly had lost her virginity at the age of eleven, her mother, a Christian Scientist, spent the next year trying to beat the sin out of her. At the age of twelve Polly spent several months stealing all the money she could without arousing suspicion, packed her rucksack with portable valuables and left her mother lying on the repro lino with an antique stainless-steel vegetable knife in her groin and the instruction to pray for stitches. As far as she was concerned she'd never really had a mother and the only person she valued any more than herself had been Marjae. But now there was only shadow.

With her rain film belling out around her and her hood up, Polly headed back through streets already turning slick with a cloudy drizzle. Every now and again a gust of wind wafted the smell of sulphur dioxide from where the acid in the falling rain reacted with discarded Coke cans or other garbage. In a few minutes she reached the door to her tenement, fumbled her keycard into its slot, then shouldered the door open. In the cold light cast by everlasting bulbs she climbed the stairs with her hand ready on the small taser in her handbag. She'd been rolled in here before and she wasn't going to let it happen again. Reaching the plastic door to her flat, she checked behind her before using the card again and entering.

'Lights,' she said, quickly closing the door behind her. The lights flickered on just in time to reveal the man in Task Force fatigues as he stepped up close to her and slammed her back against the door.

'Nandru!' She was more surprised than scared, but that soon changed.

'You touch it, you know, and it calls to you . . . calls to you all the time,' he hissed, his breath rank, his eyes not tracking properly.

'Nandru . . . what is it?'

His hair was filthy and there was a week's stubble on his chin. He looked out of it – on something.

'But *they* are U-gov – straight out of Brussels,' he said. 'Vat grown, I'd bet.'

'I don't know what you're talking about,' Polly said.

'You know what it means to be hunted?' he snarled.

She shook her head.

He gestured with the gun as if for emphasis, but when he did so, Polly flinched. This wasn't his usual UN-issue stunner, nor was it hardware commonly found on the streets. Polly recognized the weapon as a favourite in the latest smash-em-up VR interactives: it was a MOG 5, a weapon that fired depleted uranium bullets, seeker rounds, and mini high-yield grenades capable of turning a house to pebble-sized rubble – if the interactives, the ints, were to be believed.

'Do you know?' he yelled.

Polly stared at his bloodshot eyes and ravaged face, then lowered her gaze to the cluster of barrels he was waving under her chin. She carefully reached out and pushed him away, then, unhooking her handbag, stepped past him to the sofa, where she sat down. She found her lighter and cigarettes, lit up and blew a plume of smoke.

'Why don't you tell me?' she said, slurring only a little despite the vodka she'd been downing all evening.

He gestured with the miniature Gatling barrels towards the window – streaked now with neon-lit rain, the colours changing every second as the bar sign across the street went through its sequence. Walking over to the pane, he stood silhouetted against it for a moment.

'It's all shit,' he said. 'If it's hunting you, you're nothing – you don't mean anything to the future. You're just a taste, a scrap of protein, and there's nothing you can do – *nothing*. Christ, we're just fucking morsels to it, and it can have us any time it likes. It's going to have me. It knows it. I know it. Just a game to it.'

Still by the window, he leant his shoulder against the frame, the gun resting in the crook of his right arm. With his left hand he reached out and smeared the condensation on the glass – it was hot in her flat – and he sighed, suddenly looking very tired. This had to be about Marjae.

Because of their trade, she and Polly had received the World Health download for free. Polly had watched it during an evening taken off to allow the prescribed drugs she was taking to clear up her latest recurrence of herpes – contracted before Marjae had finished training her in the hygiene discipline of their trade. The most recent and rugged HIV caused New AIDS, the download had informed her. This particular bug could survive outside the human body for as long as an hour and could be passed on with the same ease as hepatitis A. Public toilets came under stringent health restrictions and in some levels of society it was already fashionable to wear masks outside the home. On the street there was a rumour that the virus was able to survive in the proboscis of a mosquito and that this information had been suppressed. It wasn't a new rumour. Marjae was found to be HIV positive during her monthly test a year after they'd laughed at that download – presented by a supercilious doctor program – and they'd been certain that they were not stupid enough to end up infected. She died from one of the pneumonias a year after that. PS 24 probably, as that was the one rife at the time. It was Marjae, Polly remembered, who had observed, 'The man said it's like the wars, y'know? We're getting wise enough to number 'em.'

Marjae: lying skeletal on a bed in the confinement hospital. One last little chat while she lay with the euthanizer in her lap, a finger poised over the button. Polly's replies muffled by the surgical mask she wore.

'It ain't easy any more. It'll kill you. Get out. Get out while you can.'

Her finger rattled on the button until a little red light came on, and the killing drugs shot through the pipes to her catheter. Ten minutes later she was asleep, ten minutes after that she was dead and, Polly realized as she left the hospital, in another half-hour Marjae would be in the incinerator. Those hospitals had a high turnover and U-gov efficiency targets to meet.

When Marjae euthanized, Nandru had been out with Task Force, cauterizing the latest haemorrhage of fanaticism spreading from oil wells run dry. He must blame her for his sister's death. Polly decided she needed something a little stronger to get her through whatever was coming. From the back of her cigarette packet she pulled her last H-patch, stripped off the backing and pressed it into the crook of her arm.

'Look . . . I'm sorry about Marjae,' she said.

He turned from the window and stared at her in confused bewilderment, then his expression sharpened when he saw what she was doing.

'You stupid ignorant little bitch. You want to end up like my sister?' he sneered.

'AIDS and sep,' she managed as she pressed the H-patch tighter against her skin and shuddered with expected pleasure. 'She was jabbing. That's real dumb.'

'So *you're* the sensible girl?' he hissed at her.

Irony, that was. Polly knew what irony was, even now. The hit from the patch was weak; it in fact seemed to sober her rather than take her anywhere pleasant. She needed to use the chaser – the second patch – but knew that to do so would probably further piss off Nandru. He moved close now, leaning over her.

'Well, sensible girl . . . I've seen it, stretching further than the eye can see: a hell of flesh and teeth and bone and, of course, the scales. Just a glimpse, mind. Just a glimpse past the feeding mouth it used to take four Binpots, then Leibnitz, Smith . . . Patak.'

Fucking insane.

She must have lost it for a moment then because when she

came back Nandru was sitting on the arm of the sofa, the weapon resting greasily against one of her cushions. In his hand he held an object that glittered.

'. . . too much of a literary reference, don't you think?'

'What? What?'

He was staring at her again with that sick crazy look. 'I haven't got time and you're too smashed to understand.' He reached into the pocket of his fatigues, took out a roll of money, and showed it to her. 'You get this after you've followed my instructions. I'd give it to you right now, but I know you'd be useless to me if I did. Hopefully I can get this done before it gets me. You see, I'm a marked man – I've been selected from the fat stock.' He paused, suddenly looking very angry. 'You know, they didn't give a fuck about the rest of us – had us confined and wired so they could watch and learn while it took us. Well, I'll take *them*. You just watch me.'

Polly stared at him in bewilderment. Some animal had killed his men and was hunting him. Who were *they*? Different from the animal? What was he talking about? She eyed the money as he slipped it back into his pocket.

'I took it to our place, you see. You remember? Our party place before the two of you went shit out . . .' He leaned closer and shook her hard. 'Do you remember!'

'Yeah! Yeah, I remember. Back off, for fuck's sake!'

She'd sucked down a real interesting piece of blotting paper while camping out in the Anglia Reforest. Why it was called that she had no idea, as there hadn't been forest there before the flood and the reclamation. East Anglia had been mega-fields and factory complexes stretching from the outskirts of London to the coast. Maybe the name referred to the far past; way back pre-millennial, before the European space station and the Big Heat, back when knights in armour charged after dinosaurs and all that crap. Polly was hazy about the details.

Their camp had been next to a ruin that was little more than half-collapsed breeze-block and brick cavity walls, the cavities packed with estuary mud sprouting stinging nettles and thistles. This ruin had stood in the shadow of a thermal generating tower, built there when the place had still been under water. The holiday had been Marjae's idea. They'd spent two days on bennies and disiacs, partying with Nandru and one of his comrades from the Task Force: screwing amid the rough grass and stinging nettles, stopping only when the chemicals ran out and they began to feel real sore.

'The old house under the tower,' Nandru reminded her. 'I won't tell you exactly, in case they put a bend on you. I'll instruct you when you lead them there. You know, they didn't dare feed it . . . kept it in Isolation while they studied it.'

Polly accepted that there was some valuable object out there and that somehow she would be involved. She smelt money. She smelt danger. Now she turned her attention to the glittery thing he held.

'This is state, diamond state. They got some in Delta Force and maybe in the SAS. Like I said before, they're called Muses.' He must have told her when she was out of it. She studied what he was holding out to her. In his palm rested a fancy ear stud and a teardrop of aluminium the size of a cigarette lighter. 'It's AI, got about a hundred terabytes of reference, can fuck any idiot silicon within five metres.' He caught her by the shoulder and pressed the teardrop into the hollow at the base of her throat. It hurt. It hurt a lot.

'What is it? What are you doing?'

He was at her handbag and in a moment had found what he wanted. He held up the second patch for her to see, and she nodded, choking as the pain spread from the base of her throat to the back of her neck, as if someone was slowly sawing off her head. Moving in front of her, he parted her legs, then reached up to press the patch against her inner thigh, just hidden there by her leather pelmet. DP they called it: double patching. The second patch was an 'endorph gate naltraxone derivative' – or a 'pearly', to those who used them. It reactivated over-backed neural receptors, brought the H-hit back on line; made it like it was. The pain faded and Polly lay back to stare at the pretty lights. Vaguely she heard a door open and close.

At five in the morning Polly woke on the sofa with post-euphoric depression, undressed and went to bed in a foetal coil round the pain in the top of her chest. She didn't know what Nandru had done, but she could feel the metal lump bedded above her breastbone. She tried to get back to sleep, but as well as the pain everything else nagged at her: not only was Marjae's brother back on the scene with some serious weaponry and a serious fuck-up in his head, but there were the prosaic and sordid facts of her everyday life.

The rent was overdue, she'd used the last of her patches, her DSS card had been revoked because she'd been caught soliciting without a U-gov licence, and now the Revenue were after her for back taxes for the 'public service' she had provided. But she was determined they were not going to get her on any of the social projects, which was the usual way things went in this situation. She had friends who'd done that and who were classified bankrupt, the result of this being revocation of citizenship and full indenture to U-gov. The chains were plastic cards, location torcs, but nobody dared call it slavery.

At seven Polly rolled out of bed and got herself moving. She kept herself busy to hold depression at bay. Without somagum she had no chance of sleep now. Anyway, the temperature was in the upper twenties already and the day looked likely to be a holezoner. Standing before her grimy mirror, she studied the ear stud Nandru must have inserted in her lobe while she was stoned.

It looked a lot nicer than her usual topaz so she left it in place, before turning her attention to the teardrop of metal. With her hardened fingernail, she tried to lever it up from her skin, but it was stuck solid there. He must have used skin bond – the stuff comedians had put on public toilet seats before all the public toilets were closed down. No doubt she would see him again sometime when she wasn't out of her skull and he wasn't out of his, then she could demand an explanation. For now it could ride: there was the morning trade to catch and she had work to do.

She dressed in absorbent knickers, loose vest and padded knee boots, then sat in front of her mirror and did her face. Her flat was squalid and her credit breadline, but she was proud of the fact that she could sling on any old charity-shop rag and, with a bit of eyeliner and lipgloss, look good enough to walk into Raffles or Hothouse. She grinned at herself, exposing her white and even teeth. Best thousand euros she'd ever spent, having those done: no tooth decay, nothing stuck to their frictionless surfaces, and no pain. And the force of the blow required to break them would likely kill her, so she had no worries on that score. Suitably tarted she strapped on her waterproof hip bag and stocked it with the essentials of street survival. Into it went condoms, tissues and spermicidal spray, a neat Toshiba taser the size of a pistol grip, her smart cards, money, cigarettes and lighter, and her last joint. She would save the joint to haze things for the inevitable rich ugly bastard she usually ended up blowing. Thus set she headed out into the streets of Maldon Island.

Granny's Kitchen had only just opened by the time she arrived. She sat near the window and tapped up coffee and toast on the holographic menu that had appeared in the glass top of the table as soon as she sat down. Windows opened from each of these asking how she would like them prepared. She punched her selection then 'send' before any more windows could open. When her order arrived Polly ate one of the slices of toast and shoved the other aside, before lighting up her first cigarette of the day. Smoking and sipping coffee, she watched the street.

Already the island town was filling up with foot traffic and those zero-carbon hydrocars allowed within the town limits. After her second cup of coffee and second cigarette, Polly decided it was time to go to work. She quickly left Granny's and walked up the High Street with her hips swaying. Within a few minutes she had taken up her usual position outside the Reformed Church of Hubbard. There she stood with her hand on her hip and smoked yet another cigarette. She had been told that no one smoked a cigarette quite so provocatively as she did. Her first customer approached her ten minutes later.

'I need a blow job real bad,' he said. Polly recognized him from the week before. By his businesswear, he was an executive of TCC, and carried on a shoulder strap a laptop disguised as an old book.

'Fifty,' said Polly, upping her price by ten euros.

'OK.'

Polly led the way round the back of the church. As she went she sprayed spermicide in her mouth and left her hip bag open so she could grab the taser at any moment. The alley behind the church was scented by the blossoms of a jasmine sprouting wild up one synthewood wall. On the cobbles were used H-patches, the slimy remnants of degrading condoms, gum wrappers and a smashed VR helmet. Polly noted a splash of blood on the walls and on the leaves of the nearby vine before turning to her customer and taking a condom from her bag. He was already undoing his trousers. She knelt down in front of him, grateful for the padding in her knee boots. It didn't take long, and after she'd cast the condom in a corner to degrade with the rest of them, he transferred the money straight across to her card.

'See you next week?' he asked, eyeing her almost possessively.

She remained wary and noncommittal, and deliberately sprayed spermicide in her mouth while he was watching to bring home to him the basis of their relationship. She'd had hassle before with a guy who got too hooked into her and started causing problems. When he was on his way, she took up her station again. By midday she'd made seven hundred euros. Not bad, even though the last hundred had left her walking somewhat gingerly. She reminded herself not to forget her gel next time. And as she walked away she promised herself to give this all up before she turned sixteen. That still gave her six months' leeway.

With customary eagerness Polly headed back to her flat. She'd made good money this morning and turned half of it into DPs, an eighth of Moroccan, ten fifty-gram packs of rolling tobacco plus papers – her local smuggler had been out of packet cigarettes – and a litre of Metaxa. Niggling at her conscience was the thought that she should have put some of the money aside for the rent and taxes, but she'd worked hard providing for the pleasure of others and now it was time to provide for herself.

Online tactical. Tech-com unavailable. Instruct?

Polly whirled round from the door, groping in her hip bag for her taser, but there was no one standing behind her. She surveyed the street, her attention finally coming to rest on the customers sitting at the tables outside the bar across the road. A few men were looking at her, but that was nothing unusual: dressed as she was, there were few men who wouldn't give her the eye. No one over there was laughing, so it likely wasn't some joker there with a directional speaker. It also seemed unlikely that she'd been targeted by advertising com. Turning back to the door she used her keycard, and was quickly inside.

Going mute until further instructions.

'Fuck! Who is that?'

There was now no one anywhere in direct line – no one to

point a directional speaker at her. That meant there had to be a phone hidden nearby.

Muse 184, came the toneless reply.

'What the hell is this?' Polly asked, but something was nibbling at her memory. Hadn't Nandru mentioned the word 'Muse'? She tried to recall the conversation, but found there were blank and hazy spots, as there always seemed to be nowadays. Suddenly she remembered the gun he had carried: state-of-the-art hardware like in the interactives. And what were those other things they called 'Little Buddies'? She touched the metal at the base of her throat. Shit, what the hell had he given her?

'Who is that speaking to me?' she asked.

Muse 184, came the reply again.

'What the fuck are you?'

Adaptech AI Muse 184 tactical and reference system. Interdiction enabled. Note: tech-com is unavailable and should be reported to com central. Instruct?

'Shut up!'

Going mute until further instructions.

Polly ran up the stairs to her flat, fumbling her card to get her through the door. As she dropped her shopping on the sofa and sat down beside it, she was shaking. After a moment she took out a foil-wrapped block of resin, opened a pack of tobacco, and began making a joint – the familiar action calmed her shaking more than the smoke she eventually took in. She tried hard to think straight. According to Marjae, Nandru had been hinting about an important job he'd got in Task Force, so he must have been into something a bit more serious than smearing a few Binpots. But it didn't make sense. Why had he come here, to her, and fixed on her this . . . thing? Suddenly she had an idea.

'Muse, er, I want to . . . take you off me,' she said.

Awaiting detach code.

That was no good then. 'Go mute,' she said.

Going mute until further instructions.

Shaking her head, Polly stood and walked over to the the kitchen area, found a glass, then back at the sofa filled it to the brim with Metaxa. After draining half of that she began to think about the patches tucked into the secret compartment at the back of her hip bag. On another level she knew that none of this constant intake was helping her to think about her problem – she was just abandoning thought altogether.

Polly, time to rock and roll.

'I thought I told you to go mute,' she said with irritation. Then she realized what she had just heard. 'Nandru?'

Yeah, your ever loving. You didn't think I teched you up with forty grand of hardware just so's you could look pretty? This is utterly untraceable.com. Anything else and they'd have zeroed me in seconds.

'What the hell are you talking about, Nandru?'

Within the next hour some serious scumbags are going to be paying you a visit. You see, your Muse was mine and it's bugged, and thinking they're tracing me they'll find you. Shame I can't do that myself with the monster, but at least I'll be wiping up some shit.

'You've done this because of Marjae,' said Polly. She then downed the last of her brandy, shoved the cigarette makings into her hip bag and headed for the door – if someone nasty was going to find her she'd rather be out in the open and visible to lots of witnesses.

You're wrong there, my little slot machine. You're my mouthpiece and my goat. When they find you, they'll ask you where I am and where I stashed the fucking scale they want so badly. You'll tell them the truth and lead them to our place, and through you I'll talk to them.

He was talking crazy again? Scale? She was halfway down the stairs before she asked, 'And when you've given them what they want, what happens to me?'

Don't worry, you'll live if you do just exactly what I tell you. Also, you don't really have much choice in the matter: you cannot remove

Muse, so they will find you. And if you don't follow instructions, they'll take you away and peel your skull until there's nothing left.

Outside in the blazing afternoon of the street Polly shaded her eyes and, once a gap appeared in the stream of hydrocars, headed across the road to the bar. The place had a reputation for being a bit retro, hence the sinister look of many of the alfresco patrons in their mirror shades and wrap-arounds. Finding a plastic chair that had been tucked under one of the outside tables, and so was not scalding to sit on, she took up a position with her back near the plate-glass window, where others gave her some cover and from where she had a view of the street. As soon as she sat down the table surface displayed a turning array of beer bottles and spirits. She tapped a bottle of Stella passing under her hand, then hit the edge of the display to turn it off. The table's appearance returned to its customary granite finish.

The waitress who came out with her beer eyed her dubiously. 'You know we don't allow . . .' began the girl, embarrassed.

'It's OK,' said Polly, dropping a five euro on her tray. 'I'm only here for the beer.'

The first swallow was rapture in that dusty heat. The breeze that suddenly began blowing was really nice as well. Polly tilted her head back to enjoy it and only then heard the low thrumming that accompanied it.

'Willya lookit that!' exclaimed the man at the table next to hers – the man who had been conspicuously not ogling her, since he was sitting opposite his wife or partner. A shadow drew across them and Polly opened her eyes to observe one of the new Ford Macrojets sliding across the sky above, its four turbines uncannily like eyes staring down into the street. The vehicle hovered for a while, then shot away to spiral down to the infrequently used connection platform up the hill and just off the High Street. It was predicted that in another ten years most traffic would have taken to the sky. This did not concern Polly as she had never accumulated enough money to afford even an electric scooter.

'There it is again!' said the man ten minutes later. 'Just like Bluebird.'

Polly didn't know what that meant but, as she observed the huge vehicle turning down from the High Street, even she was impressed. Such transport spoke of wealth she was sure she herself would never own. When it drew up in front of the bar, her instinct was to try and get herself into the car and hopefully get some taste of the riches it represented. But when she saw the four men who climbed out of it, she just wanted to run.

They were U-gov meat. Just like Nandru had said: they were straight out of the Agency in Brussels. They wore their grey suits and blue EU ties like a uniform, and what need had they of mirror shades when their eyes were mirrored? One of them, a blond-haired Adonis with an utterly blank expression, looked at the device in his hand, held it up for a moment, then abruptly pocketed it and walked over to Polly's table. But for hair colour, the one who followed him was in appearance indistinguishable, as were the two standing by the car. Illegal net-sheets had men like this down as the product of some strange eugenics project involving cloning and augmentation. Of course all the official news organizations decried that as hysterical rubbish, but then they had to if they wanted to stay in business.

Already other drinkers in the bar were finding their reasons to be elsewhere. The couple at the next table gulped their drinks and quickly grabbed their shopping. The blond man sat down opposite Polly. He blinked the mirroring from his eyes to expose calm grey. With an almost apologetic smile he reached inside his jacket and removed a short, ugly, seeker gun. Pointing it at her he flipped up the frame sight and clicked a button on the side of the weapon, before putting it down on the table. Polly observed the flashing LED, and she had played in enough interactives to know the gun had acquired her.

Interdiction online. Tech-com unavailable, Muse informed her, leaving her none the wiser.

Ah, I see our friends have arrived, said Nandru.

See? thought Polly.

'Where did you get that Muse?' said the heavy sitting opposite, at last.

Polly glanced around. All the other outside tables were now unoccupied. The waitress stepped out, then quickly ducked back inside when she saw her new customers. There were still people inside the bar, standing well back from the window and observing the scene. No help there. The only possible rescue in a situation like this would be to have a few hundred thousand to slip to a eurocrat, and even then . . .

'It was given to me by a Task Force soldier called Nandru Jurgens,' she said.

The man nodded slowly then said, 'And you're linked to him now, I take it?'

Polly nodded.

'Ask him how much,' said the man.

Polly tilted her head as she listened to what Nandru told her. Her mouth went dry and it took her a moment to get enough spit to repeat his message, 'Fifty million wired direct to Usbank account PX two hundred and three, two hundred and seven, forty. He also wants to know your name.'

The man now tilted his head for a moment, and Polly had no doubt that he was listening to voices inside it much like her own, for there was a small grey pill of an ear stud in his left lobe, and she doubted it was there for decoration.

'My name is Tack,' he said eventually. 'He must understand

that the transfer cannot be authorized until I have possession of the item.'

'I'm to take you to it,' said Polly.

Tack showed no change of expression and Polly thought: *I'm going to die.*

'I find that unlikely,' said Tack. 'What is to stop us taking the item once we have it in sight?'

'He says you'll see when you see.'

Tack picked up his gun, rose, and gestured with it to the Macrojet. Polly tried to seem casual by finishing off her beer, but it was warm now and she had difficulty in swallowing. She stood up and moved ahead of the blond man towards the car. Climbing inside, she found herself trapped between walls of identical muscle. The one called Tack sat in the front passenger seat, while the driver wound up the turbines to a howl and took the car into the sky. Polly doubted the traffic police would be hitting on this vehicle. Questions of legality with people like these remained that: questions only.

The probe, Carloon thought, resembled a barbed arrowhead he had once seen in a museum, but one from an immense arrow. Mounted on the launch platform that hung geostationary above equatorial Africa, it now stood separate from the gantries and maintenance pylons, supported only by the fuelling towers that were pumping in the deuterium oxide used in its initial fusion burn, and personnel were leaving the platform in stratocars and supply ships. Suited against vacuum, Carloon floated high above the platform on a line attached to a control tower on the first giant displacement ring. He wanted to see this as directly as possible and there was nothing more to do inside the tower now. The launch would either be successful or not. The 'not' case was the reason his personnel were leaving the platform. He looked up to where he could just see the second ring a thousand kilometres out from Earth.

'If we could use time travel, we could get the probe back before it went,' Maxell observed laconically over com.

Carloon glanced across to the second figure floating a few metres away from him. That she had come to see this showed the importance of the project to the Heliothane Dominion.

'But we can't,' was all he replied.

'Explain to me the reason for that,' Maxell instructed.

Carloon sighed. He himself was only just beginning to understand the possibilities and limitations inherent in the new science. Phasing matter and matter displacement he did understand, but such things as temporal inertia, short-circuit paradoxes, and the vorpal energy generated by life, were a little beyond him. 'As I understand it, time travel is easiest on Earth and becomes increasingly difficult the further you get from that centre of . . . vorpal generation. We can use it within a limited sphere, which encompasses most of the solar system surrounding Earth; beyond that the energy levels required climb exponentially.'

'But you are using an offshoot of that technology here?'

'Yes. We're using spatial displacement to shift the probe back to its launch point as it accelerates on its antigravity engines, while feeding it the energy to accelerate – which we couldn't do if it was heading out of the solar system. If we complete twenty successful displacements, the probe will be travelling at ninety-three per cent light speed when we finally let it go. We could have used temporal displacement between the rings as well, but that would only have reduced the mission time by less than one-hundredth, and would have used over four-fifths of the Earthgrid energy output.'

'That mission time being?'

Carloon repressed his irritation: Maxell knew all this. Rather than reply, he observed, 'The probe is launching.'

They both turned their attention to the geostationary platform, where the fuelling towers were rolling back under a haze of heavy-water vapour. Then the fug was lit by the bright burn of fusion engines igniting and the probe began to rise towards them on two spears of white flame. Behind it, on the platform, structures glowed and flared in the back-blast. This was a one-off launch. Carloon found his body tensing and his mouth going dry as the probe accelerated rapidly. In a minute it was close, then it passed through the displacement ring, travelling at five thousand kph, in eerie silence. He watched it rise high, accelerating for the next ring. When it was almost invisible, the fusion flames flicked out.

After taking a drink from the pipe by his mouth, he said, 'It now accelerates on AG only.'

'How long until the first displacement?' Maxell asked.

'Minutes, but we won't see much.'

'And how long before it arrives at its destination?'

'Sixteen years years before it reaches Proxima Centauri. But before we get any results . . .' Carloon shrugged.

Minutes later the probe reached the second displacement ring a thousand kilometres out. Space distorted in that ring and the probe just disappeared. Instantaneously it reappeared inside the first ring and continued to accelerate – its AG motors working against the gravity of Earth. Again and again it ran that course, energy being fed into it by microwave transmitters in the displacement rings themselves, enough energy to power a solar civilization for years. Finally that civilization let it go. The probe headed out into darkness, to confirm or deny a theory about the existence of life on Earth.

2

Astolere:
It was a move of desperation to attempt a ground assault on the Callisto facility, and one for which the Umbrathane have paid dearly. But we have yet to learn the full extent of the payment we might make in using this infant technology. My brother Saphothere's venture into the past, using one of the bioconstructs, we knew would have unforeseen consequences in itself. That he took with him an atomic weapon to place at the point of the assault force's arrival, we knew could only make things worse. Eight thousand of those ground troops died in the conflagration – and as for the rest of us? We now all have memories of two parallel events, while living in the future of only one. And we all now know that such manipulation of events, so close to us on the time-line, has pushed us down off the main line, and that we are one step closer to oblivion.

Tack was inherently immoral. He had been grown for immorality and trained for it. He knew the rules, all of them, and he knew how to break them with a thoroughness that was frightening. The rule he knew how to break most efficiently was 'Thou shalt not kill' or any legalese derivation of such.

Tack did not have a mother or father in the usual sense. He had been cloned from a particularly efficient CIA killer, and vat-grown two hundred years after that same killer had paid a visit to a crematorium furnace without the benefit of being dead. The burned killer's genetic tissue had been taken from him years before as part of one of the top-secret loony projects of that time. Tack's accelerated upbringing had consisted of, during daytime, an enforced training that had killed off many of his classmates – all surprisingly similar in appearance to himself – and at nights being hooked up to a semi-AI computer via the surgically installed interface plug in the base of his skull. At the age of ten he was physically an adult, mentally an adult, but mentally something else as well. His intensive knowledge of both Eastern martial arts and modern weaponry blended into a coherent whole that made him the supreme killer. His understanding of the world at large came not from personal experience but via uploading. In him his makers and masters had achieved their goal: they had both soldier and secret agent, and did not have to worry about whether or not he would obey orders, for he was *programmable*.

Glancing back now at the little whore, he wondered what Nandru Jurgens hoped to achieve with her, for it was evident to Tack that she was as dispensable to the Task Force soldier as she was to Tack himself. Some time soon the sale would have to be made and in any such transaction there was always a point where one party must, however briefly, be prepared to trust the other party. And it was in such brief intervals that Tack operated most efficiently. He expected some kind of threat and some kind of double-cross, but was confident of his own and his comrades' ability to circumvent this; confident that by the end of this day he would be in possession of both the item itself and the money, and that Jurgens and this little whore would be dead.

'Where to?' he asked.

'Head for the Anglia Reforest and put down by the old thermal generating tower,' Polly replied.

As the driver changed course, Tack faced forward again and briefly scanned the console on the side of his seeker gun. Since first pointing it at the whore it had, by laser and ultrasound scanning, recorded her recognition pattern and now it literally contained bullets with her name on them, though they were not the ones he had it presently set to use. Right now the gun was programmed to track the one whom Tack considered the greater danger: Nandru Jurgens himself. Tack would probably not need to use the gun on her anyway, since he intended to keep her close, and for close work he preferred the seven inches of kris flick knife in his pocket.

Soon they were heading out beyond the residential areas and passing over the old wall that had held back the sea before the U-gov-sponsored land-reclamation project – one that, like all such projects, had spiralled out of control costwise and was now on the brink of failure. Below lay the plain of the Anglia Reforest, seeded with nettle elms, binding grass, and endless brambles, thistles and stinging nettles. The Green contention that the place would become overrun with GM rape and maize had been fallacious – man's small tinkerings with code were yet to prove effective enough to counter billions of years of evolution.

Tack pointed to the tower rising like a giant iron tulip out of a copse of small oaks. 'The clearing. Down by those ruins,' he told the driver.

The man nodded and brought the Macrojet spiralling down towards a clearing that had probably in the past been a farmyard.

Tack turned to Polly. 'You will now take us to the item. Understand that I will kill you if there are any problems. There will be no problems?'

'Look, I don't wanna be here. Nandru roped me into this without asking me,' Polly replied, her hand flicking up to the Muse at her throat.

Only the presence of that device caused Tack any qualms, for even he did not have sufficient clearance to know its capabilities. It was recently developed military tech and, as such, an imponderable in this situation. However, he judged it to be tech whose purpose was merely informational, not some form of weaponry, its presence being only required by Jurgens as a secure comlink.

The Macrojet landed, blasting about it, like confetti, old crab carapaces whose owners had probably been washed inland during the over-flooding of the incompetently built sea wall that lay some miles to the east. Immediately the two either side of Polly piled out of the vehicle and ran to investigate the surrounding buildings and tangled vegetation, pulling guns from concealed holsters as they went. Tack glanced at Polly and gestured her with his thumb to the open door, before himself climbing out. He did not rush for cover – he had every confidence that the other two had the area covered sufficiently. The driver remained in the car.

'Where to now?' he asked Polly.

She held a finger up to the earring that he reckoned had to be an inducer. Tack understood the technology because he too wore a device that used electrostatic induction to vibrate the bones of his inner ear – in his case to relay instructions from his Director of Operations in Brussels. After a moment she pointed to a nearby ruin – all tumbled breeze blocks and heaped mud. When Tack made no move to head in that direction, she frowned and led the way.

Walking behind, Tack scanned his surroundings. The sunlight was bright, so he flicked up his polarized nictitating membranes, once again mirroring his eyes.

No one in the immediate area, Glock told him over comlink.

Traffic control hasn't got anything within five kilometres, said Airan.

There is the tower, though, added Provish, the driver.

'Stay alert and keep all detectors on,' said Tack, getting a querying look from Polly. 'This guy took out two in Prague with a door mine.'

As they reached the ruin, the whore froze and lost all interest in her surroundings. Looking past her, Tack saw that the item was there, resting on a large fragment of polystyrene, and it was on this that her attention was now riveted. Tack knew about this reaction, but had never felt it himself, perhaps because of his programming. He then noted the explosive charge fixed to the side of the item, and began to guess what Jurgens's game was.

It calls to you . . . it calls to you all the time.

The nettles were dead and dry in the cavity walls, and the grass was brown and crunched underfoot. Glancing at her stolid and lethal companion, Polly stepped sideways into the shade cast by the low oaks. She was thirsty, and scared, not only because of her present situation but of the reaction she had immediately felt. For a moment she thought the thing was some chitinous object washed in by the over-flood, like the pink and white crab carapaces all around. It looked like a mutated crustacean from the sea, and some weird things had been turning up in seas greenhouse-cooked and radioactive. However, white plastique was jammed around its thorny outgrowths, and the miniscreen of a matt-black detonator connected to this explosive displayed a revolving spiral of red lights.

There it is, Nandru told her, and she was bemused by the avidity in his tone.

'What do I do now?' she asked out loud.

The heavy was staring at her but offered no reply.

Tell him the detonator is net-linked and programmable. I know he's monitored and in constant com. His DO can run a diagnostic probe from wherever he is and that won't cause a detonation. He'll find a hard link from the numbered account.

Polly relayed Nandru's words, while still staring at the object. It was seemingly all thorned glass and silver; a perilous thing to slip onto her forearm – as she desperately wanted to do. Groping in her hip bag for a smoke, she spotted Tack immediately pointing his seeker gun at her.

Interdiction initiated. Seeking . . .

Ignoring the dead voice of Muse 184, she slowed her movements but did not stop them, as she was aching for that smoke.

With shaking hands she opened her tobacco pouch and rolled a cigarette. Lighting up, she turned directly towards Tack, deliberately away from the temptation of the strange object, and blew smoke towards him provocatively. His air was somewhat distracted, he was obviously listening to his comlink, but the barrel of his weapon never wavered from her face.

'The hard link has been found and the diagnostic probe is in,' said Tack. 'What is the purpose of this?'

After listening to Nandru, Polly replied, 'He tells me you'll find that, when the specified sum is transferred to the numbered account, the detonator will shut down.'

'And we are to believe this?' asked Tack, his tone conveying respect at the neatness of the set-up.

'He also tells me that at some point there has to be trust.'

Tack was silent again, for long-drawn-out moments. Polly could feel sweat trickling under her blouse. She did not convey what Nandru told her next.

As I thought, the fuckers are trying to break the hard link. No way in, dickheads . . . They'll have to do it – they're too desperate for the damned thing.

'It is agreed,' said Tack after a moment. 'The transference of funds will be made. Inform Mr Jurgens that if the detonator does not shut down then, or if there are any other . . . mishaps, I will personally hunt him down and feed him into a trash compactor.'

I can hear you, fucker. And your hunting days are over.

Polly eyed the spiralling lights on the detonator's screen and stepped back into the hot sunlight, preparing to bolt. Suddenly the lights went out and, realizing she just was not far enough away, Polly closed her eyes and cringed inwardly.

'Transaction complete,' said Tack.

Polly opened her eyes to see him stepping in towards the object and its clinging explosive, his weapon again concealed while he pulled on surgical gloves. He stooped, pulled off the detonator and cast it to one side. He then stripped away the plastique, balled it, and tossed it in another direction.

You know, Polly, if it hadn't been for you, Marjae might still be alive. You can tell your friend there that I acquired him and his companions when they were walking over. The deal's done and now it's payback time.

The detonation came from behind and Polly turned in time to see the underside of the Macrojet as it turned in a conflagration. Two other hits swatted it along the ground as if it was fashioned of balsa and papier mâché, blowing it to pieces. Glancing back, she saw Tack raising his seeker gun and she ran for the trees.

Interdiction find.

The mosquito whining of seeker bullets was suddenly all around her – their winged shapes whipping through the air like June beetles. Coming out of brambles some way ahead of her, with leaves stuck to his long coat, she saw one of Tack's companions levelling his gun at her. Then he doubled over, and the dull thud of a muffled detonation spread his insides across the dry grass.

Not target. Interdiction pause.

Behind her she could hear the killer, Tack, pursuing. She turned to her left as there came the low coughing of a nearby gun.

Interdiction find.

A seeker round whined past her and hit a sapling just ahead, blowing it in half. Another round whined overhead, made a strange whuckering sound, then spiralled into the earth directly in front of her and exploded. She leapt the smoking hole and just kept on running. The shots were missing her and she just did not understand why.

Provish was right. In the fucking tower! In the t—

That was Airan, the remains of whom Tack passed only a

minute later. The seeker round had taken off his head, which was especially unlucky for him because he, like Tack, had taken the precaution of wearing a moly-Kevlar undershirt.

Firing again at the girl dodging between the trees, Tack watched in amazement when the round – programmed to hunt her down – veered left and slammed into the remains of an old brick wall. With no time to check his weapon, Tack thumbed off its programming facility, took careful aim, and held his finger down on the trigger. Retaining their casings the rounds now went where he aimed. Trees flared and burning bark showered down, as the girl jumped a drainage ditch. Too many trees and she was moving fast. Tack sprinted after her, only to hear a familiar whining behind him. The round fired from the tower slammed into his back, knocking him face-down next to the ditch. He struggled upright and another round exploded on his chest knocking him backwards into the ditch. Briefly he caught a glimpse of the girl turning and sprinting back towards the ruins, then he blacked out.

Well, there went the super-killers and you are still in one piece, little Polly.

Gasping, Polly stumbled into the ruin and flopped down in some shade with her back against the breeze-block wall.

'You fucking bastard, you nearly got me killed!'

Only a little bit and, anyway, you'll get paid because now I have their money and their precious objet d'art.

Polly stared across at the thing he referred to and once again felt a powerful urge to just go over and pick it up – to slip it onto her forearm like a piece of baroque jewellery. What the hell was it? It looked organic rather than made, was a tube seemingly rolled from a holly leaf the length of a person's forearm, that leaf itself fashioned of white and silver metal. As she contemplated it, she found herself standing, inexorably drawn to it. Somehow, it had the same attraction for her as a roll of drug patches. She could feel the yearning, the *addiction* . . .

I'll be with you in a moment. Just you wait there for me.

Polly squatted by the object, reached out and touched it. Inside her something snapped shut and she knew exactly what she had to do.

Polly, keep away from that! I said, fucking keep away from that!

It was heavy. She had to take it up with both hands, and as she did her hands bled. The pain was ecstasy. She slid it over her right forearm. Skin peeled and flesh parted like earth before the plough. She screamed as blood jetted from slit arteries, and she fell to her knees.

Don't! Don't! It comes when you touch it directly!

Very quickly she ceased to bleed. She stared at the thing. It was bonding to her flesh. She could feel it bonding to the bones beneath. Looking up, she saw Nandru running towards her, his weapon braced across his chest.

'What the hell have you done?' he shouted.

The air distorted, and something harsh inside her dragged her upright. She could feel something washing through her like citrine fire. The drugs and the dullness they induced were going. Elements of her mind blossomed and opened out. True wakefulness hurt as no physical pain possibly could, and she understood why so many humans spent most of their lives fleeing it.

'Oh Jesus.'

In the distortion Nandru turned to face a flaw in reality. The flaw opened out to expose two vast rollers of living tissue turning against each other. Polly realized they were land and sky composed of living flesh. Out of this, looming into the day, came a living door, throated with teeth and shadows, and lipped with razor bone – the horrifying terminus of some huge trainlike tentacle that stretched back into that landscape of flesh.

There came a roaring sound, a high-pitched keening, then the stench of carrion.

No! No! I don't want to . . .

It closed on him, drawing him in

Casualty link established. Uploading . . .

Nandru was gone, eaten alive. She watched him go, torn apart and ground away.

Then the flaw snapped shut thunderously, and all distortion fled. Polly saw everything clearly now and did not for one instant believe she had been hallucinating. Just as she wasn't hallucinating the killer, Tack, who was walking out of the trees towards her.

He was gaining on her. That first burst of adrenalin had taken her some way but she was quickly tiring. The thing on her arm had made her thoughts oh so clear, but it had not repaired a body damaged by years of drug abuse. Glancing back, she saw him raising and lowering his seeker gun as she dodged amid the trees. He was aiming at her legs, and in his other hand she saw the ugly glitter of a knife. Her shoulder clipping a tree, and with brambles tangled round her feet, she sprawled and knew terror. The killer was so close. Then he was standing over her, a look of cold satisfaction on his face, his mirrored eyes reflecting the surrounding green.

'Get up,' he said.

Polly looked into the mouth of the gun, then at the knife. As she stood he holstered the gun and she knew only panic at what he intended to do. She turned to flee as he stepped in with the knife held low for a disembowelling cut. He grabbed her arm, then grunted in pained surprise and released her. Glancing back while stumbling away, she saw he was walking after her now, knowing he had her. Polly had to escape. The flaw – that distortion. She felt herself reaching out with something within her that was linked to the thing on her forearm. Twisting that something, she fled in the only direction available to her and fell into waves of darkness below featureless grey. Screaming only blew what air remained from her lungs, and in her next breath she took in nothing. Then came a slow wrench as if she had just penetrated some meniscus. Suddenly she was face-down in cold and dark; salt water filled her mouth. Pushing down, her hands sank into slime. She jerked herself up, breathed and shook her head to clear her eyes, and found herself lying in a foot of sea water under the same trees as before. Only now the trees were without leaves and the air was cold. Heaving herself to her knees, she observed crabs scuttling away through the water nearby.

'What is this?' The killer was still with her, standing up to his calves in the water and looking around disbelievingly.

Then he focused on Polly once more. He stepped forwards, grabbed her by the arm that was not enclosed in the object, and hauled her fully to her feet. She tried to knee him in the testicles, but he turned his hip into the blow, and in a flash had the point of his knife poised just over Muse 184.

He tilted his head and said, 'Tack here. Mission status?'

Polly watched his expression shift from puzzlement to outright disbelief.

'What do you mean "doubled signal return"? Where's my DO?'

Almost irrelevantly, Polly noticed that his clothing was torn and burnt away over his chest, exposing the body armour he wore. This then was how he had survived the seeker rounds Nandru had fired from the tower.

Bastard that . . . The voice whispered in her skull, its phrasing human but its tone machine-like. Perhaps all this clarity of thought was an illusion and she had recently taken some bad lysergic. But she must discount that possibility and react only to circumstances as she saw them. Right now she was a hair's breadth from being killed. Certainly this man would think nothing of cutting her throat, then sawing off her arm to take the object wrapped around it back to his masters.

His face pale with shock, Tack now dragged her towards dry ground, where earth was mounded against one of the ruin's walls. He pushed her away from him down onto the patch.

'Stay there and don't move. You try to run and I'll carve you,' he said, then put away his knife and rolled up one bloody sleeve.

Polly stared at him, then shifted again.

Ignore all irrelevant distractions. Focus on the target. What was *irrelevant*? When his hand had closed on her arm, it had closed on the item that she had somehow put on, and which now seemed to be fused to her flesh. The pain he had felt was more than it should have been. Now he stared down in momentary confusion at his hand. His palm had been sliced open and there was a fragment like a thorn of coral embedded in his wrist, blood oozing out around it. She had been getting away. No distraction. He had felt the first shift and how he had been caught at the edge of it and drawn in, somehow, by this lump of material embedded in his wrist. Seeing the leafless trees and drowned landscape, he had for a moment considered the possibility of a memory lapse: one of those blank spots associated with reprogramming. However, his subsequent garbled communication with Operations had confirmed what was real. No one there had heard of his Director of Operations, and no one had heard of Tack either. And by their response to him he just knew they had been sending a kill squad to deal with an anomalous agent – himself.

The girl had done something; moved them. This second time it happened validated his crazy idea about just *what* she had done. He gazed around and saw that they now stood upon a plain of drying mud, deep with cracks and scattered with growths of sea sage and plantains. There being no trees here, this time, he could see the distant sea wall straddled by a huge slab-facing machine. Nearby the ruins were not clearly defined, mounded as they were with mud and yet to be weathered out of the ground. To his right the thermal generating tower stood tall and pristine, and from it a macadam road led back through the old inner sea wall towards the industrial complexes outside Maldon. People were working in and around the tower, and from it a high-mounted crane was lowering a dismounted generator to a low-loader.

Tack glanced down from this bewildering view and saw he was up to his ankles in the mud. With some difficulty he pulled his feet free. The dry mud was in his shoes, in his socks. The girl was sprawled in the mud and looking as bewildered as he felt, and now Tack realized he must keep her alive. He enjoyed books and the interactives as much as normal people, so he knew about the concepts of time travel, and how leading quantum physicists had stated that it might be possible.

He looked up again to scan their surroundings. The first shift had taken them back to the time of one of the over-floods: two to ten years. This second shift had brought them back to the time just after the new sea wall had been built and the land area enclosed by it reclaimed. Tack had seen documentaries about the furore the project had caused, reclaiming land considered by all insurers as unsafe because of the chances of over-flood – a prediction subsequently proved to be true – and therefore a place deemed by all developers unsuitable for any sort of building. The project had cost millions, and millions more as it had rendered useless many of the thermal towers, which required sea water to operate. And this had all occurred half a century before Tack himself had been a twinkle in his creator's test tube.

'It would be inadvisable to go further,' Tack warned the girl.

She looked at him with her eyes wide, panicky. With slow

deliberation Tack squatted down before her, making himself appear less threatening. He wondered if she had any idea what she was doing. He inspected his own injured limb and noted that, even though his hand was still bleeding, the wound in his wrist had sealed around the thorn. Distraction. Trying to exude calm, he rolled down his sleeve and looked at the girl.

'You go any further back and this place will be under ten metres of sea,' he told her.

She glanced around then pushed herself upright. Her clothing pulled up dry mud with it; was packed with the stuff. She pulled her blouse out of her pelmet and flat pieces of mud fell out, contoured on one side to her body, as if she had been lying in it as it dried. Tack felt no confusion about this. Land levels change through time, she had travelled, the dry mud had been displaced by her body. It all made perfect sense to him. What did not make sense was why the trees and other parts of the landscape had not been dragged along too. Why her clothes, him, his clothes?

'How have you done this, girl?' he asked, expecting no coherent answer – she still looked bewildered, probably not yet grasping what was happening. Certainly all this had been caused by the object on her arm, about which he knew only his DO's instructions: *Come back with it, Tack, or don't come back at all . . .*

'My name is Polly.'

Tack considered for a moment. It was always best not to use the name of a potential hit, not to consider them as anything more than disposable. He considered what he should do now: a swift head shot would prevent her doing anything more, and he could next cut the object from her arm. But what then? He had no idea how to operate the thing, and suspected that she was only doing so at an instinctive level.

'You have not answered my question,' he said.

'You're going to kill me. Why should I?'

Tack nodded and stood up, stepping closer to offer her his hand. 'You must take us back . . . you must take us forward again.'

'Why the hell should I!?'

She rolled and came to her feet, backing away from him. Observing her expression, he was surprised at the sudden intelligence he saw there and realized he had little chance of gaining her trust. There was only one option: he must retrieve the object and learn how to use it himself. Stepping forward, he drew his seeker gun from its chest holster. Momentarily the controls snagged on his damaged clothing. He saw her take a deep breath and close her eyes.

'No!'

He fired, realizing as he did so that, in snagging the gun, he had switched it back to seeker mode. The bullet shot out, dropping its casing even as it left the barrel, opening its ceramic wings to swerve itself away to one side of her. Swearing, he slapped it back to manual. Then one moment he was sighting on her forehead, and the next moment his lungs were filled with brine.

Water pressure closed over him like a vice and he did not know which way was up. He struggled and he kicked and fought. Breaking the surface, he spewed water and fought for every coughing breath. She was over there, steadily swimming away from him. He knew he needed to stay close, but it was all he could do to stay on the surface and breathe. The sea was rough, rain hammering down, and lightning stalked the horizon. She shifted again, leaving a hollow in the water that closed with a sucking rush. Gone.

With a dogged determination to survive, Tack shed his coat and shoes and swam for the barely visible sea wall – the original that had been well inland after the reclamation. Years of physical training, both when linked to a computer and in the field, enabled him to get to his objective through the cold rough sea, when many others might not have made it. After fighting his way through a mat of bladderwrack, he wearily pulled himself up onto the slabbed face of the wall and coughed dregs of burning salt from his raw lungs. His hand ached and he felt feverish. When he reached to pull the thorn from his wrist he saw that it had spread out into a small hard plate the size of a drawing pin, and was now covered with smaller hairlike thorns, which bloodied his fingers when he tried to pull the thing out. It came part of the way up like a scab, but when he released it to get a better hold, it drew back against his flesh. When he tried again with the tip of his knife, he found he could not move it at all. The thing had now bound itself to the bones of his wrist. He clambered to the top of the wall and looked around, shivering in his soaked clothes.

He knew now that he had to be at least a hundred and fifty years back, in the time before the ascendency of U-gov. His DO was not yet alive, and both his programming and his training had no way to incorporate this. He tried to concentrate on essentials: right now he wanted to be warm and dry. He was also hungry and thirsty. His base programming allowed for that – for him to deal with these needs.

As her sodden knee boots wrapped themselves to her legs like sheet lead, Polly fought to peel them off without swallowing any more sea water. Free of them at last, and now fighting to swim to a shoreline etched by the orange light of the setting sun, she felt horribly weary, but understanding came at last from the killer's recent words: *You take us any further back and this place will be under ten metres of sea.* She had travelled back in time, just like in the movies or the interactives, but in none of those had the heroine been immediately drowned after transit – she always arrived at some hugely interesting point in history where she could influence important events of *recorded* history.

Closer to the shore and she saw wooden frameworks supporting vicious tubular nests of barbed wire. Up on stilts behind this defence was a wooden cabin and below it a sandbag bunker, from which protruded the recognizable twin barrels of a gun.

Second World War, at a guess. Not many aircraft attacking during the First.

'What?' she managed, swallowing water. 'What?'

That's an anti-aircraft gun. The onomatopoeic ack-ack, I should think.

She really just did not have the breath at present to carry on a conversation with Muse, and she did not have the energy to wonder why the device attached below her throat was talking to her in such a conversational manner in *Nandru's* voice. Struggling on, she could feel her reserves of energy depleting, and was beginning to notice that if anything the shore was now getting further away. But perhaps this was an illusion caused by the descending twilight. The sun was gone now and the shore was silhouetted against a sky of bright red and dull iron. Behind she heard the low thunder of engines and glanced back to see a squadron of bombers only just distinct through encroaching darkness.

Now those are Heinkels with a Messerschmitt escort, it would seem. That confirms it.

'Nandru . . . Nandru, is that you?' she managed.

She ceased swimming, to tread water, and realized to her horror that she was being dragged out to sea. The planes were closer now and suddenly she was blinded by a strobing of light. The sound impacted a second after, as guns all along the coast opened up and powerful searchlights probed the sky from somewhere further inland. Ahead, when the gunfire paused long enough for her eyes to clear, she saw more planes appearing high against the blood-red western sky.

Spitfires probably . . . now that's something I knew before . . . No, apparently I'm wrong: they're more likely to be Hurricanes.

'Nandru . . . what happened?'

You know, my memory has never been so clear – it's eidetic in fact – but every second . . . and those seconds are long in here . . . I find it harder and harder to distinguish between what's my memory and Muse's reference library.

'You . . . died,' said Polly, beginning to swim again.

And so I did, but it seems my Muse uploaded a copy of me to your Muse. I didn't know they could do that. There's the facility for transferring recordings in the event of the bearer's death, just so that vital battlefield intelligence won't be lost, but apparently you've copped the lot . . . well, as far as I know.

The red tinge in the sky was almost gone, lost in the fall of night and blasted away by cordite light as the guns hammered the air. Glancing up, Polly saw the fighter planes attacking and the flickering of gunfire like the distant glow of ignited cigarettes. Then suddenly she was pinned in the actinic glare of a new sun, and a grey wall loomed over her. Waves slapped her from side to side.

'Frank, it's a woman. What should I do?' someone shouted.

'Throw her the ring, you berk, and haul her in!' replied an older voice.

Trailing rope, a life-ring splashed in the sea beside her and, with a surge of gratitude to the unseen rescuers, she grabbed hold of it.

You'll probably be shot as a spy.

Her current gratitude did not extend to this particular incarnation of Nandru.

Systems, keyed to the Dopplered light intensity of the red dwarf it was approaching, began operating inside the probe. It flipped over and extruded long struts from around the monopoles of its AG motors, spreading them out into space. Linking struts split from the main ones and joined to others, forming a structure like a spider's web, but one that was ten kilometres across. Between these struts a silvery meniscus spread, which, like the rest of the probe, healed itself when it struck interstellar particles. It had only been a matter of luck that so far nothing larger than a hydrogen atom had got in the way – at such speed anything bigger might have obliterated the probe.

Against the tide of photons, this light sail slowed the probe, but minimally. It further decelerated when the AG motors came back online – powered by the sail, which was also photovoltaic. As the probe drew closer to the red dwarf, light pressure on the sail increased, as did the supply of power to the AG motors. But it was ten years from the probe's deployment of its light sail, before it fell into orbit of Proxima Centauri, and another two years before it found a dead, cold world orbiting that old sun, and went into orbit about that.

Far above grey mountain chains and methane fogs, the probe folded away its sail, like someone putting away an umbrella after coming in from a blustery day. It then spent a year scanning and mapping the surface of the planet. Finally satisfied, it ejected a two-metre sphere of plumbeous metal which, on independent AG, descended to the surface. Landing on a plain of black rock, this miniprobe hinged down claw arms from where they rested up against its surface like the sepals of a flower, and from the ends of these, explosive bolts thumped down into the surface. From its underside a drilling head extruded and began to turn, a haze of dust all about it as it bored down. At a predetermined depth the probe tested a rock sample, using thorium dating, then began to scan more closely the detritus from the drilling. The layer it had been searching for was penetrated a metre away from where predicted, but geological activity accounted for that. Compressed in the rock, the layer was only a few microns thick, but there was plenty enough material in that layer for the probe's intensive analysis.

The results, immediately transmitted, took four point three years to get back to Earth: a confirmation that was a happy revelation to some, a source of dread to others.

3

Astolere:
The two leaders of the remaining seven thousand troops, now pinned down by my brother's forces, but in a position from which it would cost Saphothere greatly to expel them, have surprisingly surrendered – it has ever been my previous experience that Umbrathane always fight to the death. While they go to parley with Saphothere on Station Seventeen, I can only wonder at the extent of the plan. The Umbrathane were attacking because of our development of what is being called vorpal technology (a word from an ancient rhyme I have yet to find the time to track down), so must have understood what they were facing. The failed attempt by the Umbrathane fleet to knock out the energy dam between Io and Jupiter confirms this: they knew the energy requirement for time travel to be immense, and had the fleet's attack succeeded, then Saphothere would have been unable to plant the atomic. Still, I do not think that we can afford many dangerous ventures such as my brother's, and I wonder at the consequences of what both we and the preterhuman, Cowl, are creating.

Tack tried to hold it at bay by concentrating on his immediate circumstances but, like the black wall of depression, an utter lack of purpose loomed in around him. U-gov did not exist in this earlier time, nor did the girl, nor the item she had bound to her arm, and this rendered his mission not only impossible but irrelevant. Slowly, inexorably, emergency programming was coming online, compelling him to return to the Agency for debriefing – only there was nowhere for him to return to. As he stumbled across a ploughed field in the pouring rain, he fought impulses he could not satisfy. He felt almost drunk or drugged, and could not control surges of emotion that one moment had him in fits of giggles and in another moment had him railing at the downpour.

Ahead of him and to the right, Tack caught glimpses of artificial light through a thick hedgerow. Mud was clodded on his bare feet and between his toes, and spattered up his legs. It was also smeared up his front and on his face from when he had tripped over and thumped the ground like a child in a tantrum. Eventually reaching a gate in a thorn hedge, he stooped to pull up a handful of soaking grass to clean his feet, and found his eyes swimming with tears and his chest tightening with a surge of self-pity. Swearing at himself then, he stood up and vaulted the gate. On the other side was an asphalt lane and a little way along it the glow from the windows of a house. Scraping his karate-hardened feet against the macadam surface as he went, he . . . paused as a wave of something flowed up to him through the night, through and past. He drew his knife, clicked it open, and glared around. But disquiet remained as there now seemed an abnormality to his surroundings – strangely indefinable. Advancing on the house, he found himself sliding into total-combat mode like an animal on the defensive. Soon he was stepping past a gleaming Ford Capri, which in his own time would have been seen only in a museum. At the door he hammered on wood with muddy knuckles, the knife concealed behind his back.

In a gust of scented warmth a woman in a towelling bathrobe opened the door and looked at him in surprise.

'Hello, how can I help you?' she asked.

Another age – so much trust.

'What is your name?'

'I beg your pardon?'

'What is your name?'

'Jill . . . Jill Carlton. Why do you want to know?'

Her married name obviously. She wore a wedding ring. Not

any name he recognized from U-gov or from the Agency, so it was unlikely she was an ancestor to any of his masters. He might have had qualms if that were the case. He reached out and slashed her throat. Choking red onto white towelling, she staggered back and fell, her flailing arm pulling a telephone and a basket of dried flowers down on top of herself.

'Jill?'

Drawing his seeker gun, Tack stepped over her into the hallway, then to the right into the kitchen, where a man was just rising from the table, a newspaper open to the half-completed crossword. The husband caught a glimpse of his wife thrashing bloodily in the hall behind Tack, and for a moment could not comprehend what he was seeing.

'Oh my God,' he managed, before a brief thwack from the gun and the whine of a round, flung him back against a kitchen worktop, with a hole in his cheek. Then the round exploded inside him, blowing all his teeth, and half his head across the granite-effect kitchen surface. He was dead even before the blood stopped pumping from his wife's open throat.

Tack holstered the gun and pocketed his knife before looking around. Remembering how time-travel stories traditionally went, he moved to the newspaper and looked for the date: 1997. He was even further back than he had thought. He then moved to the sink and washed his hands, coldly observing his own reflection in the darkened window above it.

'The energy required to short-jump here is immense, but I was allowed this alternate so I might see you – know you.'

His gun immediately back in hand, Tack turned so fast that his twisting foot ripped up carpet tiles. He turned again, this way and that, still unable to locate the source of that calm androgynous voice.

'I do know you now, Tack, and I have no qualms, none at all. The new Tack will be different. You end here.'

A hand, bone-white, emerged out of the empty air over the kitchen sink. The hand clasped a gun that looked laughably small and ineffectual. There came a click, an infinitely bright light, and a brief indescribable agony. Tack burnt away. This Tack.

Ahead of him and to the right, Tack caught glimpses of artificial light through a thick hedgerow. Mud was clodded on his bare feet and between his toes, and spattered up his legs. It was also smeared up his front and on his face from when he had tripped over and thumped the ground like a child in a tantrum. Eventually reaching a gate in a thorn hedge, he stooped to pull up a handful of soaking grass to clean his feet, and found his eyes swimming with tears and his chest tightening with a surge of self-pity. Swearing at himself then, he stood up and vaulted the gate. On the other side was an asphalt lane and a little way along it the glow from the windows of a house. Scraping his karate-hardened feet against the macadam surface as he went, he . . . paused as a wave of something flowed up to him through the night, through and past. He drew his knife, clicked it open, and glared around. But disquiet remained as there now seemed an abnormality to his surroundings – strangely indefinable.

A figure, tall and rangy, clad in a long coat, baggy trousers and pointed shoes, stepped out of the shadows to his right. The hands and face of this figure were bone-white, and its pale hair was tied back in a ponytail. The expression on its face held anger and contempt. Tack had only time for one breath before a fist like a bag of marbles slammed into his stomach. He went over, his knife clattering on the asphalt. He couldn't get his breath back. He had never been hit so hard in his life.

'That is for what you were going to do,' said a horribly calm androgynous voice. 'And this, and what is to come, is for all those things you have already done.'

A foot – moving too fast for Tack to even think about blocking

– slammed his testicles up into his groin. Throughout the systematic beating that followed, he heard a woman's voice asking what was going on out there and a man's voice telling the woman, Jill, to get back inside and that he would go and find out. And all the time Tack could not understand why he kept thinking: *This is wrong; it does not happen this way.*

Those thoughts carried him into unconsciousness.

The two soldiers deferred to the boat's captain, even though he wore no uniform that Polly could see. But then he was clad in a long waterproof coat and woollen hat and a uniform might be concealed underneath.

'You all right, luv?' asked the young ginger-haired soldier who had pulled her out of the sea, his concern not preventing him goggling at her. Drunk with fatigue, Polly glanced down at herself and saw that her soaked blouse was now utterly transparent, her nipples protruding as a result of the cold water, and that her skirt had ridden up to her waist, revealing knickers that had also been rendered transparent.

'I'm cold,' she said.

The youth blushed and glanced at his companion, who had now moved closer to get a good look. Polly observed that this youth carried a machine gun, whereas the first had a rifle strapped across his back.

A Sten gun and a Lee Enfield rifle – that's definitely from Muse as I wouldn't be able to identify a 'bolt-action .303 rifle' if one bit me on the arse.

Ignoring Nandru's commentary, Polly pulled her skirt back down and folded her arms across her all-too-noticeable breasts. She felt foolish doing this, considering her daily occupation, but suspected these two would not possess cash euros or chip cards. She was also experiencing a horrible cringing shame at what that occupation had been. This, she now realized, had been just one of the many reactions she had deadened with the drugs and alcohol. The two young soldiers were both now staring with puzzlement at her folded arms. Glancing down she realized what might have attracted their attention: the strange object had lost its spikes and sharp edges and was now completely moulded around her right forearm, from her wrist to just a few centimetres below her elbow. Lowering her arms, however, immediately gave them something else to concentrate on.

Leaning out of the wheelhouse, the captain called to them. 'Are you two just going to stand there ogling the young lady, or is one of you going to offer her a coat?'

Both youths moved into action. The one with the Sten gun said, 'Come on, let's get you below . . . You can have my greatcoat.'

The ginger-haired youth reached out to grip her biceps, then hesitated and turned the movement into a gesture for her to move ahead of him. On unsteady legs she preceded him to the hatch, and down splintered wooden steps into a hold heated by a small stove and thick with cigarette smoke. Without speaking, ginger hair moved past her to take a heavy army coat down from a wall hook. The machine-gun holder, following them, took up a piece of blanket from one of the cases that they had been using as seats down here, and passed it to her. Still shivering, Polly dried her arms and legs and tried to blot the rest of the moisture from her clothing, thoroughly aware of the silence of the two soldiers and how they could not keep their eyes off her. When she accepted the greatcoat, shrugged it on and moved closer to the stove, the spell broke.

'They spotted you from one of the pillboxes. How did you end up in the sea?' asked ginger hair.

'Toby, get that bloody kettle on!' came a yell from above, giving her time to try and think of a plausible answer. Toby, the ginger-haired one, moved over to where one crate being used as a small table was cluttered with cups, tea-making stuff, and two overflowing ashtrays. Taking up a large teapot, he emptied its remaining contents into a nearby bucket, which by the smell of it also served a less sanitary purpose. He then spooned in loose tea. The other soldier unhooked his Sten gun and sat down on one of the lower steps, propping the weapon against his knee. He took a pack of Woodbines from the top pocket of his army shirt, knocked out a cigarette and lit up.

Not too bright: an oil stove and cigarettes down here. You'd think they'd be a bit more careful considering the load they're carrying. But then I suppose you get blasé about that sort of thing after a while.

Polly desperately wanted to ask what Nandru was on about. She studied the crates stacked everywhere and saw stamped on them 'Corned Beef', and in one case 'Pilchards'. Over to one side were stacked hessian sacks, which she guessed contained potatoes.

Over to your left.

Polly glanced in that direction, wondering if Nandru was much closer to her thoughts than she would like, and observed a stack of metal cases roped down to hooks and partially concealed by a tarpaulin. On one of these she could see, stamped in white letters, the label '3.7 inch AA', which meant nothing to her.

That looks like a shitload of ammunition.

'Well, what happened to you then?' asked the one with the Sten gun, shaking out his match then grinding it underfoot.

I've been thinking about this and there's no easy story. Say you had a row with your boyfriend or something, and he tipped you out of his boat.

'What's your name?' Polly asked the youth.

'Dave,' he replied, hoisting his Sten gun into a more comfortable position. 'This is Toby, and the captain up there is Frank. What about you?'

'Polly.'

Dave continued staring at her, evidently still waiting for an answer to his previous question.

Polly said, 'Nandru . . . my boyfriend . . . he died and I was going to join him.'

The kettle Toby had just filled from a jerrycan clanged down on the cast-iron surface of the stove. He was staring at her with his mouth open, not knowing what to say.

'Gurkha?' Dave asked. Polly thought it safe to affirm this.

'He died fighting then, I take it?'

'Yes,' said Polly. 'I think he did.'

Oh, very funny. Now they'll ask you where and when I was killed, and we don't even know the damned date.

'Where'd he cop it then,' asked Dave.

'He was killed at . . . in the desert. They said he died doing his duty.'

Dave stared at her for a moment. 'He was with Monty?'

Polly numbly nodded her head.

Ah fuck, yes. Tell them I caught it at El Alamein.

'Yes, at El Alamein,' she added.

'Yeah, well that Rommel was a tricky sod, but the bastards are on their last gasp now,' said Dave. He gestured at the ceiling with his cigarette, and they all paused to listen to the distant gunfire. 'Probably trying to hit Marconi again. That's one they haven't given up on,' he finished.

Polly did not know what to say to this. She had heard the name Marconi once but could not remember in connection with what. Dave observed her for a moment, then took out his cigarette packet and held it out to her. Polly stepped over to him and took one, then stooped low to light it from the match he struck and cupped for her. Drawing on it, she found it tasted of nothing but burning paper and gave her no satisfaction at all.

'You were going to kill yourself?' asked Toby, then got a warning look from Dave and flushed with embarrassment.

'I was,' said Polly, 'but now I wonder if that might just be giving in to the fuckers.'

Silence immediately followed and, glancing at the two youths, she realized they were shocked by her swearing. She moved to one of the crates and sat down. Drawing on her cigarette again, she got a bit more of a hit this time, and immediately sensed movement from the thing on her arm. She took another drag, ignoring it.

'Where are you going?' she asked.

'If I told you that I'd have to shoot you,' said Dave, in mock reproach.

'OK,' said Polly. Glancing over at Toby, now pouring boiling water into the teapot, she tried to remember the last time she had drunk any tea. Her mother used to make it and, ever since, the stuff had left a bad taste in her mouth.

'No big secret,' admitted Dave. 'Cock-up on the supply front from Herne Bay to Knock John. So we're running some stuff down from Goldhangar to keep 'em going for a week or so. We all know something big is coming up.'

'Knock John?' Polly repeated, before she could stop herself.

Toby said, 'I always wanted to go out to them. I've never seen them.'

'Not many people have,' added Dave. Then, to Polly, 'Knock John naval fort is where we're heading. It's one of the Maunsell sea forts.'

Polly nodded as if she knew what he was talking about, and hoped Nandru would be able to fill her in. While she waited for his input, she sipped from the tin mug Toby handed her, and the memories became more painful than ever before.

Consciousness returned ungently and Tack found he could not move. Staring up at dusty beams, he at first thought the assailant had broken his neck. But it wasn't the beating that had paralysed him. The familiar sensation of imperatives dissolving in his skull told him that he was *connected*, as did the raw pain at the back of his neck where his interface plug was located. It was apparent someone had done some home surgery, on this dusty floor he lay upon, to access the plug and connect him up. He was being reprogrammed, and there was nothing he could do about it.

Movement to his left, but he could not turn his head to look. Someone said something in a language he did not recognize, then went on with, 'Ah, you took your time, but then I suppose that's to be expected. You AD humans are soft and riddled with imprecise genes.'

The face of the white-skinned man loomed above, his expression contemptuous.

'You knew the fundamental laws of evolution and you ignored them. You bred strong diseases and weak humans, poisoned with a shitload of inherited idiot programming. You, Tack, have been doubly programmed. And your second program is about to be replaced.'

The stranger liked to talk, that was evident. Tack listened as best he could, through the white noise in his brain, as imperatives were changed and new instructions melded into place.

'Normally we would have nothing to do with your type, but this opportunity to grow a viable tor we cannot miss.'

The man's face hovered above Tack again for a moment, then went away. Tack was left with an impression of alienness, but one not easy for him to define.

'The tor is the device you were sent to retrieve, in a future that does not exist as of here and now. The piece broken off in your wrist, given the right nutrients and conditions, can be encouraged to grow into an entire new tor. And that would be one of which Cowl has no knowledge. Perhaps through you we can get to him at last.'

'Cowl?' Tack managed, his voice grating dry in his throat.

'Ah, Cowl.' A hiss now came into the man's tone. 'Cowl is a step too far for a social species. He is the ultimate individual and, though I hate to admit it, the ultimate application of Darwin's laws. He kills every threat to him and would destroy humanity to save himself. Your existence is threatened, just as much as mine.'

Tack just didn't get it – it was all too much. But he did recognize someone far beyond him in the arts of violence, and he wondered about his captor's programming.

'You may sit up now.'

Tack did as instructed and found himself on the floor of a barn, in a space walled around with straw bales like huge bricks. Sunlight stabbed through holes in the shiplap wall and illuminated motes of dust in the air. Nearby was an old grey tractor steadily being iced with bird droppings. Tack looked first at his captor, then at the cable snaking from the back of his own neck to a strange-looking portable console propped on some rusting farm implement. The console appeared to have been fashioned from glass, in a suitable shape, then again melted and allowed to distort and sag before cooling. Turning aside, he noticed a ploughshare only inches from his right hand, but he found he could not act on his initial intention, which was to pick up the lump of iron and cleave that white face with it.

'Pick up the console and stand.'

Tack did precisely as instructed. His programming had changed and he resented it. He suddenly resented all such control: he wanted to be himself. Was this urge part of his new programming?

'You may detach the cable now.'

Tack obeyed, his fingers pulling the bloody optical plug free from the back of his neck. White-face took cable and console from him and placed them in a backpack. Returning, he reached around and pressed something against the wound in the back of Tack's neck. Tack could feel the object moving as it occupied the cavity and sealed it shut. The other man then pointed to the backpack.

'Pick that up and put it on.'

Tack did as instructed.

'Questions?'

There had never been questions when dealing with his DO. Tack asked anyhow.

'What do I call you?'

'You call me Traveller. It is a title in *our time*, and you do not have my permission to use my given name.'

Tack absorbed *our time* and wondered just when this man was from.

'What do you want of me? I didn't understand you before.'

'It's not really you we want, just what is embedded in your wrist.'

Traveller pointed at Tack's arm. Tack raised it and now saw that his wrist was enclosed in a transparent band filled with esoteric electronics and some sort of gelatinous fluid. Only just could he see the thing embedded in his wrist through all this – it lay at the centre of an array of golden connections almost like an integrated circuit.

'What's a tor?' he finally asked

'Tors are complex organic time machines: portable and biased towards the past they are sent from. Our machines, unfortunately, must push from the future into that past, against all Cowl's traps and juggled alternates, and up the probability slope he's shoving us down.'

'I still don't understand.'

'Of course you don't. You think linear. What you must be is the ultimate existentialist: only what you perceive is real. If you travel into the past and kill your father before you were conceived, all that happens is you cause an alternate to sprout from that point in time. That act, though, would shove you far down the probability slope, and you would be unlikely to be able to travel ever again. You would become trapped in the alternate you created.'

'Probability slope?' Tack felt as if he was trudging through treacle.

'The parallels are in the form of a wave and the main line sits at the apex of this wave. The other parallels fall down from this apex in descending order of probability. The further down that probability slope you are, the more energy you require to time travel. Both our lines, from our perspective, are coming off the apex. Mine is further down than yours.'

Tack discovered humour. 'Thank you for clearing that up for me,' he said.

Traveller hit him and he spun and went down, overbalanced by the pack, blood spurting from his nose into the dirt. Traveller stooped over him, and yanked his head up by the hair. Tack found his hand on the butt of his seeker gun, but he was unable to draw it.

'When we're done with you,' Traveller hissed, 'I may yet kill you.' He grabbed Tack's arm and held it up so that Tack could again see clearly the band around his wrist. 'Understand that this is all that's keeping you alive at present, simply because the nutrients it is currently drawing from your body are keeping it alive.' Traveller then hauled Tack to his feet one-handed, with the ease of a man picking up a rag doll, and shoved him towards the double doors of the barn. 'Now, get moving.'

The double doors opened onto a yard of compacted road scrapings, along the opposite side of which stood a Dutch barn sheltering a combine harvester, a tractor and the tractor's various implements. Wiping blood from his face, Tack noticed a plough with its numerous shares polished bright by recent use, and wanted to throw Traveller at this tangle of iron and hear his bones break.

'Turn to the right,' said Traveller, and Tack could do nothing but obey his new master. Glancing back, he saw a farmhouse and wondered if it was the same one from which he had heard voices the night before when he had received his beating. Ahead lay a track leading out between fields of newly turned earth, glistening like brown scales in the morning sun. It was cold, his breath steamed in the air, and he noticed frost sugaring the nettles and elder that grew in the shade of the outbuildings.

'Where are we going?' he asked, hoping this would not be a punishable question.

Traveller glanced at him. 'Out to the sea wall along from where you came in. We got you located as soon as the torbearer broke away from you, but we didn't act on that for many years. We had the tor located in your original time, but the beast was there guarding it, as it always does, until it was taken up.'

Beast?

Tack did not ask that question. He pursued his original query. 'Why are we going there?'

'There we use the mantisal that brought me here. It is presently sitting out of phase underneath the slope,' replied Traveller, impatience in his voice.

'Mantisal?'

'Enough. I haven't the inclination now and you haven't the intelligence.'

Tack realized the limit on how far he could push, so clamped his mouth shut as he tramped along beside Traveller. Evidently he was being dragged into a situation it would take him some effort to understand, but that there was a chance for him to understand it fully was an indulgence U-gov had never allowed him.

They followed the track out between the fields and round to the left, where it finished against a gate and a thick blackthorn hedge. Beyond the gate was a field that had been left fallow long enough for brambles to take hold. After climbing over the gate they worked their way around the edge of the field to where a path had been beaten by frequent use through the vegetation. The far side of this field was bordered by a barbed-wire fence with a stile at one end. Climbing this, they then crossed a grass area as wide as a motorway, and finally mounted the sea wall.

The sea did not come right up to the wall itself here, as between there lay an area of mudflats overgrown with sea sage and whitish grass, cut through with channels clogged with glossy mud and encroached by the marching growth of samphire. Traveller pointed out a wreck half sunk in the flats, its portals like blind eyes, and the mud all around stained with rust. Negotiating a course out to this, across tough grass on which crab carapaces seemed to be impaled, and avoiding the channels that might easily suck them down, they came at last to the edge of a muddy hollow containing the mass of black wood and corroding metal. Traveller stood there for a while with his eyes closed and his head tilted back, a salt breeze whipping loose strands of hair around his face.

Observing the man, Tack was struck by just how *different* he appeared. It was not so much the albinism, but the bone structure underneath. Traveller was elfin . . . or demonic.

'When it comes, you climb inside and make yourself as comfortable as you can. While we shift, you must not extend any part of yourself outside its structure or that part will ablate in interspace.' Traveller opened his eyes and gazed at Tack, and his eyes were now brighter, more intense. Tack saw that they were almost orange in colour, and could not understand why he had not noticed this before. He nodded dumbly, not really understanding.

Traveller gestured in the direction of the wreck and, in the empty air between them and it something began to phase into existence. It was spherical, at least five metres across, a vaguely geodesic structure formed of glassy struts ranging in thickness from that of a human finger to a man's leg. As it slid closer to them, Tack saw that within its substance veins and capillaries pulsed, and that the thicker areas were occupied by half-seen complex structures that sometimes looked like living organs and sometimes tangled masses of circuitry. From the outer structure, curving members grew inwards to intersect below two smaller spheres, which were only a little larger than human heads. The curve of these members left enough space for Tack and Traveller to occupy, overlooked by the two spheres. Only when he gripped what felt like warm glass and hauled himself up behind Traveller into the cavity, did Tack realize just what the twin spheres actually were. They were huge multi-faceted eyes positioned above fused-together glassy feeding mandibles, a spread-thin thorax and the beginnings of legs that blended into the curving outer members, and thence into the surrounding sphere. He had just climbed inside some insane glassmaker's representation of a giant praying mantis turned inside out.

'It's alive,' Tack observed.

'Where I come from,' Traveller replied, 'defining what life is has become a little problematic. Now be silent until I tell you that you may speak again.'

Tack felt the power of this order operating through his new programming, and knew that were Traveller to abandon him right then he would never be able to speak again unless reprogrammed. Inside the strange creation he found a place to jam the backpack, a ridge on which he could seat himself and one of the internal struts to hang on to.

Traveller stood before the mantis head and reached out towards the eyes. His hands sank into them as if into syrup, and the surrounding structure took on the tint of molten glass. Then the world departed and Tack found himself weightless in a glass cage flying through a grey abyss over a sea of rolling darkness. In this he saw a vastness beyond comprehension, combined with an impossible lack of perspective, and in trying to comprehend both of these felt something straining to break away in his mind. After a moment he closed his eyes and wished it would all go away.

4

Astolere:
Upon seeing the creature in its growth tank I had to ask why it is now so large. Cowl informs me that the greater the mass of organic complexity, the greater the vorpal energy generated (that word again). This is self-evident, but it seems to me that our research requirements of this energy are small, while what the creature might generate is potentially vast. Even so, I have been informed that Engineer Goron, the de facto governor of Callisto, damn him, is to cancel further research until such a time as the full consequences of time travel can be ascertained. Palleque tells me that the real reason for this research halt is that the Engineer trusts the preterhuman not at all. When I asked Palleque why this was the case, he replied, 'Sister, after their attack on the energy dam the Umbrathane escaped by displacing their ships. Work it out.'

Not much to work out really. I know because I built the first displacement generator, using an offshoot of Cowl's research. The Engineer must think Cowl has passed on schematics to the Umbrathane and is therefore a traitor. Moreover, how did they know enough about the dangers represented by his research to risk such a suicidal attack? Of course doubt remains because, had their attack succeeded, Cowl himself might have been killed. Unless the attack was actually a rescue attempt . . .

The gunfire had ceased by the time Polly returned to the deck and the moon was up with its horns sinister. She made out structures like a squad of Martian war machines frozen mid-stride in the sea, and from one of these a searchlight speared down, as the boat decelerated and turned.

'Red Sands army fort,' said Dave. 'Did a run out there a couple of weeks back, so it's not the usual supplies we'll be taking in. They're stocked up until the next changeover.'

They moved back along the deck to the wheelhouse, where Frank stood by the helm, gently guiding it with one hand while puffing on a pipe. Polly stared at the thing in his mouth and remembered that the last time she had seen someone smoking a pipe, it had contained a cocktail of crack and an LSD derivative. She suspected, from the strata of strong tobacco smoke in the boat's interior, that these drugs were not Frank's particular penchant.

'So, who are you then?' he asked.

'Seems she went to take a swim without any intention of coming back,' said Dave, leaning back against the wall of the cabin. Outside, a metal chimney was belching steam as Toby put out the fire in the stove, as per Frank's recent instructions.

Frank eyed her for a moment then said, 'Now why would you want to do that?'

'Because my husband died at El Alamein,' Polly replied.

'I thought you said boyfriend,' interjected Dave, lighting up his nth cigarette.

Oops, now they'll start getting suspicious. Tell them you called me husband out of habit, as extramarital sex is somewhat frowned on in this particular time.

Smoothly Polly explained, 'Habit. Where we lived it was best for people to think we were married.'

You're rather good at this. Had I known, I might have made different use of you.

Polly would have liked to explain to Nandru that, prior to putting the object on her arm, she would have had difficulty finding her backside with both hands. She was thinking an order of magnitude more clearly than heretofore and, as every moment passed, she could feel the crap being further cleared from her system. What worried her now was what would happen when withdrawal hit. It hadn't yet, but she felt sure it must.

'Do you still intend to take that swim?' Frank eventually asked.

'No . . . it would be a betrayal of his memory. He was a good man.'

Ha-de-fucking-ha. Because of Marjae I wanted you creamed. I can't feel it now, but back then, when I was alive, I thought you a noxious insect that should be stepped on.

'We loved each other,' Polly added, and heard hollow laughter in her head.

Frank and Dave both looked embarrassed at this.

Frank said, 'This will all have to be confirmed, you know. They don't like any unexpected visitors on these forts, even if you hadn't any intention of coming out here.'

'I've no problem with that,' said Polly, glancing out at Toby, who was now manipulating a hoist to raise a crate from the hold.

Frank brought the boat to a near halt below one of the constructs, his hands delicate on the controls to keep the vessel in position. Polly saw a net, attached to a line, thump down on the deck and watched as Dave went out to retrieve a small pack taped to the line, and then help Toby heave the crate into the net. A torch flashed from above and Dave returned the signal with his own torch. Polly did not need the clearness of thought she now possessed to figure that this particular delivery was unscheduled.

'Likes his malt whisky, does Lieutenant Pearce,' commented Frank as the other two returned to the cabin and they got under way again.

Conversation thereafter became muted and Polly felt herself fading into the background as the three men discussed a war that was not even a memory to her. She learnt that both Dave and Toby were still in basic training and anxious to join the fighting, and recognized Frank's tired look when he heard this enthusiasm. And she wondered at such naivety.

In the next hour Dave pointed out another fort far to their left and announced, 'Shivering Sands.'

Later, Frank said, 'Knob Sand,' gesturing to some half-seen marker buoys while swinging the boat to the port. 'And there's Knock John.'

Polly was impressed. The naval fort loomed like an old-style battleship raised up on two thick pillars. No lights were visible on it, but in silhouette against the star-studded sky she could discern guns and radio antennae.

'Frank here. Coming in from the south,' Frank spoke into his transceiver.

They drew into Knock John's shadow and slowed by a wooden jetty being hinged down from a scaffold running up the side of the nearest pillar. Only then did Polly get a true impression of the size of the fort. Dave and Toby cast ropes to the men who came out onto the jetty when it was in position, before unclipping the deck hatches to access the cargo below. Above them a crane was swung across and it lowered a cargo net straight into the open hold.

'Best you come with me. Feel up to climbing that ladder?' Frank asked her.

Polly stared at the ladder, now made visible by the lights that had just been turned on within the scaffold, and wondered if she could manage it. She suddenly felt weak, slightly sick and incredibly hungry – more hungry than she had felt in years.

'Brownlow should have the stew pot on by now and some tea brewing, and his tea is better for some additive.' Frank patted the shoulder bag he had just picked up.

'I can handle it,' said Polly firmly, then something lurched inside her and she found herself closing her mouth on a welling up of saliva. What surprised her most was that it wasn't a drink she wanted so much as the food. Following him down onto the jetty, then along to the iron ladder, she rolled up her dropping coat sleeves and cursed her lack of footwear . . . abandoned somewhere in this same sea. Someone at the head of the ladder rushed over to help her as soon as he realized she was a woman.

'My daughter,' explained Frank to those who had stopped to stare, then led her across, under the shadow of the crane, to an open doorway. Polly glanced up and noted the barrels of an anti-aircraft gun before following him inside. They negotiated further stairs and ladders, and Polly received a blurred impression of somewhere crammed with men and equipment and fogged by cigarette smoke, until eventually she found herself in a canteen, where she could concentrate on nothing but the smell of cooking.

Soon all her attention was focused on a mess tin filled with unidentifiable lumps, which was thrust in front of her, and the hunk of bread plonked down beside it. Everything else faded into insignificance as she picked up a fork and began to eat. It seemed only moments later that the tin was empty and she was mopping up the gravy.

'I take it you could do with some more?' said Frank.

Polly nodded dumbly.

Three mess tins later, Polly glanced up into Frank's amused regard. Huge fatigue then trammelled her, and she had time only to push the mess tin aside before her forehead hit the table and sleep dropped on her like a black eiderdown. Then, seemingly with no transition, someone was shaking her.

The sea of blackness turned to white and the sky took on a more familiar aspect of grey cloud split against cerulean blue, and gravity took hold of him and dragged him down against the hard bones of the mantisal. Tack stared at the colour, and took it in like a man starved. That was it about the between place: no colour at all. For a moment longer, though, everything seemed unreal, and Tack noticed Traveller warily scanning their surroundings. Then the man shifted one hand inside a mantis eye and they *completely* arrived.

'Out. Out now,' said Traveller, withdrawing both his hands from the two spheres.

Tack grabbed up the pack and pulled himself towards the gap through which he had entered the mantisal. He fell and, bracing himself for impact, was grateful to drop into a snowdrift. As he pulled himself out of this, brushing it from his ruined coat, Traveller dropped into a squat on some grassy ground nearby, which was only lightly dusted with snow, then stood upright. Tack glanced up at the mantisal and, seeing it dropping back into that ineffable dimension, quickly averted his gaze. When he turned back it was gone and all that remained was the sky, punctuated by the occasional bird silhouette. He took up the backpack, slung it on and turned to Traveller.

The strange man's face was lined with fatigue, and Tack noticed that his eyes were now brownish-gold in colour, as if dulled by the extent of his weariness.

'Over there,' Traveller said, pointing to a distant line of dense forest, and they began trudging in that direction. After a moment he went on, 'You're not curious about where, or rather *when*, we have come?'

Tack stared at him dumbly.

'Ah,' said Traveller. 'You may speak.'

'I *am* curious,' admitted Tack, now free to speak again.

'Welcome to the early Pleistocene,' said Traveller, gesturing about himself with both hands. 'Neanderthal man is dominant at present, but humans like yourself are appearing, and it will only be another hundred thousand years before their ascendence. The belief, in your time, was that your people drove the Neanderthals to extinction. The truth is that a disease crossed a species boundary, contracted from the animals they hunted as food, and killed most of them off. Many of those who survived mated with your own kind and their DNA still exists even in my time.'

How very interesting, thought Tack, knowing that to voice such a thought would probably result in him getting a beating. He looked around and instantly realized that he was in no place that he knew, for in his lifetime he had never seen a landscape completely untouched by the works of man. Perhaps there had been such places in those portions of the Antarctic still not inhabited in his own era, but someone like himself did not get to travel there – his business usually involving very close contact with other human life, however briefly, not the shunning of it.

Traveller paused for a second to kick at a pile of dung before moving on. 'Mammoth, probably. I brought us down in an interglacial period, so they've moved up while the ice sheet retreated. Some big animals around in this time – we definitely don't want to run into any of the predators.'

Tack noted the massive footprints in the snow, and suddenly it felt as if a huge emotional backlog had caught up with him. That the girl had dragged him back in time he had figured with stolid logic – which was understandable since U-gov programmed its killers for dispassion. Now he experienced a surge of emotion that flipped his stomach over and made the world grow vast around him. *Mammoth*, he remembered from his early schooling. *Smilodons* . . . As they walked, he turned away from Traveller to scrub tears from his eyes. Then, his voice catching, he brought the subject back to their immediate circumstances, 'Is that mantisal thing alive?'

Without looking round, Traveller said, 'It is alive in the only way that matters.'

'I don't understand . . .'

'Vorpal energy,' Traveller stated succinctly and by the man's mien Tack knew that to push him further might result in renewed violence.

More advanced, maybe, but certainly more bad tempered, thought Tack.

However, when Traveller now glanced round, his expression changed utterly. Tack registered frowning surprise in the man's face, then a hint of amusement. Traveller explained further, 'Only life can travel in time and time travel is only possible in the time life exists. It is a self-fulfilling prophecy. Reality is patterned in circles, spheres, convolute and twisting dimensions. It is not required to be amenable to your logic. The linear mind finds this difficult to grasp.'

Tack felt the urge to make some sarcastic quip, but quickly repressed it.

Traveller added, 'The limit, for life, of travel into the past is the Nodus. It is that point in the Precambrian when multi-cellular life first evolved.'

'Why is multi-cellular life the limit? Why not single cells?' asked Tack and waited, half-expecting to have his nose set bleeding again.

'Ah, a sign of intelligence at last.'

Tack couldn't help but breathe a sigh of relief.

Traveller went on, 'That point is much debated. The energy gradient steepens into those aeons, and time travel is possible but unfeasible. The answer is connected with the quantity of living matter extant on Earth, and the amount of vorpal energy that generates.'

Something dubious in that explanation, thought Tack. 'I do not know what vorpal energy is,' he said.

It seemed Traveller did not attack him when he asked questions, no matter how they were posed. The first beating must have been only to disable him for capture, and the second time he was struck was because of his voicing sarcasm.

'I could give you the equations, but you do not have the weight of knowledge to absorb them. It is just a kind of energy generated by the slow interaction of complex molecules. It was discovered some hundreds of years after your time when separate sciences were beginning to meld together.'

Tack surprised himself by beginning to understand. He had forgotten nothing of their discussion in the barn and now a picture was building in his mind. He had a vision of time sprouting from that point called the Nodus, branching and multiplying between facing mirrors of probability, expanding from one point towards infinity. This vision carried emotional weight and it frightened him.

As they finally reached the forest, it became evident that, behind the clouds, the sun was setting. Here, once they had pushed a little way in, they found the ground thick with pine needles and dead wood, and only sparsely scattered with snow.

'Here. You may take off that pack now.'

It was dark under the trees and Tack was very tired. His training and his superb physical condition had carried him this far, but even he could not sustain indefinitely the kind of punishment he had received over the last – he glanced at his watch – twenty-five hours.

'We light a fire now, eat and rest. You will take the first watch for three of your standard hours, but understand that there are only beasts here, so it is likely that the most that will be required of you is that you keep the fire going. You understand?'

In this forest glade, sheltered from an icy wind that propelled flecks of snow as from a grit blaster, they built a cairn of wood, which Traveller lit with a weapon only briefly revealed to Tack. The gun itself looked quite silly and ineffectual, but focused enough energy in that instant to incinerate half of the woodpile and send a huge cloud of white smoke ascending into the trees. The two of them then piled on more fuel and huddled close around the blaze.

*

Polly opened gritty eyes, but her vision was blurred and it took a moment for her to discern Frank standing over her. She sat up slowly and looked around. She found herself on a bed in cramped sleeping quarters, with a blanket thrown over her.

'There a toilet?' she asked muzzily.

Frank stepped back as she sat up and put her legs over the side of the bunk. 'Back there.' He gestured to the door behind him. 'But, first, I found these for you.'

He placed a bundle on the bed: army fatigues, a small pair of boots and a couple of pairs of thick socks because the boots most certainly would not be small enough. She accepted these gratefully, then stood and walked unsteadily to the door. Following her, he directed her down a short partitioned corridor to another door. Once inside she locked herself in, took off the coat, and found blessed relief on the toilet while she took off her hip bag and checked its contents. Luckily the waterproof lining was intact, the seal-strip had remained closed, and the inside was dry. She checked the contents and was not sure what she was most glad to find, her hairbrush, rolling tobacco or her taser. At the sink she cleaned herself up as best she could, brushed her hair and applied a little make-up. Then she pulled on the fatigues, up underneath her pelmet so it held them in place like a cummerbund, then pulled on the socks and boots. Thus fortified, she rolled a cigarette and put on the coat before stepping outside again. Frank was waiting for her, glancing impatiently at his watch.

'The sun's near up and it's time we got back to shore,' he told her.

Outside, in morning light, Polly observed the navy personnel starting about their business on the fort's superstructure. Frank led her around the side, down a short ladder to the same door through which they had entered. Soon they were down on the jetty and into the boat and pulling away, Dave and Toby greeting her cheerfully.

Suddenly she was feeling very good – full of energy and anxious to be . . . somewhere. Turning to look back at the fort as they pulled away from it, she now had a perfect view of the structure, with its waves of camouflage paint undulating across the stocky pillars that supported it, with its radar tower and the guns.

Impressive, isn't it?

In her head, Polly replied, '*Yes, I never knew about things like this.*'

Do you know anything about this war they're fighting?

'*You can read my thoughts?*' she subvocalized.

No, only those ones that are on the edge of speech. Any deeper and things get a bit confusing. But tell me, what do you intend to do now? You are in an age you do not know, and I wonder what chances you have of going back to your own era.

'*I'll survive – and maybe I'll do better than survive. I made this thing on my arm take me back to here, so maybe I can make it take me forward again. If I can successfully travel in time, then there will be nothing I cannot do.*'

Big plans from such a little whore.

But her plans did not take into account the three who awaited her on the jetty.

Lightning ignited over the horizon like the flares of a distant battle, and the low rumble of thunder was constant. Visible through the trees, another glow lit the opposite horizon, as red and ominous as a furnace. Tack guessed there must be vulcanism over that way, but did not consider it worth the risk of seeking confirmation. Soon they were eating from Traveller's supplies of spicy food, which Tack did not recognize but did not dislike either, then they used melted snow to make themselves hot coffee, which he felt certain he would require over the coming hours. Traveller he noticed, laced his coffee with the contents of a hip flask, but none of its contents was offered to Tack. Shortly, Traveller searched through his pack and came up with a pair of slip-on boots, which he passed to Tack. While Tack pulled them on, Traveller also unearthed two thermal sheets. One of these he tossed over to Tack, and the other he laid out on the ground for himself beside the fire. However, he showed no inclination yet for sleep.

'Can you tell me more about this Cowl?' Tack asked, between sips of steaming coffee.

'Cowl is Cowl,' said Traveller, something hard entering his voice. Then he shook his head in irritation. 'I suppose it is best you know . . . Cowl is a genetically altered being from my own time, superior in intelligence, vicious, dangerous, unviable, and in our opinion not really human. He hates us because we *are* human, just as he hates everything else that is not of his own creation.' Traveller stared into the flames, 'And from beyond the Nodus he is trying to kill us all.'

Traveller made no attempt to hide the loathing in his voice. This man and Cowl had a *history*, Tack realized.

'But . . . you said earlier you can't travel beyond the Nodus?' he said.

Traveller shrugged. 'I don't know everything.'

Tack decided not to comment on this particular first.

Traveller continued, 'He shuffles the alternates, seeking to bring to the main line one in which the human race did not evolve and where only his kind is viable. He does this by adding his own DNA to the protomix in the seas. He is constantly experimenting and to test his results he samples the future. Tors, like the one worn by that female you were with, are the way he does that.'

'She is a sample?' Tack asked, thinking this explanation too pat.

Traveller met his gaze, and Tack saw that some of the colour had returned to the man's eyes. 'A sample, yes, and when Cowl has learnt what he wants, she will be disposed of as such,' he said bitterly.

Tack was not sure how he felt about that. He had intended to kill the girl himself, but that some monster roosting at the beginning of time would do so, almost negligently, affronted him. He gazed at Traveller and again saw signs of irritation. Nevertheless, he risked one more question.

'I don't really understand. How can you travel back in time to stop him? If he succeeds, he *has* succeeded, and that is in the past. You would now be off the main line, so unable to travel back to him.'

'Concurrent time,' said Traveller almost dismissively, and lay back on his thermal sheet.

'What is concurrent time?'

'If Cowl succeeds in his mission, say, ten years after his arrival at the Nodus, we – my people – will be shoved off the main line ten years after he departed from us.'

'But that won't kill you.'

'No, but we will no longer be able to travel in time. We'll be somewhere down the probability slope in a prison of linear time, and closer to oblivion. That would be death to us.'

Tack had an entirely different idea about what was death; it involved horrible gristly sounds, blood and burnt flesh. He gave Traveller a final glance before spreading out his own heat sheet and sitting down on it with his seeker gun ready. At no point did he think to aim the weapon at his captor – it just wasn't in his programming.

The three men wore trench coats and trilbies. Two of them looked to have been built in a tank factory, but the leaner one seemed to have been fashioned for a more vicious purpose.

'You'll come with us right now,' said the lean man as soon as she stepped off the boat. He was taller than his two accompanying heavies, and good-looking in a cold sort of way.

'Who the hell are you?' asked Frank.

'None of your concern,' said the thin man, his gaze still fixed on Polly.

'I'm making it my concern,' growled Frank.

One of the heavies calmly took out a large revolver and pointed it at the boat captain. Perhaps seeing that things might get a little out of control, the leader turned his full attention to Frank. 'Fleming, military intelligence.' He displayed some paperwork from his pocket.

'Oh.' Frank backed off. 'I suppose someone from Knock John got onto you. Look . . . she's all right. We dragged her out of the sea . . .'

Fleming held up a hand to silence him. 'I'll get to your story in good time.' He glanced at Toby and Dave as they too stepped off the boat, and slipped his hand menacingly into the pocket of his trench coat. Indicating the man who had drawn the revolver, he went on, 'Garson here will return for your statements tomorrow, so I want the three of you here on this jetty at eight sharp. We will meanwhile take this young lady away and have a chat with her.' He turned towards the shore, where a car was parked. The second heavy took hold of Polly's biceps and guided her firmly in that direction.

See. What did I tell you?

Polly shot a look of appeal at Frank and the other two as she was marched off, but they just stood staring at her with growing suspicion.

I reckon it'll be electrodes, and a body massage with a length of hosepipe, then a firing squad at dawn.

'*What about you?*' Polly subvocalized. '*Will you die with me, or will you continue existing in the head of a rotting corpse?*'

Oh . . . yes . . .

'Take the coat off,' said the unnamed heavy once they reached the car. She did as instructed and he took the garment and tossed it to Garson, who began to search it. 'Take that off, too,' the man then ordered, gesturing at her hip bag. 'Carefully.' Again she did as instructed and the item was passed on to Fleming this time. As the three men now studied her, their attention came to rest on the object on her arm.

'Now what is that?' enquired Fleming.

Polly glanced down at it and could think of no reasonable explanation. Nandru came to her rescue though.

Tell them it's scar tissue. Tell them you were badly burned. The damned thing looks like part of you now, anyway.

That explanation was only accepted when it became evident to her captors that the strange covering would not be separated from her flesh, and was apparently part of it.

'Now, hands up on the car.' Glancing back she saw the still unnamed one pulling on tight leather gloves. She turned her face away as he did an intimately thorough body search and, wincing, she wondered if surgical gloves had yet been invented. The greatcoat was finally returned to her, then she was pushed inside the car, her searcher squeezing into the back beside her. Garson slid behind the wheel and Fleming got into the front passenger seat. Nothing more was said as the vehicle started up and they drove off, but Polly became aware of Fleming's interest in the contents of her hip bag.

'We have been expecting infiltration of our sea forts for some time,' said Fleming, eventually closing the bag and placing it on the dashboard. 'I have to admire the way you went about it. I supose you intended to build up a relationship with Brownlow?'

'I'm not a spy,' said Polly grimly.

Fleming laughed quietly. 'You'll tell us everything eventually, so why not make it easy on yourself? Tell us all we want to know and I can promise you'll go to Holloway rather than up against the stained and bullet-pocked brick wall in Bellhouse.'

'I'm not a spy,' Polly repeated desperately, realizing her story about a lover killed in North Africa would soon be proven untrue. Possessing no identification papers for Fleming and his kind – no history here whatsoever – she foresaw the questions would be never-ending because no answer she could give would ever be believed or confirmed. Her only option was to escape and hide, but how? She looked at the object clinging to her arm and realized that perhaps there was another option.

Immediately upon thinking this, she felt a tension of forces webbing through her body from the alien thing. For a second her environment seemed to grow dark and she had a deeper vision of a vast colourless continuum, over which all her present surroundings seemed a translucent moving watercolour. Then suddenly she panicked and clamped down on it all, somehow, and the world around her returned to normal.

What happened then? Muse 184 has the facility to monitor your biorhythms, and they just went crazy. It is now transmitting a 'wounded soldier' warning.

'*I have my way out of this situation, but I'm too scared to take it. The thing wants to take me through time, but I don't know where to,*' she subvocalized.

Perhaps you'd better save that option for when they apply the electrodes.

'*Thank you for your comforting words.*' Polly winced.

Including the car she rode in, every machine she now saw would have been classified as a serious antique in her own era. The few tractors on the fields were small machines, grey or dull red, pulling ploughs little bigger than were once pulled by a team of horses, but of a suitable scale for the little fields they occupied. There were many laid-over hedges, and many other fields contained livestock. The roads they drove upon were unmarked by lines and never wider than double-track.

Occasionally they passed khaki-painted military vehicles and clusters of armed soldiers. Twice they were stopped, but Fleming's papers quickly got them moving again. Old propeller-driven aeroplanes frequently thundered overhead. The people in the villages were dressed for historical drama. Polly was feeling increasingly lost.

'Here we are, Ramsden Bellhouse,' announced Fleming at last.

The village looked no different from any of the others they had driven through. They turned into a drive barred by a counter-weighted gate. A guard carrying a Sten gun walked over from the log he had been sitting on to enjoy a crafty cigarette. He peered into their car and after a moment nodded to Fleming, then went to raise the gate. Soon the vehicle pulled up beside a large old house that was ancient even in this antique age.

'I'm told this place has an interesting history,' said Fleming. 'It's about four centuries old and supposedly haunted by some headless woman, but then don't all buildings that old have their resident ghosts? It's ideal for us though: not too far from our bases or from the railway station, but just isolated enough so that the civvies don't hear or see something they might not like.'

Polly was hustled out of the car and into the building. She just had time to observe a large old-fashioned kitchen, a table scattered with ashtrays, empty cigarette packets and the detritus of terminal tea consumption before she was herded up some narrow stairs, along a drafty high-ceilinged hall, and into a wood-panelled room. It contained only a single patinated desk and two chairs, and looked cold and inhospitable. But then she had expected no different.

'Sit down,' said Fleming, as he closed the door. Polly noticed the other two men had not joined them, and heard the ominous clonk of the door being locked from the other side. She gazed through leaded windows across the surrounding trees and a patchwork of fields. Glancing lower, she noticed a low roof about two metres below the window, and wondered if, given the opportunity, she could scramble that way to the ground without breaking her neck. Sitting, as instructed, she observed stains on the desk's surface: some were obviously teacup rings, but she wondered about some of the others.

Fleming deposited a notebook and Polly's hip bag on his own side of the desk, then walked past her to the window, taking out a packet of cigarettes. She saw that his brand was rather fancy – quite long and bearing three gold bands. He struck a match and lit up.

'Do you mind if I smoke, too?' she asked.

'Go ahead,' he said nonchalantly.

After a moment's hesitation Polly reached over and pulled her hip bag closer. Opening it, she saw that her taser, her lighter, and some make-up items were missing. Taking out her pack of tobacco, she rolled herself a cigarette, all the time aware that she was being closely watched. As she brought it to her lips, Fleming's hand shot round in front of her to light it with her own lighter. Once her cigarette was lit, he dropped the lighter on the table and walked round to his own seat.

'Interesting little gadget that,' said Fleming. 'I haven't seen anything quite like it, but then the Germans are quite clever at making interesting little devices.' He reached across the desk and dragged the hip bag back in front of him. Taking out Polly's purse, he flipped it open and examined the contents again. As he studied the chipcards, euro notes and coins his expression became increasingly puzzled.

Watching him, Polly realized what was probably bothering him – all the coins and notes had dates on them.

After a moment he said, 'Do your masters in Berlin honestly think we would fall for such a silly ruse. Just because *we* haven't made bonfires out of Mr Wells's books does not mean we cannot distinguish between the fact and fiction of them.'

'I don't understand what you mean.'

'I too have read *The Time Machine*.'

'I still don't understand . . .'

'The Time Machine' was a novel by a guy called H. G. Wells. It was about time travel. That's what he's referring to.

Fleming turned his attention to Polly's watch. He stared at it for a long moment, then said, 'Give me that.'

Polly slipped it from her wrist and slid it across.

'I see I can't fool you,' she said sarcastically.

He studied the LCD display, pressed some of the buttons and called up the miniscreen then the texting service, which was obviously offline. After a moment he obtained the calculator function and, using the buttons to control the cursor, actually got it to carry out some basic functions. This certainly seemed to unnerve him, so he inspected the strap, then turned the watch over. He then took out a penknife.

'I see that a lot of preparation has gone into this. What was the idea?'

He flipped off the back of the watch and when he saw the workings his face went white. 'Very interesting,' he said uncertainly.

'You win the war in 1945,' Polly said.

I'm not sure this is the brightest idea you've had.

Polly explained, 'I come from about two hundred years in the future, as you can see by the dates on the coinage.'

Fleming just stared at her, before clicking the back of the watch into place. He then began examining closely all the other contents of her hip bag: the wrapping of her tobacco, her cigarette papers, the condoms and even a packet of sweets. He took out the spermicidal spray and tested it on the air. Next he took her taser out of his pocket.

'What is this?'

When he clicked the charge switch, it whined up to power immediately and he quickly dropped it on the desk. The green *ready* light came on and after a moment he picked the device up again.

'Some sort of camera?' he suggested, studying it close up as he fiddled with it. With a crack the two wires spat out from the end of the device driving their needles straight into his forehead. With miniature lightnings flickering around his head, he jerked upright with a nasal groan, then crashed backwards out of his chair.

Polly was round the desk in a moment. She grabbed up the taser, its wires winding back in automatically as she took hold of it. A key was clonking round in the door as the taser recharged its capacitor. Then one of the heavies was stepping through the door, drawing an automatic pistol. Polly fired, the two wires striking him in the middle of his chest. Making the same sound as Fleming, he slammed back against the doorjamb and slid to the floor.

'No, not a camera,' murmured Polly, moving to the door as the taser's wires withdrew and it wound itself up to charge yet again.

The second heavy was not out in the hall, or anywhere visible, but she dared not risk escaping through the house, as there were possibly others around. The taser would not have enough power to deal with more than one more assailant. Thereafter the device needed to be left out in the sunlight to recharge the lithium battery that powered its capacitor. With a struggle, Polly dragged the comatose heavy into the room, then closed and locked the door from the inside. Quickly she gathered up her belongings and, not inclined to let the opportunity pass her by, searched the two unconscious men. When she eventually stepped out of the window, she had acquired an automatic and a spare ammunition clip, a lethal stiletto, and Fleming's wallet and cigarettes. A scramble down a sloping roof brought her to where the car was conveniently parked below her. She dropped onto its roof, and slid to the ground. Then she was up and running just as the startled second heavy piled out of the car.

'Stop or I shoot!'

Immediately Polly panicked. Always, in films and interactives, people could run while others were shooting at them and survive. This was reality – the reality of a heavy slug slamming into her back, snapping her spine before smashing through her. She stopped and turned slowly, her hands in the air. In that moment it seemed to her that she had tried all she could, but got nowhere. She allowed some internal grip to relax and that freed the tension which networked her body from the alien object on her arm.

As the heavy stood with revolver aimed, and growing confusion on his face. Polly could see the vastness accumulating behind him – a black rolling sea and endless grey sky.

'Come back!' the man shouted, and his revolver boomed, its sound oddly distorted and echoey, the bullet an ablating red streak over fading air. Then he was gone, the whole world was gone, and Polly was falling endlessly through dark and cold. She screamed, but the sound, along with her breath, was sucked away.

5

Astolere:
It is quite probable that the Umbrathane fleet remains somewhere in the Jovian system. Even I know that the energy requirement to displace them out of it would have been detected. Their fleet is a large imponderable, and Heliothane forces remain on alert. Saphothere's negotiations with the two Umbrathane leaders have gone surprisingly well. It seems that the particular faction comprising the ground assault force is always used in such risky missions because it is one whose beliefs are not so harsh as those of the Umbrathane majority. Apparently those leaders are prepared to accept imprisonment on Ganymede rather than face obliteration. Meanwhile I must return to the facility and supervise the temporary shutdown of Cowl's research program. I have to say that this is something about which I feel trepidation, especially when I tell the preterhuman himself that the torbeast (his name for it, and mountainous it is – other staff at the facility have jokily named it 'Jabberwock', though I've yet to understand the humour) must be vented out on the surface of Callisto.

Through the foliage above him Tack could see that the sky was a cloudless pale blue. A new day, in this unfamiliar time, had begun. Moving his arm up out of the covering fold of his heat sheet, he checked the time and saw that he had slept a further two hours since his second spell of watch ended. Traveller was moving about the campsite, but Tack did not want to turn over yet to see what the man was doing. He wanted to keep still for a little longer and get a chance to contemplate what he had thus far learnt.

Traveller wanted the tor that was growing on Tack's arm as,

somehow, this device would enable his kind to get to a creature called Cowl, who was trying to destroy the entirety of human history. There were so many holes in that explanation, and so many questions to ask, Tack could not even think of where to begin. The simple fact of time travel being a reality raised an insuperable wall of questions. However, lying there, Tack realized there was one question he had yet to ask: to where, or rather *when*, was Traveller taking him?

When Tack smelt coffee brewing and the mouth-watering aroma of roasting meat, he finally flipped back his sheet and sat up. He saw Traveller squatting by the fire and poking at it with a stick. A coffee pot rested on the hot embers, with skewered next to it the gutted body of a small animal.

Traveller gestured at the carcass with his stick. 'Wild pig. I'm surprised the racket didn't wake you.'

Tack looked at him queryingly.

'Something got its mother back in there.' He gestured with his thumb into the deeper forest. 'This one was hiding in bushes nearby.'

'Why didn't you bring the mother?'

'Not much left of her. Cave lion, I think. Best not to remove what was left of its kill in case it comes back for more of it.'

As Tack absorbed this, he noticed that Traveller's eyes had returned to that weird orange colour and that he seemed to possess more energy this morning than on the night before. Transferring his attention to the roasting flesh, he discovered in himself a touch of squeamishness, as the only meat he had ever eaten had come out of numerous layers of plastic – disassociated from its true source. He stood up then and moved away from the fire to urinate behind a tree. When he returned he found his squeamishness disappearing under the onslaught of growing hunger. Soon he found himself stuffing greasy roast pork into his mouth.

'Where are you taking me?' he asked eventually, cleaning his hands in the snow.

Traveller stared at him through the steam rising off his cup – his eyes now demonic. 'If you look upon time as a road, then in the wrong direction at present. We need you back in New London, where we have the technology to ensure the survival of your nascent tor. But that thing embedded in your wrist attracts the notice of Cowl's particularly nasty pet and it is, on *our* time, very active in proximity to *your* . . . natal time.' Traveller paused, his expression pained. 'I find your language particularly unsuited to any sensible discussion of time travel.'

'How do you finally intend to get back to this New London?' Tack asked, realizing he must keep doggedly to just one line of thought at a time, for every answer that Traveller gave him promulgated a whole new set of questions.

'We have an outpost called Sauros based in the Mesozoic, and between it and New London, a sub-temporal wormhole – a time tunnel.'

Tack sipped his coffee and considered. 'Mesozoic?'

Traveller grinned over his coffee. 'Think of dinosaurs,' he said. 'But we have some trips yet to make to get there. I was already tired before the one we just made, so I possessed only enough energy for limited symbiosis with the mantisal. That means we only managed about a million years. This next jump should take us back at least fifteen million.'

Tack felt his mouth go dry and suddenly, despite the hot coffee, he felt cold. With a hand that trembled only a little he placed his cup on the ground, took up his heat sheet and draped it around his shoulders.

'And this is the coldest it will be for us,' Traveller added. 'From now on things start getting hotter – in more than the literal sense, too.'

Tack waited for the punchline.

Traveller gestured about them. 'This is about as restful as it gets. Between us and Sauros lie about eighty million years of appetite.' Traveller stood up and gestured meaningfully to the backpack. Tack finished his coffee and folded the cup, inserting it into a compartment inside the coffee pot. This and the heat sheets went into the pack, which Tack then shouldered. As they emerged from the trees, Tack noticed dry grass showing through where the snow had melted away. Far to his right he saw a huge elephantine shape standing still as a rock before it turned back into the trees.

'Mammoth,' he breathed.

'Mastodon, actually,' Traveller corrected him. 'Mammoths customarily move around in family groups.' He paused and studied the spot where the creature had disappeared. 'Though there are the rogue males, of course.' With that he set off, quickly following their own tracks in the snow, back to where they had disembarked from the mantisal. Tack hurried along behind, scanning all about himself for something significant, since he felt sure this was a time – if not place – that he would never see again. But all he saw here was snowy grassland and forest, and earlier that one enigmatic shape, before the mantisal folded out of thin air before them, and they climbed aboard.

The nightmare darkness receded into memory and it seemed she had been in this forest for an age, with nothing to accompany her but the sounds of birds and the wind in the trees. But now she heard bells tinkling, the murmur of conversation and an occasional burst of laughter. Somewhere nearby there were people, and in Polly's mind that meant the possibility of food, for she was racked with a hunger that had already compelled her to chew and swallow a handful of acorns before vomiting up the whole bitter mess. Drawing hard on her second hunger-quelling cigarette, she then discarded it and moved on eagerly. Pushing through the bracken below towering trees, she soon lost any sense of where the sound was coming from and began flailing forward in a panic, then stumbled down a slope onto her knees. Before her, like an epiphany in the damp leaf-litter, grew a single yellowish-white toadstool. She reached out for it.

What the hell do you think you are doing?

'I'm hungry,' Polly replied, her mouth still full of nauseating bitterness.

Well, that would certainly cure any future hunger. Muse has it listed as Amanita virosa *or the Destroying Angel. I thought it was a death cap, but that's only a small disagreement of memory and acquired memory. Either way the results would eventually be the same.*

'You don't really know that,' said Polly, reluctant to deny herself this potential snack.

Muse 184 has a hundred terabytes of reference, remember. I'm living in its damned RAM, so I'm not taking up any space. Do you know what that means?

'No . . . no I don't.'

Put it this way, it knows more than any single human is ever likely to know on any subject you could think of. And being as its purpose is military, it particularly has everything in here you'd want to know about poisons and other causes of death. You want me to detail what will happen to you if you eat that thing?

'No, I don't need that.' Polly stood up and moved off, irritably kicking the toadstool to snowy fragments across the leaf litter as she went.

It's that damned scale on your arm. By my clock you ate four tins of pilchards and half a loaf of bread only six hours ago on that boat. It must be sucking you dry somehow. They knew it was parasitic . . . alive in its limited way.

'Why do you call it a scale?'

Where it came from, my little slot machine. You saw the . . .

creature that killed me? Well that thing on your arm is a scale from its back – if back it had.

'You said something about all this, but nothing made sense then.'

What's to tell? We raided a suicide bombers' school in Kazakhstan, and that creature hit at the same time. Fucking chaos. It chewed four of them down, and shed that thing on your arm in the process. It was just one of many arranged like scales on its surfaces, though whatever the creature is, we never saw enough of it to . . . just call it a monster, something vast from another place.

'What other place?'

I haven't got a clue.

Polly looked around her. There, the bells again . . . somewhere over that way.

'What happened then?' she asked.

One of the Binpots wanted to put it on his arm. Leibnitz put a clip into him before he got a chance, then the monster hit Leibnitz and Smith. I bagged the scale and ran with it – I knew it was important – and Patak and the others covered me. The monster took him when we got back to HQ. Next thing the last of us were in a U-gov facility with the big brains talking temporal anomalies. I was interrogated under VR with drugs I'd never heard of, then was sat out in a compound with the rest as bait for the . . . monster. Wired up like lab rats, we were. I knew it wanted me, see, from the moment I killed that guy who had been about to put the scale on himself, like you did. It attacked – chaos again. I was able to escape, grabbing the scale and some other tech as I went. The scale tried to get me to put it on, but it left me alone when I wrapped the fucking thing in plastique . . .

Polly found herself standing at the edge of a rough track. Distantly she could again hear the tinkling of bells, and that muted conversation and laughter.

'But what *is* it? What's it for?'

Christ knows. But I heard enough then to know that somehow time travel was involved, and that the monster it came from hunts through time, taking victims that are somehow irrelevant to the future. You know, if that thing hadn't attacked when it did, we would have still been around in an area that was subsequently carpet-bombed. I've thought about this a lot. I think it was coming to take dead men before they died.

Thinking about that made Polly's head ache. She turned onto the track and headed towards the human sounds. Shortly a covered wagon rounded a corner, pulled into view by a big white shire horse. The vehicle was hung with the bells she had heard, and painted with the words 'The Amazing Berthold' and its woodwork was intricately carved. Polly paused in its path as it approached, the driver and his elderly companion peering at her suspiciously, then she moved to one side of the track. As the wagon drew alongside her, she observed a young dark-haired man holding the reins, his clothes straight out of some historical interactive, and his broad flat hat sporting a couple of pheasant feathers. He pulled on the reins to halt the horse, then reached down to haul up the wooden brake.

At last it was ending, and the world was returning in coloured flashes like a strange species of lightning. Gradually revealed through the mantisal's glassy spars was a landscape seemingly little different from the one they had recently departed. They rematerialized above grassland a few hundred metres away from the edge of dense forest. Then Tack began to note the subtle but disturbing differences. Here the cloud-dotted sky was a deeper blue, the green of sprouting grass was hazing up through the trampled sea of older stalks, and everywhere were scattered yellow, red and lavender flowers. The distant trees were also tinged with the green and yellow of new growth, and there were birds racketing up into the air. A balmy breeze, carrying with it the smells of hot spring, dispersed the cold from the skeletal cage of the mantisal.

'Best get to the trees as quickly as we can,' said Traveller. 'Out here we're likely to get stomped.'

Tack saw that the man was tired again and his eyes lifeless. Traveller gestured to a distant elephantine shape coming towards them.

'Mammoth,' Tack said.

Traveller snorted. 'Wrong. They're ten million years in the future. That thing over there is a deinotherium – a rather larger and more bad-tempered ancestor of the elephant. So let's move.'

They dropped out of the mantisal and walked away from it. Glancing back, Tack saw the strange thing fold out of existence, leaving a cold mist that swiftly dissipated. Nearby he saw huge skins of excrement covering the ground, some old enough for plants to be pushing up through them, and some new enough to be covered by legions of flies contesting ownership with dung beetles the size of golf balls. Avoiding these, they tramped on towards the trees, keeping a wary eye on the approaching beast.

'How big is it? I can't really tell,' Tack asked.

'About four metres high at the shoulder. We could bring it down with our weapons, but even this far back in time every drastic action we take creates difficulties for the mantisal.' Seeing Tack's puzzled expression Traveller went on, 'We come from the potential future, and no matter how careful we may be our actions here affect that future.' He gestured all about them. 'Our presence here is even now moving this time-line down the probability slope, leaving as the main line all this without our presence. Therefore, in each jump through time we make, the mantisal takes us not only back in time but back up the slope to mainline time. And the more we influence each time we are in, thus affecting our probable future, the more slope it has to carry us back up on the next jump. Luckily, the further back we go, the less we affect our probable future.'

Reflecting on their previous conversations, Tack said, 'I'd have thought the danger would increase the *further* back we went.'

His expression showing his customary irritation, Traveller glanced across at him. 'Which shows just how little you understand. As I said before: kill your father before your conception and you'll end up right down the slope, where it would take the full energy output of the sun tap for a whole day to propel you back onto the main line. But to achieve the same screw-up here, you'd need heavy weapons – and as far back as, say, the Jurassic, nothing less than a tactical nuke.'

'I don't understand.'

'No, of course not.' Traveller said nothing more for a while then, relenting, added, 'Errors like that do not accumulate through time. There's an effect called temporal inertia. By travelling back in time and killing your father, you push yourself down the slope because of the paradox you've created. Kill your direct ancestor a hundred million years in the past, and you'll still be born.'

'But doesn't that mean . . . predestination . . . some controlling intelligence?'

'Only in the way that a tree is predestined to grow towards the sun, and only in the way that some god might have made that tree. Evolutionary forces are macroscale as well as microscale.'

'But—'

'Enough. Just think about what I've already told you. It is doubtful you'll be able to understand it all anyway. You still think linear.' Just then the deinotherium let out a roar and was suddenly charging towards them, kicking up a cloud of dust.

'It is probably in must,' said Traveller. 'Pick up your pace.'

Tack did so readily, glancing back the way they had come as he broke into a trot. 'Perhaps *that's* pissed it off,' he commented.

Traveller looked back, too, and his expression changed. The mantisal had returned, hovering just where they had previously abandoned it. Tack now did a double-take – it clearly wasn't their mantisal, since it contained four individuals who were even now scrambling out of it.

'Umbrathane,' Traveller hissed. 'Run!'

The order was reinforced through Tack's programming, so without conscious volition he found himself obeying. As he ran he drew his seeker gun, and he wondered if he had received some subliminal instruction to do that as well. A triple flash to his side: Traveller was firing with that weapon of his, then sprinting past Tack to turn and fire again. Suddenly the grass to their right was burning and the air full of smoke. Again the deinotherium roared, and now they could feel the thunder of its progress.

'Shed the pack!'

Still running, Tack obeyed, regretting the loss of the equipment it contained. But regret was dispelled when Traveller came sprinting past him with the same pack slung from one shoulder, as if its weight was of no consequence. Tack glanced back and saw the four newcomers heading directly towards them. Then the elephantine mass of the enraged animal thundered in between, drawing a veil of dust between them and their pursuers.

'Move faster!'

From somewhere inside himself, Tack found his last few ergs of energy and accelerated. But no matter how fast he ran, or dodged from side to side, Traveller was in front of him, behind him, to the side, crouching and firing, then up again and sprinting away. Traveller was *fast*, more so than any human Tack knew of, and the man made Tack feel slow and clumsy, which he had never felt before.

Behind them, the deinotherium's aggressive roaring changed to a panicked trumpeting, and Tack glimpsed back to see it turning aside, smoke boiling off its hindquarters, as black-clad figures moved quickly past it. Suddenly a tree exploded to Tack's left, and it was only then that he realized they had finally reached the forest. Loud detonations and flashes continued to move off to his left – the direction Traveller had veered in as they entered the trees. Tack just kept running as hard as he could. In fact he could not stop, and knew that if Traveller did not cancel his last instruction soon, he, Tack, would die of a ruptured heart.

Stop.

The order at last came through Tack's comlink as he was running, in the agony of lactic overload, down a black tunnel of trees. He immediately sprawled forwards on the ground, his muscles locking with cramps and his lungs feeling torn as he gasped for breath. Distantly he could still hear the trumpeting animal.

Hold your position and, excepting myself, kill anyone who comes to you.

It was some minutes before Tack could even pull himself to his knees. His seeker gun was clasped tightly in a hand as white as tooth enamel, and it took him a severe effort of will to unclench his fingers and drop the weapon. For a while he tried to massage the agonizing cramps from his legs, then taking up his gun again he dragged himself to cover amongst dense ferns beneath a fallen forest giant, partially supported off the ground by its own massive side branches. There he lay still and listened to the deinotherium's cries of outrage fading away.

After a hiatus, the birds started singing. He found nothing in their song to comfort him as he lay with his jaw still clenched rigid, while he tried to rub the agonizing knots from his legs. Slowly the pain was dispersing, but it would be some minutes before he would be able to get about on them again. As yet no suspicious sound or sign of movement.

Then the birdsong suddenly stopped again, and the most glorious face Tack had ever seen gazed down at him – before a hand like a nest of steel bars grasped the back of his collar and hauled him out of hiding.

The watcher, mind and body in glass, had tracked the course of the tor over brief centuries from this particular vorpal sensor, finally turning it out from interspace to track her progress in the real world. Upon seeing the girl thrashing her way through the woods and talking to herself, it was not difficult to surmise that this was one torbearer who would not survive long. But the omniscient voyeurism was almost addictive, and there had been something odd about those insane monologues . . . After a brief exchange with the girl, the wagon driver, presumably the Amazing Berthold advertised, jumped nimbly down to the ground and swept off his hat. And the watcher decided to listen in.

'Dancing before the King at Court, or standing at the bows of some ship travelling to far Lyonesse,' the man said, perhaps in response to an earlier question from the girl, which the watcher did not feel inclined to track back to.

The man went on, 'Perhaps standing at a window of the Bloody Tower, awaiting the harsh fate bestowed upon the beautiful and innocent. Maybe far away on—'

'You are as interminable as a three-onion fart, Berthold,' said the older man on the wagon, before replacing in his mouth the stick he had been gnawing.

The girl was studying both men intently, obviously starving because of the parasitic drain of her tor, perhaps fascinated by their smallpox-scarred faces, which were inadequately covered by the neatly trimmed beards they wore.

'But, Mellor, it is my interminable rhetoric that puts the groats and pennies into my pouch and the pheasant pie into your mouth.'

Mellor removed his stick. 'No, I would venture to suggest it is the juggling and pratfalls which do that and your athletic servicing of either lord or lady.'

Berthold frowned, then returned his attention to the girl. 'You have the face of an angel, my lady. Tell me, whence do you come, and whither do you go?'

The watcher noted now that Berthold was eyeing, with some puzzlement, her clothing, his attention finally resting on her army boots. It must be the odd clothing that caused him to use the honorific 'my lady', for in this age skin unscarred by smallpox was the preserve of milkmaids naturally immunized by an earlier infection of cowpox.

'I'm a traveller from . . . the East,' said the girl.

'Yes,' said Berthold, 'it is said that their garb is most strange and that the women wear trews. Most interesting.'

Ah, the human capacity for self-deception, thought the watcher.

The girl at last found something to add. 'I am also a hungry traveller.'

Bertold turned to Mellor. 'How far to go?'

'Another six miles, by my reckoning, and we were instructed to arrive not before tomorrow morning. Berthold, what is in your mind?'

'I am thinking that the nobility value novelty most high, and are never averse to the sight of a pretty face.' Berthold turned to her. 'Climb up here with us and travel a little way. We shall soon make our camp and I am sure Mellor has some pie to spare. Tomorrow we shall eat like kings in the house of a King, and shall leave it with as much as we can carry.'

The watcher wondered if the girl had any idea what age she

was in and how lucky she was not to have ended up dumped behind a tree with her throat cut.

Mellor snorted then spat a gobbet of phlegm over the side of the wagon, but he shuffled aside to allow the girl to sit beside him. Once Berthold, too, was up beside her, squashing her up against Mellor, the watcher felt some sympathy for her, and some amusement at her expression. By her dress she must have come from an age where people were not so unconcerned about body odour or about the things living in their beards.

'Geddup there, Aragon,' said Berthold, as he released the brake and snapped the reins across the horse's rump. The animal looked back at him, let out a snort identical to Mellor's, then slowly began to trudge up the track. After listening for a while to Berthold's subsequent 'three-onion farts' as he described interminably his adventures as a travelling entertainer, the watcher tracked forwards in time.

Late afternoon inexorably slid towards evening, and before sunset Berthold pulled the wagon over to a clearing below a huge oak tree. While Mellor freed the horse from its harness, the girl and Berthold collected fallen wood from around the tree. When Berthold then struggled to use a tinderbox to get a fire started, the girl took out a propane cigarette lighter, thought for a moment, then hurriedly put it away again.

Very wise, the watcher whispered in her glassy domain. The consequences for the girl might be proximity to more flame than would be healthy.

Soon a good blaze was going and beside it rested enough wood to keep it fed for some time. Only then, in fading light, did Mellor fetch a sack of food from the back of the wagon. The bread looked stale and the hard pies seemed to contain, along with meat, fat and jelly, the occasional bone and unidentifiable organ webbed with rubbery tubes. But for someone who had earlier tried eating acorns, it was doubtless all ambrosia. Though eating plenty themselves, Mellor and Berthold watched the girl's guzzling with awe.

'You *were* hungry,' commented Berthold.

Pausing to wipe crumbs from her face, the girl said, 'Yes, I was . . . and you say there'll be more tomorrow?'

'Tomorrow I shall entertain the King himself, then our pouches will be filled with silver and our sacks filled with salted venison and pork, pheasant pies and sweet pastries.'

After washing down, with small beer, her latest mouthful, the girl prompted, 'The King, yes . . .'

Berthold obliged her, 'Yes, good old Harry himself – Henry the VIII, under God alone King of this fine green country.'

The girl choked on another mouthful of pie and had to cough it into the fire.

The woman tossed Tack out into the open as if he were an empty coat, then slowly approached as he struggled upright. But, as he brought his gun to bear, she was on him in a second, slapping it out of his hand.

'Pishalda fistik!'

Under the impetus of Traveller's last order, he swept his foot out towards her legs, while aiming a straight-fingered blow to her throat. She caught his outstretched hand and twisted it so hard that he must follow it round or feel it break. Pulling his kris flick knife from concealment, he clicked it open and swung it towards her neck. Next thing he knew he was on the ground again, flat on his back and disarmed.

'Esavelin scrace, neactic centeer vent?' she said, casually inspecting the flick knife before closing it.

'Yeah, about four o'clock in the afternoon,' muttered Tack, hauling himself to his feet and preparing for attack again.

Desist.

Tack paused, grateful for this order from Traveller, aware that he had as much chance of killing this woman as he had of killing Traveller himself. Now, inactive, he had more time to study her. Approaching two metres in height, she moved with the same wiry strength as Traveller. Her face was utterly beautiful but strong, her cropped hair a dyed black that was growing out bright orange, and her eyes the colour of strawberries. She wore loose black fatigues, and a loose shirt underneath what looked like a sleeveless Kevlar jacket. Some sort of gun was holstered across her stomach, and various odd-looking instruments were affixed to her belt. His knife she now placed into a pouch also attached to the same belt.

Tilting her head she studied him with apparent confusion. 'Century twenty-two primitive. With you want what they?'

Tack could only suppose that somehow Traveller was watching this scene from nearby, and wondered why no shots had been fired. Unexpectedly, Traveller answered that same question as if the link between them ran deeper than just the comlink.

I am five kilometres south of you, and will be with you in fifteen minutes. Try to stay alive and try to delay.

Tack did not know how Traveller could see what was going on, though he guessed at some sophisticated sort of bugging – which should not be so difficult for a race advanced enough to travel in time.

'Answer me!' the woman spat.

'What was the question?' Tack asked.

The woman paused, as if listening, then, carefully articulating each word, said, 'What do the Heliothane want with you?'

'I would tell you if I knew a Heliothane from a hole in the ground.'

By now the woman's attention was fixed upon his right arm. Abruptly she stepped forward, grasped his forearm and lifted it to inspect the device now enclosing the fragment of tor embedded in his wrist.

'Fistik!' she spat, then, dropping his wrist, grabbed his shoulder and turned and shoved him stumbling forward. He got only a couple of metres before running straight into a wall of flesh. The hands that gripped his shoulders were huge and solid enough to compress the flesh off his bones. This man was enormous, dressed much the same as the woman, and by his features probably related to her. While he held Tack immobile, he and the woman exchanged a machine-gun conversation over his head, in their distinctive staccato language, then the man shoved Tack past him and on. Tack glanced back to see them walking behind him, the male with his weapon drawn.

The woman waved him on impatiently. 'What is the name of heliothant with whom you travel?'

Tack stopped and turned towards them. 'He didn't give me his name – said I hadn't yet earned that privilege. He told me just to call him Traveller.'

The man said, 'That is believable. Now you will keep moving ahead of us and answer our questions as you proceed. If you delay again, I will burn off your legs and carry you.'

Tack quickly turned and kept on moving. He had no doubt this would be his only warning.

'Describe this Traveller,' demanded the woman.

After Tack did so, there ensued another of those staccato conversations. Abruptly the male and female were up on either side of him, catching him each by an arm and running with him. He found himself half running, half floating, and when he stumbled being lifted and carried forwards. In a few minutes the cramps returned to his legs and he began stumbling more frequently, terrified that the man would carry out his earlier threat. Apparently these two had no time to spare even for that. The woman released him and, still running headlong, the man hoisted Tack up and slung him over a shoulder. Then the mysterious pair accelerated away at a stupendous pace. Soon they were out of the trees and onto the grasslands again.

'Deinth!' the woman shouted a warning.

Tack saw the huge animal suddenly bearing down on them. This close he saw how it did resemble an elephant, but with a short powerful trunk and shorter tusks protruding from its lower jaw. But it did not need to have recognizable characteristics for Tack to know that its earlier trauma had left it very pissed off indeed. It roared triumphantly as it thundered down on them in its own surrounding dust cloud, shaking its massive head from side to side. Tack expected his captors to veer away from it, but instead they ducked low and were under the red mouth and compost breath, between its forelegs then out through the side between foreleg and rear, then up and running again. Behind them the bellowing creature turned to pursue them, its two-metre legs making it a match even for these two apparent superhumans. The bizarre chase continued ever further out into the grasslands, the deinotherium neither gaining nor giving ground.

'Fist mantisal-ick scabind!' panted the the woman.

Tack saw her whirl round and drop into a crouch, drawing a weapon that bore some resemblance to a long-barrelled Colt Peacemaker. It emitted an arc-welder flash, then a dull and actinic explosion blew to gristly fragments most of the creature's head. It skidded down on its knees, only its trunk and lower jaw still attached by a gory bridge of flesh to the stump of its neck. Its momentum was such that it nearly somersaulted, but such was its huge weight that it flopped back and slumped onto one side. Before Tack could see more, the man came to halt and unshouldered him ungently to the ground.

'Saphothere,' hissed the woman, as more weapon fire erupted. Tack managed to raise himself to his knees just as a mantisal appeared above them. The woman was firing out over the grasslands as the white-haired figure of Traveller wove towards them, blasting away. Something else was happening that Tack could not quite fathom: there were sheets and lines slicing through the air, against which the weapon discharges flared impotently. The man guided the mantisal lower, then gestured for Tack to climb inside. As Tack hesitated, he reached out to grasp his arm and, wrenching his shoulder, threw Tack aboard. Then the female was screaming, her right arm burning like wax caught in a gas torch. Once the man was in the mantisal, the strange thing began drifting towards the woman as she loosed a fusillade towards Traveller. Then she too was safely inside and the world just folded away.

6

Traveller Thote:
The temporally active scales the beast drops, which Maxell named tors, it guards until they are taken up by a suitably vulnerable individual. Usually this person will be someone who would have died, so the beast is naturally attracted to events in recorded history where it can easily select its candidates. By this means it creates a lesser paradox to affect its own position on the probability slope. Already it has initiated three torbearers in Pompeii just before the eruption of Vesuvius, two from Nagasaki, and three hunters who had the misfortune to be in the Tunguska River valley in 1908. It is impossible for us to detect these initiations until they are made in the time-line concurrent for both Cowl and us, thereafter the torbearers become increasingly difficult to detect as they are dragged back through time. But once they are located in time, it is then only a matter of how much energy we are prepared to expend to get to them. And get to some of them we shall, for they may be our only access to Cowl.

Polly gazed at a huge house, glimpsed through the trees, with bustling activity all around it: people disembarking from carts or dismounting, grooms leading their horses away, groups of others standing chatting – colourful fabrics bright in the sunshine.

You've moved in space as well as time. You earlier shifted just outside this place and it has taken some hours of travel to reach it again.

Ignoring Nandru, she asked, 'King Henry VIII lives here?'

'Oh dear, you have not travelled much in our fair country have you?' replied Berthold. 'This is one of our King's hunting lodges.

He is here for the stag and boar, and for all-night drinking and tupping – as a rest from his toils in our great city of London.'

Mellor grunted contemptuously, 'Toils,' and spat over the side of the wagon.

Then again, it would be surprising had you not moved in space as well as time. I have to wonder how the scale puts you down so gently on the Earth's surface, considering that not only is the planet revolving, as it hurtles around the sun, but it's precessing and wobbling at the same time. Just thinking about the calculations involved would make my head ache. Had I a head . . .

'*Nandru, just shut up, will you?*' Polly replied subvocally, wondering if it was just her imagination that Nandru seemed to be displaying a babbling nervousness at the prospect of encountering such a famous historical figure.

As Berthold drove the wagon out from the woodland, four guards wearing steel breastplates and helmets over padded clothing stepped out onto the track ahead. Two of them bore pikes and the other two carried crossbows. One of the latter, who wore a brocaded velvet jacket over his breastplate and a sword at his hip, held up his hand until Berthold drew the wagon to a halt. 'Get down from there. I'll not crick my neck to just speak to the likes of you,' he ordered.

Berthold leapt down, swept off his hat and bowed. 'Good Captain, we are here at the express invitation of Thomas Cromwell, the Earl of Essex himself. Myself having entertained him in the Saracen's Head in Chelmsford, he thought my skill sufficient to have me perform before His Majesty.'

The captain withdrew a thick sheaf of paper from a leather wallet at his belt. 'Name,' he demanded.

Watching this exchange, Polly realized that over the centuries it was only the clothing of tinpot officials that changed.

'I am the amazing Berthold, premier juggler and entertainer, whose stunning verse may draw a tear or arouse laughter, and whose fame spreads far and wide!'

The captain merely raised an eyebrow and continued checking his lists.

Berthold glanced back at Mellor. 'Some pies and bread, I think.'

Mellor reached behind him to pull out the food sack. After groping inside he tossed a couple of meat pies to Berthold, who caught them and began juggling them so deftly they appeared to be turning a circle in the air without his hands ever touching them. Mellor then tossed a third pie, which joined the wheel of food turning before Berthold. All the other guards were now watching with evident appreciation, and one of them guffawed loudly when Berthold momentarily diverted one of the pies to take a bite out of it.

'Have you ever seen such skill? But this is nothing. My lovely assistant Poliasta, who comes from the Far East, where I learnt my trade under the rigorous eyes of a great wizard, will now join me, and together we shall give you a show!'

Polly's stomach lurched, not at being given a name that sounded like a wall covering, but at the prospect of bringing herself into notice. However, she had not expected to be fed for free so felt she must at least make an effort. Quickly she shed her greatcoat, accepted the food bag Mellor was thrusting at her, and leapt down from the wagon. The guards, who had clearly never seen a woman so strangely dressed, nor with unmarked skin – their own was as pock-marked as Mellor's and Berthold's – stood and gaped at her. She noticed the gaze of one straying to the scale on her arm, and wondered if this was such a good idea.

'An apple would clear the palate of the clag from so many pies,' suggested Berthold.

Reaching into the bag, Polly took out the required fruit.

'Here is an apple for the amazing Berthold,' she proclaimed, tossing the wizened fruit gently towards him.

'Thank you, my lady Poliasta.' The apple joined the turning circle as smoothly as the third pie had done. He took a bite out of it, then a bite out of another pie so that his cheeks were bulging and food spilling out of his mouth. This was high comedy to the guards, and even the captain was showing signs of amusement now.

'Now, sir, if you would hand the Lady Poliasta your dagger?'

The captain's humour disappeared for a moment, till he glanced at his armed colleagues and saw little harm in such a request. Shrugging, he drew the blade, flipped it over, and held it out hilt first to Polly. Taking the weapon, Polly felt immediately doubtful, as it was very heavy.

'Like the apple,' Berthold prompted her.

Out of the corner of her eye Polly could see several of the nobility approaching, but all her concentration was focused on throwing him the dagger. She turned it so as to reach him hilt first, but miscalculated when she threw. The dagger turned in the air and dropped low to one side of him. But, professional that he was, Berthold stooped and caught it effortlessly, and set it spinning in the midst of the never-faltering wheel, now comprised of three pies and an apple. He too, Polly noticed, had obviously spotted the approaching group, and now began to up the ante. Polly saw how the guards bowed and moved aside. The dress of the nobility looked fantastical to her: so layered in rich fabrics were the men that their bodies appeared ridiculously huge over their unpadded stockinged legs. The women's clothing was more understated and to Polly seemed almost suited to a nunnery. But there was power here – she recognized it in the arrogance of expression and pose.

'Let us test the edge of your dagger, sir.'

Polly stared as Berthold briefly snatched the dagger and flicked out with it. The apple was now gyrating in two halves, and his hand movements were becoming ever more complicated. He juggled for a while behind his back, took another bite of pie, then stuffed one apple half into his mouth.

'Mffofle gloff floggle,' he muttered through a mouth crammed full.

He had been feigning not to see the presence of the new arrivals as he tossed the various items ever higher. Then pretending to notice them, with a parody of startlement, the chewed food exploded from his mouth.

'Your majesty!' He bowed dramatically low. The dagger went whickering aside to stab into the ground between the captain's feet, and one after another the three pies then the remaining half apple thumped onto the back of Berthold's lowered head. The response from the central figure of the finely dressed crowd was a wheezy laugh followed by limp applause from his beringed fat hands. The rest of the group applauded sycophantically. Polly stared up at the huge man for a second, then quickly bowed her head. Mellor had climbed down from the wagon to make obeisance as well.

'So the amazing Berthold has arrived,' rumbled King Henry VIII. 'I see the measure of your report does not overextend itself, Cromwell.'

Polite laughter greeted this quip.

'Let you, King, look again on the visage of one who is a king of laughter.'

Keeping her own head bowed, Polly observed Berthold straighten up. His hair and beard were dusted with crumbs.

'Well done,' said the King, looming over Berthold.

'Your Majesty is too kind,' said Berthold, then clamped his mouth shut as Henry moved past as if the juggler hadn't spoken.

'And what is this gracious face?'

The beringed hand caught Polly's chin and put gentle pressure under it to bring her head up. She didn't know who the question was directed at so, like Berthold, kept her mouth shut. The King looked her up and down, his attention mainly focusing on how amply she filled her blouse.

Don't lose your head over this guy, Nandru snickered.

'*If he calls me a "pretty little thing" I swear I'll kick him in the nuts*,' Polly snarled.

Finally dragging his gaze from Polly's breasts, the monarch glanced over his shoulder. 'Cromwell?'

A bulky man, who, amongst all this noble finery, appeared like an obese vulture, stepped from the respectful position he had held a pace back from the King. 'No doubt a new member of Berthold's troupe, my prince.' Thomas Cromwell then turned to Berthold. 'What say you, fool?'

'The Lady Poliasta has only recently joined us on our journey of entertainment and joy, my lord. She came to us from the Far East and knows many of the wiles and diversions of the Orient.'

'I shall be glad to know more of them, I think,' said Henry, his gaze once again resting on Polly's bust.

Well, they do say yours is the oldest profession.

'*One I no longer intend to pursue*,' Polly subvocalized angrily.

The King released her chin and moved on. 'One ryal, I should think, for this brief entertainment, Cromwell?'

The Earl of Essex delved into his pouch and passed a coin across to Berthold. As the entertainer took it and bowed, Cromwell frowned at him briefly before moving on after the King. Soon the entire group of nobles had departed in the direction of the house.

'I'll show you where you may encamp, then where you may break your fast,' advised the captain, who was holding his dagger and eyeing it speculatively. 'And tonight you will be most careful with any dagger you might use, else you might find yourself juggling with the sharp end of a crossbow bolt.'

Still gazing with reverence at the coin resting in his grubby palm, Berthold did not even hear the threat.

Her arm was charred to the bone and on that side of her body the skin of her neck was severely blistered and leaking plasma. Her male comrade thrust his hands into their mantisal's inner eyes and the creature violently shifted through colourless void. Making small whimpering sounds, the woman pulled a flat oval of metal from the pouch on her belt, and pressed the object against her neck burns. Immediately she sighed with relief and relaxed, before more closely studying her damaged arm. After a moment she abruptly thrust it outside the confines of the mantisal's glassy structure, and from it a contrail of red cut across the colourless space. When she pulled back, the entire charred portion of her arm was gone, right up to her biceps.

The two of them now conferred, and Tack understood none of it. All he imagined was that they were a greater danger to him than Traveller.

'Where are you taking me?' he hazarded asking.

The man glared at him. 'What is your name, primitive?'

'Tack.'

'Well, Tack, I am called Coptic and my partner is Meelan. Now, with those introductions over, you will remain silent until we directly address you. Any disobedience will be punished severely.'

Tack nodded, his mouth clamped shut.

As Coptic and Meelan returned to their conversation, it swiftly devolved into an argument in which Coptic apparently prevailed. A moment later, reality crept back in all around them. With warm drizzle misting all the mantisal's surfaces, thick subtropical greenery came into view below a leaden sky, forest reared to one side, and an inky lake spread on the other. In the forest some large beast issued a deep booming bark, and this seemed to decide

Coptic, who was already gazing out at the damp vista with distaste. This reality jerked away as the mantisal turned back into the between space. Then, after a second, another one folded into place.

Once again they were beside a lake, but now the sky was a clear amethyst dotted with dawn stars and the moon was ascending. There was no forest, just dense greenery covering the ground below the black skeletons of trees. This vista stretched away into shadow for as far as Tack could see, only relieved by the occasional stone outcrop. Greenery also extended across much of the lake's surface, in the form of huge lily pads centre-nailed by blowsy yellow flowers.

'Out,' Coptic ordered.

Tack did not hesitate, moving to a gap in the mantisal's structure and dropping to the ground. Immediately he found himself up to his chest in vegetation, and his skin crawled when he heard an insectile scuttling near his feet. Looking towards the lake, he saw the reflected glitter of eyes from bulky shapes resting in the water, and it occurred to him that his seeker gun might now be a million years away from him.

Coptic and Meelan disembarked together, then the mantisal floated higher like some strange and gigantic Christmas decoration, before turning itself out of that world.

'You go there, ahead of us,' Coptic told Tack, gesturing towards one of the rocky outcrops, then turning to pick up Meelan and following as Tack forged a path. Glancing back again at the water, with his eyes adjusting to the the dearth of light, Tack saw that the wallowing creatures resembled hornless rhino, and were grazing on the plentiful waterweed. That they plainly weren't carnivorous was no comfort, since the deinotherium they had earlier encountered had been a herbivore. Obviously a vegetarian diet did not necessarily guarantee an even temper or a convivial nature.

'Just watch where you're going,' said Coptic. 'Moeritherium are only dangerous if you get between them and the water – they'll not come out of there after you.'

Moeritherium?

Tack wanted to know how these two had so quickly acquired his language, to the extent that they could easily name varieties of prehistoric beast in it. And he wanted to know what they intended for him – and if he might survive it. Soon he reached the edge of the vegetation and climbed up onto an expanse of mossy stone. Coptic followed him, setting the incapacitated Meelan down on her feet again, then shed the pack he was wearing and opened it up. Tack noted that its contents were much the same as Traveller's, and guessed they must derive from the same time.

Coptic removed a heat-sheet sleeping bag and unrolled it over a level area coated in a thick blanket of dark green moss. Without a word, Meelan climbed inside the bag. Once she was comfortable, Coptic keyed a control on the oval object attached to her throat. She sighed and instantly lost consciousness. Coptic now took a box from his pack and, with the various implements it contained, set to work on Meelan's injuries. Squatting nearby, Tack watched the big man trim back her arm stump until he reached white bone and bleeding flesh. A pumping artery he closed with a small clip, before sealing the whole stump under some sort of spray-on dressing that set in a hard white nub. The other lesser-degree burns running from the arm up to her neck, he now revealed by cutting away her clothing, then he covered the area with another spray that set in a pink skin. Finally satisfied with his work, he rocked back on his heels and gazed at her intently.

It struck Tack that Coptic was contemptuous of him, for during this entire procedure the man had not looked round once. But judging by the man's abilities, perhaps he had that right. Tack turned away and stared towards the imminent sunrise.

Abruptly Coptic swivelled, stood, and walked over to him. 'Come with me.'

He led the way to a jut of crystalline stone rising a couple of metres high at the end of the outcrop and, gripping him by one shoulder, pulled Tack up beside him so they both stood before this glittering face. Coptic then reached out and pressed the flat of his hand against the surface, which immediately took on a strange translucence. Something like a tangle of tubes – some complex mechanism – came out from the depths of stone and seemed to bond to Coptic's hand. Then slowly a face became visible behind this – a woman bearing characteristics similar to those of Traveller and both Tack's kidnappers. She spoke, obviously angry as she berated Coptic in their staccato language.

Coptic turned to Tack. 'Hold up your arm.'

Tack obeyed and observed the avidity in the woman's expression when she saw the band around his wrist. Coptic's riposte was brief and at the end of it he gestured to where Meelan lay. The woman in the rock dipped her head in acknowledgement, said something more, then faded. Back by the fire, Coptic stared into the flames for some time, then with a hint of suspicion glanced at the rock before speaking.

'The one you name "Traveller" killed Brayak and Solenz, which is the inevitable result of a violent encounter between a heliothant of his status and low-breed umbrathant,' he stated flatly.

Tack remained silent, having not yet been given permission to speak. He guessed who the two named were, for it hadn't escaped his notice that four individuals had originally disembarked from the mantisal they had used to get here.

'Such is natural law,' Coptic added. 'But we are high-breed Umbrathane and shall prevail. And when Cowl sweeps the Heliothane from the main line, we shall travel to him beyond the Nodus to be at one with the new kind.'

Who, Tack wondered, was this man really addressing his words to? It seemed to Tack that Coptic was speaking accepted doctrine because he thought the woman in the rock might still, somehow, be listening.

'You may speak,' said Coptic unexpectedly.

'What do you want of me?' Tack asked him.

Coptic nodded slowly. 'We detected only the travel of a heliothant through interspace, so sought to sabotage whatever plans the Heliothane might have. But now we have you and the means of learning some things Cowl would not allow us.' He gestured to the ring around Tack's wrist. 'No doubt the Heliothane themselves sought to assassinate Cowl. But they would not have succeeded – they are low-breed by comparison.'

'So, like Traveller, it is only the tor you really want?'

'Tors he allows us, when he brings us to him.' Coptic stared at him. 'From the one that is growing on your arm, and about which he knows nothing, we can learn a great deal.'

So, despite their doctrine, there was little trust between Cowl and the Umbrathane.

'You say that you are an "Umbrathane", and that Traveller is a "Heliothane". Are these two warring factions in the future? What are you trying to achieve?'

'You will now remain silent,' said Coptic.

Tack nodded and turned away, watching the sun finally breach the horizon.

Using the sensor's facility for penetrative scan, the watcher tracked the girl inside the house to its kitchens, then through boiling steamy chaos observed her sating her ravenous appetite. The travelling entertainer, Berthold, had set up camp on one of the big house's lawns, where the staff and servants of the various nobles here were also encamped. The watcher now tracked the girl, Polly, out of the house to where she helped erect the awning that extended from one side of the wagon, and under which she had slept like a corpse the night before – though a corpse, it had to be noted, with its hand on the automatic under its greatcoat. Afterwards, at Berthold's insistence, Polly practised his act with him.

'Do you mind me doing this, Mellor?' Polly asked after Berthold, satisfied with the way she threw him objects, and her ridiculous prancing around him as he juggled them, had gone off to chat to the men in a neighbouring encampment.

'Not really.' Mellor grinned at her with bad teeth, then held up his hands and wriggled his fingers. 'Gettin' stiff as dead rabbits nowadays, and someone who looks like you do should help pull in the shillings.'

'But I won't be around for long.'

Mellor gaped at her. 'What you gonna do then?'

The watcher knew, and wondered just how Polly intended to explain herself. Already she must be feeling the pull from her tor, and must be preventing it from dragging her downtime at that moment.

'It seems I have a journey to make,' Polly replied.

'Where?'

The girl did not know, could not know, and the watcher pitied her.

Polly said to Mellor, 'I don't know yet, but I do know that when I assist Berthold tonight it will be for the one and only time. Then I will be moving on.'

'Oh.' The old man appeared genuinely disappointed. The unseen observer supposed he had been relishing the new-found prospect of a life of ease and pheasant pies. Then scanning forward to evening, as nothing of note seemed to be happening, this watcher observed the King's hunting party return: all those richly clad men on their richly caparisoned horses, a chaos of hounds milling about below mud-spattered hooves, and servants trotting along behind with cut larch poles bearing the blood-dripping kills. The womenfolk came out of the house to greet the returning hunters and to congratulate them shrilly on their successful venture. The scene was bright and gay and appropriate to its time, and hopefully appreciated by Polly, what with all she would suffer soon enough. Smiling then, enclosed in living glass, the watcher observed Polly giggling on seeing Berthold dressed up in his diamond-patterned suit, silver bells and ridiculous footwear with turned-up toes. It wasn't enough, could never be enough. It was like seeing a child walk smiling into a bear pit.

After sunrise the moeritherium departed the lake to graze their way through the thick surrounding vegetation, mooing and grumbling as they went. They passed close by, but their only reaction to the three humans was to pause while they chewed and peered up with close-set eyes, before snorting and moving on. Seeing these creatures' continual munching reminded Tack of his own hunger, and he wondered if Coptic would ever bother to feed his prisoner.

'There is food in the pack,' said Coptic later, but only when the sun was high. All morning the man had been sitting utterly still and silent in a lotus position, next to Meelan. 'And I would appreciate coffee now. If there is anything there you do not know how to use, you are permitted to ask me how it functions.'

Being already familiar with the contents of Traveller's pack, Tack found himself some food and the makings of coffee, and had only a little trouble setting up the small electric stove. Taking up a collapsible water container, he folded it open and stood dutifully waiting until Coptic looked his way.

'Proceed.' Coptic gestured irritably towards the lake.

From their outcrop Tack walked back along the trail crushed by the moeritherium herd. As he stooped down by the water's edge, he became aware that if he wanted to escape now was the time, since Coptic, though possessed of superhuman speed, might not be prepared to leave Meelan's side. But what would he be escaping to – a lonely, possibly all too brief life in a prehistoric wilderness? For he had no idea how to summon a mantisal. After filling the container, he returned to the outcrop, where Meelan was now sitting up and looking much healthier.

Ignoring the muttered conversation of the other two, Tack filled a kettle and set it on the stove, and while watching it, sought to untangle his confusion. Though Traveller had reset Tack's loyalty, the man had left him greater free will than he had previously experienced. Working for U-gov, Tack never had the time or inclination to consider his life as a whole. He had been nothing but an organic machine, but now he had acquired a wider compass. Now he genuinely wanted to know more about the workings of his surrounding world, to participate fully, to experience and to truly *feel*. To fulfil this hazy aspiration he must be free; freedom from programming and the will of others must now be his ultimate goal.

The three of them drank coffee and ate some of the supplies in the pack, while cautiously observing the nearby wending progress of three large bovids. These strange creatures bore a resemblance to both oxen and deer, but could not be firmly identified as either. Tack knew that with Traveller he could have satisfied his curiosity, but not with his present companions. Their repast finished, Coptic instructed Tack to put all the implements away and take up the pack. As with Traveller before them, Tack must act the beast of burden, though he suspected Traveller regarded him as somewhat less of a beast than did Coptic and Meelan. At the lake's shore the mantisal again folded into existence in response to some inaudible instruction. They embarked, Coptic once again piloting the bioconstruct, and instantly fell into achromatic void.

*

Upon entering the hot and noisy banqueting hall, Polly reeled at the wave of human stench that hit her, and gazing round decided she had never seen so much bad skin gathered in one place. This was something all the historical dramas and interactives had never been accurate about.

'God, they're ugly!'

Poxed, the lot of them. There's no vaccinations in this period. What you are seeing here are the few who have survived to maturity. It's probably why Berthold thinks you're such an asset – you're a rare unmarked beauty. But then Berthold doesn't know you like I do.

'Bring on the juggler!' bellowed the King.

'Let us begin,' whispered Berthold, turning to Polly with the bells on his jester's hat jingling. He then cartwheeled onto the empty floor between the tables, finishing upright after a somersault. The King threw a chicken leg that bounced off Berthold's face. To a tumultuous roar, other food was hurled at him from every direction. He sinuously dodged these items, then held up his hands.

'Enough! Enough I say, good sirs! Would you bury me in your generosity?'

To much hilarity, the rain of food finally halted. Berthold stepped to a table and gathered up a goblet, half a loaf of bread and a chicken leg.

'Good crowd tonight,' said Mellor from behind Polly. She turned and stared at him, wondering if he was quite mad. Suddenly she felt the overpowering urge for a cigarette – elsewhere.

'Now, let me introduce to you my beautiful assistant: that Far Eastern Princess, the lady Poliasta!'

Polly walked out to catcalls and shouts of, 'Get yer dumplin's out!' – and not all of them from the men. Following Berthold's earlier instruction, she bowed elaborately towards each table, holding out to one side a sack containing the various items

Berthold would use in his act, and into which she must secrete any coins tossed onto the floor.

'Let me begin with a simple demonstration of the juggling art!'

Berthold set the three items he already held into motion. His competence was quite evident and even caused the surrounding uproar to quieten a little.

'But such skill is not easily acquired. I had to travel to the far realms of the East, where I found my lovely Princess here, and there I learnt this craft under my wizardly master, the Great Profundo!'

With that Berthold stepped on a stray pheasant carcass and slipped onto his backside – the chicken leg bouncing off his head, the loaf of bread rolling away, but the goblet dropping neatly into his hand. He pretended to drink from it.

'My master, Profundo, always used to say "Watch your footing."' This comment was almost drowned by the howls of laughter. A few coins tinkled on the floor and, as instructed, Polly set about collecting them. And so it went. The crowd particularly loved Berthold's obscene juggling act with the painted wooden phalluses, especially when he caught one in his mouth. His knife act he curtailed because this crowd stopped laughing and began to watch him warily. The performance closed with him juggling seven wildly different items, including a codpiece that somehow ended up stuck over his face, before the other props rained down on his head. Finally Berthold and Polly were summoned before the King.

Henry VIII was red-faced, and obviously too pissed to see or talk straight, so it was Thomas Cromwell, leaning in close to him, who began relaying his words.

'The King congratulates Berthold on his skilled and entertaining performance . . .'

The King showed signs of anger, and Polly surmised that

Cromwell was not relaying the royal sentiments with any precision.

'The King wishes Berthold to accept this purse . . .'

Cromwell picked one up and tossed it to Polly, who expertly caught it in her open prop bag, then curtsied.

'The King now wishes to retire.'

Evidently that was not precisely Henry's intention because he was still giving Polly a look that should have been censored. Then Cromwell helped King Henry to his feet, and away to his bed.

After the royal departure the party swiftly dissipated – spreading to some of the tents pitched outside for those who wanted to continue.

'God's blood!' Berthold exclaimed, counting out the money collected, and eyeing the sack of leftover food Mellor had collected from the tables. 'We could go right now and live on this for a year or more!'

'But not yet,' insisted Mellor.

'Two more nights at most,' Berthold replied. 'By then they'll start losing interest.' He unstoppered a jug from a nearby table, and took a deep slug of its contents.

Between the layers of black and grey something was becoming visible; glittering like nacre and expressing rainbow hues at the edge of the visible.

'Fistik,' spat Meelan, now much recovered.

This word being one Tack now identified as a curse, he more closely studied what was angering her. The thing extended as a line between the two surfaces, stretching in either direction to far-off dimensions beyond where Tack could easily focus without feeling as if his brain was tearing away inside his head. Occasionally this object drew close enough to take on substance – the only apparent solidity in this place beyond the confines of the mantisal itself. As he stared at it, Tack felt a growing frustration at knowing he could not ask. But time spent gazing into this etioliated infinity took its toll as his vision blurred and weariness descended on him like a brick. He dozed off, coming half-awake later to see Meelan thrusting her remaining arm into one of the mantisal's eyes. Meanwhile, Coptic withdrew and turned away, his eyes suddenly dead black.

Then a brightly coloured crowd was feasting nearby and throwing food at a man who was juggling clocks . . . while, with the insane logic of dream, Tack collected up the shattered amethysts into which the dropped timepieces had transformed. All was now colour and that colour became the smell of heated sand, then a boot inserted under Tack's side rolled him rudely into wakefulness, falling onto that sand.

Coptic's laugh was hollow as he too dropped down beside Tack, its humour buried in weariness. Meelan also seemed weary, her eyes turned black like her partner's. Lying there, Tack observed the mantisal disappear, folding itself away in exactly the same manner as when viewed side-on. He stood, taking up the pack that had dropped beside him, and panted in the sudden heat.

Again they were on a shore – only this time it was a seashore. Scattered along the strand were turtle shells, mounds of fly-blown weed, and nearby the desiccated remains of a shark being pecked at by birds like raggedy miniature vultures. Behind the shore lay a coniferous forest, its trees gigantic. A constant din issued from amid the trunks, some of it identifiable but much of it utterly strange. The singing of the birds was harsher here and possessed an angry immediacy. Occasionally a mournful hooting crescendoed and somewhere a sonorous groaning bemoaned the constant racket.

'What age is this?' Tack asked, forgetting himself.

Coptic's huge hand caught him hard on the side of his head, knocking him to the ground, with lights flashing behind his eyes.

'Did I permit you to speak?' the big man asked.

Tack said nothing more, waiting for the inevitable beating, but Coptic was disinclined to take things further and turned to Meelan, who was studying a device she held. After a moment she gabbled something obscure and gestured disgustedly at the forest. Coptic spat a brief reply and pointed out to the sea, whereupon Meelan nodded. More conversation ensued as both of them inspected the instrument, then eventually Coptic turned to Tack.

'We must rest here and recoup. *You* will go that way.' He pointed along the beach. 'In about three kilometres you will come to an estuary. Walk up it until you find fresh water.'

Coptic took the pack and squatted down to open it. After emptying it of most of its contents, he passed the collapsible water container to Tack. Tack then paused for a moment to observe the big man assembling what, futuristic as it might be, was still identifiable as a fishing rod. He saw no more than this, for Coptic glared at him and gestured him away.

When Tack came to the desiccated shark, he expected the miniature vultures to take off, but the birds ignored him and continued feeding, their pecking beaks making sounds like pencils beating against cardboard. Amid the empty turtle shells he saw the bones and beaked skulls of the armoured reptiles, and noticed that all the shells had been broken into, and bore large teeth marks. Moving closer to the forest, he nervously eyed the sea, wondering what kind of creature out there had the jaw strength to crack open living turtles like sherbet lemons. Perhaps the dinosaurs Traveller had mentioned? This seemed unlikely to Tack, as he did not see how his two captors could cover a distance through time which Traveller had said would need many separate shifts. Most likely this current era was some ten or twenty million years before that of the deinotherium, which meant perhaps forty million years preceding Tack's own time. He shivered at the thought, despite the warmth.

As the beach curved round, Tack's two kidnappers were soon out of sight, and he realized that he was turning into the wide mouth of an estuary, its further shore now visible to him. He estimated that he had covered just over a kilometre so far. The forest to his right now included the occasional white-barked deciduous tree, bearing autumnal leaves and translucent fruit. Below one such tree he spotted two large animals resembling cats, but which were squabbling over fallen fruit. He picked up his pace, not wanting to discover if they might turn out to be omnivores. After a few hundred paces, he heard their squabbling grow louder – then suddenly cut off. Glancing back, he witnessed a nightmare stepping out onto the beach, and understood why the cat creatures no longer wanted to attract any attention.

Fear closed its leaden claws around his guts.

7

Traveller Thote:
The attempt to remove the tors from the two Russian hunters, who actually remained together through a number of time jumps, was a failure that killed both of them and Traveller Zoul when we tried to transplant one tor onto him. It seems these organic time machines genetically encode to their hosts. Zoul was dragged back by the next shift, but the web of temporal energy the tor created in him did not match his physiognomy and what arrived at the shift's end died, thankfully, very quickly. We need to get to torbearers earlier in their journey, before the jumps accelerate, to give us more time to complete our task. Our chances of doing this are good, as more and more torbearers are being detected every day.

It was leopard-skinned and it was gigantic. Comparing it against the trees it had just emerged from, Tack estimated it to stand nearly two metres at the shoulder, and be five metres long. Though doglike, its movement was feline, its sinuosity only hampered by its huge weight. But this thing was to the family pet dog what a great white was to a goldfish. And no animal should have jaws of that size: they seemed unnaturally out of proportion, like some cartoon depiction of Father Wolf.

Tack considered just keeping on walking, in the hope that the beast wouldn't notice him; he would, after all, provide only a snack for it. But it swung its huge head in his direction, paused for a moment, then began loping along the strand towards him. Tack turned and ran just as fast as he could.

The sand hampering his progress, he moved to the more

compacted ground at the edge of the forest. Glancing into its shadows, he considered heading for one of the fruit trees, which appeared eminently climbable. But the creature behind him looked big enough to stretch its jaws up to the highest branches, and heavy enough to push the trees over. Sweat broke out all over him, soaking his ragged clothing and trickling into his eyes. In this kind of heat he might keep up his pace for a few kilometres only, but wouldn't have the energy for anything else, least of all defending himself.

The nearby estuary was narrowing now, and Tack thought about taking to the water, until he noticed that those floating seabirds were in fact fins. No escape that way, then. The forest had become mainly deciduous, but still the trees were too small. Glancing again at his pursuer, he saw that it did not seem in any great hurry to catch him. It kept loping along like some great big dog, as if too lazy to put on that last spurt of speed. Nevertheless, its long stride was eating up the distance between them.

Keep running, as you are now, and when I give the word, turn immediately into the forest.

'Traveller!'

There came no reply, but Tack felt suddenly so very glad. Not only did Traveller have the weaponry to bring down this monster, but he would then once again reclaim his charge, and Tack was sure his chances of survival with Traveller were higher than with his more recent companions.

The creature was now so close that Tack could see a red tongue lolling from its panting mouth between teeth as large as cannon shells, and wide bloodshot eyes dispassionately observing him. The greatest horror, he felt, was that should it catch him he would be one brief crunch then gone; he would be killed with neither anger nor hate and for no more purpose than to assuage an ever-recurring hunger.

Now he could hear the regular tread of its great splayed paws thumping into the sand. Though it did not possess claws, that was more than compensated for by the sheer quantity of ivory in its huge mouth.

Now.

Tack turned instantly, dodging trees as he ran. The beast turned in behind him, clipping a pine and releasing a shower of cones, branches and needles. With its snout raised, there seemed an excitement to its mien – the chase was finally becoming interesting.

Further to your left.

Tack changed course again.

That's enough. In a moment you'll see a large tree ahead of you. Climb as fast as you can. I don't want to have to fire on friend andrewsarchus there, as the umbrathants would detect the energy spike.

Tack soon spotted the tree, and slowed to ascertain his route up it. Then a deep mooing bark behind accelerated him on. He hit the trunk with his right foot, running almost vertically up it for a couple of paces, before grabbing branches at random and hauling himself higher. Under his feet he caught sight of a wide furry back passing like an express train. Pulling even higher, he saw the monster swerve and shoulder into a pine trunk. The tree snapped and went down whip-fast. The creature turned, ploughing up debris from the forest floor. It launched itself towards Tack, its massive paws tearing bark from the tree trunk as its head crashed up through the lower branches. Its mouth opened into a glistening red well, then its huge jaws slammed shut on a bough Tack's foot had just left. Then the creature slid to the ground, growling in exasperation.

'It would seem you're hardly even out of my sight before getting yourself into terminal danger,' said Traveller.

Tack glanced up at the man lying comfortably along a wide bough, his feet wedged against the trunk.

'What did you say that thing was?' Tack gasped, continuing upwards until he was higher than Traveller.

'Andrewsarchus. You've just evaded the largest carnivorous mammal ever to roam the Earth. Don't you feel privileged?'

Tack gazed down at the monster sitting doglike at the foot of the tree, its head tilted to one side as it observed them.

'Oh, I can think of better ways to pass the time.' Tack then clammed up, remembering how Traveller's tolerance of him was only slightly greater than Coptic's. Traveller seemed unperturbed, though. His eyes were dead and his expression weary as a result of vorpal travel, but he seemed quite relaxed.

'Can you summon the mantisal to us up here?' Tack asked hopefully.

'Now why should I do that?'

Tack gestured to the andrewsarchus. 'So we can escape him, and those two lunatic umbrathants, and continue our journey.'

'Ah, you are learning. However, sometimes one's plans must remain protean to accommodate opportunities.' Traveller paused to gaze at an instrument propped on his stomach. 'You know, arriving in a time like this, and observing the evidence of predation scattered all along the beach, the seasoned traveller should first locate a handy tree as a refuge. Such caution is only sensible, yet Meelan and Coptic have not bothered to do so, which is a sign of both inherent arrogance and stupidity. That neither of them has bothered scanning the hardware inside your head is another sign.'

The andrewsarchus, growing bored with sitting waiting, was now up and prowling around below them. Many metres above it they might be, but if the mantisal could not be summoned up here, then at some point they must climb to the ground. Tack did not find the prospect inviting.

'What might they have found in my head?' he asked.

'Let me put it this way,' said Traveller. 'No matter where or when you are, *I'll* always be able to find you. Though I might not have the required energy to get to you.'

'You put a bug inside my head.'

'Not quite what I would call it but, in essence, yes.'

'So now you've found me shouldn't we continue our journey to this Sauros place?'

'No, because of those protean plans I mentioned. Now, detail to me what has happened to you since I last saw you.'

Tack told him about the brief journeys, and that strange communication with the woman in the rock.

'Iveronica: the leader of an Umbrathane cell that has been a thorn in our side for too long,' Traveller explained. 'They seem to follow no coherent plan, so are not amenable to prognostic apperception. We have never been able to predict when they will strike, nor to locate their home base. Her hostility ably demonstrates how Coptic and Meelan are not entirely trusted or accepted by her. It seems those two have never been allowed to that base, but that now you are their ticket there.'

'You seem to know a lot about all this,' Tack observed.

Traveller showed him the screen of the instrument he was holding, and on it Tack saw the woman again as he had earlier seen her through his own eyes.

'You see what I see,' Tack stated.

'I see a recording of what you've seen – and I've only just been going through it.'

Tack stared at him and guessed what was coming.

Traveller continued, 'Iveronica has supplied Coptic and Meelan with an energy feed to track back to the Umbrathane base. I have availed myself of the opportunity presented and will continue to follow – parasitic on the same feed.'

'But you cannot follow them unless *I* am with them?' added Tack.

Traveller shrugged. 'Should you escape, Iveronica might learn of it and cut off that feed. You stay with them.'

Tack felt that the andrewsarchus said all he himself wanted to say by approaching the bole of the tree, cocking its leg, and pissing like a waterfall before finally sauntering away.

'You must not leave us,' Berthold implored Polly, after taking his nth draught from the second jar of strong beer he had opened, then wiping his foam-covered beard on his filthy sleeve. He had not even bothered to change out of his jester's suit, which smelt strongly of stale sweat and chicken grease – not the most appealing combination.

'As I already told you, it's not something I have much choice about. I cannot explain why, Berthold, and I'm not sure I need to.'

Anger flashed in the man's expression, as it had done more and more frequently since Mellor had relayed the bad news before himself slumping into drunken slumber.

'Think of the coin! Think of the excellent food we receive!'

The coin was irrelevant to her, but Polly was thinking more and more about the sackful of bread and pies and shrivelled apples, for indefinable power now networked her body from the scale, hooking into unlocatable places in her and pulling taut. Soon, she knew, she must again travel through time. Presently she might have the choice of when this would happen, but if she left it any longer, that choice would be taken away from her. She had hoped Berthold would drink himself into a stupor, so she could quietly take her leave along with the food sack. But he had passed through the mournful weary stage of drunkenness, and was now growing ever more insistent and aroused.

'You must stay!' he repeated, staggering towards her and grabbing her arm, eyes glaring bloodshot in the lamplight cast from a nearby tent.

Polly merely shook her head. But this suddenly became too

much for Berthold, for he put down the jug and grabbed her by both arms.

'My Lady Poliasta.' He pinned her back against the wagon, pushing his face to hers. She turned her head aside, to avoid a mouth that smelt as if its tongue had died and putrefied inside it. Undeterred, he groped inside her greatcoat, first fondling her breasts then trying to find access to her crotch. When her clothing defeated him, he started trying to tear it away.

'Well, *this* doesn't exactly convince me to stay with you,' said Polly.

'I will wed you. You'll be both my wife and exotic companion. Together we'll travel the country and people will marvel at your beauty and at my skill!'

Worse offers than this had been put Polly's way – as had better ones. She didn't really need to consider further, since she knew she was out of choices anyway. Swaying her hips closer to his hand as if to encourage him, she brought her knee up hard.

Doubled over, Berthold staggered back clutching his codpiece, and made a sound like a duck being flattened by a steamroller. He collapsed onto his side, still coiled up tight. The things he said between agonized groans were a revelation to Polly – she hadn't realized such words had such a *history*. Quickly she ducked under the wagon's awning and grabbed up the food sack from where it rested by the snoring Mellor. Stepping out again, she saw that Berthold was up on his knees now, his face lowered to the ground as he clutched his testicles.

'I'm sorry. I have to go now,' said Polly quietly, turning and walking away into the night.

The grass was already dew-covered and her breath misted the air. Shortly she reached some trees and turned to look back. The King's hunting lodge looked warm and welcoming, with lights in its windows and smoke billowing from its chimneys, as did the encampment outside it, where the raucous party showed no signs of flagging.

Time to go – and to go into time.

'I always felt that you were full of wit,' she told Nandru, aloud. 'Or was I thinking of some other word?'

'Poliasta!'

Berthold.

'Damn,' she said. 'Doesn't he know when to give up?'

I'm sure he's full of ardour.

'Shut up, Nandru,' she growled.

Polly concentrated on relaxing her control of that internal tension generated by the scale, and she felt a tug into the ineffable.

'Polly! My pretty Polly!' Berthold gasped. 'We must drink together and toast our union!'

Berthold was staggering closer clutching a beer jug in his right hand, yet still, somehow, she found herself unable to leave this time. She drew the automatic earlier secreted in her coat pocket.

'Come no closer, Berthold!' she warned.

The man who shot at her during the Second World War had not been dragged through time with her, but *he* had been at least ten paces away from her. But the killer, Tack, from her own time, had been much closer.

'Stop where you are!'

Berthold ignored her, for how could he possibly realize what she was pointing at him? Aiming to one side, she pulled the trigger, and whatever fates existed were on her side in that moment. Her shot went closer to him than expected, smashing the beer jug. Knocked off balance, Berthold staggered and fell on his backside. But that humiliating position was still more inviting than where Polly now fell.

'Polly!' his cry echoed after her, and died away. Moving through chill blackness, Polly pocketed her gun and kept a firm hold on the food sack. As the scale pulled her through a void without dimension, she gazed down at the roiling of an impossible sea in all shades of non-colour. Her mind strained to breaking point as it sought to encompass something outside the scope of its natural evolution. Her breath burst from her in a groan – then she was sucking on nothing. There seemed some sensation of movement this time, of actually travelling, rather than the brief black hiatus she had previously experienced. Soon it must end, surely soon . . . but it went on interminably and Polly discovered how horrible it was to asphyxiate. And even this dark world went away as she blacked out.

Collecting the water container from where he had abandoned it, Tack then headed for the tributary to which Traveller had directed him. The andrewsarchus was now, according to Traveller's instruments, somewhere over on the other side of the estuary. Tack knew that when he did finally attain his freedom, he wanted it to be accompanied with a shitload of the technology these strangers used.

Finally coming to the stream, he expanded the water container and filled it, then headed back to the beach as quickly as he could. Already he had been gone for longer than he should have been, and though he had a plausible explanation – like climbing a tree to save his life – he wondered if Coptic would allow him time to explain. Building up a sweat as he lugged the heavy container, he soon spotted Coptic jogging down the beach towards him, his weapon drawn.

'You took too long,' Coptic said. 'Put down the water container.'

Tack held onto it firmly, knowing this was all that might stop Coptic attacking him. But Coptic stepped forwards and backhanded him, the blow lifting Tack off the ground so hard he felt sure his neck had snapped. He thumped down backwards on the sand in a daze, and coming to he saw that somehow Coptic had rescued the container from spilling its contents.

'I think you have disobeyed me.' He adjusted the controls on his weapon. 'Now, tell me why I should not cut off your limbs, leaving only the arm we require.'

'I'll die of shock,' Tack managed, crawling backwards.

'No, we can keep you alive in that condition, and you'll not be a burden to us safely strapped inside the mantisal. Once at Pig City your arm can be removed to be preserved in a nutrient tank, and the rest discarded.'

Tack looked wildly about himself, to try and find some way out of this. Then he saw it. He pointed up the beach. 'There, you can see the tracks it left.'

Coptic glanced up the beach with a look of bored irritation, then he abruptly did a double take. 'Remain exactly where you are,' he said, walking up to inspect the trail left by the andrewsarchus. After a moment he returned. 'Get up.' Tack obeyed. 'Pick up the water container and proceed.'

Walking ahead of him, Tack was thoroughly aware that though multiple amputation might not be imminent, there could still be further punishments for disobedience.

Shortly they regained the encampment, where they found Meelan crouching by a fire over which a large fish was spitted. After a brief exchange between her and Coptic, she stood and stepped forwards, glancing up and down the beach. Then she took out an instrument similar to the one Traveller had been using. Tack set the water container down by the fire, and when Meelan returned to her previous position, he presumed andrewsarchus was no danger to them at present.

After Meelan and Coptic had eaten their fill of the roasted fish, Tack was allowed the remains. Such was the sheer size of the thing that he found plenty of flesh left on the bones, and inside the armoured head, which he managed to crack open with a stone. While Tack snacked on parboiled brains, Coptic unrolled his sleeping bag and lay on top of it, while Meelan prowled, keeping half an eye on Tack, but mostly her attention was focused on the instrument she held. Coptic was asleep in an instant, snoring gently. Feeling revived by a full stomach, Tack stood and walked down to the shore, strolling up and down a section of beach that did not take him out of Meelan's view.

As well as the debris left by the feeding andrewsarchus, the remains of the shark and the piles of seaweed, he saw other things that apprised him of how very far from home he was. Here were green mussel shells like the split horns of cattle, scallop shells the size of dinner plates, and a multitude of spiral shells decorated with Mandelbrot patterns in primary colours. He found a shark's tooth that covered the entire palm of his hand, and pocketed it in case it might provide a handy substitute for the knife Meelan had taken from him – though he doubted he had the proficiency to use it against her.

'There are bivalves buried in the shallows. They will serve as bait.'

Tack whipped round to see Meelan standing right behind him. Observing her closely now, he noticed that the dressing over the stump of her arm looked inflated and oddly distorted. Seeing the direction of his gaze she merely glared at him, then tossed him the fishing rod Coptic had been using earlier. Catching it, he inspected it more closely. The rod itself was telescopic, and the short length of line extending from its tip was as fine as a hair and terminated in a barbed hook, which was intrinsic to it rather than attached separately. Halfway along the line were a slidable bubble float and two weights. The reel itself was a cube with curved edges and no winding arm, only a small console on one side.

'You will now catch more fish for us to eat before we depart.' She turned away.

Tack was damned if he was going to ask her how to operate the console, so began pressing at random. After a while he found the button for extending the rod – in an eye blink – to its full three-metre length. He next found the button to release line from the reel – sliding frictionlessly from the far end of the rod into a tangle on the ground – then the button to wind it in again. Contenting himself with using only these three controls, for there were many others, plus a small screen displaying pictographic script, he laid the rod down and went to dig up some bait. Quite soon he found himself fishing on a prehistoric shore, hauling in an armour-headed fish with broad scales as bright as mercury. And for that brief time he realized he had *never* before enjoyed himself so much – not once in his entire life. But it ended all too soon, when Meelan announced that he had caught enough.

After Coptic had slept for a straight six hours into twilight, Meelan woke him up and took her turn on the sleeping bag. Without a word Coptic cooked and ate one of the three fish Tack had caught, then sat down in the lotus position to keep watch over the instrument Meelan had used earlier. Tack, weariness catching up with him, and on receiving no contrary instructions, curled up on a mound of pine needles in the bowl of a tree, and fell asleep. It seemed only an instant before Coptic was kicking him awake. But already it was dawn and, checking his watch, Tack discovered he had been oblivious to the world for a full eight hours.

'Pack up the supplies. We're moving on,' ordered Coptic.

Looking around, Tack saw Meelan down on the beach gazing out to sea. Gathering their equipment, he followed Coptic down to join her. Both of them, he saw, were well rested now, for their eyes glowed like embers. He did not see how they summoned it, but instantly the mantisal folded out of the air ahead of them, cold mist pouring off it to dissipate above the warm sand. Tack followed the two of them aboard and took up his accustomed position. Again they shifted.

One has to wonder if it matters at all to that thing on your arm whether you arrive at your eventual destination alive or dead. It seems parasitic – so perhaps it will continue feeding on your corpse as it drags it back through time.

Polly's head was aching abominably, her mouth felt terracotta dry, and her body felt battered. Her hands and face were stung all over, not as a result of time travel but of landing in a patch of nettles. Still gasping on welcome air, she rolled over and sat upright, then wished she had not been so hasty as her vision darkened and a wave of nausea washed through her. After a moment this was supplanted by that familiar gnawing hunger. Glancing down at her hand clenched white around the neck of the food bag, she eased her grip and delved inside it, retrieving a large pork pie, but it was frozen as solid as granite.

You have to wonder if you have an eventual destination, or if there is any purpose at all to your journey. Maybe you're just a piece of temporal flotsam?

'Nandru, I don't suppose you could tell me where to find your OFF button?'

Touchy. I was only trying to make conversation.

After staring at the inedible pie for a moment longer, Polly cursed, returned it to the sack, then sat upright. She was sitting in patch of vegetation at the edge of woodland, and it all looked little different from the countryside of Henry VIII's time. Getting unsteadily to her feet, she gazed around.

The nettles grew in a band along the edge of forest, separating it from grassy heath scattered with patches of teasel and thistle and dotted with wild flowers. This open heath extended some hundreds of metres to a wall of parsleys, displaying glimpses of reeds and more forest beyond. Nowhere visible was there any sign she recognized as from the hand of man.

'How far back have we gone now?' she wondered aloud.

Oh, speaking to me again are you?

'Yes, I'm speaking to you,' she snarled.

That's good, for after a few more of these jumps back through time, I'll be the only one left you can speak to.

'What do you mean?' Polly carefully trod a path through the nettles, as she made her way out into the open.

Well, your time-jumps are getting longer and longer, and remember human history isn't that long, relatively speaking.

'Go on,' Polly snapped, acutely aware of how little history she knew.

OK, like it was once explained to me at school: if you compared the whole sweep of Earth's history to one day, then human history occupies about the last two minutes of that.

'Don't be ridiculous.' Polly suddenly felt very cold.

I'm serious. Earth is four billion years old, and modern humans have only been around for about one thousandth part of that. Dinosaurs, which I'm sure you've heard of, existed for about a hundred and sixty million years, yet died out some sixty million years before we appeared.

Even as he said it, Polly recalled with painful clarity the small facts she herself had picked up almost by osmosis while watching films and taking part in interactives. She recited, 'And before the dinosaurs, hundreds of millions of years of life on land and in sea, and before that only in the sea, then even more time without life at all.'

You're now getting it. Seems your brain is waking up.

'Yeah, seems like it.'

Polly trudged towards the reeds where she assumed she would find a river, as that seemed as good a destination as any. Upon reaching the high parsleys, she reached out to brush them aside.

Stop right there.

'What?'

Those plants are hemlock, so don't get their juice on your skin – they're poisonous.

Polly veered around the stand of hemlock and headed for a gap through to the reeds. Soon she found herself alongside a fast-flowing river, its bottom sandy and pebbled, underneath a slow ballet of strands of waterweed. Soon she found a shallow part, the water's surface broken by a pebbled prominence, where she crossed and began to walk upstream. Eventually she found a fallen log to sit on. Her hunger had become a constant gnawing in her gut, so she took out her tobacco and made a roll-up, in the hope that it might still the pangs. Staring down into the debris caught where the fallen tree's branches penetrated the river bottom, she froze suddenly and found her hunger the last thing on her mind.

'I think I know what time we've arrived in,' she whispered.

And how do you . . .? Oh.

'You see him, too?'

Trapped amid debris, with water flowing over it like a transparent skin, lay a rotting human corpse. White bone and grinning teeth showed through where much of his face had slewed away, white fingerbones dotted the river bed, the remaining flesh was washed almost colourless. But the leather helmet, breastplate and one leather sandal remained. Tatters of cloth flowed about his hips. His eye sockets were empty.

Your leaps through time are indeed getting longer.

'He's a Roman soldier, isn't he?'

A legionary, yes, so this time you've shot back over a thousand years. The Romans were here from about 100BC until around AD400.

Polly continued puffing silently on her cigarette. When the scale moved her backwards next, who could know *when* she would end up? How could she make any plans for her own future when she kept regressing further into the past? She stood and continued upstream.

'I don't know what to do. What am I supposed to do?'

All you've ever done, really: survive.

The era of the andrewsarchus was like balmy spring compared to this period. It seemed as if someone had just opened a furnace door, and Tack did not relish the prospect of stepping from the mantisal when they landed. Coptic, who was currently controlling the bioconstruct, remained where he was, as the mantisal slid on through the air, ten metres above the ground. Meelan began whispering urgently to Coptic and gestured to the structure encaging them. Coptic spat a reply, nodding ahead. Tack assumed this exchange was something to do with how the mantisal's glassy struts were becoming clouded, as if filling up with smoke, though he had no idea what this might signify.

Gazing downwards, Tack observed dense scrubland broken only by striated rock formations and red earthen tracks. Looking ahead, he saw that this arid landscape extended as far as distant misted mountains crouching above the flat shimmer of heat haze. Immediately below them, creatures resembling a cross between camel and deer went crashing into concealing scrub. Others, like deer with elephantine snouts, spread honking along well-trodden trails. A lone beast like a rhinoceros, but with twin club-shaped horns on its snout, looked up, then stamped its feet, before lowering its head and charging away. Then, slowly becoming visible through the haze, appeared a sight that did not belong in this distant age at all.

Behind a high steel palisade rose a conglomeration of cylindrical structures like a chemical plant, but painted in various shades of burnt sienna, green and yellow, so as to blend into the landscape. To one side of this complex lay the gutted ruins of huge craft. These possessed stubby glide wings and bloated nacelles, now gradually decaying into the plain. Spaceships perhaps, but Tack wasn't to know, nor could he safely ask.

'Pig City,' muttered Meelan, her attention focused on the newer structures rather than on the once-streamlined vehicles.

Tack noted a hint of contempt in her voice. She now turned her attention to her arm stump. He watched her pull away the strangely distorted dressing, as if it was a dried-out scab, and drop it out between the lower struts of the mantisal. An embryonic limb was revealed. She grinned at Tack triumphantly, and he quickly switched his attention elsewhere.

To clear the palisade, Coptic took the mantisal higher. Now the clouding throughout the construct's cagelike body was resolving into black veins, and its flight was becoming erratic. Tack suspected some problem. He returned his attention to their destination, where he observed, mounted on a tower set in the fence, some sort of gun tracking their progress.

'Why is it called Pig City?' he risked asking, and received an irritated glare from Coptic.

Meelan was more forthcoming. She gestured to a herd of animals gathered outside the palisade. Though these battle-scarred monsters bore some resemblance to wild boar, their mouths were crocodilian and crammed with broken teeth, and they themselves were the size of a rhinoceros. 'Enteledonts. I'm told the Umbrathane here regularly give them little treats and provide them with water, and in exchange can rest assured that no one is likely to approach on foot – which is why we aren't.'

Two of the fearsome monsters were between them tearing apart a bloody mess of bones and flesh, and Tack assumed this must be one of those treats. When he glimpsed a boot nearby with some of its owner still inside, he swallowed dryly.

Coptic brought their transport in over the wall and down.

'Out,' he ordered, withdrawing his hands from the mantisal's eyes, which now were black at their core.

As Tack dropped to the ground, he observed four people walking over towards them. Two men and two women. They were Umbrathane he knew because he had been told, but otherwise he would never have been able to distinguish them as a different kind from Traveller. One of the women he recognized at once as Iveronica – the woman in the rock. Following Tack out of the mantisal, Coptic snared him by the collar and marched him forward. Behind them came a familiar rush of chill air as the mantisal began to disappear. Tack glanced back and watched it folding away slowly and unevenly, its structure beginning to evaporate. Coptic jerked him towards the approaching four. A harsh, staccato conversation ensued, Meelan sounding by far the most vocal. Listening intently, Tack recognized the name 'Saphothere', and frequent use of the word 'fistik' while Meelan gestured at her newly growing arm, but otherwise their exchange was lost on him. Glancing to one side, he spotted a grinning woman standing by the palisade tossing from a small tin what looked like sweets out to the enteledonts. The beasts fought amongst themselves as they gobbled them up, thick drool hanging from their jaws like glass rods. Tack now had no doubt where he would end up once he was no longer of any use to these people. At that moment he felt Coptic grab up his arm, to show Iveronica Tack's nascent tor.

'The heliothant you with that want?' Iveronica said. Before he could begin to formulate a reply another staccato exchange ensued between them. Tack's attention was drawn back, by the roaring grunts and a crashing, to the woman at the palisade. As she rattled her tin against the bars, the creatures beyond it were going wild, chewing on the metal, trying to force their way through, even biting at each other. Abruptly Coptic shoved Tack down to his knees and stepped back. The woman who had just asked the question stepped forward and walked all around him.

'Are you a Heliothane agent?' she demanded.

She unhooked something from her belt and held it up. After studying it, she turned to Coptic and spat some command at him. The big man jerked Tack back to his feet and began probing his scalp with iron-hard fingers. They finally located the base of Tack's skull, where Traveller had inserted an interface plug in order to reprogram him. A finger drove in, and Tack groaned as something was levered from the cavity. Coptic tossed his pink and gelatinous discovery on the ground, and Meelan drew her weapon and fired once, turning the object into a puff of black smoke.

Be ready, came Traveller's voice over Tack's comlink.

Tack felt a surge of adrenalin. He reached into his pocket with his one free hand and closed it around the shark's tooth. Iveronica was now barking instructions to her fellows, who obediently moved away. Pausing to gaze contemptuously at Tack, she then gestured to one of the cylindrical buildings behind her.

Then it hit.

There came a vivid flickering as of numerous flashbulbs going off in sequence. The woman clanging at the palisade dropped her tin and stumbled backwards. Bright lines travelled across the fence's surface like flame on ignited fuse paper, so it was eaten away and fell to dust. With the root of the tooth braced against his palm, Tack turned and drove it up hard, slicing into Coptic's neck and up under his chin. Next twin explosions took out a couple of towers. A huge gun barrel entangled with debris dropped away and crashed to the ground. Staggering wildly, Coptic scrabbled with bloody fingers at the tooth embedded in his neck. A woman screaming briefly, an enteledont shaking its tormentor like a red rag. More of the creatures piling in behind. Meelan, yelling as she points her weapon at Tack. Shots dogging his steps as he runs. Another explosion nearby, and out of it a ragged figure cartwheeling through the air, then a red man-shape, peeled from head to foot, bellowing as it drags itself along the ground. Over the rampaging enteledonts a mantisal hurtles in, and it slams to a halt right above Tack, instantly shrouding him in cold mist. Tack reaching up and grabbing, hauling himself inside as the construct ascends.

'Push that out,' said Traveller, nodding to pumpkin-sized mirrored sphere attached loosely to one of the struts. Tack pulled it free and slipped it out through a gap in the structure. Glancing down he saw other mantisals appearing all round, and people running to board them. Then they were up and away from Pig City, hurtling out over the scrubland.

'Don't look back. It will blind you,' warned Traveller.

Tack turned away just in time from the burst of harsh white light, which refracted through the body of the mantisal and threw midnight shadows beyond rocks and trees on the landscape below. Momentarily he glimpsed the familiar shape of a nuclear explosion, before the mantisal folded them into between space.

But even then it was not over. Against the surrounding blackness he saw a spreading cloud of escaping mantisals.

'Don't look,' Traveller warned again.

Fire bled through and painted red light across colourless space. Immediately after, they flew on through the vorpal and human wreckage evaporating in a place unable to sustain it.

'I saw you get the one called Coptic,' said Traveller.

Tack merely nodded, too stunned still to speak.

'My given name is Saphothere,' Traveller conceded.

8

Engineer Goron:

The energy dam still functions, but with the orbit of Io perturbed I don't know how long this will last. We assumed there was to be another attack when the Umbrathane fleet displaced into orbit around Callisto, and in response missiles were launched from Station Seventeen. They didn't impact, for the fleet shifted inside the temporal barrier englobing the moon. What readings we were able to take showed us that the entire moon was a few degrees out of phase. Attempts at tachyon communications failed. Luckily Seventeen did not orbit Callisto, since, like the rest of the stations that were there then, it would now be drifting erratically in the Jovian system – the phase change having negated the moon's gravity-well before the final apocalyptic event. It seems stupid to ask how we could not have predicted this when we have access to time-travel technology. But who would have thought only a month ago we would have needed to look to the immediate future? It is certain that the entire population are all dead. It was only the Umbrathane fleet and the research facility that shifted.

As they thawed, the apples became pulpy, but Polly still managed to eat four of them. Then she gnawed her way through to the frozen core of her pie as she walked some miles along the watercourse. Finally stopping to rest with her back against an oak tree, she slept until what was, in her estimation, midday. When she woke her mind seemed a lot clearer.

'I don't want to just survive. I want a life as well,' she abruptly stated.

Nandru's reply was some time in coming, as if he too had been dozing.

You are alive.

'I want to understand, to experience. So I should view this . . . journey as an opportunity. There is so much I can learn.'

All you ever wanted to experience before was as many highs as possible with the fewest hangovers.

Polly unbuttoned her coat to check the contents of her hip bag. It still contained some heroin patches and pearlies.

'No, I've changed,' she insisted.

She ignored the patches, taking out only her tobacco to roll herself another cigarette. It occurred to her that she only had enough for a few more days. Not having experienced withdrawal from the other drugs she had used before placing the scale on her arm, she might avoid tobacco withdrawal as well. She had no intention of getting hooked again on patches though, so considered throwing them away. However, they would serve as analgesics should she be injured – which was now looking increasingly likely.

So your plan is?

'To learn, to experience. I need to *see* things in this time before I get dragged back again.' She assessed the food bag. 'I have enough supplies here for a few more days, but what after that? I'm hardly equipped for this kind of life.'

You've done pretty well so far. You've acquired rather more suitable clothing than that you started out with – as well as a gun and a knife – and, of course, you've still got your taser.

Reminded of this last item, she removed it from her hip bag and studied it. It was not yet recharged, so she moved back to the open area by the river and rested the taser on a log, where its solar cells would benefit from direct sunlight.

Yours seems an admirable aim, but surely, in a such a barbaric age as this, you'd do better to keep your head down and wait for the next time-jump.

'But then I'd continue doing nothing – just existing.'

Then, when your taser is fully recharged, we must go and look for whatever passes for civilization here.

When later she came upon it, the military encampment was undoubtedly the work of man, but whether civilized or barbaric was still to be seen. Polly had entered an area at the forest's edge where some trees had been felled, coming in sight of a tented city surrounded by an abatis and earthen banks. Outside these, soldiers stood in neat ranks facing funeral pyres – Roman legionaries burning their dead. Seeing heads already turning in her direction, and word being passed along, she sat herself on a stump and started chewing on another pie. Shortly after, a small group of heavily armed legionaries was approaching her, their cloaked commander riding along behind. She noticed how clean-shaven and neat these people were, how polished was their steeped-leather armour, how their short swords gleamed. She also noticed how frequently their attention shifted to the forest behind her.

They suspect an ambush.

'Well, I'm not going to ambush them, unless they get nasty,' Polly replied out loud.

The men gazed at her in puzzlement as she finished the last piece of pie crust.

'Quis's, pro Ditem?' asked the legionary now closest to her – a brutal-looking man whose clean-shaven skin only revealed more clearly an ugly scar across his face.

'I haven't the slightest idea what you said just then,' said Polly, standing up and sliding her hand into her pocket to grip the comforting weight of the automatic.

He said, 'Who the hell are you?'

'You can understand what they're saying?'

Just about. In here Muse has dictionaries for about a hundred languages. By simultaneously accessing all European languages, I can get a rough translation, as many of them have Latin as their root.

'Fugite,' said the mounted officer, urging his horse forward. The men parted to let him through. He dismounted and tossed the reins to scarface. 'Qua loqueris? Certe nil horum barbarorum.'

'Sorry, I'm just an ignorant savage and don't understand what you're saying.'

I think he just said you don't sound like an ignorant savage.

'What's he saying now?' Polly asked. The officer had turned to scarface.

He's pointing out that you are talking in your strange tongue to someone apparently unseen, so you are either fifty men short of a cohort or touched by the gods. I suggest you continue talking to me out loud, so that they may retain that opinion of you and not think to satisfy their curiosity by means of the numerous sharp objects they seem to favour.

'A cohort is one tenth of a legion, and usually consists of between three and six hundred men,' said Polly, shivering.

Yes. So what?

'That's something I never knew before. So how do I know it now?'

You haven't figured that out?

'Apparently not.'

When I put Muse 184 onto you, it immediately established a nanonic linkage through to your spine and up into your head, where it has since been making numerous connections – an example of this being that you no longer really need the inducer in your earlobe to hear me. Its library – and something of me too – have been bleeding over into your mind ever since. You didn't notice it at first because the heroin abuse kept you on the edge of moronic most of the time. Then the scale cleaned out your system and ever since you've been growing continually more knowledgeable. Besides that, Muse has also been upgrading your linguistic ability in English, so that you would become more able to communicate with it coherently.

The Roman commander turned and gestured towards the encampment. Scarface reached out to take hold of Polly's arm, but desisted when the commander spat another order at him. Looking round, Polly saw awe in the faces of the soldiers, and something like fear.

'But I'm talking like I've always talked,' argued Polly.

Another soldier now moved in beside her, while the commander remounted. Scarface gestured towards her food bag. She handed it over and he peered inside, wrinkled his nose at its contents, then tossed it to the other man to carry. Whatever happened now, Polly was determined not to hand over any of her weapons. But Scarface baulked at the prospect of searching her further, after nervously eyeing her clothing. Perhaps he thought she might put a curse on him, or perhaps he thought she had fleas. After a moment he ushered her on ahead of him.

Polly returned to her exchange with Nandru. 'Can you control my upgrading? Can you . . . teach me things?'

Not at present. The Muse element of myself follows a program originally designed to supply necessary information during battle. It operates mainly when you are under stress, and opens sections of its library to certain connections in your brain only when specific types and quantities of neurochemicals are present. Believe me, it's complicated enough in here – I don't want to interfere recklessly and end up lobotomizing you.

The smell of burning pine wood and burning flesh became stronger now. Perversely, the aromas caused her further pangs of hunger. The pyres were burning low and the legionaries beginning to march back to their tented city beyond. But a grey-haired old man wearing elaborately chased armour awaited Polly and her escort. This personage was obviously someone most important, for a gilded litter with bearers in attendance awaited his pleasure, and a cohort of men in splendid armour stood by. As they drew closer, the mounted commander hissed warningly to Scarface.

Well, you certainly seem to be receiving the grand tour.

'What's that supposed to mean?'

The old fellow waiting there is the Emperor Claudius no less. I'd advise you to take your cue from others in showing due signs of respect. The Romans weren't exactly distinguished for their record on human rights.

Finally they reached the Emperor's presence and, though bows and salutes were exchanged, she noticed there was no outright grovelling. Polly remained standing meekly where she was while the commander dismounted and explained the situation with numerous gestures and puzzled frowns. At an imperial signal, two of the Emperor's personal guard approached her. Both possessed a polished Teutonic look: one of them as slim as a whippet, while the other appeared capable of crushing walnuts with his eyelids. They had no reservations about laying hands on her and half carried her before their master to thrust her down on her knees before him.

'All right, no need to get tetchy!' she protested.

Walnut eyes seemed about to strike her, but desisted when Claudius raised a finger. He then crooked the same finger at her.

'Surge.'

'What did he say?'

I think you can stand up now without getting thumped.

Polly stood and waited in silence. The guards stepped back a little way as the Emperor folded his hands behind his back and limped one circuit around her. Stopping in front of her again, he reached out and felt the fabric of her greatcoat, touched each of its brass buttons in turn, then stared at her boots. After a moment he gave voice to some drawn-out utterance, stammering his words, and smearing his chin with spittle.

'What was that?'

I'm not entirely sure. Translation is difficult enough for me with clearly spoken Latin. I think he wants you to take off your coat, but maybe it would be better if you pretended not to understand too much.

She addressed the Emperor, 'Sorry, I haven't a clue what you're talking about. You see, I'm a time traveller, and your language died out quite some time before I was born. I'd like to oblige you, but no way are you getting your mits on my gun.'

The Emperor tilted his head, listening to her closely and frowning in puzzlement as he wiped the spittle from his chin. In a circular gesture he indicated her coat, then putting his hands together, parted them and moved them each to one side, clearly indicating that she should remove it. Polly considered pretending further that she didn't understand, but walnut crusher was staring at her with alarming hostility. She slowly undid the buttons then opened wide her coat. The Emperor's puzzlement increased when he saw what she wore underneath. He again made that removing gesture. When she did nothing, he flashed irritation and pointed at her hip bag.

'I guess I'm going to have to act now before they strip me of everything. You said they might be thinking I'm touched by the gods?'

Be very careful, Polly. I would hate to lose you now – what with all you mean to me.

Polly grinned at the Emperor, pointed up to the sky, then held out her hands in some strange gesture of welcome. She then reached into her hip bag, removed the taser, turned quickly to one side and fired at the walnut crusher. The result couldn't have been any more spectacular. He went up on his toes, with small lightning flashes zipping around his inlaid breastplate, then down flat on his back like a falling log. Weapons were drawn all around, the soldiers shouting and moving in. The whippet had his sword poised to stab her, and looked terrified. Calmly putting the taser back in her bag, Polly surveyed them all in her most queenly manner, then returned her attention to Claudius, going down on one knee before him and bowing her head.

Oh, fucking wonderful, and there I was thinking you were getting brighter.

The uproar all around continued, as Polly waited for the sword stroke that would take off her head, and almost not caring. When it died down, she glanced up to see the Emperor had raised his hand again. As he addressed his men, it was evident some of them found him incomprehensible, so badly was he stammering. When he gestured Polly to rise, she did so quickly.

'*Can you tell me how to say, "He is alive"?*' she subvocalized.

Try '*Vivit.*'

Polly gestured to the prostrate soldier, and repeated Nandru's words. Claudius, his expression frightened, spat an order and swords were immediately sheathed.

'That seemed to work,' said Polly cheerfully.

Well, they haven't nailed you to a tree yet, so that's a plus.

The soldiers loaded walnut crusher onto the litter, and he was rapidly born back to the encampment. Polly followed on foot beside the limping Emperor.

Tack was foolishly pleased to be given the honour of addressing Traveller by his true name, though Saphothere was a mouthful to someone from an age when appellations of more than two syllables were considered excessive.

'Saphothere.' He tried it out. 'What was that weapon you used on their fence?' he asked, staring into the darkness outside the cave mouth.

Saphothere turned on some kind of palm torch to illuminate the interior beyond. 'Molecular catalyser. The palisade was constructed of a steel composite and ceramoplastic. The catalyser caused them to react with each other: the iron in the steel combined with the oxygen in the organic molecules of the plastic, turning the fence into a powder consisting mainly of iron oxide and carbon.' He glanced at Tack. 'Understand, Tack, I have given you permission to use my name, but you will also use my title. The correct form of address is "Traveller Saphothere". Your actions at the Umbrathane stronghold were admirable, but they do not entitle you to overfamiliarity.'

Tack grimaced as he followed Saphothere deeper inside. Studying the cave floor, he spotted broken bones and the skull of some bovid that had been crushed by the large teeth of a predator, and was grateful that Traveller had retrieved and returned his seeker gun.

'What period are we in now . . . Traveller Saphothere?'

Saphothere looked at him askance, perhaps regretting the leeway he had granted. 'It's the Palaeocene – sixty-three million years in your past. There are not so many large animals around just now, as an extinction event occurred not long ago in evolutionary terms.' The man then noticed the direction of Tack's attention and added, 'Some carnivorous dinosaurs did survive, but they will not survive the coming competition with the mammals.' At that moment Saphothere's torch revealed something that – like Pig City – did not belong here: a steel door.

'They knew of you: Coptic and Meelan. She spoke your name when they saw you running towards them . . . Traveller.'

With no evident movement from Saphothere, the round door suddenly released from its surrounding metal frame and hissed inwards, revealing a well-lit room stacked with equipment.

'The Umbrathane should know my name – for most of my life I've been hunting and killing them across half a billion years.'

Saphothere led the way past the stored equipment and into a spartan living area. Here, there were rough wooden chairs around a table, bunks for four people, equipment that might have been equally domestic or the control system for launching atomic weapons for all Tack knew, and supply boxes containing packets of food and drink. Saphothere touched a console as he walked past it, and a horizontal bar rose above it, dragging up behind it a screen of translucent film on which image-enhanced exterior scenes were instantly displayed, along with scrolling pictographic script and mobile Euclidian shapes that meant nothing to Tack.

Glancing towards him, Saphothere explained, 'Security system – but of an order of magnitude more efficient than the pathetic one that guarded Pig City.' He dropped into a seat and rubbed his eyes. 'Getting to that place was more difficult than destroying it. I hadn't realized they had so much energy to squander.'

Tack dropped against a wall the pack that had belonged to Coptic and Meelan. Saphothere, after already checking through its contents, had returned it to him with the injunction not to use any of the more complex devices it contained without instruction. Still eyeing the pack possessively, Tack took a seat on the other side of the table.

'I don't understand,' Tack began.

Saphothere looked up. 'Those enteledonts were from twenty million years in the future, and by establishing them as guards, the Umbrathane pushed their city far downslope. It has been difficult for me to bring us back to the main line. To reach here we travelled sideways in time.' Saphothere was studying him carefully, perhaps waiting for questions his explanation would no doubt provoke from a linear mind.

But Tack understood. 'Where did they get their energy from?' he asked instead.

Saphothere nodded in approval. 'They used fusion reactors dismounted from their spaceships, and perhaps some sort of parasitism on the wormhole. Easy enough, as energy is projected along it from New London all the time – it's what our mantisals recharge from, mostly – and its available abundance in the ages between there and Sauros is the reason we were able to jump so accurately to here.' Saphothere gestured at their surroundings. Then with a nasty smile he added, 'Though such accurate time-shifting raises the danger of running into yourself, which would cause a short-circuit paradox – something you could only risk inside the temporal barriers of somewhere like Sauros.'

Tack absorbed this for a moment then asked, 'So the time tunnel, the wormhole, is a conduit for this energy . . . the energy you all use?'

'You might say that. Better to say, though, that the time tunnel *is* the energy – it's comprised of that.'

Tack nodded slowly. He understood only a fraction of this now, but hoped to grasp more as his relationship with Saphothere progressed. He no longer felt desperate for immediate answers now he knew they would be forthcoming anyway.

'You need food and rest now,' Tack said, gesturing to the nearby stocks. 'That's food?'

'It is, but I'll have to show you how—'

'I'll learn,' said Tack, standing up. And Saphothere was too tired himself to even be annoyed about the interruption. He rested his forehead on his arms, while Tack taught himself how to cook with the alien equipment. Finally he brought a lavish meal to the table, and they ate in silence, Saphothere growing visibly stronger with each mouthful he consumed. When they had finished, Saphothere got up and brought a bottle of amber liquid and two glasses to the table.

'One of the better products of your time . . . well . . . quite near to your time. In the nineteenth century Sauros sat for a while in the sea underneath the Arctic ice cap. I managed to acquire five or six crates of this before our next shift. I don't have much left now,' he explained.

Tack and Traveller proceeded to drink malt whisky – for Tack a first-ever experience.

The Emperor was persistent in his attempts at communicating, the watcher noted. He sat impatiently on the edge of his couch, rather than reclining on it like his subordinates did on theirs. But the words were becoming increasingly mangled in his mouth as the wine flowed, and Polly was unsurprisingly showing signs of confusion, despite the fact that the AI device she carried was obviously offering some sort of translation. Perhaps it could not explain to her why the Romans seemed both excited and scared upon hearing her name. The watcher herself ran a search through her own database and came to the conclusion that this was because of its similarity to 'Apollyon' – the Greek name for the Lord of the Abyss, Satan.

Then Polly said out loud, 'So they think I'm some sort of demon now?'

Demon, messenger, oracle . . . they don't seem able to make up their minds, the watcher opined, noting the slave standing behind the girl, scribbling down her every utterance on a piece of parchment. Talking out loud to her AI companion, had probably been what had clinched it because it was quite obviously not an act.

Now also sitting on the edge of her couch, the girl listened and responded as best she could when Claudius addressed her. Otherwise, her attention was inevitably focused on the platters of food the slaves kept bringing: fish served in a fragrant sauce, meats with sweet and crunchy coatings, dried figs and fresh apples. She even worked her way through a whole platter of oysters. Noting Claudius eating his way through a large plate of mushrooms, and then checking her database again, the watcher whispered to herself, *Now that's a preference he'll come to regret.*

But there was little enough going on here, and tracking forward the watcher observed that guests not yet departed were falling asleep on their couches. Claudius himself was snoring like a malfunctioning chainsaw and soon four slaves came in to pick up his couch, and carry it out of the tent – the troop of Germanic guards falling in behind. Two female slaves entered silently, but shortly made it understood that Polly should accompany them. She was led off to another tent, lit by an oil lamp, and containing a bed covered with furs and silks. The girl imperiously waved away the slaves when they attempted to undress her and, taking off only her boots, collapsed and was instantly asleep.

Enjoy it while you can.

The watcher skipped over the night into the next day and observed the killing.

'About two thousand years in your future,' Saphothere replied to the question Tack would have liked to have asked him long ago. 'After the Muslim jihad and the ensuing resource wars, after the nuclear winter that resulted from those wars, and after the fall of your whole civilization through your tendency to breed weak humans and strong plagues.'

Tack dared to reach out for the bottle and topped up Saphothere's then his own glass. 'Weak humans, strong plagues?'

Saphothere took up his glass and downed half its contents. 'You were already witnessing it in your age: hospital superbugs, variant pneumonias, air-transmitted HIVs. Ignoring the fundamental facts of evolution, you used antibiotics in excess, by this artificial selection process thus producing bacteria resistant to antibiotics. And that is only one small example.'

Much was already being said to that effect in his own time, Tack remembered, but there had seemed little genuine will to do anything about it. How could doctors refuse a dying man further treatment on the basis that this would eventually lead to the treatment itself becoming ineffective?

'Weak humans?' Tack nudged.

Saphothere stared at him, a faint smile twisting his features. 'Not something entirely applicable to yourself, but you and those of your kind were a persistent exception.' He did not explain further, but went on, 'The ordinary people of your time were coddled in the extreme with drugs and medical treatments, and in your soft, malformed societies the weak and the stupid were allowed, even encouraged, to breed indiscriminately. As the centuries passed, the human gene pool became weaker, while plagues became more common. The second Dark Age began with a neurovirus – for most of humanity a plague contracted in the womb. Like syphilis it ate away at the brain and claimed its victims by the time they reached their thirties. That sorry age lasted a thousand years, until the rise of the Umbrathane.'

'The Umbrathane preceded you then?'

Saphothere was now grinning openly in a way that could only be described as nasty. 'Oh yes. They arose from a small interbred group who had managed to maintain a cerebral-programming technology that enabled them to live, individually, decades longer than anyone else on the planet. They spread out from their enclave and took control. Umbrathane: meaning those bringing the land out of shadow. But does any of this sound familiar to you?'

Tack was at a loss to know why it should. This all occurred in a future he would never have reached in his natural lifespan.

'They came before you?' Tack repeated, hiding his mounting irritation.

'Before us, yet with us always. They bred the weakness out of the human race. The Nazis and the Stalinists of your own recent past were nothing in comparison to them: hundreds of millions of weaker beings were exterminated in their camps, and their own breeding programs lasted for centuries. They made the human race strong and succeeded in taking it out into the solar system – before fracturing into various sub-sects perpetually at each others' throats.'

'So when did the Heliothane come into being?'

'There was a catastrophic war . . . millions killed on the surface of Mars, incinerated by sun mirrors originally used to heat the surface of that planet, but then turned into weapons by a sect which decided that the adaption of the human form to exist in those airless wilds was sacrilegious. Before we named ourselves Heliothane we controlled those mirrors, the giant energy dam in orbit between Io and Jupiter, and other energy resources in the solar system. We were engineers, on the whole, and finally became unable to countenance the destruction of our projects in these petty wars. Finally deciding to act, and with so many power sources at our disposal, we had outreached the Umbrathane technologically and industrially within a decade.'

'And then?'

Saphothere drained his glass, then refilled it. Tack's glass was still full, for though he was enjoying the buzz from the alcohol, he had forgotten to drink while this story unfolded.

'Those who did not escape, and did not accede to our solar empire, we exterminated,' Saphothere explained.

'And when did time travel come into this equation?'

'During that war. For centuries it was known to be a possibility, but that huge energies would be required. One of our own people finally worked out how it could be done, so it was used by us in a limited fashion as a weapon – shifts of a few hours or days only, for we understood how huge a threat this technology could pose to our very existence. Had we gone back to attack the Umbrathane at the period they destroyed the Mars mirrors, we would also have shoved ourselves far down the probability slope. Near the end the one who had first worked out how to use the tech gave it to the Umbrathane and they and he fled into the past. To pursue them, we needed larger energy resources and so laboured on the great project. Two centuries from the destruction of the Mars mirrors, we completed the sun tap.'

'Cowl, you're talking about Cowl? This is why you could not kill him in his own past because to do that you would lose the whole technology he was responsible for.'

Saphothere eyed him. 'You're not so stupid after all. Perhaps this whisky is loosening some of the knots in your brain. Now, have you worked out the origins of both the Umbrathane and the Heliothane?'

Tack said, 'The Heliothane are direct descendants of the Umbrathane – if not Umbrathane themselves with a slightly different name and a different agenda.'

'That is correct. Now consider the original Umbrathane maintaining a cerebral-programming technology for a thousand years. Tell me, how many of your genetically engineered and programmable kind exist in your own time?'

'Hundreds . . . but not thousands,' Tack replied, getting an intimation of what Saphothere was telling him.

'Perhaps only ten or so years on from when you were pursuing that girl, your own kind break their thraldom to U-gov and become able to choose their own programming. They then become an independent organization, selling their skills to the highest bidders in the wars that follow – as mercenaries. The Umbrathane are the descendants of your own kind, Tack. I am, too. Which is why, for so long in our own period, even though we knew about you being dragged along in the wake of that torbearer, we dared not touch you. But now we are more frightened of what Cowl is doing.' Saphothere abruptly stood up, drained his glass, and slammed it upside down on the table. 'Now I must sleep, and build up my own resources for what is to come. One long leap will bring us to Sauros. Then will come the easy journey through the tunnel, back along and beyond all this way we have recently come, to New London.'

As Saphothere ensconced himself in one of the bunks, Tack drank another glass of whisky and tried to fathom all he had just been told. The whisky didn't help though, so, after silently toasting Sauros and New London in whatever direction they lay, he headed for one of the bunks himself.

Thadus knew that, in the terms of the people here, he and Elone were untypically old. His hair was grey, yet he did not drool or fall over, and was not dying. Which was why, he supposed, the naked youth up in the oak tree behind them, had not fled and now watched them with fascination. The boy had also probably never seen clothing like this, or the devices they carried, unless in pictures found in the ruins below. Thadus raised his unclipped rifle sight to his eye and scanned the ancient city. He could see one or two cooking fires so some knowledge must survive, despite the fact that everyone here was moronic by the time they reached their twenties and did not live beyond their thirties.

Elone blinked down her nictitating membranes to mirror her eyes. 'The census figures from the satellite put the population in the region of three thousand.'

'No sign of anyone developing resistance?' Thadus asked.

'None; the opposite, in fact. The population has been dropping steadily over the last thirty years. And what with the new enclave being built a hundred miles north of here . . .'

Thadus snorted. It was, of course, sensible for those uninfected by the neurovirus, those umbrathants who just by living longer were becoming the rulers of the Umbrathane, to protect themselves from reinfection. He said, 'I was just wondering if there were any who could be extracted before we cleanse.' He stabbed his thumb over his shoulder towards the oak tree. 'The boy there seems pretty well coordinated.'

Elone turned and gazed up into the tree. 'He's about twelve years old and malnutrition has delayed his puberty.'

'Alpha strain, then?'

'Yes. The hormones produced in puberty trigger the more

destructive stage of the virus. Right now only about a quarter of his brain has gone. After another ten years he'll lose half of what's remaining, before the virus starts targeting his autonomic nervous system and kills him.' Elone frowned. 'But you know all this.'

Thadus turned to her. 'And I want to hear it again and again. You're the umbrathant on the ground, and if you've any doubts I want to hear them. Do you know how many places like this I've cleared out?'

'You were working on the south coast.'

'Damned right. Eight old cities all with populations similar to this one, all alpha strain. I know there's no other answer, but I can still smell burning bodies.'

Thinking about the past, Thadus realized his memories were not so clear as they had been. He checked the monitor inset into the muscle of his forearm and saw that in another five days his mental template would need to be uploaded again to replace memories and abilities lost to the neurovirus he himself carried. By this, and by the cocktail of drugs developed over the last century, he kept the destructive virus at bay. But these only delayed the inevitable and at best two years remained to him. But, then, he was tired and after this last extermination would be unemployed. The rulers in their enclaves would no longer have any use for him and certainly he would not be allowed to live amongst them.

'What will you use here?' Elone asked, surreptitiously checking her own monitor.

Thadus tilted his head to the now audible sound of engines. 'The perimeter's closing in and any outside the ruins will run for home – that's what they usually do. We then drop compound B, and do a ground survey while your people collect samples. But we don't want too many delays. We drop incendiaries before evening.' He looked beyond her and pointed. 'There.'

Further along the ridge to their right, overlooking the city, two individuals broke from cover. One was naked, the other wore rotting skins and carried a primitive spear. They bolted down the slope into low scrub before the buildings. Behind them a tree went over with a rushing crash and an armoured car emerged from the forest. All this activity became too much for the boy in the oak tree behind Thadus and Elone, and he scrambled to the ground. In one smooth motion Thadus clipped the sight back onto his rifle, aimed and acquired the boy as he scrambled past. Thadus then lowered the rifle.

'See?' he said. 'They run for home.'

In an unconscious gesture, he now pressed a finger to the comlink in his ear. 'Dolure had to flame out a cave some were hiding in, but otherwise that's all of them. The bomber's on its way over.'

Both he and Elone detached masks from their belts and donned them. All around the ancient city troops and Elone's monitoring personnel were walking out of the surrounding forest, and other armoured cars were now driving into view. Then came a different engine sound as high up the tricopter bomber droned overhead and took up station above the city. There it shed its load like a sprinkling of black peppercorns. With his rifle sight back up against his eye, Thadus watched the gaseous detonations and the haze of compound B spreading between the buildings.

He checked his watch, gave it ten minutes. 'Let's walk,' he said.

And as he and Elone did that, the Umbrathane perimeter also closed in on the city. It was only minutes later that they started seeing victims of the poison gas: family groups gathered around fires, some clothed in animal skins, others so far gone in cerebral breakdown that they had been unable even to maintain this primitive clothing; individuals who had run and been felled by the gas; older victims of the plague curled up in stinking cavities in the fallen masonry, where they had survived only if their kin remembered to feed them; others rotting in those same cavities. While Thadus walked with his rifle propped across his forearm,

Elone went to rejoin her people – infected umbrathants like himself and his men – who were now spreading out to take tissue and blood samples. His own men checked for anyone alive, but in a desultory manner – Thadus had never found a survivor of the gas in all the cities he had cleansed.

Then he saw the boy.

For a moment Thadus thought he was seeing some ape that lived in the ruins with the people. Often there had been troops of macaques, chimpanzees and baboons – escaped from zoos and living wild for centuries now. But compound B was tailored to kill them as well, as they also carried the neurovirus. He gave chase to the figure darting amongst the ruins, realizing he was seeing the boy who had earlier hidden in the oak tree. How was it he was still alive? Thadus needed to bring this boy to Elone for study. He grimaced to himself, remembering his rifle had already acquired this youth. Elone did not need the boy to be alive for her tests. Finally getting a clear view, Thadus halted and raised his rifle to his shoulder.

'Thadus, the tricopter is coming back,' Elone told him over com.

Thadus hesitated. The 'copter wasn't due back until the evening. Then, just about to fire, he saw two of his men round a crumbling vine-cloaked pillar ahead of the boy.

'Grab him!' he shouted. And that shout seemed to unleash nightmares.

Thadus looked up and saw the tricopter looming over the ruins, its bay doors opening. There was no confusion in him about that. Here was a neat solution for the enclave dwellers: exterminate inconveniences like himself, Elone, and their people, along with the last of the feral humans. But then he looked ahead and saw that behind the two men the air shimmered and distorted as a line of heat haze cut it vertically. Then that cut began to evert, exposing something monstrous.

'What the hell?'

Screams were now coming over com, not from the two who were after the boy, for they had yet to see the horror looming behind them, nor from his fellows who had seen the 'copter – Thadus knew they would not scream at that. He scanned to his right and saw a terrifying vertical mouth, three metres high, its inside turning like toothed conveyers, hoovering up corpses and running umbrathants, sucking the living and the dead into a meat pulverizer. More screams. To his left a similar mouth being propelled down a street by a huge tentacle, slamming shut on four umbrathants, then withdrawing to snap up at its leisure the scattered corpses of feral humans. All around, death. Above, incendiary cylinders tumbling down through the sky from the tricopter. Ahead his two men, torn apart and turned away into an organic hell, which then closed out of existence.

Thadus stared at the feral youth standing there. He was naked, perhaps less confused about what was happening, having less expectation of the world. Something strange enclosed his right forearm: a weird thorny growth. Thadus did not know why he pulled the trigger, for they were both dead anyway. The boy seemed to turn away from the bullets and just disappear. Explosions all around, then. From beyond where the boy had stood, a wall of fire fell on Thadus. He rested his rifle across his shoulder, closed his eyes, burned.

9

Modification Status Report:
The biostatic energy generated by complex molecular interaction is inversely related to tachyon decay. Because this is a function of which I have little knowledge, I am wary of further complicating the genome, but this seems unavoidable, so further research into this 'energy' is required. Discarding parasitic DNA has made room for some additions: a strengthened endoskeleton, the growth of an exoskeleton, and increased muscle density to support these. However, this is not enough. The hostile environmental parameters I have input necessitate a more efficient sensorium and concomitant growth in nerve tissue, and then there are the brain alterations required to support all the above. Complication of the genome is, unfortunately, inevitable, especially if I am to give my child the direct brain-interfacing ability. I had hoped that my pursuit of perfection would result in a simplification of the blueprint. I had hoped my child would possess the straightforward utility of a dagger.

The racket started before dawn and grew steadily louder and more persistent. Polly awoke clear-headed and full of energy – rather how she remembered waking in those days before the alcohol and drugs. The moment she threw back the covers the two slave girls from the night before entered her tent, bearing a bowl of warm water that contained steeped bunches of lavender, some wash cloths, a dress and sandals. When they started plucking at her clothing, she shooed them away and stripped herself. They gaped at the alien scale on her arm, which was even now webbing tension through her body. But she ignored them and cleaned herself from head to foot.

Sufficiently clean, Polly donned the dress and sandals, then turned her back to the two slaves as she transferred all the items from the pockets of her greatcoat to her hip bag, before cinching it around her waist. She then ran a comb through her wet hair and tied it back with a scrunchy, and the two then watched in fascination while she applied lipgloss and eyeliner. And, thus fortified against the world, she stepped past them into the raucous daylight.

The camp was in turmoil on this bright morning. All around her, legionaries and slaves were taking down tents and packing away equipment. Carts were loaded, canvas backpacks filled, as horses were saddled and fires put out. Polly turned and walked over towards the Emperor's tent, two of the Praetorian guards who had ringed her tent throughout the night falling in behind her. His tent flap was opened for her by yet another guard, but she ducked in to find the interior empty. She turned and looked queryingly at the guards. One of them bowed to her first, then indicated a horse being led over by a bearded old man who smelled as if he had rolled himself in dung. Mounting the horse was awkward in the long dress, but she managed it with some dignity. He then led the horse through the encampment, two guards walking on either side.

Gazing around, Polly felt a surge of happiness. This morning held great clarity for her: the smells of the encampment and of the summer seemed so utterly *real* to her, the cacophony seemed *inclusive* of her, and all the colours so bright and immediate. Outside of the camp she proceeded between ranks of legionaries standing neat and silent below the hum of bees flying over the surrounding heath and the high clear song of skylarks. Coming at last to an open-sided pavilion, she dismounted, and entered to find Claudius was seated at a small desk, surrounded by various senior commanders.

'Quid agis hodie, Furia?' he asked, sharpening a quill. All conversation in the tent ceased at this greeting.

I think he's decided you're a demon now. He just asked about your health or some such. Probably doesn't want you to keel over before you reach the sacrificial block.

'You are a cheery bastard, aren't you, Nandru?' Polly grinned.

All the men present listened to her with polite puzzlement, then turned their attention to an approaching party of soldiers escorting four men to the Emperor's presence. These four were certainly not Roman: their hair and beards were long and braided, their clothing brightly dyed in clashing colours, what scraps of armour they wore were daubed blue. They were also wearing a lot of gold jewellery. Polly at first took them to be captives, but this could not be so for they all carried shields and weapons. Halting some ten metres away from the pavilion, they laid their armaments on the ground before approaching. As if taking part in a historical interactive, Polly prepared herself to be entertained.

Come to negotiate peace terms with him, I reckon.

'I suppose those pyres we saw yesterday were for the bodies of soldiers who died in some battle the Romans just won,' murmured Polly, crossing her arms.

Claudius glanced up at the four barbarians and smiled crookedly. Several of his soldiers stepped in between the men and their weapons, then grabbed the four and dragged them before Claudius, where they were forced to their knees.

I don't think they've heard about the Geneva Convention.

Polly's stomach tightened, and in a second she felt suddenly very vulnerable. This stuff was real – she must never mistake it for entertainment. She glanced aside to where the remains of yesterday's pyres were now nothing but black smears in the trampled grass. Turning back, she watched as Claudius stood up from behind his desk and walked forwards. He glanced at Polly and beckoned her over. Walking with a suddenly leaden stomach, Polly moved to his side.

'Taedet me foederum, ruptorum,' Claudius said abruptly, and

made a cutting gesture with the flat of his hand. Watching, Polly could only think that this should not be happening: horror proceeding so easily into a glorious day. The soldiers shoved the men down on their faces, both captives and soldiers yelling loudly. Short swords, glinting in acid sunlight, rose and fell, red now streaming from their blades. The condemned took a long time dying, despite the repeated hacking. With bile rising in her throat, and an urgency to escape pulling ever tauter that tension webbing through her body, Polly watched one of the groaning victims dragging himself across the blood-soaked grass, the back of his jerkin split to expose butchered flesh and shattered bone. He finally became still when one soldier caught him a blow that opened the top of his head.

The gladius is a stabbing weapon. They could have killed them more quickly . . .

All Polly could wonder was why the skylarks were still singing. Ignoring whatever it was the Emperor was now pronouncing, she turned and began walking back towards the main camp.

Barbaric times: an Empire based on enslavement and slaughter.

'Shut up with the fucking moralizing, Nandru. I'm not in the mood.'

No one tried to stop her progress, though she was surrounded by a desperate babble as she walked. Back at her own tent, she found her clothing hanging outside it on a wooden pole, fairly damp but clean. She hauled it from the pole and into the tent with her, where she quickly donned it, soon stepping back out into a morning now bearing the taint of the abattoir. Claudius and his guards were coming towards her, their pace limited by the Emperor's limp. She stared at them for a moment, then turned to head in the opposite direction. Suddenly guards were all around her, blocking her way. Walnut crusher was amongst them, staring at her with vicious satisfaction. An order stammered from the Emperor had his men closing in tighter. Unlike the rest, walnut crusher was furtively drawing his sword. Polly opened her hip bag and groped inside, her hand closing on the handle of the automatic this time, rather than the taser.

'How do I say, "I must return to hell"?'

Mihi redeundum in infernos.

The Emperor uttered something else and limped nearer. Walnut crusher glanced briefly at his imperial master, then closed in, obviously intent on his own agenda. Polly took quick aim and shot him once in the chest, the impact hurling him back into several of his comrades, then crashing to the ground. All the soldiers froze where they were. Polly stared down at the dead man.

'And how do you say, "He is dead"?'

Mortuus est . . . Polly.

She turned to Claudius and repeated both statements. The Emperor fought to reply, but couldn't manage it. Polly turned away, straight towards a wall of soldiers, who reluctantly parted to allow her through. She had put some distance between herself and them before they finally came to their senses. As the silence turned to an outcry behind her, she turned briefly to watch the squads of men running towards her. Placing the automatic back in her hip bag, she shifted again – and folded that bloody world away.

Saphothere's face looked ravaged by fatigue as it turned to Tack in the light of prehistoric dawn. Removing one hand from the mantisal eye, he pointed out of the glassy construct towards the distant horizon. It took Tack a moment to drag his attention away from the ground just twenty metres below – Saphothere had promised dinosaurs and he was damned if he was going to miss seeing them.

For a moment Tack reflected that the sun appeared very strange here, until he realized that the sun was actually behind him and what he was seeing on the horizon was a titanic iron-grey sphere, misted by distance.

'Sauros?' Tack guessed.

Saphothere nodded briefly and returned his hand to the construct's eye. The mantisal jerked forward and began drifting towards the horizon.

'Damnation!' said Tack, when something he had first taken to be a lichen-covered boulder raised its shielded, horn-decorated head from grazing a low groundcover scattered with lush red flowers. It looked up with vague bovine curiosity, as it munched in its beak enough ferns to roof a jungle native's hut.

'Styracosaurus,' explained Saphothere, glancing down. 'They move into areas like this that have already been grazed down by the duckbills, and feed on the subsequent low growth. But this isn't the time of the titanosaurs, so not every tree in sight gets flattened.' He gestured to the many strange arboreal plants widely scattered across the landscape. Their trunks were very wide at the bottom, narrowing up to comparatively small heads of foliage.

'What about tyrannosaurus rex?' asked Tack.

'Oh yes, he'll be about somewhere.'

Tack returned to studying the ground below and realized that, after Saphothere's latest comforting reply, the mantisal was descending.

'Can't you take us straight to the . . . city?' he asked.

'The mantisal's natural environment is interspace. More than ten minutes in atmosphere would kill it.'

'Coptic and Meelan flew theirs to Pig City,' Tack told him. 'Its structure became clouded first, then veined with something black.'

'Nitrogen absorption,' Saphothere explained. 'Enough of that will kill a mantisal, but then the Umbrathane wouldn't care about that – they regard mantisals as machines rather than living creatures.'

'Do *you* consider this,' he gestured at the hyaline cage enclosing them, 'a living creature?'

'I do. It is both manufactured and grown. Its genome forms the blueprint for most of its structure, but many other processes are involved. The final result is a living machine with about the intelligence of a dog, though that is not strictly true either, as the bulk of that intelligence is applied to dealing with senses and abilities no living creature on Earth has ever possessed.'

Tack reached out and touched the glassy structure. It was hard, yet there seemed a lightness to it. Deep within it he could see organic or advanced electronic complexity.

'What's it made of?' he asked.

Saphothere glanced at him. 'The main structure is a material manufactured since long before your time: aerogel – the lightest solid in existence then. It was originally used as an insulator. But, having a wide molecular matrix, there is room in it for the submolecular components you see. Underneath your hand is just one product of the unification of the sciences – call it bioelectronics or perhaps electrobionics. Maybe a good illustration would be for me to point out that Heliothane technological capabilities are of such scope that it is possible for us to *grow* a gun, an electric drill, or even a microwave oven.'

'Oh,' said Tack, unable to think of a more appropriate answer. He turned his attention back to the fast-approaching ground.

Seeing them close to, Tack realized that the red flowers were the product of vines spreading in a mat across the other groundcover, and sometimes climbing the trunks of the trees. This vegetation was penetrated by cycads, tree ferns sprouting from wide stumps next to the decaying fallen cylinders of their original trunks, stands of more familiar shrubs, young giant horsetails spearing into the air, and dark green bushes like laurel but scattered with small yellow apples. Dropping from the mantisal, when it was low enough, he was glad to sink no further than to his ankles into a carpet of vines. Beside him Saphothere unshouldered his pack, while the mantisal fled back to its natural and chemically neutral environment.

'So we walk?' enquired Tack, fingering his seeker gun and scanning his surroundings suspiciously.

Saphothere merely glanced at him then squatted down and took from his pack a device that looked like a mobile phone fashioned of perspex, before being heated then twisted out of shape.

'Your comlink?' Tack asked.

'No, my comlink is very similar to yours, though embedded in the bone behind my ear and with a subvocal transmitter linked into the temporal lobe of my brain.'

Tack reached up and touched his own ear stud. His comlink was solar-powered, so was necessarily external to his body. It operated by bone-induction, so any communication he received only he could hear, but any reply he made had to be spoken out loud in order to be picked up. He supposed he should be grateful this device had not been torn out of his ear lobe, considering all that had recently happened to him.

Saphothere opened out his phonelike device to expose two twisted screens, the lower of which switched on to show shifting virtual controls. He continued, 'The defences of Sauros block external comlink communications because of the possibility of computer viral attack. This – ' he held up the device – 'is an encoded tachyon transmitter imprinted to me. If anyone but me tries to operate it, they'd find themselves getting turned inside out through a vorpal singularity. The result is not pretty.' His fingers followed the virtual controls, and the upper screen lit to show someone's face. Saphothere addressed the face in the same language used by Coptic and Meelan, then he snapped the device shut.

'What now?' Tack asked.

'Now we wait, if our friends over there allow us the opportunity.'

Saphothere pointed somewhere behind Tack, before returning the tachyon communicator to his pack. Whirling round, Tack saw three creatures approaching through the low vegetation, some hundred metres away. As these slim-boned dinosaurs moved, heads and tails extended horizontally, they stood no higher than a man's waist, but every now and again they stopped to peer about them, raising their heads much higher. Their precise movements were reminiscent of herons, but their long hind legs were built for speed, their foreclaws for ripping apart living flesh, and though their heads were narrow and ophidian, they possessed mouths large enough to swallow the lumps they might rip from their prey.

'Don't tell me,' said Tack, remembering an interminable film series on dinosaurs. 'Velociraptors?'

'Wrong. The name for these in your own time is troodon, or wounding tooth. Velociraptors are quite smallish feather-covered egg thieves, so they would avoid us. Hopefully these will too, as they usually go for smaller prey.'

'And if they don't?' Tack aimed his seeker gun at one of the advancing creatures, but the gun refused to acquire – its template being for human recognition only. Tack lowered it again and punched in the code to set a blank template. Flipping up the square sight he aimed at the leading one. A small grid flicked up in the square and froze the creature's image, which told him that the template had been established and his target acquired. He then acquired each of the other two creatures in turn. Saphothere watched him with paternal amusement.

'I never scanned that weapon of yours,' he admitted. 'How does the round guide itself into the target?'

'The initial charge fires a cased round,' said Tack. 'The case is dropped when quite close to the target, then the explosive shell opens wings powered by synthemuscle. The target template is uploaded to a micromind in the shell – running a program that is a direct transcription from the mind of a wasp attacking a human.'

'Interesting,' said Saphothere, then raised his own little gun and pointed it at the vegetation between themselves and the approaching troodon. The weapon emitted a muzzle flash like that of a machine gun firing in darkness. Involuntarily, Tack staggered back, blinking away after-images, as a swathe of vegetation a couple of metres wide ignited as if soaked in petrol. Squawking and cawing, the hunting dinosaurs turned tail and ran.

Quickly holstering his weapon, Saphothere nodded towards Tack's seeker gun. 'You see, such surgical precision was not really required.'

Feeling foolish, Tack returned his weapon to its holster and, following the direction of Saphothere's gaze, spotted an object approaching at speed from Sauros itself. Soon this resolved into a hemisphere of grey metal, its curved surface facing downwards. Soundlessly, it settled in towards them and landed. Running around the inside this object was seating, and at its centre a single column supporting a basketball-sized globe.

'In,' Saphothere instructed, and Tack clambered aboard.

Once seated, Saphothere reached over to the globe, which split like a flower head to reveal a hand-shaped indentation.

'Wrong person puts his hand in this thing and the globe closes, snipping his hand off at the wrist,' Saphothere lectured.

As the hemisphere rose into the air, he gestured over the side with his other hand. 'Now a little fire would not have put *him* off.'

Looking over the side, Tack did not need anyone to tell him that he was seeing his first tyrannosaur. As the monster stepped delicately through the vegetation, tilting its enormous head from side to side to observe the rising pall of smoke, Tack felt a surge of joy at the sight, tempered with gratitude for not being at ground level. Here was a creature that even the andrewsarchus might flee.

'Beware the jabberwock, my son,' said Saphothere. 'The jaws that bite, the claws that catch.'

Tack looked askance at him.

'Beware the jub-jub bird, and shun,' the traveller continued, 'the frumious bandersnatch.'

Tack peered back at the ground, wondering if he might see such creatures.

After blacking out again because of lack of air, Polly felt a creeping horror that this would happen to her again and again, until someone or something killed her. There was an aching weariness in her and the flesh felt loose on her bones. But, as was usual, the hunger impelled her more than the need for rest. Pushing herself to her knees, she looked around. The surrounding marsh was still and eerie, and even though the sun was shining the air was cold and damp.

'Where and when the hell am I now?' she asked, her voice rough. 'And why didn't I grab some food before I shifted?'

If you'd taken time to grab some food, I suspect you'd have received open-heart surgery without the benefit of an anaesthetic. As to when we are, I suspect that each jump you make takes you back a multiple of the previous one, so this is certainly more than a thousand years before Claudius came across the Channel to slaughter the ancient Britons.

By now she realized there was no going forward again. This time, as a sensation much like huge acceleration took hold of her, she'd been able to sense, somehow, the direction she must go in order to travel forward in time. At the root of her being she had known that the scale could take her forward, but all effort to shift in that direction had been thwarted – as for a swimmer fighting against a riptide.

Finally finding the energy to stand, Polly was alarmed by a nauseating movement, until she realized she was standing on a mat of reeds that ringed a small island. Moving inwards to firmer ground, she glanced from side to side and all she could see was an expanse of water dotted with more islands. Licking the water soaked into the sleeve of her greatcoat she found it salt, so it seemed that not only was there no prospect of food here, but nothing to drink either.

'I wonder if I could get this thing off,' she said, running her hand over the surface of the scale, which was now utterly smooth to the touch.

Why? Do you want to stay here?

The minimum she wanted was to be back in her own time, with access to the comforts of civilization, but with her head as clear as it was now. But she was ambitious for more. She wanted the advantages 'Muse Nandru' gave her and continued use of the scale, so she could choose exactly where to travel in time.

'Somehow I have to learn how to control it,' she muttered.

An unlikely possibility. Monitoring your blood sugars has confirmed that it is some kind of parasite, and that basically for it you are only an energy source powering each of its leaps through time. That's why you feel so hungry on each occasion – it burns away every available resource inside you. On the plus side, you'll never get to be a size twelve.

'Fucking ha-ha.'

Uh-huh, here come the natives.

Looking through Polly's eyes, Nandru had spotted him first, for on one of the salty waterways a coracle was coming into sight. As it drew closer, Polly noted that the man sitting inside it was short and squat, with dark oily hair and a knotted brown body. He wore breeches of some kind of animal skin, a sleeveless top of rank-looking fur, round his throat a necklace of shells. Once he saw her, he immediately stopped paddling and snatched up a spear with a long serrated-bone blade. Gazing at him Polly wondered if this time might be the Stone Age. She had found that mentioned in an encyclopedia disc left behind in her apartment PC by the previous owners – a disc she had studied for a little while till growing bored and using it as a coaster.

'Stone Age?' she asked.

Probably, so watch yourself. This guy probably hasn't heard of female emancipation.

She watched the intruder put down his spear, a look of infinite distrust still on his face, and take up his paddle to row the coracle closer. Wondering if it might now be judicious to take another jump through time, she tested the webwork lacing through her body, but received only a sluggish response. Reaching her island, the prehistoric man took up his spear again, probing the mat of reeds with its tip before stepping ashore. He gabbled something, in which Polly could identify no single word.

'What did he say?' she subvocalized.

My best guess would be, 'Who the fuck are you?' I'm getting nothing through my translation programs.

The man repeated it louder and more insistently, gesturing first at her with his spear, then towards the coracle. He was eyeing her in a way she recognized and was strangely reassured by. At least his intentions were not entirely hostile. She gave him a smile and after a fleeting frown he smiled back. Retaining a half smile, she stepped forward, clutching at his arm to steady herself over the carpet of reeds, and climbed shakily into his coracle. The primitive followed her, and the coracle dipped alarmingly as he took his place. When he spoke again, she merely smiled at him again, but this now seemed to annoy him. He reached out, yanked her towards him, then pushed her down into the belly of the coracle, where he pressed one filthy possessive foot on her.

The Heliothane here were all beautiful, but in the same way as tigers – they were endowed with a grace and symmetry best admired from a safe distance. In one of the many narrow corridors leading outwards to the viewing windows, Tack encountered a goddess over two metres tall. Her skin was the colour of amber and possessed some of that gem's translucence, her yellow hair intricately braided, and her eyes utterly weird – gold irises set off by black sclera. She wore clothing much like Saphothere's: a long coat of black leather, loose trousers tucked into spear-toed boots, and a shirt of rough red canvas. What jewellery she wore – in her ears, around her neck, and threaded in her hair – was of polished bone. Gaping at her, Tack did not realize he was blocking her path, until, showing a flash of irritation, she slammed him into the wall and strode past. Winded, Tack continued on towards the windows, as directed by Saphothere, where thankfully there was more space to move.

Gazing out over the vista below, Tack first located the dying fire, then the tyrannosaur. The controls, set low in a corner of this particular window, were not so simple as Saphothere had suggested. Trying to track the moving virtual buttons, Tack managed to flick the window to infrared, which only worsened the view.

'What are you trying to do?'

Tack froze. Thus far no one but Saphothere had spoken to him in his own language. Thus far he had found it prudent to avoid all other Heliothane. Apparently it had taken much persuading on Saphothere's part to prevent some of these people from just cutting off Tack's arm and lodging it somewhere safe. He turned round slowly.

Whereas most of the Heliothane that Tack had seen were tall and rangy, this man was of a more normal height, which he more than made up for in breadth, for his shoulders had to measure one full metre across. He wore a loose shirt and trousers of a material resembling thick white cotton. His skin in contrast was jet black, features negroid, and eyes mild brown. Tack also noticed that much of his exposed skin was laced with fine scars.

'I'm trying to get a closer view of a tyrannosaurus out there,' Tack replied.

The man humphed and reached out an arm as thick as Tack's leg, which terminated in a boulder-crushing hand. Half expecting to receive a blow, Tack jerked back, but instead the man ran his fingers over the virtual controls, and the window flung up the required view of the creature outside, tracking it as it moved in its endless search for prey to chew on.

'An impressive creature, but strictly speaking it has evolved only to exist within narrow parameters.' He looked at Tack. 'You realize that people of your time were misguided in their belief that tyrannosaurus was merely a carrion eater? That all came from their softening outlook on existence – a political correctness engendering the attitude that at their root all creatures are good. They were in fact right the first time: tyrannosaurus is a vicious predator that will rip apart anything that moves, usually to devour but sometimes for the fun of it.'

Tack grunted in understanding.

'Another myth was that their front claws serve no purpose. Try telling a creature with a set of teeth like those that two handy toothpicks are useless. They like their meat fresh, not trapped decaying in their mouths.'

Gazing back at his companion, Tack noticed over his shoulder the tall woman he had earlier 'bumped into' entering the viewing area and heading in their direction. She appeared distinctly irritated. Noting the direction of Tack's gaze, the big man looked round. Coming to a halt, the woman licked her lips nervously before starting to speak in the Heliothane language.

The man interrupted, 'Tack here does not understand our language, Vetross, so to use it in front of him is impolite.'

The woman bowed her head. 'My apologies, Engineer.'

'So, tell me, what so urgently requires my attention?'

'The spatial scroll extending . . . has will extend . . . stretch . . .' Vetross paused before saying, 'This is not a suitable language for the subject.'

'The mind, like the body, requires exercise,' said Engineer. 'You are just using different muscles this time. Think about it for a moment, then continue.' He turned to Tack. 'Have you seen enough of your dinosaur?'

Tack nodded. In truth he could have watched the beast for hours, but he did not think this was the answer Engineer wanted, so Tack wasn't about to argue.

Engineer continued, 'When Vetross finally gets around to telling me her news, I suspect that Saphothere's departure, and yours, will be brought forward. Do you know where he is at present?'

'In the recovery ward.' Tack removed from the pocket of his new coat the palm computer that had belonged to Coptic, and which Saphothere had reprogrammed specially for him. Once he opened it, the device – consisting of what appeared to be two sheets of smoked glass hinged together – displayed a map of the interior of Sauros. In one corner was a small icon of a control panel which, when touched, expanded to fill one half of the computer with a static virtual panel. Using this, Tack was able to confirm Saphothere's location.

'Ah, simple but exclusive of some useful information,' said Vetross suddenly.

Both Tack and Engineer turned towards her.

She continued, 'The energy dam in New London is functioning

at full capacity and all abutments are field stable. We are ready for the shift. All that has to be decided is whether or not we maintain the one light-year span, or allow the one-third light-year extension.'

'You see, it's not so difficult. I will join you shortly to begin the shift.'

Vetross nodded sharply and, without even looking at Tack, moved off. Engineer turned back to him. 'Tell Traveller Saphothere that I require him at abutment three.'

Tack risked, 'What was all that about?'

Engineer smiled. 'The energy required to shift Sauros back in time a hundred million years is now available. And, while making that shift, the tunnel's span will become unstable, which is why you must go now.'

The big man turned and began sauntering away, adding over his shoulder, 'Tell Saphothere not to delay. A solar flare could crack the dam, which would put the project back months in New London time, if that place were ever to survive the event.'

Following his map, Tack negotiated the corridors of Sauros, by travelling ramps and walkways whose floors flowed like mercury but somehow maintained a surface solidity. In the vast interior spaces of the city he observed massive walls of balconied dwellings, around which travel hemispheres buzzed like insects; immense machines labouring to some unknown purpose, but which caused some sort of inductive tug at his skin; huge ducts and conduits, and spaces curtained with nacreous energy fields. Everything was composed of metal, plastic and other manufactured materials, and all served a definite purpose. There were no statues, nothing built for simple aesthetics, no gardens, yet the place possessed an awesome functional beauty.

The recovery ward lay at the rear of one of the residential blocks, its panoramic windows overlooking a well, at the bottom of which rested a machine consisting of what appeared to be randomly cut concentric gear rings shifting against each other, as if searching for some final combination. Every time they shifted it seemed as if the very air changed all its directions of flow and some force pulled at Tack's insides. Saphothere lay on a metal slab, pipes conducting his blood from a plug in the side of his chest to a wheeled machine nearby – which, so Saphothere had informed Tack, cleaned out the poisons and directly added nutrients along with complex enzymes that accelerated tissue repair and the growth of fat cells, so in effect Saphothere was being endowed in just a few hours with what would otherwise have needed days of rest and sustenance. As soon as Tack entered the room, Saphothere opened his eyes and glared at him.

'I told you to keep yourself occupied for five hours,' he said.

Tack told him of his encounter by the viewing windows.

'Engineer?' Saphothere sat bolt upright, then leant over and made an adjustement to the revitalization machine. After a moment its pipes were clear of his blood, then one of them filled up with some emerald fluid. Saphothere gasped in pain, picked up a wad of white material from an inbuilt dispenser, waiting until the emerald fluid cleared, then yanked all the tubes from his chest, slapping the wad quickly into place to soak up any spill of blood. None of this surprised Tack now. His surprise had been earlier, when Saphothere, without assistance, had opened up his shirt, placed the plug against his chest, and explained through gritted teeth how its connection heads were now digging inside him, searching for his pulmonary and ventricular arteries. It seemed Saphothere had no time for anaesthetics or the ministrations of a nurse, had there been one in evidence.

'I take it he is an important man?' asked Tack.

'He's the Engineer,' said Saphothere, as if that was all the explanation required. He swung his legs off the slab, kicked away the wheeled device, which rolled back to the wall, sealed up his shirt and stood. 'I would have liked more time here, but it seems your education will begin sooner than expected.'

'What do you mean?'

'I will not be flying the mantisal all the way to New London.'

Even Ygrol, the toughest and most dangerous member of the Neanderthal tribe, was tired and knew he was fighting a losing battle. The aurochs he had killed would keep his fellows supplied with food for some time yet, but no matter how much meat he brought to the encampment, his people were still weak and incontinent, blinded by the blisters around and on their eyes, still dying. Only Ygrol was still physically untouched by this terrible malady, though it hurt him in many other ways.

Inside the yurt he wrapped the dead girl in a tanned goat fur to keep her warm for the journey and began sewing it shut. He did this because it was always how the dead should be honoured, though he would not bury her, for the one on the mountain demanded the corpses. After dragging her outside the yurt, he first went over to check that the stew, in its hide pot over the fire, contained sufficient water, for without it soaking through the hide, the pot would burn and the contents spill into the flames. From the other yurts he could hear the moaning and the demands for water and food, but ignored them – that they were making a noise meant they were still alive. Returning then, he threw the girl's corpse over his shoulder and walked back through the forest towards the mountain, where *it* awaited.

Nothing seemed to satisfy the monster, and Ygrol had tried every means at his disposal. It had taken the remains of the mammoth meat from the storage cave, and twice took his kill when he left it unguarded for but a moment. He thought perhaps to satisfy it with the gift of other sacrifices, and so began killing the flat-faced outsiders for it, and dragging them to the mountain.

But that seemed to make no difference at all. Now all it seemed he could do was make his people as comfortable as he could while they died, then take their bodies to the mountain as offerings. But then what, when they were all dead?

The gift still rested on the stone where the tribe had butchered smaller carcasses and spread out hides for scraping and, sometimes, the need to go and take it up nearly outweighed Ygrol's duty to his people. But he knew that to do so would somehow take him away from them. He knew that the creature on the mountain wanted this of him. But he dared not leave the tribe with no one to provide for them.

Something thudded against the goatskin wrapping the girl, and he thought a carrion bird had just dive-bombed him. He pulled his bone club from his belt and looked around at the trees. Then he saw the two flat-faces running towards him, and glanced aside to see the arrow penetrating the sad parcel over his shoulder.

Ygrol considered fleeing. He did not have his spear, and he knew just how lethal were the flimsy-looking weapons these people carried. But to run he would need to leave the girl and, even though he was taking her to give to the monster, he would not leave her to these excuses for human beings. Pulling her lower, so she rested across his chest, he roared and charged. Another arrow thudded into his package, went through the girl's leg and just penetrated his chest. The bowman was down on one knee, struggling to string another arrow as Ygrol hammered into him, smashing him aside with one sweep of the club, his head split right open and his brain almost completely out of his skull. Not pausing, Ygrol continued after the other man as he fled. He threw his heavy bone club at the back of the man's legs to bring him down, then was on him in a moment, and did not put down the corpse of the girl as he stamped the life out of this upstart Cro-Magnon. On the mountain he left his two victims on either side of the girl to assist her on her journey, then headed home, trying to figure out how to work the bow and arrows he had taken.

Back at the encampment it did not take long for the Neanderthal to know that something was badly wrong. First he smelt burning meat, then, upon walking into the clearing, heard no one moaning. The stew hide had been torn open and emptied and the smell arose from the few small pieces of meat in the fire. The yurts had likewise been torn open and emptied – all that was left inside them was the occasional bloody animal skin. Ygrol shrieked his rage and ran to leap up onto the butcher stone. He cursed the gods of sky, rock and earth and damned the spirits of all the ancestors who looked down from their fires in the night sky. And as if in reply, the very air over the encampment split and the mountain monster appeared, but this time nothing was hidden. Ygrol saw then the spirit of every animal he had slaughtered for the pot and knew some accounting was due. He looked down at the gift, where it rested between his feet, considered smashing it with his club, but then picked it up.

Deep in the forest the Cro-Magnon men heard a scream of defiance and rage from the Neanderthal encampment they were encircling. But they never found the one who had murdered so many of their tribe. Not even bones.

10

Modification Status Report:
Some sensory additions will form in an aerogel grid on the exoskeleton, similar in function to the lateral line of a fish, but sensitive to a wide spectrum of radiation. The presence of this grid negates the need for eyes. This is fortunate, as the interfacing organs, which by necessity must remain close to the child's brain, occupy much of its face and leave little room for much else. I have retained the mouth in position, along with those modifications required for the more efficient ingestion of food, but the nose and the eyes are gone. Also, it being the case that many of the interfacing organs are delicate, some sort of protection is obligatory. Serendipitously, I have discovered that only a small alteration to the gene controlling exoskeletal growth (this taken, along with the mouth modifications, from the genome of a scarabaeid beetle) causes growth of 'wing cases' over the face. Already, I think, I know what my child's name will be.

He lay flat on the floor of his hut, his eyes rolled up into his head and his body rigid with ecstasy. The hut stank. The man stank. Polly grimaced down at him, then moved over to the duck skewered over the fire and tore off a leg. The two patches she had pressed against his chest, while running her hands up inside the stinking fur he wore, were taking him somewhere he had never been before. Wondering why she had chosen to do that rather than zap him with the taser, she supposed, after seeing the squalor he lived in, she had felt some pity for him.

As she sat eating, and washing down each mouthful with bitter sips from a wineskin, she could hear his woman still angrily moving about outside. He had yelled at her earlier when the woman had protested, whereupon the woman had glared at Polly with both hatred and fear. Polly realized she had to leave now before he came to and wondered what the hell had happened to him. Tossing the duck bone in the fire she reached out for the rest of it, tearing away its stringy flesh with her teeth. The remainder of two flat gritty loaves she shoved into her pockets, then looked around. But there was nothing else here she wanted – no more food anyway. With one last look at the prehistoric man she had sent into a drugged coma, Polly stepped out of the hut. The woman looked up from a quern on which she was grinding some sort of grain. She babbled something Polly did not understand. Polly reckoned her to be not much older than herself, but she appeared terribly worn, like Marjae near the end. Behind her two naked brats were squabbling in the mud. Polly strode past them all to reach the coracle moored on the island shore. The woman shouted a protest as Polly stepped into the small boat and pushed herself away with the paddle. She did not look back.

The sunset was red on the sky when Polly finally moored at another island and crawled ashore. She prepared herself a bed of thick reeds and slumped down on it gratefully. Even as cold as she felt, she was instantly asleep. Night passed in a seeming instant, and as she woke to the dawn chorus of waterfowl and frogs, and then the sound of a man bellowing and threatening. She sat up and he saw her at once and cursed as he waded towards her as fast as he could. There seemed no doubt about what he intended to do with his serrated spear. Polly turned aside, the webwork inside her responsive to the slightest nudge. But there was the suffocation to face.

Try hyperventilating.

'What?'

Breathe quickly and deeply – more than you need to – until you're dizzy.

Polly started doing just that. Soon she felt a buzzing through her limbs and became light-headed. As she stepped beyond the bellowing man's furthest remembered ancestors, the swamp grew thin and it dissipated like fog, exposing a reality of infinite grey over a black sea. Terrible cold gripped her and it seemed as if the pressure of that was aiming to squeeze out her last breath. She was falling now, hurtling through that grey void – the sensation of speed more manifest than before. Briefly she glimpsed a silvery line on some impossible horizon. Surely it must end soon. But as the air bled out of her lungs she began to panic – the scale was going to carry her to the limit again, she was going to run out of breath. Her desperation to stop seemed to distort everything around her into glassy planes, vast curved surfaces, and lines of light. What she needed was down there, and she pulled herself into it. Gasping but elated, she stumbled across frost-hardened ground into the blast of a snowstorm.

Then something growled behind her.

'Abutment three' bore the shape of a huge crooked thumb projecting over one corner of the triangular entrance that filled the bottom of this vast chamber. Tack had no wish to look down into the tunnel again, since some effect of perspective seemed to try and pull his eyes out of his head. In the distance he could see a similar abutment overhanging each of the other two corners, and it *was* a distance – looming through the mist filling the chamber, they stood at least a kilometre apart. Standing back from the edge of the platform mounted on the side of this abutment, and over the rim of which Engineer and various members of his staff were now peering, Tack turned to Saphothere.

'He told me about the shift back in time, but what was all that about spatial elasticity and the unnecessary squandering of energy?' he asked.

Saphothere glanced at him. 'At present the tunnel is one light year long, internally, and a decision must be made as to whether we maintain that physical length or extend it.'

'But if they are going back a hundred million years, surely the tunnel *needs* to be extended?'

'Distance,' said Saphothere tersely, 'when equated to time travel through interspace, is only a function of the energy you need to expend. The shorter the tunnel's actual length, the greater the energy input required to maintain it. Had you sufficient energy you could open a doorway directly into the Precambrian, though you would probably put out the sun in doing it. Zero energy input would extend such a tunnel to infinity, attenuating it into non-existence. It's quite simple really.'

Tack snorted and returned his attention to Engineer. He and the others had now finished their discussion and rejoined them.

'It is now decided,' said Engineer. 'Take your mantisal through and inform Maxell that we shall maintain the tunnel at one light year. I feel that to extend now would be premature, and that we should wait for the shift into the Triassic.'

'Yes, Engineer,' replied Saphothere, with a short bow. He turned, and almost immediately their mantisal appeared out of the hot humid air blowing across the platform.

'And you, Tack,' continued Engineer, 'I look forward to seeing again when you return, though you will be much changed.'

Tack did not know what to make of that, so he just nodded and followed Saphothere into the mantisal. Soon they were drifting out from the platform, out over the triangular well below and all its gut-churning distortion. Then the mantisal dropped like a brick, straight down into it.

The falling sensation continued until the mantisal turned, so that rather than dropping downwards as if into a real well, they were now travelling along an immense triangular tunnel. It was only a change of perspective, as the weightless falling sensation continued, but enough for Tack to get a grip on, and so not lose the contents of his stomach. Also, as they progressed, he began to feel acceleration, noticing what appeared to be faults in the silver-grey walls of the tunnel fleeing past faster. All of this was numbing, and just watching it dropped Tack into a weary fugue. He dozed, losing it until Saphothere spoke to him again. Checking his watch, Tack saw that only minutes had passed.

'Come over here.'

Tack pushed himself away from the side of the mantisal, drifting over to catch hold of a strut, then hauled himself down to a standing position next to Traveller. Saphothere withdrew his left hand from one of the two spheres.

'Place your hand in there,' he instructed.

Tack rested his palm against the surface, which felt glassy until he pushed into it, then it gave way and enclosed his hand in cold jelly. Immediately there came a prickling stinging as of numerous needles penetrating his flesh. A chill spread up his arm, across his back, then leapt up via his neck and into his skull. The mantisal suddenly appeared even more transparent than normally, and the tunnel itself changed. Now they were hanging in the flaw of a gem, in which they held their position against a waterfall of light. And beyond this, interspace was again visible – infinite grey underlined by the black roiling of that strange sea.

'What's it doing?'

'Connecting . . . and feeding as well.'

'Feeding?' Tack repeated woodenly.

'Mantisals draw energy from sources we provide for them within interspace, but that is not enough for a material creature. They separate out carbon from our exhaled breath and, in this manner' – Saphothere nodded towards Tack's hand – 'directly absorb other essential chemicals. Now, do you feel the connection?'

After trying to dismiss from his mind the fact that he was

somehow being eaten, Tack did sense something. The mantisal was tired and wanted to rest. It felt confined by the distortion of interspace around it, and was aware of that distortion in a way that – through it – Tack instinctively tried to grasp, but it defeated him. The flow of light now began to diminish, and the mantisal began sliding to the edge of the flaw.

'Don't let it stop. You must keep pushing it.'

Tack tried to put the construct under pressure, but just did not know how. Mentally pulling back in confusion, he found the alien mind sticking with him, sinking into him, becoming one of his parts. Now its weariness was his, its need to rest becoming his own. Then he *knew*, and from that part of himself which enabled him to persevere through a particularly tough fight-training session, he now found the will to drive the mantisal on. It began to slowly draw back to the centre of the flaw and the flow of light began to increase.

'Your other hand,' urged Saphothere, now seeming just a skeleton cloaked in shadow beside him – like an X-ray image. Tack watched Traveller withdraw his hand only so far that his fingertips still remained inside the eye, then inserted his own hand into its place. Upon doing this, he felt some strange species of feedback from the piece of tor embedded in the wrist of that hand, and saw it brighten under its enclosing bangle, glowing like a solid gold coin. From it, he felt resistance, as if from some infinite ribbon of elastic stretched into the far past. Only while feeling this did he realize that, in his head, time now equated to a distance, and that other elements of the mantisal's perception were becoming comprehensible to him. He remembered undertaking a simple perceptual test that involved viewing a line drawing of a cube and switching it about in his head, so that what he perceived as the rear surface became the front and vice versa. Doing the same with what he was seeing now, he brought the tunnel back into existence for himself, while maintaining an awareness of how the mantisal perceived it . . . and much else.

As the compressed ages fled by, he realized that the flaw itself was rising from Earth's gravity well, which in its turn was a trench cloven around – and within – the trench of the sun. And that they were falling towards the sun, for their destination did not lie on Earth. Reality now patterned around him in absolute surfaces twisted in impossible directions, spheres and lines of force, empty light and solid blackness, all multiplied to infinity down an endless slope. Glancing at Saphothere, who had now moved away from him, he saw just a man-shaped hole cut into midnight – but the traveller was also a sphere and a tube, both finite and infinite. Tack groped for understanding, something starting to tear in his head.

'Start pulling yourself out now, else you'll never return.'

Saphothere was beside him again: skeletal, terrifying, fingertips back in the eye.

Tack pulled away and absolute surfaces slid back into place to form the walls of the tunnel, shapes curving away into nothingness, and soon he once again perceived his surroundings in simple three dimensions.

'Now, take out your right hand.'

'But . . . I can do this . . .'

'You have done enough for now. You've been standing here for two hours and for fifty million years.'

Tack withdrew one hand and Saphothere instantly thrust his own into place. Taking out his other hand, Tack looked at his watch and confirmed that two hours had indeed passed. Pushing himself back through the cavity of the mantisal, he felt weariness descending on him like a collapsing wall.

'But one light year?' he said, as he moved to his accustomed position in the mantisal.

'Time and distance, Tack. Distance and time. You now know the answer: to fly the mantisal you had to build the blueprint of the logic in your mind.'

It was true. Inside himself Tack felt he had gained an utterly new slant on . . . everything. He thought about the tunnel and said, 'It compresses the continuum and multiplies, by orders of magnitude, the distance the mantisal can normally travel. And, like the tunnel, the more energy the mantisal uses the shorter its journey. In how short a time, for us, could it traverse this tunnel?'

'Less than an hour, its personal distance contracted to a few hundred kilometres,' Saphothere replied. 'But it would kill itself and its rider in the process.'

Tack nodded, too weary to ask anything further. Folding his arms and bowing his head, he closed his eyes and fell into a dream world, where Klein bottles endlessly filled themselves and hollow people built tesseract houses.

Being interface technician, Silleck commanded the respect of many and the distrust and horror of some. As she strode along the moving walkway towards the lift that would take her up into the control room of Sauros, she spotted other Heliothane surreptitiously noting her shaven head and the scars on her scalp from the penetration of vorpal nodes. But she was used to such attention and ignored it as she thought about the coming shift of the city. Goron had summoned her early because she was his most trusted interface technician, so that meant she would have an hour or more to scan through various vorpal sensors scattered throughout time and across alternates. It was perhaps the best part of her job – such voyeurism.

Reaching the lift shaft, she stepped on the platform and as it took her up she ran her hand over her scalp. Her head ached slightly, as it always did nowadays, for there was never enough time for the damage done by the penetrating glass fibres from the nodes to heal completely. Stepping off the platform, she noted that Goron had not yet returned from the abutment chamber. She nodded to Palleque – who always seemed to be here – then headed to the interface wall, seeing that already one of the other technicians was linked up.

The man stood with his head and shoulders enclosed in the vorpal sphere, which was also packed with translucent and transparent mechanisms. Through this distortion, nightmare hints were visible of his open skull and of glassy pipes and rods interfacing directly with raw exposed brain. From the back of this sphere, like a secondary spine, a mass of ribbed glass ducts followed the curve of his back down, before entering a light-flecked pedestal and then down into the floor. From this spine, vorpal struts spread out like the wing bones of a skate, to connect it to various mechanisms in the surrounding walls, ceiling, floor and adjacent connectware, so that the man seemed to hover at the centre of some strange mandala – the human flaw in an alien hyaline perfection.

Silleck headed to the middle of the three spheres located along the wall, beside the man, and ducked underneath to thrust her head up through the gelatinous material. As she pressed her back up against the glass support spine, she immediately felt her head and face grow numb. Her eyesight faded, as did her hearing. There was no pain, but she could feel the tugging as automatic systems opened her scalp, removed the screw-in plugs of false skull, and began to drive in the nodes of vorpal glass. She knew the fibres were growing in from the nodes when her vision began to flick back on as from a faulty monitor, and she began to hear the bellowing of some dinosaur. Soon she was seeing the standard view for which her equipment was set: from outside Sauros. Then the connection began to firm and that view feathered across time and she was seeing, and *comprehending*, Sauros over a period of hours, present and future. And if that was not enough, she began then to see up and down the probability slope, possible cities, a maybe landscape, might-have-been dinosaurs. Without the connectware and the buffering of the technology surrounding her, such sight would have driven her mad.

Eventually Silleck stabilized her connection and focused on the specific, as there was no use yet for her to have such an all-encompassing view – that would only be required during a city-shift or an attack. Scanning the near present and near future, she found little to interest her, so began to tune into the tachyon frequencies of the nearer vorpal sensors. Through one such, she observed a boy being pursued by a couple of early Cro-Magnon women. But because she had seen this all before she knew he would escape with the roasted squirrel he had snatched from their fire, would sleep under a thorn bush, then be shifted back through time by his tor, to somewhere beyond available sensors. Anyway, there had never been much interest in such individuals, for the boy was clearly from the time of the neurovirus and would not survive many more time-jumps. No, it was the view from the next sensor that most interested Silleck. The girl fascinated her, and Silleck had not yet had the free time to view everything that happened to her on this latest brief jump. The jump in itself was interesting because both ends of it were encompassed by the ten-thousand-year life of this particular sensor. Focusing her awareness, Silleck connected into the sensor near the end of its life and tracked back through time until she found what she wanted.

The girl, Polly, turned, groping inside her greatcoat for the automatic Silleck had seen her shoot at the juggler some hundreds of thousands of years in the future. Already the cold had begun penetrating her inadequate clothing, and her hand shook as she pointed the weapon into the haze of the blizzard. Adjusting the sensor, Silleck viewed the animal out there in infrared, and could hear the muffled thud of heavy paws, then a low growling. The girl pulled the trigger, then cursed herself and groped with shaking fingers for the safety catch. Out of the snowy blur a shape loomed: huge and shaggy, and with enormous, unlikely looking teeth. Polly squeezed off a shot, and in the half-light the muzzle-flash momentarily overloaded the image Silleck was viewing, so the technician did not see the snarling retreat of the beast. Polly now glanced behind herself, perhaps realizing for the first time that she stood on the edge of a cliff, over which the storm was blasting. Far below her lay an icy plain being crossed by a herd of woolly mammoths. Polly turned back, no doubt hearing the furtive approach of the beast that Silleck could clearly see. The creature had been *big*, and that shot, the technician realized, had only pissed it off.

'Really, and there I was just thinking about finding a ski lodge,' Polly said out loud.

It was this seemingly insane monologue that had first drawn Silleck's attention in the woodland, where the girl had first met the juggler. It was only on further scanning that the technician realized Polly wore some kind of AI device that seemed rather advanced for the time the girl had come from.

Polly closed her eyes then, and Silleck observed the temporal web responding to the girl's will, drawing her into interspace. She disappeared moments before the beast, a large bear, hurtled out of the storm, then came to a skidding stop by the precipice and looked about itself in confusion. That was as far as Silleck had got the last time she had looked through this sensor. Now she drew back down its time-line to the point of its arrival, after being fired into the past from New London. She then tracked uptime to the temporal signature of Polly's arrival, some five thousand years later.

The girl materialized in mid air, the tor unable to adjust, during such a short forced jump, to ground level. She hit the ground and rolled, searching desperately for the weapon she had just dropped. It rested on an icy surface, underneath which were tangles of waterweed and small fish swimming sluggishly. After snatching up the gun, she looked around.

She stood upon the same cliff top as before, but there was no blizzard or huge animal, just rocks and dirt and the bare bones of a tree stripped of its bark by a constant icy blast – all below an anaemic sky. Polly buttoned up her coat and moved away from the edge of the precipice. Still cold, Silleck observed – the girl had managed to miss a brief interglacial period.

'Yeah, yeah, you and my mother both,' Polly said out loud.

The probe not being sophisticated enough to tune in to the other side of the conversation, Silleck contained her annoyance and continued to watch as Polly walked away from the cliff. Shortly she came to a scree slope descending to a stream that was mostly ice but in which some water still flowed. She stooped down beside it, cupped her hand to sample some. Moving along the stream's course, she took some bread from her pocket and ate.

Boring, thought Silleck, phasing forward quickly as the girl followed the stream to a river that descended in occasional waterfalls down the mountainside – the moving water forming only a small percentage of it, the rest of it frozen into weird hyaline sculptures, like teeth, or many-fingered hands grasping the rocks. Soon she came in sight of the lower plain, where the river terminated in a wide pool. A bear had broken through the ice, and Polly watched it lunge into the water, then pull back without anything to show for its effort.

'Is that the creature I saw before?'

Unheard, Silleck replied, *No, but possibly a far distant ancestor.*

Crouching, Polly continued to observe the hungry creature. She waited cautiously until it headed away and was well out of sight before making her way down towards the pool. Silleck adjusted the probe to X-ray and observed salmon skeletons swimming under the ice. The girl would be starving because of her tor's parasitism, but Silleck could not see how she could possibly get herself a meal. Suddenly inspired, Polly groped in her bag, and took out some device and fired it into the water. Silleck linked into data storage in Sauros to identify that item as a early defensive taser, then wryly observed its effect. Jerking violently, two large salmon floated to the surface. Not even bothering to take her boots off, the girl waded in and scooped them onto the shore.

Well done, Silleck told her. *Well done indeed.*

'Sure,' said Polly to her AI companion, taking out a knife. 'You never heard of sushi?'

As the girl feasted on raw salmon, Silleck heard Goron say, 'We're ready for the shift. Let's have you all online,' and reluctantly withdrew from that distant time.

The exit from the time tunnel was much like its entrance: possessing the triangular distortion that it was painful to look at and with huge abutments poised over its three corners. The mantisal rose into albescent space beside a tornado of rainbow heat haze which penetrated to the centre of the triangle. Only as they moved away from this did Tack notice distant walls and realize they were in some vast chamber. Eventually reaching one wall, they entered a passage, delving into a horizontal city composed of either buildings or machines, then into a long curving tunnel.

Tack decided that he definitely wasn't in Kansas. They ascended into what must be vacuum and the close glare of the sun, between the giant buildings of a vast city complex that, as the mantisal rose, Tack now saw bordered the face of a gigantic disc.

'How is it we can breathe?' Tack asked, once he remembered to breathe again.

'The mantisal generates oxygen as a waste product, after absorbing the carbon from the CO_2 we exhale.'

That sort of answered Tack's question, but not quite.

'I mean . . . how come the air isn't lost from inside here?' He waved at the open spaces between the struts.

'In simple terms: a force field, generated all around the inside of the mantisal, contains it – though a more correct description would be a temporal interface.'

'Oh, that's all right, then.'

Saphothere shot him a warning look, which Tack acknowledged with a shrug before returning his attention to the fantastic view.

Here were towers of such immensity that they could have contained the entire population of a major city from Tack's own time; titanic engines – their purpose unknowable to him; and huge domes covering dense forests, parks, and in one case a sea in which leviathans swam and upon which ships rode. Tangles of covered walkways and transport tubes linked these structures, and various transports, some of them mantisals, swarmed about them. Above this city, perhaps unloading their cargoes, hovered enormous spaceships constructed of spheres bound together by quadrate dendritic forms. The centre of the disc was void except for a single immense dish, and nothing moved above that, for there space was distorted by the transit of lethal energies.

'New London,' Saphothere announced.

Tack could think of no sensible response.

The mantisal was now heading towards the edge of the disc. Apparently this environment was not harmful to it, for Saphothere seemed in no hurry to get it to any destination. Below them the city unrolled and just kept unrolling. Tack looked up towards the sun, which was surprisingly dim. He should not be able to look directly at it like this.

'Do you see the sun tap?' Saphothere asked.

Sun tap? The man had repeatedly referred to that, but Tack had never wondered what it might mean. Silhouetted against the face of the orb he noticed a rectilinear shape, minuscule in proportion, but then, to the sun, so was planet Earth.

'How?' Tack was at a loss.

'It sits in the chromosphere, using more than half of the energy it generates to power the antigravity engines that hold it in place. Entering the same AG fields, the sun's radiation accelerates and is focused into a microwave beam with which you could fry Earth in half a second.' He nodded towards the distortion above the dish. 'A fraction of that beam hits splitting stations, before reaching here, and is diverted to conversion stations spread throughout the solar system, which in turn provide the energy for our civilization.'

'Conversion stations?' Tack asked.

'One such station, over Mars, converts microwave energy into the full spectrum of light – from infrared to ultraviolet – which serves as our replacement for the sun mirrors destroyed by the Umbrathane. It is the reason that planet is now no longer entirely red.'

Tack considered that. 'You said just a fraction?'

'Most of that beam hitting the dish here, is used to power the wormhole – the time tunnel. You have to understand that we originally built the tap specifically for that purpose, and that the greening of Mars became just a side benefit. Tap and wormhole are inextricably linked and neither, once created, can be turned off. There is, in fact, no physical means of turning off the sun tap as the antigravity fields that sustain its position also focus the beam – as I mentioned – but if you did, the wormhole would collapse catastrophically and Sauros would be obliterated by the feedback. Also, if the wormhole was independently collapsed, the energy surge would vaporize New London. The project was therefore a *total* commitment.'

They now became weightless inside the mantisal as it dropped past the outer rim of New London, and soon Tack observed that, just like a coin, the city had two sides. When the construct swung in towards the other side, Tack felt his stomach flip and bit down on a sudden nausea. Now he felt the pull of gravity from the second side as they descended towards a building on the very edge of a city, which sprawled across the entire underside of the disc. This structure was shaped like the rear half of a luxury liner, but standing on end so its stern was pointing into space. Except this would have been a liner that made *Titanic* look like a lifeboat. The mantisal now curved in towards the 'deck' side of the building, where other structures protruded at right angles. Tack saw that, like a silver foam, thousands of mantisals were already attached to these protrusions. Eventually they came in amidst them and descended onto a platform resembling a weird melding of a giant oyster shell and a helipad.

Withdrawing his hands from the mantisal's eyes, Saphothere said, 'You remember the mask in your pack? You'll need it to get to the entrance, as it's vacuum up here.' He gestured to an oval door at the juncture of the landing platform with the main building. 'You'll have to run, though.'

Tack opened his pack and took out the mask. When Saphothere had originally explained its function to him, Tack had hoped he would never have to use it. It looked organic, like the sliced-off face of a huge green cricket, its interior glistening wet. As he pressed it against his face, its soft interior flowed around his features, moulding itself to him. For a moment he was blind, then a vision screen switched on, with complementary displays arrayed along the bottom. Breathing involved only slightly more effort than usual. Apparently the mask stored pure oxygen – after sucking it in from its surroundings – and, when being worn, released it.

'Come on now,' urged Saphothere, his own mask in place

as he leapt out. Tack followed him, running for the door. Initially his skin felt frozen, then suddenly it was burning. He saw vapour rising off his clothes and dissipating. Saphothere, trotting along beside him, seemed completely at ease in this environment. As they reached the oval door, Tack glanced back to see the mantisal floating over to one side of the landing pad, where others of its kind were gathered. Grabbing the protruding handle, Saphothere pulled the door open and led the way into an oblate airlock chamber. As soon as he closed that door, air began blasting in, and after a moment they could remove their masks.

'Now what?' Tack asked.

Saphothere proceeded through the next door into a chaos of sound and colour. Tack could hardly take it all in: a vast chamber containing dwellings in all shapes and sizes suspended in gleaming orthogonal scaffolds; gardens and parks, some of them even running vertically; walkways ribboning through the air; transports of every kind hurtling all about the place; and Heliothane everywhere, thousands upon thousands of them. Glancing at Saphothere he saw the man was operating his palm computer.

'You are too slow and too weak, so would get killed in here' – he gestured to the surrounding mayhem – 'within minutes, probably by accident. This is not for you yet.' So saying, Saphothere operated some other control on his computer. Tack felt the all-too-familiar sensation of a reprogramming link going in. He tried to object, but instead simply shut down. Everything started to grey out and the last thing he felt was Saphothere catching him as he fell.

Rain like a vertical sea hammered upon her and, slipping in the mud, Polly went down on her face. Her nostrils filled with the stench of decaying vegetation and in the darkness she could hear things hooting and screeching.

'Yes, I know – not a good place to be,' she said, then wished she hadn't spoken when the animal noises fell silent.

Pushing herself upright, she looked around at the darkness and at huge trees looming behind curtains of rain.

'You've got nothing to say?' she asked him nervously, terrified she might now be genuinely alone.

Oh, always something to say. But at present I'm trying to use one of Muse's military logistics programs to calculate your acceleration back through time.

'*You'll be able to predict what era I'll arrive in next?*' Polly subvocalized, sure she could hear baleful movements out there.

Well, I have some dates to work with . . . within vague limits. Thus far it would seem your acceleration is exponential, though what the exponent is it's difficult to ascertain. All I do know is that if the increase continues at its present rate . . . a few jumps more and you'll be going back millions of years at a time.

'*You're not serious?*'

Oh yeah, but, as I said, the parameters are vague. If you follow the curve I'm now trying to plot, you'll end up off the graph – achieving a jump that is infinite. But then I might only be viewing part of that curve and who's to say you'll be following a curve anyway? Thing is, you are now learning to control the shifts, and Christ knows what other factors might come into play. The next one might easily be one year or one million years.

'Oh, screw this,' Polly said out loud and reached down inside herself to grasp hold of that webwork and bend it to her will. This time there was no transition over that previous black sea and she was immediately into that Euclidian space she could manipulate, if only in a small way. She gave it a few seconds only, then pulled herself out, dropping down on her back into soft leaf litter in a raucous daylit forest. She gasped in a lungful of cold morning air.

Of course, every time you do that, you just screw up my calculations further.

Polly did not know whether to laugh or cry.

Cheng-yi dragged himself out from under the mounded dead and looked around in disbelief. The attacking unit of the People's Army had bayoneted the survivors and the wounded ponies, then looted the bodies. All that now remained of the largest robber band in Miyi county was butchered corpses strewn along the valley. That none of their attackers had dragged Cheng-yi out and searched him he put down to his being covered in blood and the plenitude of loot elsewhere. Climbing unsteadily to his feet, Cheng visually checked himself from head to foot. None of the blood appeared to be his own, which was miraculous considering he had been riding beside Lao when the machine gun opened up, and there was not much left of *him* that was identifiable. Cheng gave a little dance and shook his fists at the sky, then he looked round again, completely at a loss.

What little drug smuggling or gun running they had managed across the Himalayas since Mao's revolution, would not be available to him alone. And also, since that revolution, pickings had been poor in the Xiang region – most of the thieving already done by Party officials. Cheng was damned if he was going to rejoin China's current society: thankless toil and the grey and boring clothing did not appeal to him. One option remained: he would head towards the coast, for Kowloon and Hong Kong, and see how his fortunes would fare. Not for one moment, as he exchanged his clothing for the best available remaining on the corpses, and looted them of anything the soldiers had left, did he feel any grief. They hadn't been a bad lot, but none of them had really appreciated his qualities and, anyway, his emotional spectrum encompassed only terror and lust. The former came into play again when, just as he was ready to set out, the monster came.

The huge and horrible thing fed on the dead. He saw it bow down over the body of a pony and suck it down with a crunching gulping. The human corpses it took down with less trouble. Crouched behind a rock, Cheng-yi sobbed with terror as he listened to the macabre feasting, then when the sounds ceased, he choked back his sobs and held his breath. Perhaps it was gone now? Perhaps it had never been there . . .

Cheng-yi looked up straight into the mouth of hell poised above him and screamed. The mouth turned away and, from the flank behind, one of the monster's scales fell and thudded in the dust beside the Chinaman. He watched as the scale, at first leaf-like, coiled up into a cylinder as if rapidly drying. Lust was Cheng's next emotion, and he did not hesitate to grab the thing up and pull it up over his forearm. Then, the monster gone, he wondered what madness it was that had made him see such monstrous visions. But this was not his last.

11

Engineer Goron:
It was some staffer of Maxell's who had the idea of using cerebral programming on the next torbearer we managed to intercept. Sir Alex seemed the best option as he had been combat trained from birth. Our team had eighteen hours to work on him before his next shift and all seemed to go well: the programming took and there was even time to provide him with physical augmentation and a Pedagogue weapons' instruction download. Apparently, though he accepted our weapons, he utterly refused to shed his armour. But even with his armour and his weapons and his new abilities, he must have failed. The team, remaining at the location where they had intercepted Sir Alex while they recharged their mantisals via a portable fusion/displacement generator, were attacked by the beast only minutes after his concurrent arrival beyond the Nodus. So we can only suppose that Cowl killed the man, but was angry enough to retaliate directly.

Pedagogue was an unseen presence directly downloading information into his mind and, with the true brutality of a surgeon, wrenching into shape those structures in his mind that could utilize it. But this, this he didn't understand:

The trip was due to take another five hours. Tack *knew* there were three ramscoop fusion engines, set on outriders protruding from the main cylindrical body of the ship, belching white blades of flame. Mercury resembled a cindered sphere to his left, but with a sprawl of bright-silver installations spread in a maze across its sooty flank and cigar-shaped stations orbiting it. Tack was apparently standing before one of the triangular screens that ringed the bridge sphere – earlier in its life, the only place possible for humans to survive here. Now the ship was lethally radioactive. How such a vessel managed to operate in these conditions Tack was only momentarily bewildered to consider, but then, almost off-handedly, he dowsed the extent and capabilities of Heliothane materials and field technology.

Ahead, the sun loomed large – like a hole cut through space into some hellish furnace – and against it was silhouetted the tap itself. The thing was stupendous, like some vast tanker crossing an ocean of fire.

'Why . . .?' He didn't really voice the question – it was just there.

Would you prefer . . .

Instantly Tack found himself submersed in some viscous clear fluid, and in a world of pain. He couldn't scream as the fluid was in his mouth and lungs and, as he began to struggle, he discerned optic cables snaking away from the back of his head. Looking down, he saw himself flayed, red muscle revealed, tubes and wires connected down the length of him, metal cuffs enclosing his joints, the cowled head of some surgical robot excavating into the side of his chest. Then the horrific vision was gone and he was back on the sun ship, gasping and clutching at his chest, shivering. But the pain faded and the memory of pain swiftly blurred.

'When we have rebuilt you, you will be more sufficient to your task.'

The disembodied words meant the same in every one of the many different languages now available to him, for Pedagogue was speaking to him in *every* language that he now knew. He thought of Heliothane weapons, realized he knew how to strip and rebuild a multi-purpose carbine, and how to program molecular catalysers. And these were just the tip of the berg of knowledge expanding in his mind.

'I have questions . . .'

'And I have answers,' Pedagogue told him flatly.

Tack reached out, touched the screen, actually felt its warmth. 'Cowl must overcome the temporal inertia of four billion years to succeed.' He tilted his head. 'I see, one billion.' Now he knew the Nodus Cowl had travelled a few centuries behind was situated just before the Precambrian explosion – when complex life really began to take hold. 'That inertia – to overcome it Cowl must do something . . . cataclysmic. And even if he succeeds he'll just push himself and his new history down to the bottom of the probability slope.'

'Cataclysmic . . . Nodus. What maintains the relative position of the alternates on the slope? Why does father killing confine you in the new time-line you have created by that act, down the probability slope, rather than make that line the main one?'

'Cause and effect. The paradox shoves you down the slope.'

'Correct. But that paradox can only come into being because you are *contradicting* what came before. You are acting counter to temporal *momentum*. Before the Nodus there is virtually zero momentum and therefore zero to contradict.'

Tack saw it then. He conceived the image of time as a sheet tossed over a table, against the surface of which already rested a long rod, the uppermost point on the sheet, where it was lifted along the length of the rod, being the main line. The rod was also tilted up from the edge of the table, so that the slope of sheet, down from it on either side, grew longer the further in from the edge of the table you went. The edge of the table was the Nodus itself, and the rod protruding from the edge was held in a hand that could, given sufficient pressure, swing the rod, thus altering the position of the high point in the sheet and the slopes on either side. That hand belonged to Cowl. Tack swallowed dryly, seeing that he had no choice but to believe what he was being told: if someone's hand is hovering over the detonator switch of an atomic bomb, you do not hesitate to shoot them should you have the opportunity; you do not ask what their intentions are.

'There's more I need to know.'

'Yes . . .'

In his mind he now sensed a wave of information, poised just at the edge of perception and ready to break over him. Before him the triangular screens turned black for a second, then came back on to show an entirely different display. He stepped forward, for a moment was submerged in viscous fluid again, and briefly glimpsed his raised arm, skin growing back across it like white slime, the material of his tor grown to the size of his palm. Pain was a brief suffusion, then he was standing on a walkway beside the glass of an aquarium wall behind which something shifted. A nightmare turned towards him.

Well, look at the pretty horses now.

From the start the place had seemed idyllic: warm balmy sunshine, wild plums scattered below the trees fringing the forest – fed upon by small lemurs who maybe preferred the slightly decayed fruit for its intoxicant effect – amid lush green grass scattered with giant daisies and enough dry wood with which to make a fire for the coming night. But before she had a chance to set about gathering some, a herd of miniature horses galloped into view – scattering the lemurs in panic. Polly knelt in the shadow of a tree to eat the plums she had collected while she watched the cute creatures' antics. Then *it* had appeared, and now she crouched behind the same tree, the taser in her left hand and the automatic in her right.

You're way back now. Bastards like that died out about forty million years back.

The monster hurtled in on the pastoral scene with a scream

like a klaxon. Swinging and clashing its parrot beak, it eviscerated one of the little horses, then took the head off another, and stamped its talon down on a third, while the rest of the herd fled. It began eating the pinioned animal, tearing it in half and tilting back its head to gobble down the quivering hindquarters. In moments it finished the first horse, then it strode across to another, pecking up a decollated head on the way. Before feasting on its third victim, it paused and shat out a spray of white excrement.

I think it's getting full now.

So it appeared, for the monstrous bird, after eating the head and forelegs of the third horse, was pecking at the rest in what now seemed a desultory manner. After a moment it gave up completely, scraped at the ground like a chicken, before letting out that klaxon squawk again and moving away.

And that was only a small one.

Polly was aghast, for the horrible creature had stood higher than herself and its killer beak was the size of a bucket.

It's called Gastornis, Nandru explained.

Seeing the bird was now some hundred metres away, Polly began to move out from under cover.

Wouldn't it be better to stay in the trees?

Ignoring this advice, she glanced all around to make sure there were no other unpleasant surprises in the offing, then ran over to where the bird had been feeding.

Are you insane?

Stooping, Polly grabbed a bloody chunk of the last little horse and ran for cover again.

'Waste not want not, as my mother always used to say,' she sang, running still deeper into the forest.

Later, with her stomach full of roast horse, she gazed out from her camp and noticed how her fire's glow reflected on eyes out there. After throwing a bone out towards them, she could hear things squabbling in the darkness over it. But at least they sounded small.

The nightmare bore the shape of a man, but a tall, long-limbed man in whom the ranginess of the Heliothane had been taken to its extreme. It had no face – its head was a slightly beaked, utterly featureless ovoid, of the same shiny beetle-black appearance as the majority of its naked body. However, as if this was not strange enough, the black carapace revealed a network of hyaline veins and ribs, so that, when the light caught the network, it looked as if something horribly skeletal stood there.

'A woman used a semi-AI prognostic program to predict the future development of human DNA, and on the basis of that started recombination experiments on her children. In her terms, her first experiment was a failure, though the offspring survived. Cowl was not a failure, so there is much speculation as to what those terms of hers were.'

Tack flinched as Cowl started to walk towards him, but the dark being was then frozen mid-stride as Pedagogue continued lecturing.

'We don't know what external pressures were input, because DNA has no purpose in itself other than its own survival and procreation, so intelligence or physical strength are only increased should they have a direct bearing on that. Should the survival of human DNA entail you needing to lose your big brains and filter food out of the soil, you would all become worms. It can only be supposed that her program posited a future where the highest levels of intelligence, ruthlessness, speed and strength were required. Cowl killed his own mother while in her womb, thereafter escaping by internal caesarean much like a chick escaping from the egg with its beak spur.'

'But he became one of the Heliothane,' Tack stated. The

information was now just there, in his mind. He saw how Cowl's survival had initially depended on the Heliothane, how he had deliberately become a very valuable member of that society. It was not so difficult – ruthlessness and intelligence being much admired. The misjudgement had killed many. One of them a top scientist called Astolere – Saphothere's sister.

'I see,' said Tack woodenly.

And see he did. He saw Callisto, a moon of Jupiter, exploding, with the blast contained in some unseen barrier and the moon just winking out of existence. Four hundred million Heliothane gone in less time than it took to draw breath.

'Cowl, having made his alliance with the Umbrathane, and passing on much of his research, caused a temporal anomaly on Callisto, where his research facility was based, putting a pico-second future version of that moon in exactly the same place as the original. The physical composite of the two moons, forced to exist however briefly in the same place, went in a fusion explosion, the energy generated thereby powering his flight, and that of the Umbrathane fleet, into the past.'

'And I am supposed to kill this . . . creature?'

'Yes, that is your task.'

Back aboard the virtual ship, Tack was bathed in incandescence. The screens now revealed a side view of the sun tap. It was a leviathan wood planer shaving the fiery surface of the sun, raft-like at its two extremes but humped in the middle. The view was filtered – it would have incinerated him otherwise. Then, suddenly, he was gazing upon the vast cliff that was just one side of the tap. This close it seemed to extend to infinity in every direction, beyond planetary scale – immensity impossible to encompass. He blinked and drew his attention away from it, studying his closer surroundings. The inside of the ship had become a furnace: plastics were beginning to smoke, coatings were peeling from metal surfaces, spots of red heat were appearing on bare metal, and smoke-hazed air being drawn away through vents. And so the unreal world Pedagogue had created came to an end. When the ship's fields collapsed, actinic light obliterated everything and Tack began to wake.

She was running out of air, and now the force of her will was pushing the scale in some other way. She found herself being dragged sideways back into that dimension of black sea underlining a grey void, but drawing along with her part of the previous place. From the scale itself barely visible lines of light sprang out and turned back in on themselves, all looping at precisely the same distance out from it, so she appeared to rest at the centre of a huge, luminous dandelion clock. Then this spheroid took on a glassy quality, the light draining out of it and its surface splitting and coalescing into veins and ribs, as of water poured onto something greasy. Encaged in this cocoon she fell, gulping at nothing in the darkness, consciousness fading. But still she had some will left and attempted to force her way back into her own reality. Around her the black sea rose up, and gravity grabbed her and slammed her down on a floor of hyaline bones. She gasped in frigid air, grateful for each painful breath. Rolling upright, she found herself still encaged in the sphere, hovering now over frigid ground, a dark grey sky above, strange frozen trees to her right and a snowy plain to her left. Terrified that she would be snatched away from breathable air again, she scrabbled for a gap in the cage wall, but even as she found it and fell through, the cage itself began to fold away into that other place.

'What the fuck was that?' Polly managed, recovering her breath after landing on her back on the unforgiving ground.

Well, as about the nearest thing to an expert in temporal travel we have here, I have to say I haven't a clue.

Polly looked around, then hugged her arms close around her

body. 'I thought it was your expert opinion that it was supposed to be warmer before that last ice age.'

Sorry, but there were more than one of them. You got a few in the Pleistocene age, but I thought you were beyond them, then some in the Carboniferous . . . Let's just hope you've not gone that far yet. This is probably just some sort of hiccup: a bad winter, maybe a bad millennium. You've been covering millions of years, remember.

Polly tried not to think too much about that. Absentmindedly she opened her coat and removed from her hip bag a remaining lump of eohippus meat, and methodically devoured it.

'Any idea at all what period this is?' she asked.

None whatsoever. The thing that manifested around you might have altered the circumstances, and your previous time-jumps have been too out of kilter for me to easily work out a curve. I would guess you're getting pretty near to dinosaur country, though.

Polly grunted an acknowledgement and continued eating as she stared about her. 'Perhaps I'm just in the Arctic here – you said my position in space seems to be changing as well.'

I don't think there was an Arctic, as we know it. I'm not sure, but I think that, in the region of time we should be entering, even the poles weren't frozen over.

Polly nodded and started walking towards some nearby trees, since there she might find some shelter from the cold, and might even be able to get a fire going. At the forest edge she found it heavy going, as the snow had drifted thickly against boulders and fallen trunks. Eventually she reached a clearing and scanned the surrounding vegetation.

Looks like bamboo over there. That's odd.

Polly immediately spotted what Nandru was referring to: the segmented trees spearing up like telegraph poles. Below these she discovered mounds of dry tendrils – light as balsa and only the thickness of her finger, segmented like the trunks they had dropped from. These fragments ignited easily and they burnt with a smell of pine. Polly was quickly able to build up a big fire, since it was apparent that every tree here was dead and their wood freeze-dried. It rapidly made the transition from campfire to bonfire: flames roaring up from the plentiful fuel. Polly sat on a nearby stump to soak up the heat. Scraping up handfuls of melting snow, she quenched her thirst. Then she noticed a strange regularity to the stump, and abruptly stood and stepped away. The fire's heat continued to melt the snow and reveal what lay underneath it.

It was soon revealed as the head and forelimbs of some huge creature. The beaked head was covered by a large bony shield adorned with three lethal-looking horns.

Triceratops. Polly had seen enough films to recognize it.

'I bet dinosaur meat tastes like chicken,' she said, trying find some levity to quell the panic growing inside her.

Sixty-five million years.

Polly was appalled; she almost instinctively reached out to shift, and again found that glassy cage materializing around her. The shift this time was brief and the grey was suddenly displaced by a subliminal glimpse of burning jungle, furnace red, choking smoke and hot ash below a cyanosis sky. Intense heat washed over her, flames clawing in through the glassy structure around her, before she shifted again just to stay alive. Again jungle: cycads and tree ferns and horsetails, huge, strangely shaped trees which were mostly trunk and bole, with a minimal head of greenery. As the cage disappeared, smoke dissipated around her – having been transported through with her. She collapsed on her knees, coughing desperately.

It brought the atmosphere of that last place along with it. It's almost as if the scale has conceded to your needs, so it can get on with its own journey without you fighting to control it.

That was not Polly's most exigent concern at that moment.

You know, I think you just witnessed the dinosaur extinction.

Polly knew that. Her concern was that she was on the side of it she would rather not be.

Panicked by her discovery of the frozen triceratops, the girl shifted back beyond the vorpal sensor, and Silleck did not know if she survived the meteorite impact and firestorm that had preceded that killing winter and placed a full point at the end of the dinosaur aeons – that mercy killing of the diseased and dying populations of the great beasts. This, as Silleck knew, ended another of those long-drawn-out evolutionary wars between the large animals of Earth and their constant viral killers. Only humans had survived such a conflict, just.

Silleck now drew herself back down the aeons to where Sauros settled into the soft ground of the Jurassic. The city's bones were still creaking, and the inner sphere had not yet turned to bring the floors level, but already Engineer Goron had abandoned his station to head for his customary place at the viewing windows. But the interface technicians remained where they were: Sauros, though slowly building up its energy reserves after such a journey, was still vulnerable to attack.

Silleck scanned the nearby slope, where the city was multiplied to infinity in all its incarnations, as if sitting between two facing mirrors. She scanned up and down time as far as she could without using sensors dropped in other ages, but there seemed no danger. Then she pushed her awareness downtime to a vorpal sensor often visited by her fellow technicians, to a brief period at the end of the Triassic and somewhat downslope, which had been named by them 'the boneyard'.

Here there was some wrinkle in time that many torbearers missed. But it was a trap for many others, which killed their momentum should they fall into it. Thus they were caught for many days and without nutrition became the food for their own parasitic tors. Many of them were starving and half-dead when they arrived, and found no succour in this barren place. Silleck gazed down at the hot dry landscape, where human bones had been cleaned by grave beetles and small vulpine pterosaurs. She chose one scattering of bones and tracked it slowly back in time, seeing it reform, become fleshed and reinflate with moisture, and the brief instant when the tor reappeared enclosing the arm it had later torn away and disappeared with.

The man, who wore a turban and sarong, had walked for many days following a half-seen figure, before just giving up and sitting down to die. The figure, Silleck discovered, was an Australian aborigine, who survived and prospered in this arid hell, before being again taken away by his tor. There were other scatterings of bones, and other desiccated corpses. But it was all too grim, and the interface technician took herself back to one of the furthest sensors resting in the Permian epoch, where she knew another torbearer had been observed, but even as her awareness arrived in this sensor she began to pick up the waves of disturbance travelling uptime and upslope, through interspace, and knew that something was coming.

Gazing across the waves to where the plesiosaurs were mating – rolling in the sea, their great flukes arcing up fountains of water, their long necks slamming against the surface, and then rising and intertwining – Tack found he had acquired a deep and secure certainty about so many things. Foremost was the conviction that Cowl had to die, there was no question of that, and any of the wretched Umbrathane who got in his way should be eliminated as well. Raising his gaze to the dome enclosing the aquapark, and to the hard starlight beyond, he felt impatient to be on his way. At the sound of someone stepping onto the viewing deck behind him, he turned whip fast.

'Be calm, Traveller Tack,' said Maxell.

She much resembled the woman who had slammed him against a corridor wall in Sauros. Her skin had that same amber translucence, though her eyes were blue and her hair a straight waterfall of white. But unlike the other, she would not be slamming him into any walls. For, since being taken offline from Pedagogue and coming out of the regrowth tank, Tack had quickly discovered that he was now the physical equal of many of the Heliothane, and superior to very many more. His musculature had been boosted, his martial skills greatly enhanced, and the body of knowledge now available to him was huge. However, he realized that many of these people still viewed him with hidden disdain, for to attain such new heights had required his body to be stripped down and totally rebuilt, with everything from bones being increased in density to cerebral grafts. He even possessed implants, which were anathema to them. Their pragmatic view was that if any man was not strong or clever enough to survive using his natural gifts, then he died – plain and simple.

'What type of plesiosaur are they?' Maxell asked him, nodding at the sporting creatures.

'Elasmosaurus,' Tack said quickly, giving them their twenty-second-century name despite her having asked in the language of the Heliothane, and despite his having access to over three hundred other languages.

Maxell frowned at this. 'Still keeping to your old habits, I see,' she said, now switching to the same language. 'It appears we could not root everything out of you.'

Tack held up his left arm, displaying the tor, which had now attained full growth. 'Does that really matter? I know what I have to do now, and you know that you can do no more to improve me. This thing on my arm started to reject once you tried genetic recombination. And no one else can wear it.'

He had been told that they had first tried to remove the parasitic scale from him in order to place it on someone else, but had failed. He also knew that, had they succeeded, he would have been dispensed with like so much garbage, and there remained in him a core of resentment over that. What puzzled him was why this knowledge had not been kept from him.

'We already know why it started to reject. Cowl is using them to sample the future, so recombination would have defeated the tor's initial purpose. It read your genetic code the moment it attached.'

She came up to stand right beside him and pointed down at the sea, where a huge shark was cruising past, doubtless attracted by the thrashing of the plesiosaurs. There was no guard rail along the edge of the platform, but that did not surprise Tack from a people who walked bare-faced through vacuum. The Heliothane did not coddle themselves with their technology. The lack of a rail was just another sign of their life view – if you're stupid enough to fall in, you deserve to get eaten.

'There will be sharks in that era, but no elasmosaurus – they were most prevalent in the late Cretaceous.' She turned to look at him. 'I sense you have been impatient, and wonder why we delay. The simple answer is that Engineer Goron's shift back into the Jurassic has not been without some difficulties. Even now the tunnel has not restabilized, though we predict conditions will be ready for your transit through it in eighty hours.'

Holding up his tor-covered arm again, Tack asked, 'Do I use this thing to take me from Sauros onwards?' An implant kept the tor in abeyance, but he could still feel the thing's temporal field webbing the inside of his body.

'No, because your supplies will be limited by what you can carry, and though you can obtain food during much of your journey, there is still a large stretch of it where food would not be easily available. Saphothere will take you, by mantisal, as far back as he can.'

Tack was glad to hear that – if there was ever such a thing

here, he considered the man his friend. Saphothere no longer showed disdain for Tack, rather respect. But then those entitled 'Traveller' were not so insular in their thinking as the rest of the Heliothane.

'After that I go on by myself – and tear Cowl's throat out,' said Tack viciously.

'Oh yes, certainly that.' Maxell smiled.

Tacitus peered down through the spray at the rowers and damned himself for the sudden sympathy he felt for them: they were the spoils of war, slaves and the property of Rome, not citizens. Anyway, should they be freed from their chains their ending now would be no different from everyone else on this galley if it went down. In this sea they would all drown. He looked up to where the weird lights still played about the mast and reefed sail, asked a blessing from Mithras then made his way forward.

His sodden cloak flapping in the gale, he gripped the safety ropes tightly as he edged along the gantry above the rowers. It was then, in the howling night, that lightning struck the mast and leapt down to the prow with a sound like mountains breaking. Tacitus went down on his knees, thinking this must be the end of him. Behind he could hear some of his men shouting prayers at the storm. Looking ahead again, he kept blinking to try and clear his vision, for surely he had seen something looming there out of the night, but then he saw only smouldering wood and sylphs of flame. He continued forging ahead until on the foredeck he found wreckage and the bodies of two of his men, their armour smoking and their skin blackened. This was a cursed voyage, he knew that now. Then his gaze fell upon the strange object cleaving to the wooden rail like a burr.

It was a vambrace, he knew it at once. It was a gift from Mithras for some battle yet to come. He reached out to grab it and yelled as its thorned surface cut into his hand. A big wave hit the side of the galley and, swamped in water, the galley slaves screamed and struggled. Falling down, Tacitus held onto the object, and it pulled from the rail. Without hesitation he thrust his arm into it. Agony, and a deep gnawing pleasure that was almost sexual. Blood poured from his arm and the vambrace closed about it and bonded to him. In only minutes it was firmly in place and his blood washed away by the sea and the rain. He held his arm up in a fist salute to his men at the stern of the ship. Then the jealous god Neptune sent one of his monsters against the ship.

The giant serpent rose up out of the sea, the great loop of its body curving up into hazy night, then its eyeless head and awful vertical maw turned and slammed down on the edge of the galley. Tacitus was again knocked off his feet. Struggling up and stumbling to an inner guard rope, he looked down and saw that the monster had taken out the side of the ship and was now feasting on the slaves. The inner parts of its mouth revolving like some engine, it drew them in, screaming, by their chains. There was no question that the ship would go down, so perhaps this was the battle he was being called to. He drew his gladius and leapt down into the chaos. Knocking aside those begging him in pidgin Latin to release them, and grabbing at him in desperation, he made his way to the horror that was chewing on the ship. He raised his weapon and drove it into a wall of flesh. Once, twice, but seemingly to no effect. Then a tentacle snapped out of darkness beside him and knocked him past a revolving hell of teeth and out into the storm. He struck a scaled flank that lacerated his legs as he fell past it, and then he was down into the sea, still clutching his gladius. He could not swim and he prepared himself for death, relaxed for it. And something took him away from the storm, into some nether hell, then out into bright sunlight.

Tacitus fell face first onto a soft surface, coughed and gasped as he fought for breath, then hauled himself upright and turned, ready to attack the figures that loomed over him. Then, in the presence of gods, he went down on his knees, his blood leaking into briny sand.

'So this is the torbearer,' said the tall golden woman in her strange white clothing. Tacitus did not understand the words then, but the time would come when he did.

The man, who had to be Apollo, said bitterly, 'The galley went down – that was always a matter of historical record. The beast didn't cause any paradox it couldn't sustain by eating everyone on board.'

The man now reached down, grabbed Tacitus by the shoulder, and with infinite ease, hauled him to his feet. In the Roman's native Latin he said, 'You will help us to better understand that thing on your arm, before it takes you on your way again.'

'Thank you, Lord . . . for saving me,' Tacitus replied, bowing his head.

'You may yet wish it otherwise,' the woman told him.

Tacitus did wish it otherwise when these beautiful violent people learnt all they could from him with their strange questions and stranger engines. And when they then paralysed him and probed him and tried to take the god's vambrace from his arm. Evidently failing in this endeavour, they freed him, handed back his sword, and told him to enjoy his journey to hell. It was a journey he could never have imagined – the time he spent with them being a comparatively harmless interlude – and throughout it he came to understand what the woman *really* meant.

12

Two Heliothane on Station Seventeen:

'The Engineer wouldn't let me see the recording from the internal security system – all we managed to get out before some sort of temporal barrier shut off all communication with the facility.'

'Brother, I want to know.'

'Goron's been otherwise occupied, trying to push his project, so I managed to break into the system . . .'

'What happened?'

'Cowl's creature killed Astolere.'

'That can't be . . . the amniotic tank was supposed to vent onto the surface of Callisto, where the beast would have died.'

'That didn't happen.'

'Then the creature must be destroyed.'

'There's more than that.'

'Show me.'

. . .

'What is that?'

'Some kind of feeding mouth that can be extruded from the main body. It wasn't there before.'

'That glass should have been able to withstand any force the creature could exert.'

'Yeah, does that include displacing parts of its molecular structure through time so that those parts aren't even in the same location?'

'Scan shows this?'

'Damned right it does.'

'Cowl does not try to help her.'

'No, he just allows it to consume our sister. She was the brightest

and best of us all, and though she was there to supervise the shutdown, she was perhaps, excepting the failed preterhuman, Cowl's greatest advocate.'

'Then Cowl must die.'

Engineer Goron gazed fondly upon the Jurassic, where giants were demolishing a forest to fill their titanic ever-hungry stomachs. Even with the damping fields of Sauros operating, it was possible to feel the vibration of their gargantuan progress – what palaeontologists of Tack's time gave the overblown term 'dinoperturbation'. This herd of camarosaurs, though impressive, was nothing to what he yet had a good chance of seeing, for he had arranged for Sauros to come out in this specific locale: where brachiosaurs roamed. He could also have aimed to bring them out twenty million years later, in the time of the seismosaurs, but conditions had been optimum for this time and place, and he doubted he would have got that one past Vetross. Goron also hoped that when Tack returned there would be a chance for the twenty-second-century primitive to view these creatures along with him, as Tack, stupid in ways Goron could not even conceive, seemed to possess an appreciative awe of these giants that Goron's fellows did not.

'What is it, Vetross?' He'd spied her edging towards him. 'More calculations for me to check? More energy measures for me to approve? I appointed you as my second for a good reason, you know.'

'It's coming,' Vetross replied.

Goron turned towards her and read the fear in her expression. This moment had been inevitable as soon as they had begun the push. Cowl would not countenance them getting close, without attacking. And attacking meant only one thing.

'On *our* time?'

'Ten hours. It's pushing up the slope towards our Carboniferous, otherwise it would not retain the energy to bring enough of itself to bear. We've got travellers located back every fifty million years. Canolus slowed it with a neutron warhead quarter-slope relative to our Silurian, but while he recovered ground, it got him in transit.'

'Canolus always tended to be premature. What about Thote?'

'Mid-Devonian. Took out a small percentage of its mass with a displacement sphere. Damaged his mantisal, however, and now we can't locate him.'

Suddenly Goron felt very tired, but that was unsurprising considering he had been working non-stop for three centuries. 'Get every weapon you can online, and send all non-essential personnel back through the tunnel. I want field walls projected out to one kilometre in every direction and displacement generators, set for proximity activation, scattered randomly in between. And if there's anything I haven't thought of, I want you to think of it.'

'*Every* direction?' asked Vetross.

'Damned right. The rock underneath us won't stop it – it would just need to go out of phase either physically or temporally.'

Vetross watched him hesitantly.

'Have I missed anything?'

'I don't think so.'

'Then why are you still here?'

'Because you are needed now, Engineer Goron. People are frightened.'

Goron turned back to the window and, resting his hands on his tool belt, sighed and stared at a view that he knew would soon be incinerated.

'Impressive preparations, but it is all a matter of potential energy.' The voice was utterly factual.

Goron turned. 'Like I needed you to tell me—' His words died in his mouth. Vetross was staring to one side, terrified, and Goron quickly understood her feelings.

Cowl was poised like an axle-spring stood on end, looming taller even than Vetross. Here was a nightmare they had lived with all their lives: a preterhuman of darkness and glass, utterly ruthless, utterly committed to his own ends. There was no question that death would result from this encounter. Cowl now opened the cowl over his face to reveal the nightmare underneath.

'Go!'

Vetross shoved at Goron, simultaneously pulling a weapon from her coat. Goron pushed off from the wall, diving and rolling, taking his own devices from his belt. He glanced behind him, tossing an interface generator back. He did not question Vetross's sacrifice, for both he and she had instantly calculated that for just one of them to survive this encounter, one of them must die, while the other must be extremely lucky. He dropped another generator, saw fire smear along one wall, and Vetross's weapon spiralling away. Cowl's hand was on her chest, sharp fingers penetrating between her ribs, then he slammed her round gun-shot-fast into a window, cracking armoured glass and leaving a corona of her blood on it. Cowl was almost on Goron's first interface generator when it fired up, slinging a wall of energy up before the dark intruder, but Cowl somehow pushed through it. The second generator went as Goron initiated a coded transmission while he ran. He threw a handful of seeker mines behind – bouncing down the corridor like ball-bearings. Another window smashed, then Cowl came rushing along the outside of the building like a spider. Goron turned into one of the access corridors. Smash again, and Cowl was now only a second behind him. Goron tore off a service-hatch cover and threw it in a flat trajectory at Cowl's neck, then dived through the hatch, scattering more mines. Explosions, and the cover hurled back, slicing through his calf muscle. That sharp hand groped in after him just as the displacement field, which he had already set, initiated. The service chamber blinked out, and Goron rolled out into the control room of Sauros – ten seconds before he left the service chamber.

'Change the defence frequencies right now!' he bellowed coming to his feet and heading for the control pillar. His order was instantly obeyed. Then he operated virtual controls, calling up the immediate scene into the viewing gallery, saw himself turning, then a sudden distortion.

'Anomalous warp – that's impossible!' someone said.

Five seconds later the distortion dissipated and Vetross was still dead. Cowl was gone.

'That's impossible,' someone repeated.

Goron stared down at the pool of blood he was standing in, and didn't have the will to get angry about such a ridiculous statement. Anything was possible – it was just a matter of energy, which Cowl evidently possessed.

It was vast, an animal so huge that its neck disappeared into the mist above the jungle every time it raised its head to crunch the vegetation it had torn from the low cycads. Leaf fragments rained down through the mist as it chewed, and they were the size of a car door. Its excrement would have totally buried Cheng-yi, and it could flatten him with one of its elephantine feet and not even notice. In his delirium he looked in awe on it feeding and wondered just how many tons of vegetation it could consume in a day. When it farted like a thunderstorm, he could not suppress mad laughter. His amusement soon ceased when the long neck looped downwards and it inspected him with piggy eyes.

Cheng-yi quickly backed away. But the dinosaur took a step towards him, knocking over trees as high as a house. He looked down at the musket he had stolen, and which had served him well enough when the world had still been sane, then he turned and ran. Dodging into a dense stand of cycads, he crouched in shadow, sweat trickling down from his queue and also soaking through his filthy clothing.

The monster shortly returned to its feeding, but the Chinaman's nightmare was only beginning. He was no longer staring at the dinosaur. He was gaping in horror at the huge scorpion sharing his cover. Black and yellow, it was as wide as a spade, and he watched in panic as it scuttled round to face him, its vicious tail hooking up over its head. He backed away, and moved further into the undergrowth. But now, aware that the horrors here were not all reptilian, he began to notice other enormous insects: a bright blue dragonfly resting on the trunk of a giant horsetail, its armoured head the size of his fist and body the size of his arm, wings like sheets of fractured glass; a centipede the length of a python, and the colour of old blood, winding itself out from a hole in a rotten trunk; beetles big as rugby balls burrowing into leviathan turds; and some horrible clacking kin of the mosquito that kept trying to land on him, their probosces like hypodermics.

'Go away!' he shouted, and the jungle suddenly grew silent around him. It was in this quiet that his instinct for survival overrode nascent madness, and he remembered that the musket he carried was not loaded – emptied as it had been into the face of some grizzled forest monster, when the monsters had been still covered with hair. After thumping a rotting log with the butt of his musket, to make sure nothing was living in it, he sat down and, with sweaty shaking hands, reloaded the weapon. Then, feeling calmer, he moved on.

Seeing brighter light up ahead, Cheng-yi began trotting in the hope of getting out of the arboreal darkness. What he came upon was a band of devastation cut through the jungle. Tree trunks lay scattered everywhere on the ground, denuded of their vegetation. Peering to his right, he observed three more brontosaurs looming in the distance, bellowing to each other as they continued their forest clearance project. They rose up on their hind limbs to reach high foliage, their forelimbs resting against a tree until it just gave up and keeled over. Behind these giants a herd of lesser dinosaurs grazed on the remaining detritus of their passage, and behind them again, much closer to Cheng-yi, were carnosaurs – no higher than his waist – relishing the bonanza of insects exposed.

Cheng-yi knew at once that he must not let these smaller creatures see him. He stepped back into shade and kept moving. Soon he was no longer plagued by the mosquitoes, and the racket of deforestation grew distant. He stopped and, after checking it out for more leviathan insects, again sat on a fallen trunk. Resting his gun conveniently beside him, he took off his jacket to try and find some relief from the cloying heat. Closing his eyes he listened to the sound of a breeze sighing through the foliage, and found himself so weary he did not want to open his eyes again, did not want to move. Then a loud buzzing intruded. He flicked open his eyes just in time to anticipate an insect like a winged grey chilli pepper coming to land on his arm. He slapped it to the ground and, from under the trunk, a chicken-sized carnosaur darted out and snapped it up, then stood crunching it, while observing him with hawk eyes. Carefully, the Chinaman reached for his musket.

The clothing was the essence of sheer functionality, but Tack had never felt so comfortable before. The jacket sealed to the waistband of the fatigues, just as they sealed to the lightweight boots. All the pockets possessed the same impervious seal along their flaps, and there were many pockets. The outer fabric was waterproof, gloves were packed in special pockets at the sleeves, and a hood could be folded up from the back of the collar to meet a film visor extruded from the front, all sealable too. Powered by boot-heel storage batteries, which were kept charged by the outer, photovoltaic, fabric of the suit, miniature pumps set in the sleeves, the rounded collar and the boots circulated air to regulate internal temperature. In addition, the garment's insulation of foamed shock-composite served as body armour. The suit gave further protection against heat weapons by means of a superconducting mesh embedded in the composite. Tack felt invulnerable, especially when he glanced lovingly at the pack now secured by him in the body of the mantisal. The lethal toys it contained were too numerous to mention.

'Another hour,' said Saphothere finally. 'We'll stop off at Sauros while I recover my resources.'

Tack supposed that meant Traveller would once again be paying a visit to the Spartan hospital, there to be serviced like a car needing an oil change and new filters. The thought of delay frustrated him. Strapped inside the mantisal were enough supplies to take them a long way. But, in the end, this form of travel depended on the physical strength of the mantisal rider and clearly Saphothere was again exhausted, having brought them all the way down the tunnel. It was also apparent that Tack could no longer guide the mantisal himself, as his fully grown tor would conflict with its operation. For a while yet he must remain a passenger, though the temptation to take the implant offline and allow his tor full rein was sometimes unbearable. He wanted to be about the task set for him; he desperately wanted to bring into play his new abilities and strengths.

The final hour dragged past as if on leaden feet, then abruptly, ahead of them, the triangular exit appeared, growing huge as the time tunnel opened out like a funnel. Then came that feeling of huge deceleration, yet without them being hurled forwards inside the mantisal. Then they were up and out of it, rising above the abutments into the exit chamber of Sauros – and chaos.

A blast of heat slapped the side of the mantisal and sent it tumbling through the air. Tack lost his grip but, with his reactions accelerated, managed to spin within the central space and come down with his feet safely on two struts, before the momentum of the mantisal's tumble threw him sideways, where he caught hold again. He glimpsed one of the distant abutments, and noticed a cloud of fire belching from it as from a chimney. Below, nacreous waves of distortion were rolling across the tunnel interface, to break at the edges in magnesium light.

'It's attacking!' Saphothere shouted, bringing the mantisal under control and hammering it towards the chamber wall.

As the air distorted, a claw of fear twisted in Tack's stomach. A vertical pillar of heat haze opened up from roof to floor, and began to fold out, swelling at its centre. A flaw appeared in the tumescence, and broke open to expose vast rollers of living tissue endlessly revolving against each other. Then, from infinite distance, horror hurtled forwards – a mouth impelled at them by a monstrous tentacle curling up out of the writhing flesh. It was vaginal, throated with glistening teeth that tunnelled down into darkness, its lips bone razors.

'Fistik,' spat Saphothere, his eyes narrowed and his teeth clenched.

Tack knew that both of them were going to die; even his suit would not prevent it, and he had no time to reach his weapons. Then a grey raft slammed down on the approaching horror, splitting it like a head trapped under a press; pieces of bone, razor teeth and bloody saliva exploding in every direction. Twin Gatling cannons spun round in gimbals on the raft's deck – the Heliothane gunner strapped in behind them. The raft then tilted towards the flaw and the cannons screamed, spewing twisted lines of fire that thumped the reeling-out tentacle into an arc before blowing a section of it away. Simultaneously two missiles sped out from underneath the raft, bucking it violently as they went. One entered that living landscape of flesh and detonated, throwing all that was in there into white and black. The second missile sped on as the flaw slammed shut, then tumbled out of the air without detonating. Tack looked down. The severed tentacle and horrifying mouthparts were down in the tunnel entrance, drifting there as if in a deep pool, and leaving behind a misty trail of blood.

'It bleeds red?' Tack managed.

'Yeah,' said Saphothere. 'Don't we all?'

Polly avoided the river after she realized that an island, of apparently the same rock that constituted the shoreline, was in fact a crocodile big enough to supply handbags for the population of Britain. Heading some distance along the shore in the other direction, she came at last to a stream where the biggest predators were water beetles, each the size of a pack of cards, and whose diligent concerns were fortunately at the bottom of the deeper pools. Polly there drank her fill, then took off her blouse and bra and rinsed them out as best she could. She then sat down contentedly by the stream, occasionally splashing some cooling water over herself, but inevitably she soon felt hunger again. When she noticed a small carnosaur feeding on something at the tideline, she donned her damp clothing and went over to investigate.

Between plinths of rock, a small beach of pebbles had gathered. Jumping down upon it from the rocky lip, Polly was immediately assailed by the smell of things decaying. The carnosaur, hissed at her and moved away, its gait somewhat of a waddle because of its distended stomach. She moved closer to a drift of translucent white and saw it consisted of thousands of plump little squid.

She picked up one of the dead creatures, and contemplated biting into one of its tentacles, when she saw that there were others in the surf, still moving sluggishly. At least those would be fresh. She moved through the lapping waves and snatched one up, observed its little sheep eyes watching her, while it blew bubbles from its beak, then turned it over and took a bite.

Like chewing a slug I reckon?

'Delicious,' said Polly. Its taste was reminiscent of those oysters she had eaten with Claudius, but the flesh was firm and chewy. For her second one she took out her knife and by trial and error managed to squirt out the intestines and the bullet-shaped bone.

Belemnites, that's what they are! Belemnites! I used to find their fossils on the east coast when I was a kid.

Polly ignored him and continued eating, eyeing her surroundings. She noted various other things in the tideline: large, flat, snail things with ribbed shells and protruding squid tentacles, big sealice scuttling over this bounty, a single fish with an armoured head and translucent body from which a chunk had been bitten, tangled piles of seaweed and a big-headed black newt that she thought was dead until it retreated with jerky strobe-effect back into the surf. But then, when she thought she was coming to accept her circumstances, and understand that it was just her-and-Nandru and a hostile prehistoric world, she noticed the container.

'Oh Christ,' she gasped, in utter confusion, then stepped over to the object and picked it up. It was cylindrical, ten centimetres in diameter, twenty in length, and made of either plastic or metal – she could not tell. Pressing an indented button on one side popped open the hinged lid at one end. There was nothing inside it.

'Well, say something, then,' she said.

I'm just as confused as you. That is clearly a manufactured product, and nothing will be manufactured for – as far as I can judge – over a hundred and forty million years.

'Could it be alien?' Polly asked.

If you'd asked me that before this shower of shit happened, I'd have laughed in your face. Now I don't know.

Polly stood and stared out across the sea, and observed in the distance flying creatures that she doubted were seagulls. Tossing the container down where she had left her greatcoat, she decided to sideline this puzzle until the growling in her gut had ceased, and fell to gnawing on raw squid. Finally, as the little creatures became less appetizing, she walked back, gathering up her coat and the puzzling container, and headed up to the rocky margin of the beach. Pausing there to shake out her coat thoroughly and dislodge the sealice that had crawled inside, her gaze wandered back towards the stream.

The monster loomed over two metres high, though stooped forward so its hooked foreclaws hovered just above the ground. Standing still as it was, its green-and-black-striped body blended into the vegetation behind it, but its numerous bright-white teeth were all too visible – as were its yellow catlike eyes. Polly ducked down instinctively and pulled out both the automatic, now getting a little rusty, and the taser. Huddling close as she could to the rock face, she slung her greatcoat over herself and kept very still.

I don't think your automatic will do the job, Polly. But then I don't suppose its designer had allosaurs in mind. I suggest you time-shift right now.

Polly concentrated on getting the scale do her bidding, but the webwork seemed logy and slack within her – as exhausted as she herself felt.

'*I can't – it won't work,*' she subvocalized.

Nandru said nothing for a while, and when he did speak there was no reassurance in his words:

It's been fun, then.

Polly could feel a vibration in the rock as the allosaur approached, then suddenly it loomed above her, and then crashed down onto the beach, spraying pebbles in every direction. The tip of its massive tail whipped past her face as it continued on down the strand to the tideline, where it sniffed at the piles of squid, decided they were good, and started gorging. Frozen in terror, Polly watched it feed. Perhaps she should try to get away while it was distracted, but she was so terrified she couldn't trust herself to stand upright. Once the creature had emptied the tideline of squid, it turned to head back the way it had come – and came straight towards her.

The allosaur was about to leap up onto the small cliff behind her, but paused and tilted its head from side to side as if to check the view with each eye. Closer now, with its nose only a metre away from her own and its fishy breath huffing warm all around her, it took a long sniff.

Panting from exhaustion, Saphothere led the way to an escalator composed of that strange flowing metal, then to an open cylindrical elevator shaft containing a circular platform one step up from the floor. As soon as they mounted this, it accelerated upwards till the platform finally came level with the floor of a domed chamber, which Tack surmised must be at the very top of Sauros. The moment they stepped off it, the elevator dropped away, leaving an open well.

For the very first time, Saphothere seemed at a loss as to what to do next, and stood clenching and unclenching his hands and looking around him.

Goron was standing by a wide pillar of twisted vorpal glass from which sprouted transparent spheres containing multiple interior and exterior images of Sauros, as well as complex shapes: three-dimensional flow-charts and scrolling formulae which Tack now recognized as representations of ten-dimensional Heliothane technology. The Engineer's right hand was pressed inside a sphere as his left manipulated a virtual control panel. Tack saw at once that Goron's trouser leg was soaked with blood and that he had tracked bloody footprints around the column. Other personnel manipulated consoles, while still others were enclosed in other bizarre constructs of vorpal glass, and were standing at the edges of the chamber like the gods of a civilization of glass spiders. Saphothere glanced at Tack, then nodded to one side. They walked over to the windows surrounding the chamber.

'How did Cowl do that?' asked someone nearby.

'There's only one explanation,' Goron replied. 'Somehow he knew our field frequencies. That's not enough for an all-out attack, but enough for assassination attempts. He simply rode in with the torbeast.' Goron surveyed all those in the room meaningfully before returning his attention to his controls. Another man, throwing off virtual gloves in disgust, stood up and walked over to stand beside Tack and Saphothere.

'Palleque,' Saphothere acknowledged.

Tack studied the newcomer, who was tall, white-haired, and tough-looking. Though this individual had reptilian yellow eyes and a twisted mouth, he could have been Saphothere's brother.

To Saphothere the man observed, 'It would seem Cowl is somehow receiving inside information. He came through and killed Vetross – nearly got Goron as well.'

Saphothere nodded dumbly, seeming too tired to reply. Palleque glanced at Tack disdainfully and looked about to make some comment.

'Incursion. One-seventy, two-ten and lateral.' Tack presumed the voice came from one of those enclosed in vorpal tech.

Palleque grimaced. 'Three hours earlier and Cowl would have really fucked us over. But the torbeast won't be getting through now we're up to power again.'

'The push?' Saphothere asked.

'Yeah. Like riding the top of a fountain and everything gets scrambled. The constant energy feed can't be switched, so the capacitors have to be drained to the limit before we can shut off and stabilize. Took us an hour this time before we could even get the defence fields back up.'

'I don't think I need to hear any more of this,' said Saphothere and Tack could see that he was angry, gazing at Palleque with suspicion. Palleque shot a further contemptuous glance at Tack before returning to his console.

'Silleck,' Goron said abruptly, to the speaker who was warning of the incursion. 'Don't use the D-generators this time. Take a direct power-feed from one of the abutments and put a laser into the flaw.'

'Level?' asked Silleck, the woman with her head and shoulders concealed in insectile technology.

'Megajoule range – I want to monitor. Should the incursion move in, I want the level to rise comparatively,' Goron replied.

Tack stared out of the windows at the developing incursion – a pillar of heat haze opening out on the smoking landscape, his gaze veering aside to the charcoaled vegetation and to the leviathan corpses of a dinosaur herd. He watched the incursion swell and then the flaw develop, opening into that hellish alternate. But before the monster could fling out any of its feeding mouths, smoke began to pour out – glaring emerald in lased light.

'Must be running out of energy,' Saphothere opined.

'What must?' Tack asked.

'The torbeast. If it had been coming through inside Sauros, as we saw it in the abutment chamber, Goron would not have been fooling about with lasers. He's using the laser to measure the energy potential behind the rift.'

'It's not holding!' Silleck yelled.

'Put a tactical into it,' Goron stated.

A missile whipped out from somewhere below and Tack shaded his eyes. Arc light flickered and, once it went out, he lowered his hand to watch the expanding firestorm. This rolled towards the city, eating up everything on the ground that was not already incinerated. Tack prepared to get away from the windows but, seeing that Saphothere showed no inclination to do the same, he held his position. The fire reached them, roaring across all around them, and Sauros itself shuddered. Then the flame drew back into the centre of the blast, sucked in by ground winds feeding the blazing tree that rose before them. A tree that in time lost its fire and became a smoky ghost. Then the incursion was gone.

'That finished it. It's dropping back down the slope,' said Palleque. 'It can't sustain this level of loss at the moment.'

'How long before it hits us again?' Goron asked.

'Twenty minutes is the most we have,' Palleque replied.

Goron stepped away from his controls and limped over to join Saphothere and Tack.

'Engineer,' said Saphothere, with a brief nod.

'Can you manage a short-range shift?' Goron asked abruptly.

'I can,' replied Saphothere, looking even more tired.

'Then get him out of here.' Goron pointed at Tack, then turned and headed to his controls.

Tack glanced at Saphothere, who with a second nod indicated the elevator shaft. There would be no time to rest here – it was time to go.

The breath of the allosaur hot in her face, Polly knew that not to act would be to die. Thumbing its charge wheel all the way over, Polly fired her taser straight at the dinosaur's nose.

With a snarling roar the creature jerked backwards, losing its footing and collapsing on its hindquarters. It shook its head vigorously, sneezing and snorting, then swivelled round, throwing up a shower of pebbles with its tail as it accelerated away. The higher cliff on the further edge of the beach it only just cleared, sprawling on its chin as its hind feet scrabbled at the edge. Then it was off into the forest, still bellowing.

You are one lucky fuck.

Polly wondered at Nandru's definition of luck. She had survived, that was all. Slumping with her back against the rock, she waited until she felt her shaking legs could bear her, then stood up and walked back towards the stream. She was desperately tired, but dared not sleep, so concentrated on the possibilities the container had raised. After washing it out, she inspected it closely, but found nothing that revealed its origin to her.

'Perhaps there are other time travellers?' she suggested.

That would now seem the most likely answer.

'Then I must find them.'

Nice idea, but how would you go about that?

Still, the item had given her renewed hope that she might somehow escape from this insane journey. She looked around. Perhaps if she searched this whole area carefully, she'd come across some other indications of human presence. Just then a roar from the jungle discouraged that plan.

Can you shift again yet?

'Yes, I think I so,' she replied. With shaking hands she filled the handy container to its brim with water from the stream.

As she concentrated on the shift, Polly saw the strange structure growing around her once more, and the world sliding away. Jungle turned grey and black and she was weightless in a cage of glass bones over that midnight sea.

13

Engineer Goron:
The project is vast: to tap energies directly from the sun and use those energies to bore a hole back through time so that every age will become accessible, using a drill bit that will be a large fortified structure. And Maxell has agreed because this is the only way we will ever get to Cowl, or to those Umbrathane who escaped along with the preterhuman. Trying to establish bases piecemeal just does not work, as the torbeast hits them before they can be adequately defended. The only true way to establish any downtime base is to travel inside it as it moves back, as if in some vast armoured car. We will, in time, locate the preterhuman and make him pay for the dead of Callisto, but still I cannot help but feel that such a grand design is demeaned by pursuing such comparatively petty ends – so am I then guilty of hubris? We transferred our wars and exterminations from the surface of the Earth, and continued them in the solar system; how hateful it is that now we even carry them back through time as well. But, though I bemoan this, I will still go armed into that valley. Damnation! Am I a sentimental fool in that I just want to witness dinosaurs?

'It's gone,' said Silleck.

Returning to his control pillar, Goron could feel the sweat sticking his shirt to his back, and in some deeper part of himself noted that he was trembling.

Have you really fucked up, Cowl – have you underestimated us?

It seemed unlikely that Cowl would make any mistakes and that a kill could be made now, but Goron had to try, for that possibility and for Vetross.

'Is there enough energy available for short-jumping inside Sauros?'

Palleque glanced round. 'Vetross?'

'If we can,' Goron replied. 'But there's an opportunity here that cannot be missed . . . so we have to try.' He turned to Silleck and awaited her reply.

'We'll have capacitance up to a high enough level for someone to short-jump within ten minutes, just so long as that someone is not you. You were too close and the risk is too great of a short-circuit paradox getting out of control.'

Goron gazed at Palleque, who winced as if in pain and turned back to his consoles.

'Who've we got available? What travellers?' the Engineer asked generally.

'Traveller Aron is rested, and here, and possesses the same facility as Saphothere for this sort of thing,' said Palleque, his back still turned.

'Send him to the location and meanwhile patch this through to his palm computer,' the Engineer ordered, now calling up the recording he had been readying and watching it play out in one of the vorpal spheres. He saw an image of himself standing at one of the viewing windows, with Vetross at his shoulder, as behind them the incursion developed – a nacreous pillar splitting the air. Out of this pillar, like some demon sliding into the world, stepped Cowl – and Goron watched Vetross die. The recording now tracked Goron's escape – then Cowl stepping away through a second incursion. The same recording repeated, and he watched Vetross die again and again.

'Are you getting this, Aron?' he asked.

'Getting it,' the voice of the Traveller confirmed. 'How long will I have?'

'Silleck?' Goron asked.

'The potential energy levels available to Cowl are huge, but what he will *do* with them we don't know. I estimate Aron will have a minute at most.'

'*Impressive preparations, but it is all a matter of potential energy.*'

Cowl's words, but what did the being mean by them? Cowl must have known what Goron would try.

'What weapons do you have, Aron?'

'A launcher – the missile containing a displacement generator set for the Earth's core. I'll hit the incursion as he appears and with luck fry the fucker.'

'Are you at the D-generator for yourself now?'

'Yes.'

'Then be ready. Silleck will send you back the moment we have the capacity.'

Long minutes dragged by. Goron felt the sweat drying on his back and his wounded leg was now beginning to ache. He glanced down at the blood he had tracked across the floor. If they now succeeded, Sauros would be tipped some way down the slope, and all in the city would possess memories of two sets of events. But Vetross would be alive. He knew that if the blood disappeared it would mean a short-circuit paradox had developed, and the resulting cascade would drag them irretrievably down the slope. He was thoroughly aware of the dangers.

'I'm sending him now,' Silleck said at last.

The scene replayed, interfaced with the *now*. In the shimmer of displacement, Traveller Aron appeared to one side of Goron and Vetross. But something was wrong, as his appearance elicited no reaction from the other two. Aron raised his launcher to his shoulder, and it spat a missile towards Cowl as the being stepped from the incursion. The missile struck the edge of Aron's still-operating displacement field, flinging out a spherical boundary. Aron lowered his launcher and faded – displaced back to his point of departure. The scene had been changed not at all: Cowl killed Vetross and pursued Goron, then was gone.

'What happened?' the Engineer asked, his mouth dry.

'The potential energy,' Silleck replied. 'Cowl fed it into Aron's displacement sphere to keep it out of phase. The same would happen to any other we could send, had we the time or energy to spare.'

As Goron allowed that Vetross was irretrievably dead, and that this chance at Cowl was past, Silleck went on to tell him, 'The torbeast is returning.'

Goron realized that this second attack, just like the first, was not with any hope of the beast destroying Sauros, but to drain available energy and prevent them repeating their attempt to change this particular fragment of the city's past. He knew that by the time the new attack was over, and by the time they were up to capacitance again, that event would be too far down the slope to retrieve. They had failed, but then Cowl too had failed in what must have been the dark being's original purpose: to kill Goron.

Food was plentiful so long as you were not squeamish, but there was nowhere Polly felt she could safely sleep. This was not so much because of the predatory dinosaurs but more because of predatory insects. Already there was a lump half the size of a tennis ball on her arm, just above the scale, where something like a giant ant had crawled up it while she was dozing against a rock. Screaming curses as she stamped the arthropod into yellow slurry had brought her no satisfaction – only larger predators to investigate.

Run was Nandru's considered advice when she became aware of birdlike eyes observing her at the level of her own, and a long beaky mouth opening to expose translucent razor teeth and a black forked tongue. She ran, dodging between fallen trees, then dropped and rolled through the hollow under a toppled log, delaying her immediate pursuer when it jammed itself under, trying to follow her. But behind it others of its long-legged kind closed in with frightening speed. The first of those leapt onto the log and tried to smash its way through a wall of twigs and branches. Polly drew her automatic, took careful aim and pulled the trigger. The explosion sent bark flying from the log, and the creature on top of it fell back. But it was immediately replaced by another, and Polly was pulling on an unresponsive trigger. In her pocket her taser contained only one last charge, so she turned and, following some primeval instinct, jumped up into the first climbable tree. She began to haul herself up, couldn't – something snagged her coat. Glancing down, she saw one of the carnosaurs gripping the hem in its teeth. As it worried and tugged, the material ripped and a great strip of the fabric tore away, and the release in resistance propelled her up into the tree.

The four creatures below sounded like barking dogs as they tore the piece of her coat into tatters. Then, dissatisfied with this sport, they mooched around, staring up at her hopefully. Polly took out the automatic and examined it. The slide had jammed back – the gradual rusting taking its toll.

Look after your weapon and your weapon will look after you, as my old major used to say. Which didn't help him when a bomb stuck under a cafe table cut him in half.

'Just tell me how to get this working again,' said Polly.

Clean the rust from all the working parts, then just oil the damned thing. But he sounded doubtful whether it would ever work again.

Meanwhile Polly took out her taser and propped it securely in open sunlight. Making herself as comfortable as she could, she finished the last of the water from the canister. Then she began to concentrate on the automatic, rubbing away the rust with the edge of her coat and scraping the more inaccessible crevices with a nail file. How long this took her, she had no idea, but the sun had dropped out of sight behind the trees. Now the action of the weapon seemed much better, but still not as smooth as previously.

Without lubrication it will start to rust and jam again.

Polly searched through her sparse belongings till she discovered something effective. When the gun had been suitably lubricated with lipgloss and eyeliner, she inserted the clip, then stretched a condom over the weapon to keep out the damp.

I would applaud you, had I hands.

The gun safely back in her coat pocket, Polly attempted to get some sleep as she was horribly tired. After dozing for a while, she gazed down and noticed that the four carnosaurs were still putting in the occasional appearance, so felt no inclination to climb down. Instead she climbed higher to see if she could look out over the canopy.

'Oh, my God.'

Misted by distance and shimmering behind heat haze, an enormous sphere rested on a sea of greenery. She stared at it open-mouthed. Was this some moon fallen to Earth – or some strange geological formation? Focusing on it more closely, she could just discern irregularities on its surface, and indentations that could only be windows.

Some sort of ship? Perhaps even a city?

'There'll be people there, then! It must be where this canister came from.'

Don't be so sure. Who's to say it's humans that occupy it?

'OK, but I have to get there.'

Polly then remembered the roving carnosaurs and did not greatly rate her chances.

'I'll wait . . . perhaps later those things will go away.'

An hour or more passed, but the beasts kept venturing in and out of sight below her. Eventually Polly had the clever idea of securing the coat, by its sleeves, between two springy branches, and then lay back on it with her legs either side of the trunk. After that she slept deeply, only waking next morning to the sounds of the carnosaurs barking excitedly. She herself was still hungry and thirsty, but the scale had obviously taken enough nourishment from her, for the webwork was ready inside her for another time-jump. She gazed out again at the great sphere nestling in the green expanse, and felt a leaden frustration. To ever get there she must travel through kilometres of jungle, yet she was unable safely even to climb down from this tree. There was only one option.

'Screw this,' she said and shifted, intending to make the leap as brief as possible. But the webwork gripped her hard and took her all the way down.

Interspace was a chaotic nightmare of glimpses into the real, into the vast and terrible landscape of the beast, into twisting nether-space and the incandescent distortion of Heliothane weapons. Forces buffeted the mantisal with its rider and passenger, though not the sort that threw them about, but those that stretched them thinly as the mantisal deformed: at once being drawn into a worm shape, smeared over impossible surfaces; folded again into another solid shape, yet in another dimension. The scream Tack saw first as a bright red halo around Saphothere's face and a red glow on the inner surfaces of the mantisal, before he managed to dispel the synaesthesia, and he actually heard it. Briefly Tack glimpsed a neck, kilometres long and rising up out of shifting midnight, topped with a nightmare head the size of a continent. Then the mantisal returned to the corporeal world like a ball ejected from a tennis machine. It slammed against dry earth, distorting for real this time, bounced in a cloud of iron-tasting dust, bounced again and again, then rolled to stop against a massive tree.

Tack unlaced his arms from protecting his head and struggled upright. He glanced at Saphothere, who lay spreadeagled in the bottom of the mantisal, then turned to two of the packs, quickly unstrapping them from the construct and tossing them outside onto the dry ground. Then he turned his attention to the traveller. Maybe his back was broken and it would not be a good idea to move him. But nevertheless Tack gripped Saphothere under his arms and dragged him out. It was a rule of travel: get out of the mantisal quickly so it can return to its natural environment before the real world kills it – every other priority was secondary. Clear of the construct, he watched it as it jerked away from the tree and rose until touching the higher branches. It tried to fold away, but distorted, and instead went two-dimensional. It tried again and managed it this time. Tack glimpsed nightmares as it went and smelt burning flesh.

Saphothere looked wasted: his face skeletal, eyes sunken and lips drawn back from his teeth. His skin was icy and there was no heartbeat. Tack ripped open a pack and removed the medkit. Finding what he wanted, he pulled open Saphothere's shirt, placed a pulse tag against his neck, then, in a technique unchanged in millennia, injected adrenalin directly into the traveller's heart before placing a discharger against his chest. The light on the discharger flicked to green and Saphothere's back arched. It went red and he collapsed. Green again, then again, then the discharger shut off – the pulse tag on his neck now displaying the hesitant thump of his heart.

Tack rocked back on his heels and looked around. They were again at the edge of a forest, which seemed their mantisal's favoured location for bringing them out of interspace, as it gave them an easy option for avoiding hostile fauna. The dusty plain was African red and scattered with scrub and trees similar to acacia, but with yellowish needles rather than leaves. The forest rim was a dense wall of conifers and the occasional giant club moss, from which issued strange hoots and slithering movement. There seemed no immediate danger, but Tack made sure his gleaming new Heliothane carbine was ready to hand before returning his attention to Saphothere.

The diagnosticer revealed dehydration, starvation, cracked ribs, and the fact that both Saphothere's radius and ulna were broken. The traveller's spine still being intact, Tack dragged him back beside the tree and made him comfortable with a heat blanket and inflatable cushion, before setting up a drip to feed him a mixture of saline, glucose and vitamins. He then took out a scalpel and, with no more ado, sliced open Saphothere's forearm, rested one knee on the hand and pushed and twisted to get the bones, now visible, into position. He then set two bone clamps in place before using an organic glue to stick the split flesh back together. There wasn't much blood, but then Saphothere's heart was beating at a rate barely noticeable.

Now, with as much achieved as he could manage, Tack took time off to assess their situation. It was possible that the mantisal would never be coming back. Its cataclysmic arrival here might have been due to Saphothere's loss of control, or the distortions in interspace caused by the battle around Sauros, or it might be because the mantisal had been damaged by those distortions, into which it needs must return. This being the case, Tack knew he would have to leave Saphothere here and continue his mission alone. All that was required was for him to take his implant offline and allow the tor to take over.

But not yet. Despite their violent first encounter, and Saphothere's subsequent contemptuous treatment of him, Tack now felt he owed the traveller. This feeling was not due to programming, which was now such that his mission came before all else, but due to the way Saphothere's treatment of and regard for Tack had slowly changed.

Taking up his carbine, Tack stood still and looked around. There was food in the two packs, and in the two others still strapped inside the mantisal, but it was necessary to save that for the latter stages of the journey when food would not be available. But Tack was also aware that when Saphothere awoke food would be his primary need. At a rough guess he supposed them to now be in the early Jurassic or late Triassic age, so there should be plenty of meat available at least. The only problem was that this available meat might well regard them in the same light, so Tack could not leave Saphothere's side. Glancing up, he saw a flock of pterosaurs flapping over and considered taking a potshot at them, but they were very high and the chances of bringing one down close enough were remote. Refocusing, he saw that the tree above him contained fruit resembling mangoes. Accessing the huge body of knowledge Pedagogue had loaded into his mind, it took him some time to elicit that he was contemplating the outer glossy coats of a fruit much like the walnut. Propping the carbine by the tree, he jumped up to catch a low branch and hauled himself higher. Climbing with ease and speed, he pulled out his Heliothane carbide hunting knife to cut the fruit open and sample it. It was so unripe and bitter he spat it out, then tossed the fruit itself away. Where it thudded into the dust, the first of the three herrerasaurs emerging from the forest dipped its nightmare head for a sniff – before continuing to stalk towards Saphothere.

Tack just reacted, dropping ten metres straight down to land on the monster's back. The spine gave way under him with a dull crack, one of the long hind limbs splaying out at an angle, but its tail still whipping from side to side. Tack's boots slid down either side of its back ridge, and he hooked one arm under its chin and wrenched its head back, terrarium stink in his nostrils, then drew his knife across its throat, the hot blood gushing over his hand. He rolled away in time to see a second herrerasaur coming at him, its mouth open in a gushing hiss. He cut at it, sending it dancing backwards, and turned to see the last of the three stamp over its writhing companion to leap towards him. His knife angled in the wrong position, he instead caught the loose skin of its throat wattle in his other hand, and shoulder-rolled the monster, head down, into the other assailant. Both uninjured herrerasaurs went down in a dusty squirming tumble, then came up snapping at each other, but with almost telepathic consent turned on Tack again. He realized these two were just not going to stop. Any mammal might have given up by now, but these things represented ferocity honed down to its most basic elements. Snarling, their heads dipped only half a metre from the ground, they advanced. Almost regretfully Tack started to reach for the Heliothane handgun holstered at his hip.

Then the ground before him erupted in a blinding flash, throwing the closest monster back, blinking in confusion. A second then a third detonation followed, eventually causing the creatures to turn tail and run.

Leaning up against the tree, holding Tack's carbine, Saphothere croaked, 'Can't . . . leave you for a second.' With its snub barrel he indicated the dying herrerasaur – before sliding down the trunk and slumping back into unconsciousness.

Silleck hung exhausted in her vorpal connectware, watching the torbeast withdrawing into ancient past and lower orders of probability, just as she watched Vetross falling further and further down the slope.

Irretrievably dead.

Silleck had but a moment to contemplate that before she became aware of the tachyon signal coming in, using vorpal sensors positioned throughout the wormhole as stepping stones. It was a single private transmission for Engineer Goron, so the interface technician knew it could only be from Maxell – no one else had the pull to send messages this way. Momentarily shutting out exterior connections, she watched the engineer receive the communication then head away. Connecting back in again, she tracked him away from the control room and into the immediate future, where he summoned a mantisal and embarked along the wormhole and she wondered why he had been summoned to New London now.

It was over then. Goron's departure signalled more than anything that there would be no further attacks from either Cowl or his beast for the present. Silleck considered disconnecting as she was so tired, but like many of her kind she was addicted to this near omniscience. Godlike she threw her awareness back to a vorpal sensor she had abandoned when the attack had begun, and tried to find what she had merely glimpsed. The sensor she turned a hundred-and-eight degrees into interspace, and there saw the Neanderthal hurtling along in the silver cage of his pseudo-mantisal.

The glassy cage surrounding him was uneven in its formation, and in the dark interspace it reminded Silleck of some vastly expanded translucent plankton travelling above a shifting, but dead, sea bottom. The man was braced inside it and though he could not possibly understand what he was doing, she could see that he was willing himself back into the real before his tor took him to the limit of suffocation. And it worked. Turning the sensor slowly back into phase with the real world, Silleck followed him out of that dark realm, between a brightly starlit sky and a sea turned silver by moonlight.

Silleck observed his panic, but his mantisal did not fade away and drop him into the moonlit sea – tors possessed enough of their own mind or instinct to try and keep their hosts alive during the bulk of the journey. Instead it slid sideways to where dense forest formed another sea, then drifted down to an apparently rocky shoreline. Then finally the cage began to fade as it approached the ground. The Neanderthal braced himelf for a bone-jarring impact on rocky ground, but instead hit pliant mud and bounced, as the glass-like structure faded and passed through him into the ground. He rolled and came up onto his knees, pulling a bone club from his hide clothing, then he stood and looked around. When no danger was immediately apparent, he scuttled to a sandy space between edifices of the dried mud, curled himself up in the most protected niche he could find and was still. Silleck tracked ahead.

The sun had begun to peak around one of the monoliths of mud, and was warming the Neanderthal's feet before he awoke, which he did as if someone had touched him with a hot iron. He stood and headed towards the forest. Twenty feet from the trees, he hesitated – perhaps having already had some nasty experiences in other forests. Silleck noted the colourful fan-shaped leaves of the trees and realized they must be early ginkgos. Expanding her vision, she saw that the man had arrived on an island and was lucky in that, for there seemed to be no big reptiliomorphs in evidence. Not that such a primitive needed a great deal of luck. Observing the stains on the club he held, Silleck surmised he would be more able to survive the trials of these past times than many others. Though, of course, like the girl he would be unlikely to survive all the way. Cowl wasn't interested in his samples surviving.

Other stations similar to their own hung geostationary above the planet like barrage balloons, while white ceramic ships moved in constant transit between them and the installation built on the dark side of Mercury. That installation resembled a metallic mosaic imprinted on black, though occasionally blotted out under the shadows of passing storms, which in turn were lit up as if by interior flashbulbs, as those storms discharged their electric power.

'So the sum purpose of the beast's attack was for Cowl to ride in on its energy front just to get to you?' Maxell asked.

'So it would seem. Cowl knows from previous experience that he cannot break our defences in one all-out attack. That he managed a limited penetration at all is due to the fact that he had been provided with our defence frequency at that time. And he has yet to learn that our defences are not always so well maintained.'

'Risky – allowing such an attack,' said Maxell.

'For veracity,' said Goron. 'A gambit to give him the confidence to commit when he hears the greater lie.'

Maxell nodded and was silent for a moment before saying, 'I'm sorry about Vetross.'

'She knew the risks.'

Again a longer silence, Maxell changed the subject. 'The storm cycle will be impossible to maintain once the "greater lie" achieves its purpose.' She was gazing at the main screen. 'We'll lose most of this, which means a refugee population of twenty million to transship back to Earth Station.'

'If all goes well,' Goron replied, as he casually manipulated the image on a screen before him. This showed a transparent computer diagram of the sun tap, with the locations of thousands of points within it.

'Timing is everything,' said Maxell.

'Now there's a statement that can never be contested.'

'It will work?' she asked him.

'The sun tap was not designed for this. The excess of redundancy was built in, and many of the autorepair systems operate faster than anything less than catastrophic failure. But, yes, it will work – the displacement generators will do what is required of them. That, however, is not why you asked me here.'

Maxell did not look round. She continued, 'And Mars?'

'You know the new mirrors will work better than the old and that now we do not need the energy to create an environment but only to maintain it. Our loss will be great but sustainable. When are you going to get to the point?'

Maxell turned towards him. 'Only a select few of you on Sauros know what is going to happen. How do they feel about this? And, most importantly, how do you feel?'

'Three hundred years and you're asking me how I feel?'

'I am.'

Goron stood up from his console and walked over to stand beside her, his hands clasped behind his back as he gazed out at the view. 'We few who know, know the consequences of our actions: the ending of the greatest threat the human race has ever encountered, and as a result the survival of the Heliothane Dominion. Those who will die . . . I mourn them already, as I mourn Vetross, but their sacrifice is unfortunately necessary. Veracity permits it to be no other way.'

'But the Dominion's survival may not be something you'll see. You know that, without an adjacent interspace source of energy, mantisals cannot jump accurately. We'll have perhaps two hundred years of concurrent time. I've calculated the chances of us getting a mantisal to you – one mantisal, not the hundreds that may be needed.'

'As have I, and it's roughly one in a hundred thousand. And that's discounting our slide down the slope.'

'Yes.'

'We'll do well enough.' Goron shrugged. 'And there's always the chance Saphothere could bring us tors, if he survives making his kill.'

'There is also a chance that the technology will become available . . .'

'I know. But I know too that every day we exist after the event, and every day Saphothere does not come, will push us further down the probability slope. And things will change here. We'll be praised as dead heroes and quickly forgotten.'

'I'll not forget.'

Goron turned to her. 'So really all this was about was saying goodbye?'

'Yes, that's all.'

'Then goodbye, Maxell.'

14

Traveller Thote:
It was a close-run thing with the Roman. Keeping him on life support, we nearly managed to remove his tor and interface it with a mantisal. I subsequently see that it is just a question of using a quantity of the old bearer's genetic material as a buffer, plus some method of fooling the tor's propensity for pattern recognition. However, it seems I am not going to get a chance to try out my theory as Maxell has cancelled all energy allocations for this kind of work, and it seems Goron's project now has prime status. I am now to return to other duties subordinate to the Engineer. I do not mind, for we must choose the best option we can find . . . to kill our enemies.

Endless seashores. It appeared that the vambrace was intent on bringing him back into the world in the same sort of location each time. The gods were casting him into places to fight battles he did not understand at their whim. He just kept himself honed and focused on survival. He hated his gods.

The jungle was a dense wall of green, spilling into mangroves to the Roman's left as he faced seaward on the strip of sand on which he had been deposited. To his right weird trees, and other strange plants he could not identify, halted their march towards the sea at the beginning of a rocky promontory. Resting his hand on the pommel of his sheathed gladius, he headed towards that, assuming that wherever rocks were bathed by the sea there would be shellfish, which had served him well enough thus far. As he walked he suddenly felt ebullient, light-headed. The air here had a strange clarity and was as intoxicating as wine.

Reaching the edge of the sandbar, Tacitus scrambled up the rocky face and began to head out onto the promontory itself. After a moment he noted that scattered over the stone were nautiloid shells the size of dinner plates. He laughed and kicked one into the sea. Drew his sword and waved it at the sky.

'Send them now, curse you!' he shouted at the gods. 'Send your monsters and your trials!'

But there was no immediate response and, from past experience, he expected none. Usually the monsters came in the night, sniffing after him as if after spoiled meat.

He moved on towards the end of the promontory, where he squatted and gazed down into the deep water. His head was buzzing almost as if he was getting too much air, and he noted that his breathing was shallow. Observing a nautiloid drifting along in the pellucid depths, with its tentacles outstretched and its shell striped red and white, he wondered if he was beginning to see the kind of visions wounded soldiers saw before dying.

He prodded at the surface of the water with his gladius and something rose up out of those same depths, in an expanding ring around the nautiloid, like an odd piece of jewellery carved from grey rock, ivory and rose quartz. The nautiloid jetted aside in a cloud of ink and the circle kept growing larger. Then Tacitus realized his challenge had been answered.

Recognizing the apparition in that instant as an enormous open mouth, Tacitus flung himself back as a huge fish shot up over the rim of stone in an explosion of foam. Its mouth was filled with jagged teeth, its blunt head armoured. He shoved himself further away, sliding on his backside, the sea boiling behind the great creature as, with its moray tail, it tried to force itself further onto the promontory. Realizing he was getting close to the sea on the other side, he scrambled to his feet, and turned and ran. After thrashing around, trying to get to him, the sea boiling and spindrift tumbling through the air, the giant fish flipped back into the water with a huge splash, then came hammering alongside the promontory, driving a wave before it. Tacitus leapt onto the beach as the wave also reached it, and didn't stop running until he reached the wall of vegetation. Turning, he watched the fish, half emerged from the water, begin thrashing from side to side to pull itself back into the sea. He spat on the sand – recognizing this sending from Neptune – then turned to peer into the greenery.

The vegetation was so dense that there was no easy path through it. Large, unlikely insects moved about in its shade, clinging to the underside of bedspread-sized leaves, or camouflaged against the trunks of plants like green spears. He did not care to venture in there amongst those horrors, but was hungry again, and certainly didn't want to be down near the shore collecting shellfish.

'Curse you,' he muttered.

Tacitus removed, from the sack he had made from his tattered cloak a jug he had found on one of those past seashores and drank water collected from another age. Looking around, he noted how dank everything seemed inside the jungle, while at the upper edge of the beach extended a drift of bleached wood and other dried-out organic matter, including piles of triple-ribbed carapaces. Warily eyeing the shoreline, he collected some of these and, using a flint spearhead he had taken from some primitive who had been sent against him and tinder he had collected from a place as dry and hot as his native land in summer, he began the laborious process of striking sparks from his sword to ignite a fire. When it was going he piled on a log, from underneath which scuttled large horrible sealice with scorpion forelimbs, then turned back towards the jungle in search of food. Spotting a horrible insect the size of a flattened chicken, he pinned it with his gladius to one of the spear trees, then roasted it over the fire, before devouring its fragrant prawn-flavoured flesh. Later, having partially denuded the nearby jungle of similar creatures, he lay down and slept in bright sunlight, surrounded by the carnage of his meal. And dreamed of vengeance.

After carving the herrerasaur he had roasted with the microwave setting on his carbine, Tack tentatively ate a piece.

'Chicken,' he said.

'Chicken's grandad about a billon times removed,' Saphothere replied.

Tack wiped his knife on fallen needles and rejoined the traveller.

'What happened?' Saphothere asked without raising his head.

'From what point?' Tack asked.

Saphothere now looked up. 'My memory is completely blank from the moment we embarked until I came to and saw you fighting our dinner there.'

'The interspace adjacent to Sauros was . . . rough. The second attack came earlier than Goron or his people supposed, and we went straight into torbeast incursion surfaces, displacement fields and spillover from the occasional tactical being employed. We came out of it here with actual momentum. The mantisal bounced a couple of times and came to rest against this tree. I got you out and the mantisal returned to interspace – on its second try.'

Saphothere nodded, then held up his injured arm enquiringly.

Tack went on, 'I checked you over thoroughly. Besides vorpal draining you had suffered a broken arm – both bones – and some cracked ribs, and your heart had stopped. I used adrenalin and a discharger to get things going again and made some necessary repairs.'

'You saved my life,' observed Saphothere. 'Yet your programming probably gave you a choice – you could have just gone on and left me.'

'It seemed the right thing to do.' Tack sat, staring at the fire and feeling uncomfortable. 'I need you to take me as far back in time as possible by mantisal, so I can conserve my energies for the fight that follows.' But his words fell on deaf ears, for when he looked up again, he saw that Saphothere was fast asleep.

Saphothere needed five days of rest before attempting to summon the mantisal again, and it was a relief when it appeared intact. The two surviving herrerasaurs, which had been lurking around the encampment all the time and twice had to be driven off, were left to dispute the ripe remains of their kin, and the bones the two men had stripped of meat. Interspace no longer seemed as dangerous as it had done, but Tack sensed in it a weird difference, like some presence. He gazed out at the grey void overlying midnight – the nearest interpretation his customary senses could put upon the view – and noted the terminus of the wormhole, looking like a distant sliver of silver inserted at what might be called the horizon. But whatever was bothering Tack wasn't there.

'Look to the interface,' suggested Saphothere.

Tack peered at the black surface of the pseudo sea. Then, with that ability to distort perception he had acquired by riding the mantisal, he looked *harder*. There at first, infinitely deep, he observed a great tree like some vast water plant. Focusing on it was like trying to discern the final edge of a Mandelbrot pattern. Leviathan heads of tissue consisted of feeding mouths and wormish tangles of endless necks, surfaces of skin curved away into nether spaces. Thicker branches were at once serpentine torsos and the interior glimpses of bottomless intestines. Organs layered over and within each other like mountain ranges. And when at last Tack felt he was gaining some focus, some perspective, it all tumbled away and he realized he was seeing only that fraction of it his mind could interpret.

'It's quiescent at the moment,' Saphothere explained. 'Though "moment" is stretching the word – like us all it exists in its own time, and that time might bear no relation to any other.'

'The torbeast,' Tack stated.

'Yeah,' said Saphothere.

'What are you going to do about this creature when Cowl is dead?' Tack asked.

'That is a question we have yet to answer,' Saphothere replied, closing his eyes and truncating the conversation. Some hours later, personal time, the mantisal brought them down on a drizzly mountainside overlooking an endless sea of foliage. Wordlessly, Saphothere activated his tent. It self-erected into a ground-hugging dome a metre high and two metres wide – the entrance to the dome being an elasticated thing like an anus. It closed tightly behind him when he crawled inside.

Tack walked down into Carboniferous forest, armed with his newly acquired knowledge of the flora and fauna, in search of food. When he returned with a metre-long newt slung over one shoulder and a bag of cycad fruits like spherical red pineapples, he found Saphothere was fast asleep in the tent. Tack sat gazing out at the ancient forest and considered all he had now come to understand, yet he couldn't shake the feeling that he was being lied to.

Perhaps that was just natural paranoia arising because he didn't understand everything. He could see that, before Pedagogue's education of him, he would have been suspicious about things that he now understood perfectly. The length of this recent jump was a case in point. To reach this forest they had crossed a hundred and fifty million years whereas, before, half that distance had crucified Saphothere. Now Tack knew that, prior to their first violent meeting in twentieth-century Essex, Saphothere had been hunting down Umbrathane for a long time, and draining himself – and his mantisal – down to the limit continuously. Five days sitting on his butt in the Triassic had been the most rest he'd enjoyed in five years. And stuffing dinosaur meat, roast nuts and some sort of root like Jerusalem artichoke into his face had increased his physical bulk noticeably. Also Saphothere explained that the energy detritus from the torbeast's attack on Sauros had, once the danger passed, provided a rich feeding ground for the mantisal. But, no, it wasn't apparent inconsistencies like that. It was the simple idea of himself being the most effective assassin the Heliothane could send against Cowl. Yes, he understood how they could not get through without a tor but, surely, with their technology there had to be another way . . .

'Admiring the view?' Saphothere asked from behind him.

Tack turned and nodded as the traveller left his tent.

Saphothere went on, 'Fossil fuels, that's all it becomes. And your profligate society burnt it all up by fuelling uncontained growth without making any serious effort to get out of the container.'

Tack stared at him questioningly.

Saphothere gestured towards the vast forest. 'You mentioned predestination, though I should think you are now beyond such ideas. But, if you really wanted to find it, there it is spread below you. For millions of years the Earth stored energy in the form of fossil fuels, as if making it ready for intelligent use by a future civilization. With such energy to hand, your people could have powered their civilization into the solar system long before mine. It could be said that this was their destiny. And they wasted it.'

'What power did you use?'

'Nuclear fusion, bought at great cost. For your people it could have been easy, for mine it was hard.'

Tack wondered quite what he meant by 'mine', for it was the Umbrathane who had taken that step. He turned away and proceeded to gut the big newt, while Saphothere opened one of the red pineapples. The minutiae of day-to-day existence pushed speculation to the edge of his consciousness. After they ate,

Saphothere retired again. Tack dozed with his back against a rock, too lazy yet to bother setting up his own tent, even though it was hardly a difficult task. Vaguely he heard Saphothere speak, then later a breath of cold, washing across him, pulled him into full consciousness. He was staring dozily at the endless forest when something pressed against the back of his neck.

'Not one word, one movement, or I cripple you now.'

She was supposed to be dead – incinerated in an atomic blast – but Meelan now sounded very much alive.

Again the air was growing stale and Polly had to fight a rising terror to look for the other place in which she could control the careering progress of the scale and of the cage that contained her. She did not want to see more because, at the edge of perception, she just knew that a nightmare lurked underneath the midnight sea, watching her. When she did reach out, brief chaos surrounded her and she glimpsed a vast torso curving above, its edges lost in spatial distortion: an endless tangle of necks and mouths like the one that had taken Nandru; and she felt the regard of some feral intelligence.

'Oh Christ . . .'

She was groping for a way out, fear freezing her will and shoving her perception back to that of the black sea and grey void. Then something reached out, opening a surface at the end of which the coloured light of the *real* gleamed, and she fell down the slope into day, the cage smoking and dissipating as she hurtled out over cold desert and dropped down towards a rock field. She clung to the glass cage's struts, willing them to retain integrity, feeling them grow thin under her touch. But it was enough. She dropped two metres to a boulder, slid down the side of it, and rolled in a scattering of yucca-like stems, snapping them over onto ground coated with the green buttons of other primitive growth.

What did you see? I couldn't see anything.

'*That thing – I saw the thing that killed you.*'

I saw only two surfaces: one black and one grey. That's all I've ever seen.

'Perhaps you're lucky,' said Polly, standing up and brushing green slime from her coat, before looking around.

The mountains rising up to her right were jagged, unrounded by the elements. From somewhere behind them a column of smoke rose into the sky, staining the clouds in shades of sepia, black and crimson. Between them and the rock field lay a gritty plain dappled with green. The few plants were simple: constructed from a child's drawing by some inept god. In the stony ground there were occasional cracks filled with stagnant water in which miniature rainbow larvae wriggled and swarmed. Again the shift had brought her down near the seashore, for she could hear the hiss of waves beyond the rocks, though she could not yet see the ocean. Negotiating her way between some boulders, she headed in that direction, for despite her recent, near-lethal experience by the sea, it was at least something reassuringly familiar.

The shoreline was cluttered with the shells of sea creatures; water snails as big as human heads, crab things and lobster things, worm things and just plain things. Some of the shells were still occupied, and stank like a trawler's bilge, but nothing was moving. Polly kicked over a ribbed shell resembling a knight's shield and squatted down beside it to inspect the decaying creature it contained.

I don't think there's anything on the land that can attack you now.

'What makes you say that?' Polly asked bitterly.

I think you're beyond any land animal other than insects . . . or their ancient relatives.

'That's a comfort.'

About to stand up to move on, she yelled with fright. A figure was looming over her.

Dressed in dark clothing like army fatigues, the man was rangy, hard-looking. His skin looked almost bluish-white and his close-cropped hair resembled a layer of chalk. At first she had the crazy notion that he was some sort of inhabitant of this same age, then realized he could be nothing other than a time traveller like herself.

'Who . . .?' was all she could manage.

The man smiled, though it was hardly reassuring. Polly's hand strayed to her pocket and the comforting weight of the condom-wrapped automatic.

'My name is Thote – if that is relevant. I'm here to help you.'

'Now, lie face-down with your legs and arms outstretched.'

Tack considered going for her, but in this situation his new strength meant nothing and his reactions could not be faster than her trigger finger. So he obeyed, stretching out, but turning his head so he could just see Saphothere's tent. With the barrel of her weapon still pressed against his neck, Meelan tossed a small silver sphere at the tent, which burnt through the fabric like hot iron through tissue paper. The interior was suddenly filled with a phosphorescent blaze, becoming a bright lantern for a few seconds before erupting from the fabric and consuming it. The heat was intense and Tack recognized that she had hurled a molecular catalyser, like the one Saphothere had used on the palisade of Pig City and like those still contained in Tack's pack. Saphothere was not even given time to scream.

As the fire died down, a filigree of solidifying black smoke fell through the air as from acetylene flame. Tack felt the pressure of the gun barrel lift from his neck.

'I have placed on your back a small mine, which, should you move abruptly, will detonate and drive into your spine fragments of glass coated with a paralytic. Do not move.'

Tack recognized that both Heliothane and Umbrathane possessed numerous varieties of explosives that could be programmed to detonate under varying circumstances – changes in temperature, humidity, position, whatever – so he did not disbelieve Meelan. His recent education had opened his eyes to just how dangerous her kind were.

Soon after she stepped into view as she went to inspect the ruins of the tent. He watched her running the toe of her boot through the thin layer of ash. Her new arm, he saw, was now nearly the size of the other, there was some sort of brace extending down the forearm and dividing up to spread down each finger. This was clearly to prevent any deformation in the rapid growth of the limb. Unfortunately, such regenerative ability was not one the Heliothane had been able to impart to himself, along with his other augmentations.Tack then realized Meelan might not know about those. Maybe the mine's detonation was programmed to the slower movements of a twenty-second-century human, not for what he had become. Tack calculated that he had at least one and a half seconds.

With Meelan's back now towards him, he reached round, closed his hand on cold metal, and threw the object at her, whipfast. The mine blew only centimetres from where he had been lying, but by then he was rolling down the slope towards the forest, paralytic glass fragments thumping the back of his suit. In the flash's after-images he glimpsed Meelan spinning round and raising her weapon. Thrusting down with the flat of his hand, he changed the course of his roll as a series of explosions cut in a line down the slope towards him. Finally getting his feet underneath him, he sprang up, cartwheeled away on one hand while drawing his weapon with the other, and sent a spray of shots up the slope. A horsetail exploded into fibrous pulp right next to him as he dived headfirst into the cover of greenery. As plants continued to explode around him, he offered up thanks that both

Umbrathane and Heliothane were so arrogantly self-assured of their fighting skills that they rarely relied on weapons like his seeker gun.

Deep in the jungle, the continuing explosions now behind him, he was caught unawares when a white hand snaked out from behind a giant club moss to grab his shoulder. He thrust his weapon up towards a white face, and was a microsecond from pulling the trigger before its identity registered.

'I thought she'd killed you!' Tack exclaimed.

'Apparently not,' Saphothere replied, staring up at the mountainside Tack had just left.

Tack turned to look and saw two mantisals had just appeared. Later, learning that Saphothere had left his tent briefly while Tack dozed, he was grateful that even superhumans like Saphothere needed to take a shit occasionally. The traveller began climbing the tree they were standing beneath. Tack followed him up and soon they obtained a better view of their ravaged campsite.

Their packs had been propped against a rock face behind Saphothere's incinerated tent. Even as they watched, the group of Umbrathane set their defences, then leaving behind only two, a man and a woman, the other six, including Meelan herself, began scouring the jungle below. Tack handed back the monocular Saphothere had passed him.

'I recognize a couple more of them from Pig City,' he observed.

'Well, there would have been some survivors,' Saphothere replied.

'So what do we do now?' Tack asked.

Saphothere's face was locked in an angry grimace. Then he looked around. 'It's turning dusk. We hit them in full dark. Then you grab a supply pack and your weapons, and just go on from here.'

He scrambled down from the tree and Tack followed, knowing that when the traveller said 'go on from here' he meant the moment Tack grabbed those packs he must take his implant offline and allow the tor to take him back in time. From that point he would be on his own, if he survived the coming fight. Dubiously he considered their current collection of weapons. Saphothere had wisely taken a carbine with him into the jungle and had an assortment of proximity mines hooked on his belt, while Tack possessed only his hand weapon. Though containing a hundred-round clip of explosive ammunition, that was not sufficient if you went up against eight heavily armed Umbrathane.

'What about you?' Tack asked, as they pushed through undergrowth.

'I survive – or not. But your mission is vital and you must carry it out.'

'Why not just summon the mantisal here and we could get supplies elsewhere?'

Saphothere looked at him. 'We cannot afford the time.'

There it was: another of those pronouncements that just didn't make sense to Tack. Nevertheless, he nodded as if he understood.

Saphothere explained, 'When Coptic and Meelan hit us first, I was prepared to accept that as just luck on their part. But her tracking us here and being so well-prepared, I am not inclined to accept as coincidence. They are getting inside help, but most importantly they are somehow securing the energy for accurate time-shifting.'

'Cowl,' said Tack.

'Maybe,' Saphothere replied. 'Now, this is what you must do.'

Shortly afterwards Saphothere signalled that they should now proceed in silence, sliding through the foliage, stepping only on sure ground, utterly alert. Even their comlinks were unusable in this situation as they could be detected. But their clothing shielded them from infrared detectors, and the natural motion of the foliage from motion detectors. This was to be dangerous and bloody.

When Saphothere motioned for Tack to now head off separately, he did so. It was only seconds later that the firing started.

'What is your name?'

Thote's voice was calm, soothing.

'Polly.'

'It is good to meet you, Polly.'

Polly felt herself getting lulled.

Don't go all slushy for the first dick you've encountered in a hundred million years, Polly. You can bet your arse he's not just your tour guide.

Nandru's words were iced water in her face and reminded her that always, in her past, whenever someone was being nice to her they wanted a piece of her.

'If you're here to help me, then start by telling me what the hell is happening to me,' she suggested succinctly.

The man flinched visibly and got a distant look on his face. After a moment he smiled again and held out his hand to her.

'Come with me to my camp and I'll try to explain.'

Polly took his hand and allowed him to pull her to her feet. She noticed how his gaze kept straying to the arm on which the scale clung, concealed by her sleeve. Pushing for some clearer reaction she could read, she released his hand, pulled up her sleeve, and held out her forearm before him.

'Do you know what this thing is?'

'It is a tor: an organic time machine that is dragging you back to the beginning of time – to the Nodus. You are one of Cowl's samples.'

Instead of asking the questions that clamoured for attention after such a statement, Polly said one thing only, 'I don't want to go.'

The man nodded and slowly began to walk away from her. She could feel a tension in him; that he was holding something back.

She had much practice in reading men's body language. She followed him across the rockscape to a campsite, where supplies were neatly stacked and a pot bubbled on a compact stove. Thote gestured to a blanket spread on the ground and Polly sat down, while he squatted by the bubbling pot and stirred it.

'You are stretched out like elastic from your own time. There is admittedly a small risk in removing the tor; it is a living parasite and made to cling to and draw its host back in time until removed and read by its maker, Cowl. I too can remove it, though, and once it is removed you will immediately fall back to your own time. I take it you want to return there?'

Now that sounds a little too easy to me. Watch out for this fucker.

'When I left my own time someone was busy trying to kill me.'

But no, she had dragged the killer along with her . . . and what did that mean? Would he still be there on her return? Would he have never left? Thote looked at her as if reading her mind.

'You won't return at the exact moment you left. You'll arrive in what would naturally be your *own* time. You have been travelling for some days now, personal time, so that means you'll arrive back the same number of days after your departure.'

Easy as sucking eggs. He's lying to you.

Polly did not want to hear Nandru. It all seemed so perfect. She didn't want to be chewed on by bad-tempered dinosaurs. She didn't want to run into this Cowl, whose name alone sounded ominous. But Nandru was right – this whole situation stank.

'Why do you want to do this?' she asked the stranger.

'I'll do anything to thwart Cowl's plans.'

Thote ladled what smelt like fish stew into a bowl and handed it to Polly.

'Here, you'll find this tastes better than anything you'd find on the shore.'

Polly took the proffered bowl and sniffed it. The food smelt delicious, with chunks of white meat and pieces of fibrous vegetable floating in a thick sauce. She dug in and raised a spoonful to her mouth. It was in her mouth and she was already chewing, when she noticed the avid look on Thote's face. As a sudden bitterness froze her tongue, she spat the food out and threw the bowl at him, then stood, reeled, staggered back. He stood up also with a calm satisfaction.

He gestured then to a nearby rock crevice, where lay the remains of some other time traveller, the tor still wrapped like a coral on one arm, but gathered round bare bone. Empty eye sockets, bare ribs exposed through decaying clothing, some mummified flesh remaining, blond hair fallen from a bare skull.

'That will be your future if you keep going. There's a lot of time still between here and the Nodus, and few can survive the journey.'

Polly tried to shift, tried to suborn that webwork inside, but her will seemed flaccid and confusion was filling her head.

Well, what a surprise – the guy's not at all nice.

'You can't go on, Polly. Even if you do survive the journey, Cowl will kill you.'

'Like you give a shit,' said Polly thickly. She concentrated harder, trying to get hold of something, anything inside her. But the drug blurred her perceptions, ate into her concentration. Thote could sense what she was trying to do. His eyes narrowed for a moment, then he relaxed.

'Too late now, primitive,' he said. 'And, to a certain extent, I'm sorry to have to do this to you. But for two years now I've been fishing interspace with what's left of my mantisal from this shit hole.'

Polly tried to hurl a curse at him, but her mouth felt like some dentist had injected half a pint of novocaine and all she managed was to dribble down her chin.

'What I intend to try has been tried once and failed once.' He gestured to the skeleton. 'I think I have it now, though – desperation refines the thought processes. You see, Cowl is sampling genetics, which is why it doesn't matter to him if you reach him dead or alive. You are just a portable food sack for your tor, as it already has your code locked inside it – and that's all Cowl needs to find out if he is managing to destroy the future.' Thote shrugged. 'All I really need do is graft some of your skin into a vorpal strut, plasticize the tor, and wrap it around that. The field should then be magnified enough to include me – even though I am not the actual sample.'

Polly's vision was growing black around the edges, but she retained enough to see the shattered remnants of silvery cagework come folding into existence to one side of Thote. He drew an ugly commando knife from his boot, then stepped towards her.

I think we've seen and heard about enough now.

The webwork slammed into life with more power than ever. Thote's scream of rage echoed after her into black and grey, as her own silver cage materialized around her.

Some sort of projector, stabbed into the ground like a garden lantern, shrieked a warning only seconds before an explosion ripped out of the jungle wall. Tack stepped out, triggered a burst of fire towards the one visible umbrathant, then dropped and rolled as horsetails sheared over behind him. A man to Tack's left was turning his carbine towards the jungle when his legs fragmented below the knee. Saphothere came out so fast he was stepping on the man's shoulder before the same man had fully collapsed, then went into a roll from which he managed to shoot backwards, taking off the victim's head, before disappearing into shadow. Tack was back into cover by then, running at full pelt, slamming through foliage, then out and accelerating around the foot of the mountain. More explosions behind him. Someone screaming. Turn and head upslope, legs hammering down hard as spring steel. Foliage breaking behind him. Down, roll, fire. The umbrathant following him was gone – then springing up again from behind a boulder, firing his carbine, the scree slope erupting at the spot from where Tack leapt. Disappeared. Tack firing at the rock face immediately behind the boulder, his rounds set for timed detonation rather than impact. The man standing up to fire again, then screaming as Tack's rounds detonate about his feet. A second's hesitation. Enough. One explosive shell spreads the man's brains up the rock wall. And Tack was moving on again.

All the way upslope now, the battle flashes shielded by the mountain flank. The rock wall runs up the mountain like a spine and curves round above him. Already seen and studied. His weapon back in its holster, Tack heads up it like a spider, sprints across a stony plateau, drops down beside a three-metre waterfall, then descends the course of a stream in bounding strides on slimed rocks, shooting one brief puzzled glance at strange amphibians glowing with blue light in a shallow pool. Then upwards, scrambling a fern-covered slope. Finally gazing down on the encampment.

Saphothere is there, pinned down on a slope, a man and a woman firing towards him but not daring to emerge from cover. No sign of Meelan or the other one. Perhaps dead? Tack fires a single burst and the man fragments, the woman rolling aside with a horrible scream, her bare rib bones exposed. Then Tack is down the slope – the two packs resting just below him – his implant coming offline, and the temporal web inside him hardening like glass. He hits the ground and comes up in time to see a column of distortion howling up into the night, near Saphothere, bulging and breaking open on a nightmare landscape beyond. The beast breaking through! Flesh-light floods the area, in which Tack sees an explosion tossing Saphothere into the air, and Meelan hurtling in from the side, hitting him in a flat dive.

Fucking go! – over com.

Grabbing up the two packs, Tack allows the tor to take him, just as the woman with her ribs exposed hurtles down on him like a hammer. Night folds into another night. Tack glimpses the substance of the torbeast built up behind the incursion, like a forest trying to force its way through a keyhole. Hanging onto Tack's jacket, the wounded woman turns her gun towards his face. His boot goes in below her ribs, into exposed intestines. Screaming, choking blood filling her mouth, she loses her grip and tumbles away into night.

A feeding mouth uncoils out of midnight and Hoovers her up. Ignores Tack completely.

15

Modification Status Report:
My daughter is a failure that nearly killed me while she was still in my womb. Obviously my decision to retain the alleles is the cause of this – those alleles displacing both wholly and partially the alterations I made. As she continues her growth in the amniotic tank, I see that she possesses no exoskeleton, merely a toughening and discoloration of the skin. Her sensory grid is viable, but nowhere near as efficient as planned for. Her interfacing organs have been stunted by the growth of those damned human features: eyes, nose and a normal mouth, and all the concomitant sensory apparatus to support them. She has also lost some of her bilateral symmetry, which I now see is due to the fiddler-crab gene I used to supposedly make alterations to her mouth. Sometimes I damn the lack of logic in genetic evolution, when a gene controlling eye colour might also control something like fingernail growth. My instinct is to flush the tank, but much can be learnt from this growing child and, having learnt, I will try again.

There was no real danger to him in venturing outside Sauros – other than the stringencies of the environment – since Cowl would never bother to expend the energy required just to hit an individual heliothant of Palleque's minor status, so consequently there were no restrictions on such ventures for him. Had it been Goron out here it would have been an entirely different matter, for the Engineer's assassination would be an utterly demoralizing blow for the Heliothane, as it had nearly proven. Pausing on a slope made spongy by centuries of ferny growth and decay, Palleque raised his monocular and gazed back at Sauros.

Goron rarely left the city and, even if he did, Cowl might be disinclined to attack, suspecting a trap. The recent attack upon the Engineer inside the city had been unexpected and nearly successful because Cowl had known the shield frequency, enabling the preterhuman to pass through the defences at a particularly vulnerable time. And now some pertinent questions were being asked at all levels of the Heliothane.

Hooking the monocular back onto his belt, Palleque removed a small locator and saw that he did not have far to go. The communicator was on the other side of the mountain, where he had established it in a body of granite. By now it would have grown its shielding of vorpal crystal all through the surrounding rock and would be ready to use. Glancing upslope he saw that the ferns ended where the cold wind had denuded the mountain-side of vegetation. On reaching this firmer ground he picked up his pace. The Triassic push was a while away – on Sauros time – so he did not hurry because of that. He hurried because he realized time was running out for himself.

At the mountain's peak he paused to look back at Sauros again, and considered how arrogant were so many assumptions about that place. Gazing down the rear slope, he observed a swathe of devastation cut through the vegetation by a herd of sauropods, and the ensuing activity which that elicited from the attendant carnosaurs. But that would represent no problem – he now recognized his surroundings and no longer needed the locator. The communicator lay only a hundred metres below him and, by taking the slope in long bounds, he shortly reached it.

Like the wing of a downed aircraft, the granite outcrop speared up from the spread of cycads crowding this west face of the mountain. Arriving there, he pocketed his locator and reached out to press his hand against the grey rock face. Immediately the stone took on a translucence and a vorpal manifold rose to the surface to meet and bind with his hand. In the darkness behind it, a beetle-black non-face turned towards him.

'The attack was unsuccessful,' said Cowl.

Palleque nodded. 'Goron had made preparations of which no one but he was aware.'

'He used a displacement generator.'

'I've since learnt he had them placed at intervals inside Sauros, when it was first built in New London. I now have their positions mapped.' Palleque took his palm computer from his belt and pressed its interface patch against the necessary position in the manifold, squirting the information across. As he took it away again, he scanned about himself, suspicion wrinkling his brow.

Cowl bowed his head towards something, then raising it up said, 'For this to be of any use to me I will need to know a future, Sauros-time shield frequency.'

Palleque grinned. 'Now here's the good news. You won't even need that. When Sauros—'

The energy discharge hit the rock like a thunderclap. Shrieking, Palleque staggered back, his hand pulling free of the manifold, but leaving most of its incinerated skin behind. Down on his knees he groped for his weapon with his free hand, while Cowl looked on.

Stepping out from the surrounding cycads came Goron and four other Heliothane.

'You treacherous fucking snake!' spat Goron.

Palleque pulled his weapon free, but another shot slammed into his bicep and spun him round, the weapon bouncing from his grasp.

Goron turned to the fading image of Cowl. 'By all means, please, come and visit us. If you don't, we'll be coming for you.'

From Cowl there issued a hissing snarl. Goron raised his weapon and fired it straight into the manifold. The communicator fused on solid rock, all translucence behind it disappearing. Goron turned to his companions and directed two of them towards Palleque. 'I don't want him to die or suffer any unnecessary pain now.' He glanced at the rock. 'That will come later.'

She was coming out of it. Her legs felt cold and numb where they lay in the water, but at last she was able to move her arms a little and, driving her elbows into a scree of rock flakes and broken rainbow shell, she was able to drag herself clear of the cold brine and roll over onto her back. Then, still gasping, she gazed up at an anaemic blue sky smeared with washes of white cloud. Her body felt cored with lead, and as feeling returned to her extremities they felt bloated. But that core was diminishing with her every breath. Eventually she managed to heave herself up onto her knees and survey her surroundings.

The rock pool her legs had been soaking in was bright with anemones, odd shellfish, red algal growth and green weed like discarded tissue paper. She shuddered to see that it also was full of movement: trilobites sculled about in its depths like great flattened woodlice. This pool was just one amid many others left by the retreating tide, in a band of rock lying between the slope of the beach she was now kneeling on and the sand flats stretching out beyond to the distant spume of the sea. Nothing else was visible to her yet.

'How did you do that?' she managed, when she could get enough spit into her mouth.

I might as easily ask you the same question.

'No but . . . you never said . . .'

Muse is linked deeply into you and it is linking deeper all the time. Perhaps two time-shifts back I became aware that its monitoring systems were connecting up with your . . . tor. The last time you shifted I saw . . . felt how you did it, and knew that I could do it too.

Suddenly Polly felt *invaded* by the presence of Nandru –

something she had never felt before while all she could hear was his voice. Even when attending the calls of nature she had not felt his scrutiny, as he seemed to retreat to some place of his own on such occasions, as if only making his presence felt when she required it. But then she decided she was being histrionic. Nandru had just rescued her from having the tor cut away from her – along with a chunk of flesh sufficient for Thote's purpose – so he had probably saved her life.

'Thank you,' she said, at last heaving herself to her feet and getting a wider view of her surroundings.

Polly was now seeing what she would have called desert, or perhaps tundra, for only these landscapes did she associate with such an absence of life. However, the temperature here was that of a balmy spring day, and the air felt neither freeze-dried nor baked dry of moisture. Under these conditions, the landscape – strewn with boulders, drifts of powdered and flaking stone, blackened with falls of volcanic ash and divided by a sparkling river – should technically be burgeoning with life. The only evidence of such was the occasional smear of green to leaven a monochrome vista. Walking woodenly, Polly headed for the river.

There was nothing alive in the sparkling torrent. Stooping down, Polly scooped up water in the container, and drank. The liquid was cold and tasted of soda. She hadn't drunk anything so sweet in . . . a long time. She then refilled the container, pocketed it, and headed back for the seashore, wondering when she would die of shellfish poisoning.

With his breath held, and his understanding of the tor's operation complete, Tack willed it to materialize its pseudo-mantisal. But that failed when a lack of breath forced him to will it back into the *real.* He folded out of interspace in midair, the straps of each pack grasped firmly in each hand, and plummeted into reedlike growth and lukewarm water. Then, treading over a mat of rhizomes and stirring up black silt, he waded towards an island made of either mud or rock, which he had glimpsed as he fell. An hour later, exhausted, and with hunger engendered by the parasite on his arm eating into his guts, he reached the mudflat abutting a contorted hook of stone. Crawling up across the muddy slope, still dragging his packs behind him, he finally reached the remains of a lava flow and rested gratefully.

Saphothere must already be dead, or rather would be dead some indeterminate time in Tack's current mainline future. It didn't help to contemplate that too deeply as, without expending amounts of energy not available to the Heliothane this far back, time travel was not accurate enough to correct such errors – to save Saphothere's life. Now only the mission remained.

After a moment Tack stood up. Some distance ahead a gigantic tree reared out of the green battle between horsetails and ferns in a wayward promontory of forest hemmed in by the endless sea of sword-shaped emerald reeds. Gazing at this scene, Tack felt disquiet: that tree was not the right shape, the horsetails were tentacles beating at the ferns in seasonal slow motion, and the ferns themselves grew chaotically from their rhizome trunks. This seemed brute growth without complexity, a war rather than an environment, as if balance of coexistence had yet to be found. And the reeds were like dumb spectators to it all.

Just one glimpse was enough to tell him that he had arrived in the Devonian age. Here he knew that there might be a few tetrapods about, but that those ferns were loaded with cyanide, there was no fruit of any kind, and that all available tubers would have the consistency of saturated balsa and be as nourishing. He moved over to the other side of the lava flow, where it plunged down into deep water, and washed the mud from his suit. Returning above, he opened his supply pack, took out his concentrated rations and, seated on the stone, staring down the mudflat, began methodically to fill himself. He was very hungry. His tor was hungry.

As Tack understood it, a mantisal consumed a similar amount of nutrition from its temporary host as did a tor, and the length of its time-jump was also commensurate. But while the mantisal also needed to charge itself like a huge capacitor, the tor did not. It was a fact the Heliothane did not like to admit, that the tor was as far in advance of the mantisal as the hydrogen-powered aircar was in advance of the Model-T Ford. Without recharging, the mantisal jumped inaccurately – the error could be as much as a hundred million years. The tor always jumped accurately and greater control could be exerted at the point of exit. The only problem with the tors was being programmed to jump only in one direction in time: *back* towards Cowl. No heliothant had yet managed to change that programming.

While he continued eating, Tack noticed movement in the shallow trench his progress had left in the mud. Creatures similar to mudskippers were flopping and bubbling out of the water, gobbling up something he had disturbed to the surface of the mud. Which one of those might it be, he wondered. Could it be the one over there the size of a mature salmon, or the one with the purplish warty skin and eyes like tomatoes? Or was it this little one with whitish skin, sunken eyes, and large flippers that propelled it across the mud at such speed? Which one was his grandad a billion times removed? At that point the white one got too close to the warty one, and the ugly fellow snatched it up and chomped it down, so Tack assumed the warty one was the more likely candidate. This was life on land in the first days – beginning as it meant to continue.

Contemplatively Tack bit off a lump of protein concentrate and threw the remains out to the creatures. They slopped themselves away from it at first, then after a short time circled back in and began fighting over it. Eventually the warty one scuttled off with the prize in its thick lips. Replete himself, and then some, Tack set up his tent, crawled inside it, wrapped himself in the heat sheet and was instantly asleep.

With her regenerating arm locked around his neck and the snout of her weapon jammed up underneath his chin, Saphothere felt he was no longer in a position to resist Meelan. Thus sprawled on the ground, the both of them observed the incursion folding itself back into a fuzzy line in the air, as it closed then disappeared.

'Right, get up. Put your hands on your head,' Meelan hissed. 'One wrong move and you know what will happen.'

She drew away from him, keeping her weapon aimed at his back, and stood waiting while he assumed the position. His carbine lay on the ground only a metre to the side of him, but even as he glanced at it two Umbrathane women stepped out from different parts of the jungle and began jogging up the slope. As they converged on the campsite both of them studied Saphothere with evident hostility.

'Iveronica,' Meelan acknowledged the woman Saphothere recognized as the leader of the Pig City Umbrathane.

Stepping forward Iveronica said, 'I saw Coolis go, but what about the rest?'

The other woman, who could have been Meelan's double, but for the fact that her lower jaw had been replaced by a metallic prosthesis, hissed, 'Golan was dragged through with the tor-bearer. Olanda is on his way.'

Saphothere grinned at the jawless woman. 'What did you say? That wasn't very clear.'

Meelan belted him across the back of the head, knocking him down on all fours.

'Soudan, we need him.' Iveronica restrained the jawless

woman, whose carbine was now trained on Saphothere's midriff. 'Put it up.'

'What do we need him for?' Soudan lowered her weapon. 'Cowl has given us our way to him and soon all Heliothane will be extinct.' She gestured to where the incursion had appeared earlier, and where eight thorny objects were scattered on the ground.

'Information,' said Iveronica. 'Cowl won't be pleased that we didn't capture the torbearer.' She glanced aside. 'Here's Olanda now. That's all of us?'

'Yes, all,' conceded Soudan. 'That fucking primitive got Oroida and burnt Golan before she jumped him. I doubt she survived the drag-through – she was a real mess.'

'He was augmented,' said Iveronica, her face expressionless as she gazed at Meelan. 'That's why he first escaped. Golan and Oroida knew this. They made an error.'

Soudan was glaring at Saphothere, and did not seem to register her companion's words. She was probing her prosthetic jaw as if she felt it might fall away.

'Obviously not as genetically advanced as your fellows,' said Saphothere. 'How long ago in your time has it been since I just missed hitting that sack of shit between your ears?'

With a snarl Soudan swung her weapon back up. But then a shot hit Soudan squarely between the eyes, spraying Iveronica with pieces of her bone and brain. Saphothere rolled smoothly, snatching up his carbine and firing at the Umbrathane leader as she shook the bloody mess from her eyes. Meelan turned, just as smoothly, and put a cluster of shots into Olanda's chest, flinging the man back in an explosion of gore. Fire cut up into the sky as Iveronica went down, one leg blown away at the knee. She tried to bring her weapon to bear, but further shots from Saphothere smashed away her weapon and her right arm.

Saphothere stood and glanced round at Meelan. 'That could have gone better.'

'How so?' asked Meelan tightly, as she holstered her weapon and strode over to stare down at Iveronica. 'I don't see any of them getting up again.'

The Umbrathane leader, Iveronica, looked up at the two of them.

'Why?' she managed, as she bled into the dirt.

'Seven thousand of our people were on Callisto,' spat Meelan. 'When you sat in your nice comfortable ships and leapt back through time with Cowl, what of them?'

'Losses . . . were inevitable,' said Iveronica.

'You could have picked them up. Callisto was under your control once Cowl erected the phase barrier. You didn't bother because my kind of Umbrathane has always been cannon fodder for your kind. My people were reduced to less than atoms.'

'Many have died in our cause.' Iveronica managed to push herself up onto her remaining elbow. The bleeding from her shattered arm had ceased as her body already began to repair itself. 'And you have betrayed them all.'

'Do you need to hear any more?' Saphothere asked Meelan.

Meelan turned and stared at him for a moment, then abruptly stooped, her right hand closing around the supine woman's throat and her left hand catching her flailing left arm. With a raised eyebrow Saphothere looked on while Meelan slowly choked Iveronica to death. When it was over, he said, 'You know, putting that mine on Tack was a bit risky.'

'Not really.' Meelan stood, still staring down at the dead woman. 'No paralytic on the glass, and I set it to detonate far enough away from him to cause no damage as long as he was wearing that suit.'

'I meant when he threw the damned mine at you,' said Saphothere, shouldering his carbine and turning away.

After a moment Meelan followed him and they walked down

the slope to where the incursion had manifested. Reaching the bottom, Saphothere turned over with the toe of his boot one of the many active scales discarded by the torbeast – one of the tors Cowl had made it leave behind for his Umbrathane allies.

'Well, friend Tack was a little more dangerous than we supposed,' said Meelan finally. 'I think Coptic could attest to that. Anyway, who are you to talk about taking risks?' She held up her hand and shifted it in its brace, inspecting it closely. 'Maxell is not best pleased with us, you know.'

'Of course I know. She made that plain when I finally brought Tack to New London. Apparently she didn't think I should have risked losing him for the sake of finding and destroying Pig City.'

Meelan turned to look at him. 'She perhaps sees the bigger picture.' She gestured back at Iveronica. 'Like she did.'

'Perhaps,' Saphothere conceded. 'But even Maxell would have to agree that the results have been . . . gratifying.' He again nudged one of the tors with the toe of his boot. 'Iveronica would have stayed in her stronghold and never have gone to Cowl until no other option was available. With Pig City gone, and her energy sources destroyed, she and those who survived with her became just as much refugees as any other Umbrathane, and like them, needed tors to escape nasty Heliothane killers like myself.'

Meelan snorted. 'Yes, everything has worked very nicely. But why this?' She was still inspecting her hand.

'Veracity.'

Closing her hand into a fist, Meelan abruptly spun round and drove it into Saphothere's torso. He accepted the blow without retaliating, dropping down on one knee and clutching his gut.

'Veracity,' she spat.

Regaining his breath, Saphothere said, 'Iveronica would have wondered about why only you and Coptic survived, and perhaps have been less inclined to give you the energy feed leading to Pig

City. Being badly injured, your continued hatred of Heliothane would be believed and they would understand how you had neglected to scan Tack.'

'And why atomics?'

Saphothere stood. 'I had to destroy those generators and there was no time to set up catalysers or conventional explosives. I knew there would be survivors and you would be amongst them – your mantisal, though damaged, was within easy reach. I also knew that with the generators destroyed it wouldn't be possible for Iveronica to get more than a few mantisals here – I did not want hundreds of umbrathants turning up. And I knew you would be amongst the riders. It could only work this way.'

'Survivors,' said Meelan, staring at him bleakly. 'I got out about a second ahead of the blast, with an enteledont trying to chew my head, and just rode out the bleed-over of that blast into interspace.'

'Comes with the territory.'

'I sometimes wonder precisely what your priorities are, Saphothere.'

'You know my priorities, Meelan. And you knew the dangers when you signed up with me,' Saphothere replied. 'Also I hope you fully understand how things are most likely to go from now on.'

'Yes, I understand,' Meelan hissed.

The glassy skeleton around her was veined with red, like glowing wires centred in cloudy black, and the air inside it stale yet again. To Polly it seemed like an engine pushed to its limits – a malfunctioning hydrocar driven to the point where the components of its engine were growing red hot. Every now and again it vibrated, as if something was going out of balance prior to some final smash. When this was becoming unbearable, she found she did not need to use much force of will to push herself out of this hell. Just looking into the grey and black, and contemplating summoning up that place of hyperspheres and endless surfaces, was enough to push her out into the real again.

No sea was visible, or audible, this time. She glimpsed twilit sky through boiling black smoke, a river of fire snaking down from the boiling caldera of a volcano, while a cataclysmic roar filled her ears. The stink of sulphur was strong and acrid. She sneezed as something salty and stinging went up her nose, then tasted grit and ashes in her mouth, stumbled away over whorled stone, the heat from which she could already feel through her boots, and that same stone shook and jerked under her like a dying beast. A boulder the size of a family car hammered down to her right, deforming around its glowing core rather than breaking, as it bounced once, smashing the larval crust beneath it to release gouts of yellow vapour, then crumping down a second time, much of its bulk penetrating down into a gas-formed cavern.

This is not a good place.

Eyes on her footing and her hand cupped over her mouth and nose, Polly began to run. Other lumps of hot rock came hammering down. She glimpsed something the size of a railway carriage drop down behind a rucked-up outcrop, raising a cloud of the black ash that lay in drifts and sooty lakes all about. Hot flecks settled in her hair, burning into her scalp.

Shift, for chrissake, shift!

But she couldn't. There seemed nothing left – no strength, no will.

The ground shuddered underneath her, and Polly glanced back as an eruption concealed everything behind her in a boiling cloud of red and grey, hurtling towards her with ridiculous speed, seeming to eat up the landscape as it came. From somewhere there was enough – the tor perhaps realizing that, in the face of this, it would not itself survive to take back even a fragment of her arm. She shifted, glimpsed grey and black which seemed only an extension of the vulcanism, the cage not even forming around her. She came out yelling in a roll across the surface of a lake of cold cinders, sunlight above, and only a hint of sulphur in the air.

Again the pseudo-mantisal had been unable to form, but this time not due to any lack of will on his own part, nor lack of nutrition from his tor. Something had grabbed him from interspace and pulled him down, and he rolled out of it, releasing his packs and drawing his carbine from its holster – now positioned on his back. Rough shingle and broken shell gave way underneath him as, coming up onto his feet, he swung, sighting his weapon around him. No one nearby. Focusing on the rock field at the head of the beach, he advanced, weapon still ready, and checked the most likely places of concealment. Still nothing. Which meant that whatever had pulled him from interspace might not be nearby – nor whoever had used it. But certainly they *would* be coming along. His programming impetus was pushing him to shift again, but not very strongly. He fought it – rebelling on an almost unconscious level – and won. Slinging the two packs over one shoulder, while retaining his carbine in his right hand, he returned to the rock field and found cover, where he waited while tucking into his concentrated food supplies and gulping his bottled water. Leaden fatigue was eating into him as some hours later the man came limping down the beach, leaning on a strut of vorpal glass.

Tack identified him as Heliothane or Umbra, but very old – something he had yet to see in either of their kind. The man paused by the trail Tack had left and looked up the beach to the rock field. Stepping out of cover, the butt of his carbine propped against his hip, Tack waited.

The figure waved an arm and struggled up the beach. Tack observed how the old man's decrepitude had seemingly increased of a sudden, and his own wariness increased. Even so, this man looked very ill. The clothing hung baggily on his thin frame and the skin of his pallid face was as near to the skull as was possible without him being dead.

'That's far enough,' said Tack, when the oldster was ten paces from him.

The man leant on his cane of glass and wheezed dramatically. 'At last,' he said and took a step forwards.

Tack gestured with the gun and shook his head. The man took another step nearer.

'One more step and I kill you,' said Tack and he meant it.

The man halted and held up a hand. 'My apologies, Traveller. It has been so long since I saw one of my own kind I can hardly believe you are real.'

'How long?' Tack asked.

'Fifty years, or thereabouts – I lose track.'

'Who are you?'

'The name's Thote. Poor Thote, stranded here; a casualty in a war that never ends or begins. Forgotten by those who sent me into battle.'

Tack thought the guy was laying it on a bit thick.

'And you are?' Thote asked.

Tack wondered to which of the two warring factions this old man belonged, and if that made any difference to any danger he might represent. Confident that, should he need to, he could take him down, he replied, 'My name is Tack, twenty-second-century human, sent to assassinate Cowl.' He watched for the other's reaction.

'Then we are allies,' said Thote, suddenly standing more upright. 'And I know about you, Tack. You are Traveller Saphothere's protégé and perhaps our best hope. Join me at my camp for some food – since I have no doubt you are hungry. Tell me your tales, then be on your way.'

Tack returned his carbine to its holster and took up his two packs. This provoked no reaction from the old man, so Tack guessed he would make his move, if any was intended, at some later point.

'Lead on,' he said.

Thote turned and began to trudge back up the beach.

'How is it you are here?' Tack asked, as they walked.

'The torbeast reared up from its lair, in its dead-end alternate, to attack Sauros and I was sent out as a spotter, and to delay it if I could. I used a displacement sphere and took out five per cent of its mass, dropping that into the Earth's core. But it hit my mantisal when I was in interspace, damaging it and knocking me down in this place.'

'You managed to pull me down here as well,' Tack observed.

'I did that.' Thote glanced back at him. 'My mantisal, though badly damaged, remains out of phase here. It can generate enough of a field to funnel travellers down into this time.'

'Resourceful.'

'Yes . . . I can do that, but I cannot leave here, or find sufficient nutrition to keep me alive for my full span.'

Tack did feel sympathy, but knew there was little he could do. Should he try to drag the man along with him at this stage in his journey, Thote would end up with the pseudo-mantisal materializing in his body, killing him instantly. Soon Thote turned inland from the beach and led the way to his encampment in the rock field. He had built himself a small stone hut, which was roofed with large empty carapaces. Before the entrance was the remains of a fire scattered round with fish bones. To one side lay a basket woven from some of the tougher growths that grew in the area, which contained dried stems for the makings of future fires. In front of the hut, Thote eased himself down into a bucket chair, obviously carved from a boulder over a long period of time.

'I'll prepare some food shortly,' said the old man.

Seating himself nearby, Tack said, 'No need – here.' He opened his supply pack, took out one of the rations containers and tossed it over, noting the hand that caught it moved as fast as a snake.

'There's water over there.' Thote gestured to where one of the collapsible water containers used by other travellers rested against a rock.

'No need, I've drunk enough,' said Tack, now increasingly suspicious of anything this man might offer him.

Thote opened his rations and began to eat, fast, one thin bony hand pecking up the food like an albino chicken. Then abruptly he stopped eating, his face turning grey. He jerked out of his seat, grabbed up his glass staff and stumbled forward, retching. Too rich for him, assumed Tack, after fifty years on the meagre diet provided by this environment. Tack stepped forwards, and, only as the staff lashed out towards him did he spot the red line glowing inside it like a lightbulb filament. The staff merely brushed his chest as he pulled away, but the discharge of energy from it slammed into him like a spade, flinging him backwards through the air. Hitting the ground heavily, he fought against the paralysing shock, pulling his handgun just as Thote bore down on him with the butt of the staff. Thote halted as Tack levelled the gun at him.

'Um . . . Umbra . . . thane?' Tack managed, pushing himself up onto one elbow.

'Everything I told you is true,' said the man, his voice less quavering now.

'Well . . . tell me what you were trying to do?'

'Just take your supplies.'

Tack realized that fifty years alone here had also impaired the man's ability to lie convincingly.

'No, that's not it.' Tack hauled himself up onto his knees. Thote's gaze flicked to Tack's left forearm and quickly away. 'It's my tor you were after. But surely you know you couldn't use it – it's genetically keyed to just me.'

Thote's expression wrinkled with contempt. 'Is that what they told you, primitive? Is that their explanation to you for sending you alone on your pathetic mission?'

'What are you talking about?' Tack growled.

'Like the girl who passed through here fifty years ago, you're just a piece of temporal detritus. In your case primed and filled with poison, then sent on its way.'

Here was another one of those arrogant Heliothane, like others in Sauros and New London, who obviously thought Tack a waste of time and energy. With a kind of weariness he noted the old heliothant turning himself slightly sideways to present a smaller target. Any moment now he would try for Tack's gun.

'What girl?' Tack asked, trying to forestall the inevitable attack.

'She called herself Polly. Just another of Cowl's uptime samplings.'

Polly.

Almost from the instant Traveller Saphothere had captured him, Tack had forgotten the girl who had been the reason for him ending up on this insane journey. He felt a sudden loneliness – a craving to be with someone from a more familiar era. Almost distractedly he watched Thote tensing to make his strike.

'Don't try it,' Tack warned. 'Tell me about this Polly. What did you do with her?'

'Drugging her was simple,' said Thote. 'I put just a bit in the food I gave her, since I needed to keep her alive.'

'Why alive?'

'Because at the moment of a torbearer's death, the tor itself begins to feed directly on the substance of its host's body and thereafter shifts unremittingly back to Cowl.'

'What happened?'

Thote looked momentarily puzzled. 'She should not have been

able to. The drug acts on the cerebrum first before paralysing the nervous system.'

'She escaped?'

'She . . .' Thote fell forwards, his legs sagging, then abruptly he twisted round, the staff leaving his hand in a glittering wheel towards Tack's head. Like a spring uncoiling, he then hurled himself forwards in a flat dive. It was well done, and had not time and bad diet left the man so weakened, he might have been a formidable adversary. But he was not quite fast enough. Tack ducked under the flying staff, sidestepped quickly and brought his gun butt down on the back of Thote's neck. He stepped away as the man hit the ground, rolled and came up in a crouch.

'No,' warned Tack, but he wasn't getting through. Thote had that look in his eye: he didn't care. This was his last chance. Tack pulled the trigger as the man came at him again. Five rounds hit Thote square in the chest and flung him back. He collapsed in the cold ashes of his own fire, coughing blood from his shattered chest, then just tipped over into a foetal curl. Tack walked over to check his pulse; it was best to be sure. Confirming Thote was dead, Tack turned and picked up his packs, then went into the man's hut to find somewhere to sleep.

16

Engineer Goron:
The fusion explosion was contained within the temporal barrier, but even so a wash of radiation bled through the phase change. It did not take long to calculate that the bleed-over was not concomitant with the explosion that utterly erased Callisto. Had this been the case, the entire Jovian system would have been irradiated. It is certain that the bulk of the vast energy output from the explosion powered a time-jump no one believed possible. Cowl has taken himself all the way to the Nodus and, as far as we can ascertain, the Umbrathane fleet is scattered throughout the ages between then and now. The spatial shift, predictably, was towards Earth. I have to admit that what the Umbrathane might do does not bother me greatly, as I have little doubt that their ships will be unusably radioactive and so will need to be abandoned. But Cowl . . . a creature capable of snuffing out four hundred million lives so easily? Even the two Umbrathane prisoners, Coptic and Meelan, agree that something must be done now, probably because their troops also died when Callisto was obliterated.

In the rock pools there were trilobites and white slugs with hinged shells on their backs. Feverish, and aching with hunger, Polly caught both types of creature by hand, and swallowed them still alive and kicking.

Disgusting, Polly, absolutely disgusting.

Nandru was standing right behind her, for she could see his reflection in the water. But when she turned, he evaporated. She gulped down more, stuffing the horrible creatures into her mouth, all briny and stinking while her teeth chomped through their green-packed innards. Eventually she forced herself to her feet.

The sea had begun rushing back across the plain of frozen lava, and not wishing to be caught by the fast-approaching tide, she turned back towards the foothills. She was aiming for a patch of still-warm lava back there, where she had slept much of the previous night, but the tor would not allow her this luxury. Its webwork turned steely inside her and dragged her down like a claw. She shifted yet again through night, in a cage glowing incandescent, to a place barren and hammered by filthy rain. There she managed to drink her fill of bitter water, then was shifted again. In another place, duned with black sand, she staggered towards a horizon, where she hoped to find relief, something. Inside her greatcoat her ribs were now protruding. At her side walked Nandru, a frown puckering his brow.

I think it knows you will find no food here, and thus nothing to nourish it with, so it is feeding on you – using you up, killing you.

'Help me.'

And how is he supposed to do that, young lady? He's only a hallucination.

The boat captain, Frank, was standing there, chuffing on his pipe, Knock John naval fort standing tall in the sands behind him. Polly supposed that the droning in her ears must be the sound of bombers flying over.

'Stop it . . . make it stop.'

I cannot, and if I could, how would you live here?

That was Nandru, *really* speaking to her. She stared at the great maunsel fort and realized she was only seeing memory, not reality. When Fleming, the man from military intelligence, eyed her, seeming about to ask a question, she turned away from him. And in doing that she saw her own footprints stretching ahead of her, and realized she had been walking in a wide circle. As if impatient with this impasse, the tor shifted her again. And the nightmare not only continued – it grew worse.

Polly was too exhausted, too utterly depleted to care any more, and knew that the future span of her life encompassed maybe this shift and one more, but no more than that. Her clothes were now as baggy on her body as her skin was on her skeleton. She was like a fleshless waif staggering out of Belsen, whom food would probably not prevent from dying. Around her the glassy cage glowed incandescent, as if she had been trapped within tangled rods of white-hot steel, and she could see little beyond it. The shift back into the real she felt as a violent sideways motion, reminiscent of that preceding her arrival in Thote's time. Around her the world bled back into existence, in shades of iron and glass, but the cage did not dematerialize. Instead it dropped to a flat metallic surface, deforming on impact as if made of dough, while vapour began to pour from it. Within the vorpal struts the glow faded down to red filaments, as the glass itself began to splinter and crack. Polly weakly nudged at one strut and it snapped like a sugar stick. Just then a figure loomed over her and began tearing open the rest of the cage.

'Oh God . . .'

I suspect you have arrived, said Nandru.

Polly did not have the energy to scream as a skeleton wrapped in shadow was revealed through the shattering struts of the cage. Then, after a moment, she realized that this was not what she was really seeing. But still the rangy dark figure terrified her. Even some evil demonic face might have been more acceptable than the featureless ovoid that was his head. The skeletal impression, she now saw, was created by a network of hyaline ribs and veins inlaid into his black carapace.

Cowl, I would guess.

Too weird, far too weird, Polly thought.

Cowl grabbed her, one long hand closing round her thigh, and jerked her up out of the wreckage of the cage. The blood-rush to her head, as she was held suspended, made the world fade in and out of focus for Polly, but she saw that blank face tilt as she was inspected like some interesting bug. Then, with one swipe of his free hand, he tore away her greatcoat, pulling it down and over her head and off her arms. Then he caught her flailing arm, long fingers closing doubly around the tor. Inside her she felt the webwork jerk, then sensed the horror of it withdrawing, pulling back – its elements coiling up like the tentacles of an octopus dropped in boiling water. Then Cowl released his hold on her hip and she dropped, her arm wrenching painfully as she was suspended only by the tor. Cowl now gripped her elbow and pulled the tor closer to his blank face for inspection. It was as if Polly herself was utterly irrelevant – a pendulous piece of rubbish attached to the real centre of his interest. With vision now blurred, she saw him probing at the edge of the tor with one sharp finger, then drive the digit in. Polly howled.

The tor loosened, peeled up and she slid out of it like a mollusc discarded from its shell. Hitting the floor on her boots, consciousness fled her for only a moment, then she found herself lying over on her side, her arms stretched out before her face. The one from which the tor had been removed was now a flayed mess of tendons and exposed muscle.

You have to move, Polly. You have to escape.

Easy enough advice from someone who had probably forgotten what it was to be at the limit of endurance. From where she lay, Polly could see Cowl squatting, with his knees projecting way above his head, running long fingers around the inside of the tor, before abruptly sending it skittering across the floor. Gasping from an agony that just went on and on, Polly became subliminally aware of her surroundings – of curving walls of ribbed metal inlaid with esoteric circuitry, seemingly fashioned of other coloured metals and polished crystal. Above her, yellow light beamed down from a circular skylight; while, opening at intervals around the wall, were doors revealing a gleaming chaos beyond; and beside her, at the bottom of a slope, an intestinal tunnel dropped down into darkness, into which the now discarded tor had fallen. But mostly her attention was fixed on Cowl himself as he stood, with a motion both abrupt and fluid. The man – the creature? – was about to stride away, but then turned and stepped back towards Polly. This was it – he was going to kill her.

However, that was not his intention at all. Almost impatiently he snatched her up by the shin and in one motion, turning to leave, tossed her towards the tunnel's black mouth – like so much garbage.

Polly yelled as she slid down a frictionless slope, she flailed to grab at one side with her undamaged arm, but her hand slid off metal that had the feel of slime, and she plummeted down into blackness. In the brief, hurtling transit that followed, she coiled up protectively around her damaged arm. Then she shot out into yellow daylight, dropping to hit a ledge, to which she clung briefly, but seeing it occupied by skeletons and decaying corpses, screamed and released her hold. She then struck water, cold and salty, and began to sink. Polly still had some fight left in her – struggling weakly for the surface, her flayed arm burning in the brine – but in her weakness and confusion, she took in a breath, and the numbing water filled her lungs, curtailing her struggles like a body blow.

Polly, I am so sorry . . .

Drifting in golden depths, Polly now knew her ending. But then a beetle-black hand grabbed her under the chin, and some monstrous being began to haul her back to the surface.

The pseudo-mantisal completed around Tack on the next shift; then on the following one he observed the red filaments expanding in its structure as it pushed to its limits, hurtling for home.

Each time-jump he estimated to be in the region of a hundred million years. At each barren destination reached he stuffed himself with food and drink, taking glucose and vitamin supplements to stave off that point when the tor, detecting his blood sugars had dropped below a certain level, would become truly parasitic on him. This, he knew from the study of numerous torbearers encountered by the Heliothane, was the point of dying for many of those not killed by carnivorous fauna earlier in their journeys – their decaying bodies, still dragged back to Cowl, being fed upon by their tors.

Arriving here in a time when no life yet existed on the land, not even smears of blue-green algae, he set up his tent in the shelter of a frozen lava flow sculptured like some vast wormcast and, while sitting in front of it, ate and drank his fill. Thereafter transferring the remainder of his rations to the pack containing his equipment, he walked away from the tent – and immediately came upon a fellow torbearer.

She was sprawled on the ground, and wore the tattered remains of a richly decorated Elizabethan dress. There was a net of pearls holding her once dark – but now bleached-ginger – hair in an elaborate style. It confounded him how she had managed to keep it secured this way throughout what must have happened to her. Then he realized she had likely died much earlier on her journey through time, to be fed upon by her tor as she decayed. This was perhaps why her tor and the arm it had once enveloped were both gone – breaking away from the putrefying remnants of her body. The desiccating wind here had mummified her, and her hollow eye sockets gazed up endlessly into the sky. Tack turned away from the corpse and headed back to his tent.

Spewing brine from her lungs, Polly returned to abrupt and painful consciousness. The troll who had been battering at her chest now turned her unceremoniously into the recovery position and reached out to touch something recently attached to the side of her neck. Polly felt something happening – then recognized a drug hit coursing through her bloodstream.

Coughing up the last of the sea water, she rolled over onto her back and lay gasping below the lemon sky. But no matter how hard she inhaled, she was simply not getting enough air into her lungs. Then her rescuer loomed over her, a grotesque insectile mask covering its face. Polly baulked when a six-fingered hand offered her a similar mask, but she was too weak to resist as it was pressed wetly over her face.

Blessed oxygen surged into Polly's lungs. Within a moment she was feeling light-headed, but then, with a sound like a liquid kiss from inside the mask, the air mix changed to normal.

With her vision clearing, Polly studied her rescuer. The woman's skin was a metallic grey, glassy veins inset in its surface just like Cowl's. A wide and powerful body was contorted by a hunched back, and supported on bowed legs. Her arms were malformed: the left arm, grotesquely muscular, terminated in a three-fingered hand that looked strong enough to crush granite, while her right arm was of normal size, but possessed a hand with two opposable thumbs. This strange creature stooped closer and said something to her she did not understand.

'It hurts,' was all Polly could say in reply.

The other woman shook her head, muttering something that sounded foul, then stepped back towards some thing squatting behind her. Polly felt her skin crawling when she got a good look at it. The size of a pony, it rested on four spiderish legs, its jointed neck jutting forward from the thorax, then slanting back to support a wasp-like head the size of a football. The thorax itself was translucent green and packed with circuitry in which lights constantly glinted. The wasp-striped body behind was covered by nacreous wings which the woman lifted up, like the lid of a box, to delve inside. Removing something from the robotic insect's body, the grotesque woman came and squatted down beside Polly, indicating her injured arm before holding out a cylinder that hinged open in two halves to reveal a moist interior that seethed. Polly instantly made to back away from it.

She's trying to help you, Polly. That's some kind of wound dressing, I'll bet.

Reluctantly heeding Nandru, Polly held out her injured arm and the woman closed the cylinder round it. At first there was alarming movement and pain then, thankfully, her arm abruptly numbed. Grabbing Polly's upper arm, the woman hauled her to her feet.

'Abas lo-an fistik trous,' the woman said, then shook her head. Abruptly she reached over to Polly's hip bag and neatly opened it with her twin-thumbed hand. Taking out Polly's taser, she inspected the device for a moment before returning it and sealing the hip bag shut. That reminded Polly the automatic was still in her coat, but she felt no inclination to go back for it.

The troll woman then spoke words in what sounded like Chinese, then Russian. Finally she said, 'Century human what is?' before going on to try another language.

When Polly finally figured she had been asked a question, she replied, 'Twenty-second.'

The woman paused, then said, 'You are lucky . . . to be alive. Few attain . . . this . . . location, or survive long after their arrival.'

'Why . . .?' Polly asked, not sure exactly what she was asking.

'Cowl normally kills before discarding. He must have been distracted – either that or he does not care any more.' Suddenly the woman's speech was totally lucid.

Polly stared at her rescuer in bewilderment.

'It is complicated to explain. You will not be able to walk?' Testing her theory, the woman released her grip – then caught Polly as she began to slump. 'I see not.' Abruptly the strange female ducked briefly and, slinging Polly easily over one shoulder, she stepped to the insectile robot and dropped the girl down on her feet beside it, gesturing to the compartment revealed by the hinged-up wings.

'Not comfortable, but it is either that or on my shoulder.'

Polly nodded and the woman helped her into the cramped compartment, her legs dangling over the rear. Glancing round, she saw the robot's head turn to inspect her briefly, then tilt slightly, as if in query, before facing forwards again. As the woman moved off, the robot followed her dutifully, the sharp tips of its legs driving deep into the ground in sequence. It moved just like an insect, and utterly silently, with no hydraulic sounds, no hiss of compressed air. Polly had half expected to be thrown from side to side, but the compartment remained precisely level all the time.

The woman led them away from sand and out across a fragmenting lava flow. Orange-brown clouds now scudded across the yellow sky and, to Polly's right, the sea in which she had so nearly drowned reflected those colours. Wavelets foamed on a reef of jagged stones, and beyond, where the coast curved round, she now saw a huge flower-shaped citadel, from which she had obviously been ejected earlier.

Simulacra of life – excepting Cowl and this one here – and nothing else. Seems you have finally reached your destination.

'*And now what?*' Polly subvocalized.

Has anything really changed? You must just try to stay alive.

'*Maybe that's not enough any more. Maybe I'd like to do something about that faceless bastard that fucked me over.*'

A fatal course of action, I would suggest.

Polly gritted her teeth in growing anger.

With the pseudo-mantisal fighting against ablation with an outpouring of energy, Tack knew this would be the last shift, so he prepared himself. The ultraviolet light baking the Earth would be no hazard for him, since part of his augmentation had been an artificial epidermis resistant to such radiation, but the lack of oxygen was a problem. He donned the hated mask, before closing up his pack and shrugging it onto his back. With his carbine dangling before him on its strap, and the Heliothane U-sound injector clasped in his right hand, he now concentrated on the vorpal view of interspace. Cowl's tor trap was likely to be automatic, so whether or not Tack was expected, it would try to drag him quickly down into Cowl's abode and that Tack must not allow. He wanted to reconnoitre, get the feel of his prey's location, then come at him from some unexpected direction. He no longer felt any great impatience or eagerness for his task, just a stolid determination reinforced by seeing the Elizabethan corpse back there. Above all, Cowl had to die because of the suffering he had already caused and because of what he intended.

The hyperspheres and infinite surfaces, the lines of light and impossible distortion appeared in Tack's perception and he saw, in 3D representation, the trap swaying towards him like the funnel of a tornado. With rigid will, he grasped control of the webwork inside himself and forced the tor and its generated mantisal aside from the approaching funnel and down into the real. The webwork fought him, like a horse being urged at too high a jump, but Tack's will was strong because, his physical being having been bolstered by food concentrates, the tor had not managed to weaken him with the lethal parasitism that became usual at this late point of the journey. The pseudo-mantisal evaded the funnel, folded out of interspace and bounced, splintering, onto a dusty plateau. Shattering all about him on its second bounce, it began to ablate as if hit by a molecular catalyser.

As the construct disintegrated, Tack tumbled out of it in a roll. Then he was up and running, the tor so tight around his arm it paralysed his hand. He dodged into a dried-out gulley eaten down through friable rock, then along its course and came up between butts of black volcanic rock. Glancing back he saw a white rocket flame curving out from the horizon, impelling a black polygonal container. The missile hit at his arrival point, and detonated, blowing up a pillar of fire that rolled out clouds of dust.

Tack allowed himself a nasty grin – in his paranoia Cowl had given away the location of his refuge. All Tack had to do now was track back along the missile's trajectory.

Tack now stripped off his pack and slid down, with his back resting against the black rock, then pulled up his sleeve and studied the tor. It was a boiled-lobster red now, having filled itself with his blood as it sucked in the energy to fling itself to its intended destination. Inside him he could feel the webwork hardening again quickly. He pressed the injector against the tor's hard surface, feeling a brief vibration, then removed it to see a spill of chalky powder around a cluster of pin-holes, through which the catalytic poison had just been injected. Slowly the tor began to change colour, veins of black spreading across its surface and its rubescence fading to white. Inside him, Tack felt the web was dying – retreating from his extremities. Eventually the tor hung dead on his arm.

Taking up his pack again, Tack strode through the billowing dust clouds from the explosion, and set off in the direction of the missile's source. After an hour he reached the edge of the plateau and there made his camp – concealed behind a boulder starred with large quartz crystals. Inside his tent, well sealed against the external atmosphere, he paused to eat and drink his fill, before stepping outside, safely masked again, and heading to the plateau's rim. Before him lay a plain veined with rivers, encroached on from one side by a field of frozen lava. Broken rock was scattered everywhere, the detritus of some ancient cataclysm.

However, down below lay the remains of other less natural

structures, which Tack would not have recognized without Pedagogue's teaching. For here lay the remains of the entire research facility that Cowl had taken back through time, and across space, from Callisto. Witnessing this ruination, Tack recalled the gutted spaceships that lay decaying by Pig City. Clearly they were vessels from the Umbrathane fleet which Cowl had also dragged back through time.

The plain eventually narrowed into a peninsula projecting out into a golden sea, its water reflecting the lemon sky. To one side of this peninsula rested Tack's true destination – not those ruins below him, for Cowl had built anew in the three centuries since his flight.

Supported above the sea on a forest of pillars, the citadel bore the shape of an open water lily. The structure was as beautiful as it was huge. Though still ten kilometres away from it, he estimated that the tops of its petals, glowing with lights, must pierce cloud. So that was where Cowl lived – and where Tack intended him to die.

The structure squatted on a slab of basalt poised at the top of a slope leading down to the wide but shallow river they were currently crossing. It was dome-shaped, closely arched all around, so that only narrow points of exterior wall between these arches actually reached the ground. Through most of the arches glinted windows, though Polly could just see that one of them opened directly into the interior. Too tired to keep turning her head round to look at it, she gave up and faced back down the way they had come. Realizing that they were now travelling in bright moonlight, Polly tried to remember some of the journey that had brought them here, but she had been fading in and out of consciousness so often that it remained a blur.

'What's your name?' she finally managed to croak to her travelling companion.

'Before I was born, my mother named me Amanita because I poisoned her in the womb and had to be removed, completing my early growth in an amniotic tank. As soon as I could, I renamed myself Aconite.'

'Why that?'

'Because it seemed appropriate.'

Polly found she had run out of the energy to pursue this line of questioning, so bowed her head and lost it for a second. Coming to, she saw that they had now reached the other side of the river and were about to climb the slope towards what seemed likely to be some kind of house.

Aconite is an interesting word.

Nandru, who was walking alongside the robot, gazed across it with a twisted expression at the strange woman.

'How so?' Polly asked out loud.

It is an alternative name for the poisonous plant also called wolfsbane or monkshood.

'And that's interesting why?'

I see you don't get it. You must try harder; since you're now so closely linked into Muse's reference library, the information is available to you.

'I still don't understand . . .' Then Polly did get it. 'I didn't know what Cowl meant before. I see . . . cowl is the name for a monk's hood.'

Abruptly she realized her robot transport had stopped moving. She glanced the other way and saw that Aconite was standing watching her. Turning back revealed that the illusory Nandru had disappeared.

'I realize now that your words are not entirely the result of delirium.' The troll woman stepped forward and reached down beside Polly into the back of the robot. Removing a square palm console, Aconite held it in her heavy three-fingered hand while running the nimbler fingers of her other hand over the machine's display. After a moment she looked up, reached over and pulled aside the filthy collar of Polly's blouse. She touched first the muse device briefly, before reaching up to flick Polly's earring.

To Polly she said, 'Speak to your hidden companion.'

Oh-oh, looks like I've been rumbled.

'That is enough,' said Aconite before Polly could say anything to Nandru. 'Now, are *you* AI?'

Polly tried to overcome her confusion, but her brain was washing around inside her head like dirty water.

Nandru's voice issued from the palm console. 'Well, that's a moot point,' he said. 'I guess that's what I am now, but I wasn't always like this. You've caught me on a bad day.'

'You are a cerebral download,' Aconite said, disapproval in her voice. 'Yes, I see. A military log-tac computer with secure comlink, and the facility set for partial download of tactical information in the event of death. It would seem the level of redundancy was excessive and that you took advantage of that. So dead soldier, what is your name?'

'Nandru. And I resent being addressed that way, that's . . . thanatist.'

With a snort, Aconite switched off the console and dropped it back into the compartment beside Polly. Turning away, she snapped her fingers, and the robot began to follow her again.

I think she likes me.

Mounting the slope, the robot did not tilt in the least. With its back legs stretching down at full extension, its front legs bent double like a spider's, it maintained Polly perfectly level as it climbed the incline. Soon they reached the basalt slab and, as Polly twisted to look round, they began heading for the arched entrance. Close up, Polly saw that the building was huge.

Then through the entrance and crossing a wide room, with arched windows all around, containing the chaotic glinting of metal and glass – insectile sculptures or esoteric machines, Polly could not tell. A whoomph as the entrance closed behind them, then a breeze stirring up Polly's hair. The mask coming away from her face with a sucking sound. Also unmasked, Aconite picked her up from the robot's container and briefly Polly glimpsed golden eyes amid lopsided but not unattractive features. Then bright aseptic light and a soft table underneath her, clothing cut away, something cold against her chest – then a stabbing pain and a sense of movement inside her chest. Abrupt unconsciousness followed.

On waking, after long oblivion, to find some flesh miraculously back on her bones, Nandru told her, *He's her brother.*

And only later did she learn that she was the first of Cowl's samples to survive.

The cold and piercingly bright light of the full moon precluded sleep, as did the itching underneath his dead tor. Sitting in the tent, Tack picked at the edges of the thing as if it was a huge scab, and just like a scab it began to peel away from his flesh, but was frangible and snapped like charcoal. Revealed underneath it was pink scar tissue – forming so fast because of the Heliothane boosting of his body. He continued snapping away pieces of the tor and, bit by bit, broke the thing off. His arm looked grotesque and felt as if it had been burnt, so he quickly applied a wound dressing taken from his pack. His arm ached as well as itched and he realized he had very little chance of sleep now.

Once masked and outside again, Tack collapsed his shelter and stowed it away. Taking up his pack once more, he rounded the boulder and headed off. Cowl's citadel now glowed both with internal light and reflected moonlight, looking even more beautiful. Tack observed it in awe for a while, wondering why he had expected something ugly. Then he negotiated the steep slope down to the plain.

Within an hour he was back on level ground, then walking fast down a watercourse that wound in the general direction of the peninsula. He chose this route as a precaution against there being motion detectors aimed out across the plain above him. He suspected, though, that Cowl, if he entertained at all the possibility of the Heliothane getting through to him, would expect from them a massive assault, not a lone assassin.

After a further two hours, Tack reached a shallow estuary debouching beside the shoulder of the peninsula. Here he searched around until he found a trench formed by a wide crack in the granite, through which a small rill bubbled. Aiming to follow this as far as it would take him towards his destination, he was pleased when it continued meandering as far as a point adjacent to the citadel. On a nearby slab he again erected his tent, then climbed up the side of the trench to take a look.

Getting out to the citadel presented no problem. The sea would offer Tack more concealment than he had anticipated: since all his equipment was waterproof, by wearing his mask he could approach the place underwater. The problems started once he got inside it as, now gazing at the citadel through his monocular, he could see Umbrathane working on structures running round the outer surfaces of the lily's petals.

With the exception of those who had established Pig City, the Umbrathane had dispersed into cells as they had fled into the past, so presenting the usual problems of any guerrilla organization. It was not so much the damage they could inflict – their attacks were mosquito bites to the great beast that was the Heliothane Dominion – but the extravagant use of resources needed just to track them down. Saphothere had conjectured that Cowl might be gathering them to him – and this was the case. So, to locate Cowl, Tack must not only avoid the citadel's security system, but its hostile Umbrathane population as well.

Lowering the monocular, he decided that no matter what plans he made now, they would probably need to change once he entered the citadel. But the logistics programs Pedagogue had loaded him with were protean and his lethal skills at their peak. He must just go in and do what he had been sent to do. Sliding back into the trench, he opened his pack and began to extract those items that would assist him in the task.

First he donned a weapons harness, with all its stick pads and pockets to carry the necessary devices. Sliding the carbine into its back holster, next to the climbing-harpoon launcher, he hooked a further power supply and another two-thousand-round box for it at his right hip. A spare carbine he considered for one long moment, then left aside.

The five molecular catalysers – coins of red metal ten centimetres across, with a virtual console on the front – he pressed against stick pads in a line down one chest strap. Each of these was set to react with a different material, but each was also capable of being reset. Into one trouser pocket he emptied the pack of mini-grenades, and into the other he put the multispectrum scanner. The grenades were all set for a standard three-second delay – the countdown starting the moment they exceeded a one-metre proximity to the transponder in his weapons harness. Ten larger programmable grenades he attached around his belt; they were made of hard fragmentation glass and contained an explosive that made C4 look silly. His handgun, which could take the same explosive ammunition as the carbine, he adjusted for silent running – much like more primitive guns, with a silencer screwed onto the barrel, though this operated by slinging out a sound-suppressor beam in line with the bullet, generated by the same impelling charge.

Then he took from his pack the less standard items. Five field generators he attached to the other chest strap, their power supply operated from a thermal battery that burnt itself out within a few seconds. He hoped he would not need these, as it would probably mean he was on the run. The two tactical nukes – like the one

Saphothere had used on Pig City – went into a bag attached to the left-hand side of his belt. These he would use at his discretion. Finally he took out the last item: his seeker gun. It contained twenty rounds, and its system, via recordings, had already *acquired* Cowl. This he put in his thigh pocket, there being no position provided for it on the harness. He was ready.

As he climbed out of the trench and headed down to the sea, sealing his hood and pulling on his gloves, Tack wondered vaguely why he had not been provided with a long-range missile launcher, or one of those excellent Heliothane scoped assault rifles. But he dismissed that thought as he entered the water. It did not once occur to him to wonder how, once his mission was completed, he would be able to get away from this place and this time. His programming did not allow him that.

17

Engineer Goron:
We know that many thousands of torbearers have been dragged back through time towards the Nodus, but how many survived the journey we have no idea. It is also a matter for conjecture whether any who did survive the journey then survived their encounter with Cowl. His utter disregard for human life makes this seem unlikely. I have to admit to feeling some guilt at our contribution of Tack to that likely offhand slaughter, though with what is at stake it was wholly justified. But it makes me question our own regard for human survival, evolutionary imperatives and all that these entail. Is not Cowl the summit of our own aspirations? And does not our attitude to him prove the falsity of our world view?

The robot did not have a name, so Polly christened it Wasp and altered its programming so that it recognized when it was being addressed. Originally Aconite had designed it for one simple purpose: to check if those of Cowl's samples who caught on the ledge were still alive. For Wasp's wings not only served as a lid for its rear compartment; it could fly. Polly did suggest that it might be worth building an aquatic robot to retrieve those falling into the sea, but Aconite demurred. The woman liked to swim and had no wish to dispense with her reason for doing so. Consequently Polly learnt to swim as well, soon being able to cover the hundred metres out from the beach as fast as Aconite herself. But thus far neither she nor Aconite had managed to retrieve any survivors, so the accumulation of bones and slowly decaying corpses below the citadel continued to grow. Polly spent six months with Aconite before things changed.

Wasp tells me she's got a live one.

Immediately Polly rolled from her bed and stood up. Stepping naked into her shower cubicle, she switched it from water spray to UV-block, and closed her eyes while the moving shower head coated her skin with a substance that prevented her getting flayed by the ultraviolet outside. The block being quickly absorbed, she stepped out of the shower, pulled on the skin-tight garment that served as both clothing and wetsuit, slipped on her boots, whose loose upper material immediately tightened around her ankles, then took up her mask and headed outside. Aconite was trudging up the slope, with Wasp, heavily laden, following as usual.

'At last,' said Polly as she walked down to the troll woman, aware that the average had now become a live one for every two thousand dead, and that every death seemed to bruise something inside Aconite. Polly had come to realize that from childhood on it had always been Aconite's purpose to clear up Cowl's messes, to leaven his ruthless violence, and try to protect him from his own destructive impulses. She it was who had found for him a pre-eminent position amongst the Heliothane; and she it was who had come with him into the past, to continue performing her childhood duties.

'I had to knock him unconscious,' Aconite explained, holding up a sharp and perfectly maintained short sword in her heavier hand.

Studying the muscular man with his short-cropped grey hair, Polly recognized the leather armour he wore. She had seen similar armour on a corpse jammed under a deadfall in a stream in Claudian England. Tacitus Publius Severus, was the second rescuee.

After the Roman, who, they soon learnt, had encountered a Heliothane intercept squad at the beginning of his journey came three more almost in a rush. One was a feral boy without a name and without even a language, whom Polly dragged from the sea, and whom Aconite identified as from the dark age of the neuro-virus. Aconite cured him of his affliction and surgically implanted a cerebral augmentation to compensate for his partially destroyed brain; while Polly, being one to give names, called him Lostboy. Wasp, for the first time, brought in a man who had managed to cling to the ledge over the sea, and understandably he screamed all the way, beating at the robot with the rusting musket he still grasped. Identifying this little Chinaman, they made the mistake, because of the musket, of thinking him from an age earlier than from which he had actually come. He had been a thief during China's Cultural Revolution. They learnt from him how his robber band had been ambushed and slaughtered, by the People's Army, and how the torbeast had come to feast on the dead before leaving him his tor. The musket he had stolen from a Prussian soldier in a different age, and in yet another one claimed to have shot a dragon with it. The Neanderthal, Ygrol, smashed Wasp's sensor cluster with a bone club, fell twenty metres into the sea, swam ashore, then shouting all the way charged Tacitus and Lostboy, whose watch this was. With the flat of his gladius, Tacitus knocked the man out, dumped him on Wasp, then had to guide the robot back like a dog, when its sensor cluster finally burnt out.

'Why are they always men?' Polly asked, puzzled.

Because you are an exception, Polly. That you survived is a near miracle: men are built stronger, and most ages of Earth are hostile to women. Only in that distant future from which Cowl and Aconite came are women the physical equals of men. Look at those four. You have a boy who was feral; a Roman soldier who served most of his life in one of the toughest armies that ever existed; a Chinese thief and, unless I miss my bet, sometime murderer; and a Neanderthal who beats his next meal to death with the remains of his previous one.

Dangerous people: Polly had realized that as each of them had arrived. But after receiving educative downloads from Aconite's Pedagogue, they soon learnt how dependent they were on the heliothant, and kept themselves in line.

'Why me?' Polly asked – a question she had not asked in some time.

Survivors from concentration camps asked the same: how come I was caught so late? Why did that soldier's gun jam? Why was I chosen to load the furnaces? How was it they missed me under the mounded dead? Luck and statistics, Polly. Luck and statistics.

Polly knew all about statistics. Aconite had showed her only a few days after her arrival. Silently gesturing Polly to follow, the heliothant woman had led her down a spiral stair to the basement of her house.

'They are all dormant,' explained Aconite. 'Their programs run and erased the moment Cowl removed the recorded genetic information.'

Around every wall of the chamber ran racks stacked with the smooth carapaces of tors. There were thousands of the devices.

Polly fought for a suitable response. 'If . . . if all he wants is a genetic sample . . . why bring the whole person? He could take just one hair, a piece of skin.'

'To provide necessary nutrition for the tor. And because my brother just does not care.'

'Why do you collect them here?' Polly asked, realizing with a lurch that Aconite's interest in Cowl's samples might not be as altruistic as she had first thought. Did Aconite really want to save lives, or just to collect tors?

'One day the torbeast will sink into oblivion, so its temporal link to these will be severed. Then, on that day, wars will be confined to their era.' Aconite gestured to the tors. 'Those I recruit will make certain of that, for I will use them to police the ages.'

She dreams of peace, the rule of law, and right good justice. I bet every age has its idiots like her.

Polly did not consider Nandru's bile worth a response.

The seabed was littered with bones, and above it drifted the occasional negative-buoyancy corpse. Tack noted that most of the bones were from arms, so from that knew that many torbearers had not made it all the way back here intact, yet amid this decay he saw few tors and wondered why. The sheer numbers horrified even him. Recent reports of the megadeath this monster had caused had not brought home to him Cowl's utterly callous ruthlessness so much as did these sad thousands. Trudging through the skeletal remnants, weighed down by his weaponry, he finally reached a supporting leg of the citadel where it entered the seabed, and observed thick cables running down it into the detritus, then away along the bottom into misted depths. By scanning, he established the leg to be solid basalt. He fired his climbing harpoon upwards. Snaking out a thin line of braided carbon filament, it struck high, bonding with a dull chemical flash. Not bothering to hook the launcher to his harness, for the water was supporting most of his weight, he started its winder and it hauled him up.

Twenty metres from the bottom, and five from the surface, the basalt ended, the rest of the support being fashioned of metal. After scanning, he found it to be aluminium alloy, hollow, and filled with sea water. Tack pressed a catalyser against it and set the device for limited dispersement. He knew it was unlikely that this place had been built without anti-catalytic defences, so adjusting it to an unlimited setting would not dissolve everything made of this same alloy above him, but would only alert Cowl to his presence. Swinging aside on the line, he watched as the thing glowed, then a reaction spread out from it, as of pure magnesium dunked in water. The catalyser dropped away, grey and frangible, and broke up while the reaction continued. The sea grew cloudy with oxides, and pure hydrogen bubbled to the surface. When the hole was a metre wide the reaction abruptly ceased. Tack swung into the cavity and crouched on its lower rim, from where he sent a signal to detach the harpoon, which he rewound into its launcher. Leaning into the hollow of the leg, he fired directly upwards, watched the bonding glow above and hauled himself up again.

Soon he was out of the water and suspended below a domed ceiling. Scanning the metal above, he was momentarily surprised not to detect a sensor net. But then the theory still applied that Cowl had prepared himself for a mass attack rather than a lone assassin. The second catalyser got him through this ceiling into a floor space strewn with ducts, vorpal optics, and the dust and detritus that had fallen through the gridwork floor above. Here he took out one of the tactical nukes and set it for a one-hour delay, then jammed it under a duct, before going up to check the floor above him. He did not have to use another catalyser for access this time as the entire gridwork consisted of movable panels. Climbing through into a wide triangular corridor, he drew both his carbine and his handgun – the carbine set on microwave pulse – and advanced, glancing sideways into rooms that contained generators and silos, tangles of piping, and control consoles and other tech. From his psychological profile, he knew that Cowl would control all this complex from a central point – the nectary of the flower. Now Tack must find that point and the easiest way to do that was to get someone to tell him. Luck was with him, but not with the two Umbrathane he discovered working on a torpedo-shaped motor located under the floor panels.

The female was passing tools down to the male as Tack, moving cautiously, spied them around a bend in the corridor. He pulled back and observed them covertly for a second while he decided what to do. After a minute, carefully aiming his carbine, he waited until the male stuck his head above the floor plates, then fired once. The man's head split with a crack and a flare of greasy flame, steam and brains blasting up into the woman's face. As the man then collapsed back into the floor spaces, the woman forward-rolled, and came up groping for something on her belt. Tack's next two shots exploded first her biceps then her knee, and she went down with a yell. In an instant he was standing over her, holstering his carbine as she groped for the laser cutter on her belt. With his handgun he blew apart the elbow of her undamaged arm, snatched away the cutter, then jammed one of his ration packs into her mouth as a gag. Crushing down on her chest with one knee, he pressed the silencer into her eye and paused to scan up and down the corridor. No sign of action. After a moment he dragged the wounded female into one of the side rooms and, behind the insulated cowling of a generator, subjected her to interrogation techniques that owed as much to his prior U-gov training as his subsequent education by the Heliothane. When he had finished, he dumped what was left of her under the floor with her dead companion, kicking their tools in after them and sliding the grating back into place. Then he set off to find the central control sphere, about which she had told him as much as she could possibly bring to mind.

The whole place was packed with service floors and ducts, and it seemed that much rebuilding was in progress. The next man Tack came upon was supervising two spider-like robots welding plates over a long gap in the pipe running down one side of a corridor. This was the main corridor leading to Tack's destination, and by trying to circumvent him Tack knew he could get lost in this warren. With handgun levelled, he approached.

The man did not even look round, but said, 'It is going to take two hours – no less, no more.'

Tack shot him through the back of the head, then picked him

up and shoved him into the gap remaining in the pipe. The robots proceeded to plate over the corpse regardless. But such luck could not continue.

Another male umbrathant, driving a small vehicle towing a trailer stacked with struts made of vorpal glass, came around a bend, suddenly catching Tack with no place to hide. Tack hit him with a fusillade of pulses, throwing the man backwards out of his seat. The vehicle swerved into the wall, then skidded along to crash into a pillar, the trailer shedding its load in a racket of clanging glass. Tack spotted no one ahead, but behind him three Umbrathane came rushing out of a side tunnel.

Then it really started.

Tack tossed a handful of mini-grenades behind him as he ran. Spots glowed on the wall of the turning ahead, and he felt the superconducting mesh of his suit absorb rapid heating. He dropped, rolled aside in the stink of burning plastic, fired back. The first of them came over the grenades as they blew, flinging him up into the air along with some floor panels. Tack next pulled one of the larger grenades, already set for proximity detonation, pressed it against the wall low down, and ran around the corner. Now, because he might not find another chance, he yanked up a floor panel and dropped the second tactical below – its setting again for one hour. Ahead of him, more Umbrathane. He fired at them with both carbine and handgun, seeing one turned into a jerking bloody rag while the other rolled away for cover. Into a side corridor, running as the big grenade went off, blowing a wall of fire towards his back. Then he found himself where he wanted to be: out on a platform, with the inner face of the citadel curving in below him towards the central sphere, which was supported between four cylindrical pillars, each nearly as wide as it, with tangles of broad pipes spreading out like a web from its underside.

Tack dropped onto the curving slope below him and slid down

it. A figure appeared to his left on another platform. Tack flung himself sideways as shattered metal erupted in a line along the slope, flung himself forwards, then side-rolled again. Again that eruption. Then he reached one of the pipes and swung himself round it. More Umbrathane emerging on platforms. As they dropped down after him, he slapped a catalyser against the incline, set for full dispersement, and had the satisfaction of seeing them unable to stop their descent as the fire-rimmed hole spread up towards them. But no time to gloat: he hit the pillar with another catalyser, stepped behind a pipe for cover, firing at any movement he could see, while the device did its work.

Shots were coming now from all directions, slamming into the pipe and hammering the metal floor behind him, metal splinters whickering and hissing past him. He was now pinned down, but only briefly. Tossing down a field generator, he dived for the growing gap in the pillar just as the generator flung up its electrostatic wall. He dropped inside it, caught at a briefly glimpsed rail, and hauled himself up an access stair before the fusillade followed him inside. Hearing movement below, he dropped the last of his mini-grenades then set another proximity device against the wall to take out any pursuers. He continued climbing fast, entering a corridor that accessed the sphere. Here on the wall he set another grenade, this one for proximity with timed delay. Then into the sphere, where huge machines loomed in darkness, walkways spiralling around its interior wall, others reaching in towards the machines.

A dark figure was standing perfectly still on the floor below.

Cowl.

Tack felt a sudden stab of some unfamiliar emotion, which it took him a moment to identify as fear. He opened up with both weapons, turning the entire vicinity of the motionless figure into a chaos of explosions and smoking metal. But the figure just stood there, striations of rainbow light running all around it. Then a large, sharp-fingered black hand reached over Tack's shoulder and snatched away his carbine.

Tack dived to one side, came up firing his handgun. *Cowl?*

But then his attacker was gone and Tack was firing only into the falling wreckage of the carbine. Glancing over, he saw that the dark figure was still standing below. *Doppelgänger*, was his first thought, then it hit him like lead: *time travel.* Why hadn't they prepared him for this? But there was no time now for questions.

Movement underneath the walkway, a beetle head coming up beside him. He fired at it and it disappeared. He slapped down a grenade as he leapt away in the opposite direction. But Cowl was suddenly coming over the rail ahead of him *before* the grenade exploded behind Tack. Shooting again, the new arrival going up the wall and along it above him, fast. While tracking it with fire, he glimpsed the one on the floor below him disappearing. Then a hand hard as iron slammed into his back, driving him over the rail.

Tack knew then that he was dead. Cowl had supreme control in this place – possessing enough energy here to short-jump and avoid a short-circuit paradox. Tack spun around and fired as he fell, noticed the amber warning light on his gun but kept on firing until it flicked to red as it emptied.

Over a rail further below, a hand reached out and caught him, pulled him in and flung him down on the walkway floor. Cowl walking towards him. Tack flung a shield generator out as he back-flipped to his feet and turned to flee. He drew his seeker gun and emptied its magazine, firing *ahead.* A second Cowl came over the rail ahead, while the other one was somehow walking round the shields behind Tack. Seeker bullets were homing in like a swarm of bees on the second figure. There followed a blurring motion of hands, and bullets were thwacking to the walkway, where they detonated. But one, just one, missile exploded on black carapace.

This ended the game.

One black hand closed around Tack's throat from behind, and he was slammed up against the wall while, with such viciousness it broke bones and tore skin, the other one ripped away his harness, suit and all his weapons. Then Cowl flung him naked onto the grated floor. Sharp fingers then descended, piercing Tack's chest before closing, as Cowl picked him up like a cluster of empty milk bottles. Tack tried to fight back until Cowl swung his head against a wall and knocked all resistance out of him. As his consciousness waxed and waned, Tack thought it about time for him to die – but death was not a mercy Cowl intended to allow him.

The Umbrathane came and searched the house while Aconite stood with her unequal arms folded, silently watching them. When the search was completed with concision and efficiency, the leader emerged to stand before Aconite. Makali was a sour woman and Polly supposed this was because both her arms were obviously prosthetic, which meant she did not possess the regenerative gene and was thus an inferior type of umbrathant. In Polly's own time she would have been regarded as an exotic beauty, with her perfect white skin, black hair and lavender eyes; and also as a prize athlete with her future-human speed and strength. But in Umbrathane terms even Aconite was genetically her superior.

'You are inviolable,' said the woman in the Heliothane language.

'That is my brother's conceit,' replied Aconite.

To Polly, Nandru said, *Those explosions. Something shook them up last night, but it certainly wasn't an outright Heliothane attack, else we'd be sitting on a radioactive wasteland now.*

From where she was sitting, with her knees pulled up against her chest, Polly subvocalized, '*Probably a little internecine conflict. The Umbrathane always want to sort out which of them can piss the highest.*'

The woman waved her stumpy carbine at Polly and her four companions, who sat in a tight group. 'But these are not.'

Aconite slowly shook her head. 'What happened?'

'An assassin: a twenty-second-century human coming in by tor.' The woman turned and stared hard at Polly for a moment. 'But a human with Heliothane augmentations. We can only suppose some tor fragment was regenerated, as all the active tors are accounted for.'

'What about future tors?' Aconite asked mildly.

This really seemed to annoy the woman. Her face flushed and she looked ready to strike Aconite, but controlled the impulse.

'You know that's impossible. Concurrent future probability came under temporal interdiction the moment Cowl made the big jump. There is not enough energy in the universe.'

Do you understand any of this?

'*You have to think shallow so as not to tie yourself in knots. I'm just not yet able to think in circles, but it's like Aconite said: the rule of entelechy must be applied always.*'

Entelechy shmelecky. It just doesn't make fucking sense.

'*We're here, aren't we?*'

'Was it Cowl's idea for you to come and search my house?' Aconite asked Makali.

At this the woman showed discomfort. 'He would never object to such precautions.'

'So it wasn't his idea . . .' Aconite now stared at her for a moment before going on. 'My brother, not being the soul of patience or trust, has an automatic system set to obliterate any tor and its bearer who fall outside the trap. I saw the missile fired by that system two days ago. That usually means the tor has malfunctioned, or someone else has got through who should not have. I also saw the recent explosions inside the citadel. Obviously some assassin arrived and went in directly to carry out his task. So . . . why are you searching *my* house?'

'You will not always be inviolable. One day Cowl will tire of your interference, and that will be a day I enjoy.' The woman turned away abruptly, her companions falling in behind her as she marched back down to the river, where a hover-sled awaited.

Aconite gestured to the four rescuees seated with Polly, indicating that they could go about their tasks. Polly she called over.

'Go with Tacitus and watch the citadel. If anything is ejected, I have no doubt that it will be very dead, and possibly not even intact, but I want as much as possible of the corpse brought here.'

'What do you expect to find?' Polly had often brought back corpses for Aconite's forensic inspection, for Cowl's sister was looking for the same things as he was, though for different reasons.

'Makali perhaps revealed more than Cowl would like when she talked of regenerated tor fragments and Heliothane augmentations. This is a great opportunity for me to assess the extent of concurrent Heliothane technology, and perhaps to learn what might ensue in the coming years.'

'The Nodus?' said Polly. The start of that pivotal time was approaching, and though Cowl's huge geothermal taps were providing him with massive energy, they would not provide even one per cent of the amount required to jump him back behind the Nodus again. As Polly understood it, Cowl had used the torbeast to generate the vorpal energies required to push him behind the Nodus the first time, and that process had also required the energy from the fusion obliteration of Callisto, a moon of Jupiter.

'Quite, the Nodus.'

'What do you expect?' Polly asked.

'The city you saw during your journey. As we discussed before, it is no doubt the terminus of a wormhole and as such will be used as an energy source for the Heliothane, and a base from which to launch their attack against my brother. It is now a critical time. Thus far he has failed to discover the source of the omission paradox, and failed to affect the future in any way. At the Nodus this may change, and that is also the time the Heliothane will consider him the greatest danger to them. They will devote every resource they can to stopping him.'

Thote had told Polly that Cowl was trying to destroy the future, thus promulgating the theory that Cowl wanted a time-line occupied only by his own kind. Aconite claimed not to know if this was what the Heliothane truly believed, or if it was a lie to excuse their aggression. The real reason for Cowl's actions, Polly had since learnt from Aconite, was somewhat more complicated. She studied the Heliothane woman closely, realizing that something was being left unsaid – that Aconite knew more than she was letting on.

'I see,' Polly replied, then went to fetch Tacitus. As she walked away, she was also aware of how Aconite always made reference to 'the Heliothane' as if she herself was not a member of that race. And still, after all this time, Polly did not know in which camp Aconite's loyalties lay.

His adrenalin high fading, Tack began to realize just how badly injured he was and began to feel the pain. His right shoulder was dislocated; certainly some of his ribs were broken, since he could feel them shifting as Cowl carried him like a sack of shopping to the floor below, each of the preterhuman's sharp fingers penetrating through Tack's intercostal muscle. His left ankle had snapped as his boots were torn away, and his skull fractured when Cowl had slammed him against the wall. But unconsciousness did not result, since that was a luxury denied him by his Heliothane programming. Unconsciousness served no purpose, for they wanted him functional to the last moment of life. They had not seen fit to remove his ability to feel pain, however, as that did serve a purpose.

When they reached the lower floor, Tack saw several armed umbrathants departing in response to a silent instruction from Cowl. It occurred to him then that the Heliothane, as well as not providing him with suitable weapons to take a distance shot at this monster, had not provided him with any way of taking his own life in the event of capture. He knew what was coming now, something invariably enacted in all situations of this nature: he would be interrogated mercilessly.

Cowl dumped him on the gridwork floor, then seemed to lose interest in him for the moment – walking over to a vorpal control and pressing his hand into its oblate shimmering surface. Tack peered down at his chest and watched blood trickling out. No artery had been severed so a welcome death would not come that way. Perhaps he could press a finger in, locate such an artery . . . but the thought dispersed like mist almost as soon as it arose. Instead he scanned his surroundings.

There were closed doors all around, but he doubted he could ever manage to reach them, let alone open one. Nearby the floor sloped down to some sort of disposal tunnel cut down into darkness. He stared at this, confused by the conflicting impulses within him. The possibility of escape arose, but dispersed again. Then Cowl was back, standing over him, in one hand holding two objects: the tactical nukes.

'They thought to kill me with *you*?'

The voice was sibilant and seemed to issue from the air around the dark being. Then Cowl came forward in a movement so fast it deceived the eye, closed a hand around Tack's throat and jerked him upright. Tack groaned in an agony of grating bones and bruised organs. Glancing down, he saw the two nukes bouncing across the floor, their casings breaking open. Looking up again, he watched Cowl's face before him, glistening black, and utterly smooth until a dividing line appeared in it. Then the cowl split, and hinged open at either side, to reveal the nightmare underneath.

The black eyes were lidless, and a double set of mandibles opened before a mouth containing rows of spadelike teeth. Between mouth and eyes, other organs spilled hair-thin tentacles, small grasping spatulae, and sliding scales of chitin briefly revealing red cavities and other soft, unidentifiable things that quivered eagerly.

Tack tried to pull away, but he might as well have been fighting a moving iron statue. The horror pulled him closer, turned his head aside, and came down on the side of his face. He felt the mandibles sawing into his neck and cheek. With a sharp popping and grinding, something forced its way into his ear, adding a new hurt to the ever-growing waves of pain surging through his body. He screamed and tried again to struggle, but some hard probe hit a nerve, rolling out such incandescent agony that his arms and legs were paralysed. Tack screamed repeatedly until something ripped into the back of his neck and connected to his interface plug, switching off that ability in him. Then the horror only increased as Tack felt his mind being taken apart, and each part of it thoroughly scrutinized.

Memory after memory rose up for Cowl's inspection. Tack relived the moment of first awareness: a child with the mind of a killer and a hard-wired loyalty. Mission after mission was replayed: the killings, the frame-ups, the interrogations and beatings, but to Cowl they seemed worth only a brief scan. All events concerning the tor were scrutinized thoroughly, however, and Tack sensed Cowl's acid amusement over all that had occurred just before Tack's first shift back in time. As this forensic study continued, Tack felt Cowl begin delving through his U-gov programming, and the subsequent Heliothane programming: ripping great holes through them, dumping large portions of them as irrelevant, studying some sections and breaking them down into their smallest elements.

Traveller had initially beaten him into insensibility, this and subsequent events Cowl watched very closely. Flashes of black humour invaded Tack's consciousness as some of the lies he had been fed were revealed. Tack began to see how he had been cunningly primed for this mission right from the beginning. How blackly painted were the Umbrathane and Cowl, and how saintly the Heliothane in their mission to save the world. A flare of anger shot through to Tack when the destruction of Pig City was observed. And then Saphothere's subsequent history lecture was turned on its head as Tack absorbed Cowl's viewpoint: the Heliothane pushing for dominance over the independent Umbrathane polities; Cowl being forced to use his immense abilities in the service of the Heliothane, under threat of being destroyed because of his genetic variance, even though that rendered him physically and mentally superior to all Heliothane themselves; Cowl then giving the Umbrathane an escape route; and his own escape to beyond the Nodus. But Tack did not understand the dark being's hollow laughter in reaction to the Heliothane assertion that he was trying to eliminate human history.

Later, in Sauros, Cowl replayed every conversation, every image; gathering useful data for attack, for a means to crush. In New London the same, where Tack felt the last of Pedagogue's programming of him being pulled out by its roots and studied intensively. One conversation between Tack and Saphothere particularly held Cowl's interest:

'. . . *Tap and wormhole are inextricably linked and neither, once created, can be turned off. There is, in fact, no physical means of turning off the sun tap as the antigravity fields that sustain its position also focus the beam – as I mentioned – but if you did, the wormhole would collapse catastrophically and Sauros would be obliterated by the feedback. Also, if the wormhole was independently collapsed, the energy surge would vaporize New London. The project was therefore a* total *commitment.*'

Cowl then spent an age with the image of Maxell before angrily dropping it.

Back in Sauros Cowl observed the torbeast invade from the other side.

Throughout all this the progressively ravaged elements of Tack's mind dropped back into some mental abyss, devoid of motive beyond those any human is naturally born with, and devoid of programming. There they reconnected – first with the imperatives of survival, then with the untainted yearning for true freedom.

Subliminally Tack felt a loop generated as Cowl found something important in a conversation and viewed it again and again.

Palleque: '*Three hours earlier and Cowl would have really fucked us over. The torbeast won't be getting through now we're up to power again.*'

Saphothere: '*The push?*'

Palleque: '*Yeah. Like riding the top of a fountain and everything gets scrambled. The constant energy feed can't be switched, so the capacitors have to be drained to the limit before we can shut off and stabilize. Took us an hour this time before we could even get the defence fields back up.*'

Then Cowl's vicious amusement at Saphothere's reply: '*I don't think I need to hear any more of this.*'

Tack's foot suddenly hit the floor, and pain howled up from his broken ankle, but he was too physically drained even to scream. He tumbled over on his side, the taste of blood in his mouth, as Cowl turned away, his face closing. On some unconscious level Tack realized the being now had what it wanted, as it left Tack's mind to fall like snow through darkness.

Escape was now an instinctive goal for Tack, where previously his programming had not allowed it. He pushed himself up onto one elbow, the inside of his head feeling sand-blasted and nothing making any sense. With blurred vision he observed that Cowl was back at his vorpal control, the air above which shimmered and split on a nightmarish living landscape. Operating on a wholly animal level, Tack dragged himself backwards, reached the slope in the floor and stared down at the tunnel. Pushing himself over the edge, he immediately slid down its frictionless surface, grunting with pain as his shoulder hit the rim of the tunnel and he plummeted into it. A brief descent through darkness opened into bright yellow light, and the golden glitter of the sea below. As Tack fell, he bounced on a ledge and groped for purchase, but found none and went over, finally hitting the sea flat on. The sharp pain in his chest he recognized as a rib penetrating his lung. Sinking, he had no breath to hold, so breathed sea water instead. His only coherent thought as he drowned was triumphant:

I have escaped.

Engineer Goron stared at the 'CELL SECURITY SHUTDOWN' signal in one of his control spheres, until it disappeared, then he removed his hands from the control pillar and gazed around the control room of Sauros, noting how his staff had been depleted. The loss of Vetross, irretrievably murdered by Cowl, had been unexpected, even though Goron had expected casualties. Two of the direct-link technicians had been pulled dead from their vorpal connectware after the subsequent torbeast attack. And now Palleque, formerly his most trusted aide, was in a cell awaiting an interrogation that Goron was apparently putting off. At least Silleck was still with him and the personnel replacements seemed competent enough. He returned his attention to the control pillar.

The energy levels were already up to eighty per cent of requirement, and he calculated that they would be ready to shift Sauros very soon. All the field frequencies which Palleque had access to had been subsequently changed, and all weapons systems had since been moved to a separate circuit, so as not to be dependent on the power tap on the wormhole itself.

'How long?' he asked Silleck.

'One hour and fourteen minutes. Are we going for an extension this time?' asked the woman, who was enclosed in vorpal tech.

'Yes: one third of a light year.'

'Good. We were pushing it last time.'

Goron turned his attention to the man now sitting at Palleque's console. 'Theldon, is everything stable?'

'It is, Engineer,' the man replied without looking round.

'And everyone is now aware of the location of their nearest displacement generator?'

At this, Theldon looked round. 'We are . . . you are expecting trouble?'

'That last torbeast attack was a little too close to our vulnerable time. I think we managed to stop Palleque from passing on that we do have a vulnerable time, but it is best to be cautious.'

'That's all right for all of you,' grumbled Silleck. 'You don't have to detach vorpal interface nodes before hitting the generator. Anything goes wrong and I doubt I'll get the time.'

Goron winced. 'You'll be fine,' he said, putting as much confidence in his voice as he could. 'Now, keep an eye on things for the moment. I have something I need to do, but I shouldn't be away long.'

He turned away from his control column and headed for the lift platform, aware that his fellows were watching him curiously. Dropping down from the control room, he felt like a traitor.

Via moving walkways and ramps he quickly reached one of the supply centres that dotted Sauros, observing as he went the city's various citizens about their various tasks. He had a bitter taste in his mouth because what he had set in motion so long ago was now coming to fruition. Reality now bore a hard edge.

The supply-centre door opened when he palmed the lock, without requiring further confirmation of identity. Inside he walked along the racks of replacement items needed for the many different systems the city contained, until he came to a rack of empty containers – empty all bar one. This, too, opened when he palmed it, and inside rested a single device. It was heavy, the shape of a transformer with rounded edges, and it fitted his palm. He took it out, weighing it in his hand, then slipped it into his belt pouch before exiting the supply centre.

Further transit of walkways and ramps finally brought him to a residential section of the city. The door he sought was different from all those which opened automatically as soon as their residents approached, being heavily armoured and its frame recently welded into place. Reaching it, he again pressed his hand against the lock and to his satisfaction received no reaction. He took out a small key and inserted it into the manual lock beside the security lock. One turn and the door whoomphed off its seals. He dragged it open, stepped inside, and quickly closed it behind him, before turning to the apartment's only resident.

'I noticed the security system go offline,' said Palleque, banging a fist against the mesh that covered the single window out of which he was gazing. Just an hour earlier the charge the mesh was carrying would have thrown him across the room. 'I wondered if you expected me to try and escape.' Palleque still did not look round. 'Had I tried, I doubt I'd have survived long out there. It would seem a lot of my fellow Heliothane dislike me and they wonder why you are delaying the interrogation.'

'Ostensibly I am too busy with organizing our push into the Triassic. Anyone not satisfied with that explanation would put my delay down to a certain squeamishness.'

Palleque turned at last. 'The push . . . it is imminent?'

'One hour, even less now.'

Palleque let out a tense breath. 'Then it will soon be over.'

'Not for you.' Goron removed the device from his belt pouch, and put it down on the single table before Palleque's couch.

'Displacement generator. What location?'

'The same as all others now,' Goron replied.

'That is risky and may give the game away.'

'A risk I am prepared to take.'

'But am I? The torbeast swept up my sister as if she was nothing, and I am prepared to die to exact vengeance.'

Goron stared at him directly. 'Yes, I know your commitment.' His gaze strayed down to Palleque's arm, then his hand.

Palleque glanced at the dressing, then held up his hand covered in a surgical mitten. 'For veracity, as always, it had to be done. I'll heal soon enough as I have the rejuvenation gene, though I never expected to have the chance to do so. Let's hope you didn't underdo things by not killing me outright.'

'We are now not long away from that point when all such subterfuge will be irrelevant. I have no doubt that already Cowl has extracted the required information from the torbearer. Now all that remains is for us to perform our duty at this end.'

Palleque came over and picked up the displacement generator. 'I'm surprised you had any of these to spare.'

'I made sure there was one,' replied Goron. He waved a hand around Palleque's erstwhile apartment – now his cell. 'You deserve better than to die here.' He turned to go.

'Goron,' said Palleque, halting the Engineer's departure. 'Good luck.'

'Let us hope that is something we don't need too much of,' Goron replied as he left the cell.

18

Palleque:
As if he too would not sacrifice his life to that end, my brother Saphothere feels I too fanatically seek to avenge the death of our sister, Astolere. That I have become Cowl's agent he attributes to Coptic and Meelan. But those two are not really accepted by the other Umbrathane. It is fortunate that my ostensible fanaticism prevents him from asking further questions. I was always Cowl's agent, and have remained in communication with him. The destructive war between Umbra and Heliothane is an utter waste, and I considered the preterhuman the ideal candidate to rule us all. It was I who passed on the displacement technology to the Umbrathane, to enable them to escape Heliothane oppression, and much else have I done. Cowl was suspicious at first but, upon discovering that I supposedly did not know what had happened to my sister, concocted the story that she, along with the entire population of Callisto, is with him behind the Nodus. I was wrong: Cowl is too careless of human life to rule us. And at the least he must be made powerless – the very least.

When they got him ashore and Tacitus started work on getting the water out of his lungs, Polly stepped back, her hand dropping to her taser in its waterproof pouch at her hip, then sliding across to the sheath knife beside it. Tacitus did not notice this movement as the rescuee now coughed sea water and blood from his lungs and the Roman, as he had been taught, turned him into the recovery position.

'It is surprising that this man is still alive,' commented the Roman – in the Heliothane language they all now spoke after an instructive session connected to Aconite's Pedagogue machine. Tacitus then grabbed hold of the man's arm, putting a foot in his armpit then pulling and twisting, relocating his shoulder joint. The rescued man groaned, fell back into his prior position and curled up his legs.

'His name is Tack. He is the man I told you about a while ago – the killer I dragged back with me for a few shifts,' Polly told him.

Speaking out loud through a link established to Wasp shortly after Polly's rescue, Nandru interjected, 'And now things become clear. You recollect that a piece of your tor, in its still nascent stage, was left embedded in this U-gov bastard's wrist?'

'I still can't see what's worth saving here,' said Polly.

'Things have changed and we all know so much more,' said Tacitus, looking up. 'I would even save enemies of Rome, here and now, should they survive Cowl's ungentle ministrations.'

'You hear that, Polly?' Nandru asked. 'I hope so, because I've just informed Aconite that friend Tack here is still alive. Come on, you know U-gov assassins aren't my favourite playmates, but I damned well want to hear what this one has to say for himself.'

Polly let her hand slip away from her knife, not exactly sure what emotion she was feeling. There was anger, yes, for earlier this man had been intent on killing her, but that anger was no longer a savage thing within her. Where, in the end, would she be now without Nandru and then this one? Rotting in her bedsit, and perhaps moving onto the needle like Marjae had, blowing U-gov officials in back alleys when not being screwed up against a wall, dropping her price as the goods became more shoddy. The more she thought about it, the more ambivalent her feelings became.

'Come on, let's get him onto Wasp,' she decided abruptly.

For Polly only, Nandru said, *Of course, I don't think he'll live that much longer if Cowl or the Umbrathane realize he's still alive. And if they don't know yet, they can find out soon enough.*

Between them, Polly and Tacitus picked up Tack and dropped him into Wasp's rear compartment. Studying him, Polly saw that his injuries were extensive. He certainly had a compound fracture of his ankle, for bone was sticking out of his flesh. Deep wounds in his chest were seeping blood, and the medscanner Tacitus had pressed against his neck showed his vital signs on the wane. But it was unlikely he would die irrecoverably because, even if his heart stopped, Wasp possessed the facility to plug into a person's neck and keep an oxygenated haematic fluid circulating around the brain, which was all Aconite needed to maintain someone's life – other repairs she could perform in her surgical facility.

They headed back towards their hostess's home, glancing back occasionally to check for any activity apparent in Cowl's citadel, but all remained quiet out on the sea as if, having spat out the indigestible remains of some meal, the place was now contemplating what to eat next. As they reached her home, Aconite and the others came out to meet them.

'Another man,' snorted Cheng-yi, before heading back inside.

Lostboy stared long and hard at Tack before something seemed to go click in his mind. He jerked his head up, pointing out to sea. 'The beast.' They all turned to look.

Polly had wondered at the earlier stillness and now realized why. The Umbrathane customarily ceased their constant maintenance of the citadel and fled to its interior safety chambers whenever Cowl summoned all the energy from the geological taps for the purpose of linking to the torbeast. Now, the very air around the citadel seemed full of distortions and hints of nightmarish shapes, where the beast encroached upon the real.

'Coming after *him*?' Ygrol asked, stabbing a thumb towards the unconscious Tack.

Aconite shook her head. 'Cowl would not expend such energy. He'd just send Makali out here, or fire a missile direct from one of the citadel's emplacements.'

From Wasp, Nandru said, 'But not a coincidence, I'd warrant.'

'Certainly not,' Aconite replied. 'Cowl is no doubt acting on information obtained from this newcomer.' She was studying her palm screen. 'Our friend here has been comprehensively mind-fucked.'

They carried Tack inside and laid him down on Aconite's surgical table. Polly was the last to leave the room as Aconite began pulling her medical machines into place.

'He's the one I dragged back . . . the one who tried to kill me,' she said.

'So Nandru has informed me,' Aconite replied. 'Be assured, though, that this is not the same individual. The one who attacked you was a human automaton programmed by your controlling government. That automaton has since, unless I am mistaken, been reprogrammed by the Heliothane. And since then, again, has had his programs and much of his mind ripped apart by Cowl. I don't know how much there will be left of him – he might be another Lostboy by the time I've finished.'

Polly gave a small nod and exited the room.

Its hunger was immense, but each time it fed it pushed itself even further down the probability slope, yet it knew that if it could somehow feed enough, things would change for it. Thinking, as it perpetually did, in five dimensions, it was aware that oblivion lay in both directions on this temporal line. Allowing its consciousness to fall into the past, it dropped back to its secondary inception – from when its consciousness had materialized in the Precambrian. Pushing into the future, it found long slow starvation in a world in which it was the only life form, resulting, at its death, in the truncation of that alternate in vorpal and thus temporal terms. Only here, holding its position in what it defined to itself as the *now*, where up-slope energy was being fed down to it, could it maintain temporal life. Now, and always now, the energy being fed to it was huge – and growing.

The Maker wanted something of it, as he always did, but the torbeast was never anything less than utterly grateful and adoring. Every time he wanted something, the opportunities given for feeding far outweighed any concomitant pain. On many occasions the beast had suffered loss of its mass through attacks from the enemy, but with side-branched feeders it hoovered up biomass from alternates further down the slope, and this, though not commensurate, satisfied sufficiently its endless urge to *feed.* But this time there was something different. The promise this time was of unrestrained feeding on the enemy, the life system of a whole alternate to denude, without consequence – billions of human lives and vast biomass, with which it could achieve . . . *all.*

Drawing on the energy font, the torbeast shoved its mass over those alternates it had previously denuded, and which had been the cause of its fall down the slope. It manifested thus in the skies of barren Earths – a glimpse of organic hell – then shifted on. On a world where the sea was occupied only by single-celled organisms, it flooded out around another energy font, drawing all of itself through as, over the span of millennia, the first font died.

The beast's substance drew in from its secondary inception point, and in from that future of its own death. In a wave of living tissue, kilometres high, it flooded across a barren continent, ripping aside mountain chains and tearing up the plains before it. Storms dogged its progress, cloud formations boiling across the sky above it, and lightning walked across its flesh. Then, reaching the ocean surrounding the continent, this wave broke into a chaos of filter-feeding mouths like stalked whales, plunging into the waters and driving a second tsunami ahead. Spreading out into the oceans, it fed, sucking up biomass by the kilotonne, digesting lakes of organic slurry, driving on in a global apocalypse. Only the heat of volcanic vents diverted this progress, as did the steam explosion from a volcanic island chain now swamped by the wave. At the font its substance poured in slower then slower. Then, with a thunderclap that blew hurricanes across the beast's heaving landscape, the flow ceased. But by then the torbeast had met itself on the other side of the planet, and it now wholly occupied this alternate Earth.

A grey-skinned woman stooped over him. He recognized her in some fragment of his mind. At the foot of the table he could see the fleshy squid-like tentacles extending from the carapace of an autosurgeon and he felt their wet touch on his leg. As the bioconstruct straightened his ankle, pain briefly laced together the elements of his sentience, and he found enough strength to yell out and jerk upright. A heavy three-fingered hand stilled his protest by the sight of it, even more than the pressure it exerted against his chest to push him back down.

'You surprise me,' she said.

He gazed at her disparate arms and couldn't find any meaning in her words at first. Then something meshed in his mind and he understood.

'Why?' he grated. But the question was not directed at her. *Why am I? Why is this? Why everything?*

'I see that your shut-off point is graded somewhat above that occasioned by your trauma. Deliberate but cruel augmentation I think.'

That meant nothing to him. He blinked and listened to the sound of a storm outside.

'I'm Tack,' he mouthed silently to himself, and wasn't sure what that meant either.

His mind consisted of disconnected monads, now shaping

themselves to each other and searching for connection. On some level he realized he was rebuilding himself, but not quite in the same way as before – like a demolished house rebuilt with the same bricks, a house would result but the individual bricks would not be in exactly the same positions. Foundations did remain, but Tack had memory of things that no longer controlled him, found voids, and sought structure. With all the rage and love of a living man he sought to *be*, and felt dread, and a terrible yearning.

'There. The anaesthetic doesn't work, but this will.'

Blackness interminable, filled with leviathan structures falling against each other and bonding. Then terrible thirst and a massive hand supporting his head to the cool rim of a glass against his lips. He drank cold water.

He'd earlier seen the girl Nandru Jurgens had used, and whom his Director of Operations had subsequently ordered him to kill, but that he discounted as hallucination. This grey-skinned woman, with her strange hands and penetrating golden eyes, he could not deny. He stared at her as she withdrew the glass, and operated some control to raise the backrest of the surgical table further, but then she moved away about her tasks amongst the esoteric machinery that surrounded him.

Now he observed his naked body. Pipes ran from his chest to a wheeled machine nearby, and fluids – dark, clear, bloody and translucent blue – ran through those pipes. He saw that the wounds in his chest were now just sealed lines and that the autosurgeon had withdrawn, leaving an organic-looking surgical boot enclosing his foot and ankle.

'You've been unconscious for three days and I've repaired most of your internal injuries. The bone glue is very effective, but I wouldn't advise any gymnastics just yet,' the woman warned him, her back turned to him.

The voice was as calm and modulated as that of a professional killer, Tack thought. He wondered if it was this about her that bothered him, but, no, he hadn't heard her voice before, had he? He realized then what was familiar about her. Though distorted, she had much of the physiognomy of another.

Cowl.

With a lurch of dread Tack instantly realized that Cowl must not see into his thoughts again. Now, Tack's mind being in such different order, he realized that in his eagerness, Cowl had not delved deeply enough. The being had not heard the one called Thote saying, '*Like the girl who passed through here fifty years ago, you're just a piece of temporal detritus. In your case primed and filled with poison, then sent on its way.*' And Cowl had not felt Tack's later puzzlement at why he had not been provided with weapons capable of a distance hit, nor why he had been so ill-prepared for a fight involving time travel.

The woman turned to him. 'Can you now speak?'

'I can.'

'Good. Cowl's mind-fuck doesn't usually leave behind anything human, but it would appear that your mind, being so accustomed to programming and reprogramming, has retained its facility for self-organization. I suspect this is because he reamed you through your interface, thus leaving many natural, unconscious structures intact.'

'What are you to Cowl?' he asked.

'I'm his sister.'

Tack scanned the room for suitable weapons. Though a traitor, she was still Heliothane, so she would be strong and fast. But it seemed imperative he escape, and to do so it would be necessary to kill her. Then suddenly he felt how utterly wrong it would be to try and kill this woman who had tended to him, and his thoughts fell into brief confusion, out of which he re-arose, sick with anger. His immediate reaction had been caused by remaining emotional outfall from his Heliothane programming, but he should not think like that. Now he knew that he had never been an assassin, that from the very moment Saphothere had found him he had been manipulated: his sum purpose that of a sacrificial goat. He owed the Heliothane nothing.

'Don't let that worry you.'

For a moment Tack thought she was reading his mind, then he got back on track. 'Your brother nearly killed me, and tore my mind apart. So I shouldn't worry?'

'No, Tack. What he did to you was a response to the assault upon him. I will not define that as *your* attack, because we both know you had no choice in the matter. And, anyway, the result of Cowl's violence, whether intended or not, is that you are now alive in a way that you never were before.'

It was true. Tack could now make choices, decisions, and with all that came a concomitant confusion. Perhaps he actually owed Cowl more than he did the Heliothane? But no, what good Cowl had done for him was by default, and to sway in that direction would be like holding out the hand of friendship to a crocodile. From the beginning of his life Tack had never been able to choose sides for himself, to choose anything really. But now he possessed free will, so had to ask himself which side he might choose, and if he should choose any side at all. Just for a second he wished for the easier road of external programming. Just for a second.

'Does Cowl know about what you have done?' he asked.

'No, I don't share my brother's views, nor his hatred.'

'Which side are you on – Heliothane or Umbra?'

'My own, Tack.'

And there it was, and he made his choice.

Seeing this war from both perspectives, Tack realized, in the perspective now utterly his own, that he did not think *anything* could justify what Cowl had been doing – his negligent slaughter of the torbearers. And he was utterly aware that the information Cowl now possessed was precisely what the Heliothane wanted him to possess. However, Tack could not forgive the lies and the programming forced upon himself, nor the Heliothane's ruthless extermination of the Umbrathane.

Asking himself which side he was on, he found his answer the same as Aconite's: *my own*.

In interspace Saphothere murdered his mantisal by driving a tor thorn into its sensory juncture and breaking the thorn off. Shortly after this Meelan did the same, then also the third passenger, and they watched while the three thorns melded, then sprouted fibrous connections into the bioconstruct. By this means they subverted the process that would cause the tors they now wore to generate their own pseudo-shells and thus separate the three of them. Shifting back in time, they arrived in Silurian evening, unloaded their supplies and disembarked before the mantisal dematerialized. Then they made their camp in a shadowy clearing surrounded by tree ferns and arboreal gloom.

'I feel as though I have killed a trusted pet,' said Saphothere.

'It was necessary,' Meelan replied, as she watched the third member of their group move off with the collapsible water container.

'I wonder *how* necessary. We are just a sideshow to the main event.'

'Don't get all maudlin on me, Saphothere. You know how important our sideshow really is. Cowl does not know the truth, which is why he has failed thus far to influence the future, but he could still send us all down the slope into oblivion upon learning that truth.'

'Even without *his* pet?'

Meelan did not reply immediately as she had opened a rations pack and was stuffing her mouth with food. Eventually she said, 'We know he has an energy source – he's had three centuries behind the Nodus to prepare one – so he is still dangerous. We mustn't forget that what he has made he can make again while he still lives.'

'There is a second important—' began the big man, returning with a filled water container, before his words were cut off by a cough. He started again, his voice grating, 'There is another important aspect to our mission – access to tors.'

'For "aspect" substitute "hope",' suggested Saphothere.

'We have five to spare already,' Meelan observed.

'Of how many thousands that we'll need?' asked Saphothere.

'Well, in that you are optimistic – you think so many will survive?' Meelan asked.

'Cowl will have a supply,' said the third member.

'See, more optimism,' said Meelan.

The big man started to say something, but now broke into a longer fit of coughing.

'That still bothering you?' Saphothere asked.

The big man touched the gnarl of scar tissue starting at his throat and running up under his chin.

'It bothers me,' Coptic agreed.

The brightly coloured acanthostega, a small amphibian that had been feeding voraciously on the the bony-headed fish of the swamp, fled as fast as it could through mud and decaying tangles of vegetation, and into the nearby forest. The looming cliff, rising over all, cast a shadow into the amphibian's small domain, and in its simple brain it sensed the danger of its extinction. Behind it, the swamp was boiling, and tonnes of reed mat were being sucked up as if by some vast combine harvester, fast disappearing into red slits that were giant maws. Then the same monstrous cliff reached the edge of the trees, and something began wrenching the forest giants from the ground, juggling them up into the air, where they, like the reed mat, were chomped down. Wriggling up the ramp of a decaying log, the acanthostega ignored swarming termites, disturbed from their abode by the shaking of the ground – creatures which otherwise would have made it a tasty meal. At the summit of the log, with only a headlong drop ahead of it, it froze, instinct promulgating this reaction now flight was no longer an option.

As the cliff advanced, things began pushing through the undergrowth all around. Not far from the amphibian, slimy lungfish were hauled from their shallow pool by snakelike extrusions of the same cliff – only these snakes were without eyes, possessing only mouths that were vertical slits lined with incurving teeth. One such snake was squirming along the forest floor towards the small amphibian, and in response, the acanthostega arched its back, more prominently to display its bright poisonous coloration. The slit mouth rose above it and opened, then abruptly snapped shut. Then the snake things withdrew from the forest and the devastation immediately ceased. The earth still shaking, the cliff began to withdraw. Now the amphibian, sensing that the danger had passed, moved downwards along the log and began lunching on the termites.

Eventually the acanthostega returned to its little swamp but there found only a muddy cavity. Its vision was not sufficient to see the utterly denuded landscape beyond, and its mind was not sufficiently sophisticated to comprehend such concepts as 'luck'. It could not comprehend what vast beast had come to feed in its world, or how that feeding must necessarily be limited. That the beast had to cease before being forced back down an incomprehensible slope as a result of its destruction of *this* history.

'I'm not so sure I'm glad to see you well.'

That came from Polly, the girl he had tried to add to his list of victims millions of years in the future. So she had not been a hallucination earlier and he was glad she was alive. Though all those others before her were most definitely dead. He had killed them. Made mute by what he was suddenly feeling, he moved on past her to one of the arched windows and gazed out into darkness, trying to blink the strange after-images there from his eyes. In a moment he realized these were no after-images; he really was seeing shimmering hints of nightmarish shapes, as of open mouths and snakelike bodies, beyond the rain-beaded window.

'What is that out there?' he eventually asked, his voice dead.

'Something you caused.'

Tack surveyed the occupants of this strange room. That familiar voice had not come from the Roman soldier, the Chinese man, or the boy, for they were all over on the other side of him – the first two working on something inside the back of the boy's head. Tack tried to take sights like that in his stride: the boy with the back of his head open like a hatch, and two men who should have no conception of such work, probing inside with various finely polished tools, discussing in low voices what they were doing. Perhaps the boy was an android or something. Nor did the voice issue from the Neanderthal, who was sitting carving circuit patterns into a club fashioned from the rib of a large animal. Tack's attention then strayed to the wasp robot squatting beside the sofa Polly occupied.

The robot spoke again, 'It is the incursion overspill from the torbeast – that always happens when Cowl summons it up from the bottom of the slope and establishes a communication link, but not normally intruding to this extent. Perhaps, Mr U-gov *facilitator*, you can *explain* exactly what fuck-up you have caused.'

Polly, sitting with arms crossed, flicked her gaze to Wasp, then brought it back to Tack. 'You have to understand that Nandru may be even less glad to see you than I am.'

Tack stared at the robot, then looked at Polly, who pointed to the Muse 184 at her throat.

'Nandru?' he said, even more confused.

Polly just stared at him silently, a hint of a smile twisting her mouth.

'The dead soldier uploaded to the device Polly wears – and which now speaks to you through Wasp,' explained Aconite as she entered the room. 'But however he speaks, his questions are still pertinent.'

Tack was not even sure he cared, for moment by moment he could still feel elements of his mind knitting together. All those missions for U-gov, all that *facilitation* . . . even the Heliothane reprogramming had not brought him to this level of consciousness.

'So what have you caused here? Why is my brother reacting in this way?' Aconite asked.

Tack swallowed dryly and tried to shove his mangled history away from himself. He considered not telling Aconite anything, but decided he did not owe his silence to those who had sent him to this time. No matter how he felt about Saphothere, the traveller had sent Tack on a suicide mission. Tack managed to admit, 'Inside my mind . . . Cowl found a way to attack Sauros.'

'Sauros?' Aconite asked mildly, unsurprised.

Tack concentrated on the *now*, and found that by doing so he could control the horror growing between his ears. While the other three in the small group moved over, Tack told of Goron's project, of the city and the wormhole, how it fed energy for accurate mantisal jumping, and how the Heliothane were pushing backwards in time finally to get to Cowl. He then repeated, verbatim, those particular segments of conversation that had been of such interest to Cowl, and had now caused this reaction. He did not tell them what Thote had said, however, or of his own thoughts about distance weapons and sacrificial goats. That was for himself.

After a long silence, Aconite said, 'This Sauros is what you saw, Polly.' She turned back to Tack. 'I somehow doubt that either Goron or Saphothere would be so negligent, but it appears to me that this Palleque might not have been entirely in their employ.' She looked thoughtful and bowed her head, supporting her chin on her heavier hand. Musingly she continued, 'I can think of only two possibilities: if the information Cowl extracted from you is true, then Sauros will become vulnerable when it shifts, and the torbeast my brother is now summoning will kill everyone in it. Thereafter, it being impossible to shut down the wormhole without catastrophe, the beast will then push through to New London and to the Heliothane Dominion.'

'They'll be able to deal with it there, won't they?' asked Polly.

'That I very much doubt,' said Aconite. 'It will kill billions and destroy New London, thus causing that catastrophic shutdown. Most likely resulting vacuum will then kill it, but it is tough and, should it survive to somehow reach Earth or the solar colonies, billions more will die.'

'Option one don't sound so good,' said Nandru. 'You got anything better?'

'Maybe this is a trap. Perhaps, having lured the beast out fully, the Heliothane will use some sort of nuclear conflagration to destroy it. Even so, I don't see how the destruction of Sauros can be avoided, followed by the consequent collapse of the tunnel, which in turn would result in the destruction of New London – so achieving the same result. This leads me to think that maybe option one is the only one – no Heliothane plot, just my brother winning this battle at least.'

To Tack the second option seemed the more likely, and he wondered why Aconite was so dismissive of it.

'Why would that happen? Why would New London be destroyed?' Polly asked.

Tack knew the answer to that one. Keeping under rigid self-control he said, 'Remember I mentioned how interested Cowl was in what Saphothere said: "*if the wormhole was independently collapsed, the energy surge would vaporize New London.*" Sun tap and wormhole are inextricably linked, and the hole is drawing in so much energy that if it collapsed, that energy would have to go somewhere else. The life of New London, in such a case, would be numbered in seconds.'

'Then what should we do?' Polly asked.

'Nothing,' said Aconite, turning away. 'It is not our concern.'

Watching her go, Tack could not fathom the hint of amusement in her expression, but he knew how absolutely she was wrong. What he hadn't told her confirmed this for him, but he had no wish to tell her now. He hoped that the Heliothane succeeded in whatever plan they were pursuing, if only it resulted in the death of this damned Cowl. That would be repayment for what the being had done to Tack himself, would end the slaughter of the torbearers, and maybe even end the war. His silence, now, best served that purpose, and anyway he had no trust of any sibling-on-sibling conflict – getting involved on any side of that was the way to find *yourself* branded the enemy, and have them both at your throat.

But Tack's most important concern had little to do with any of that. Turning to gaze back out into the storm he felt disparate memories still sliding together in his mind. Every mission he had carried out, though having its own limited emotional impact, had lost that impact each time he had been reprogrammed. With that framework now gone, however, all those mindless missions were coming together in his head and he was beginning to really *feel*. Past sins were coming back to haunt him.

A row of nacre pillars, stretching from horizon to horizon, the incursions opened across the Triassic landscape. From a forest of low ferns and stunted ginkgos, a herd of browsing prosauropods rose onto their hind legs and started hooting in alarm. The big male charged out from the main group and, thrashing its tail from side to side, tore up the ground with its huge and lethal foreclaws, which were usually enough to drive away all but the most persistent predator. But these intruders were nothing he knew, and he began to back off as they advanced across the landscape like whirlwinds. Eventually he turned and, with his tail high in the air, charged after the more prudent females of his herd. None of them were to know that they were trapped inside a ring of the pillars, a ring eight hundred kilometres in diameter.

19

Modification Status Report:
Pain inside. The boy grows at a phenomenal rate and the early scans show that his growth is optimal. I feel his carapace hard in my womb when he moves, and twice already he has interfaced through my spinal cord. Watching Amanita build her machines, the stunted tendrils moving on her face, I wonder what the relationship between the two of them will be. Will they be friends? Will he consider her his inferior, even though it was only through studying her that I was able to achieve him? Her mind is complex and quite evidently her intelligence is high, but she is very much a human girl. When he interfaced with me I glimpsed a mind equally as complex, but frighteningly alien. But my reaction I put down to my hormonal imbalance. I should not fear this perfection I have achieved.

Sauros, a metallic sphere drawing a tail of bright energy between grey and black surfaces – inverted through vorpal vision, it was poised in the flaw of a vast gem, infinite surfaces falling away from it, while it was supported by a fountain of energy and cut by the surfaces of a hypersphere. But Goron did not need this second view to know they were heading into deep shit. Like a bullet reaching the end of its ballistic arc, the great city was now ploughing down into the midnight sea in which awaited the organic Mandelbrot patterns of endless layers of beast.

'We'll have no fields! It'll tear us apart!' That was Theldon, playing his hands over his console like a virtuoso finding he has gone deaf.

'All weapons systems are still enabled. We're getting no energy loss there. I am reading organic mass on the other side.' Silleck: grim, determined, fatalistic.

'Put tactical nukes out ahead of us – as close as you dare. Have them detonate on the other side of the interface,' Goron instructed, which was about the only instruction he could give in the circumstances, though he knew they were flea-biting an elephant.

The real world rolled in around them, distorted over hypersurfaces. The triple flash of detonation momentarily blackened all screens, and Sauros resettled, groaning, to its bones in the midst of a firestorm.

'Incursion right inside us!' Silleck yelled, before even Theldon, who was supposed to be searching for such, could yell a warning.

Goron called up a view, into the abutment chamber, and saw the huge flaw opening and the defence rafts moving in to attack. He saw a feeding mouth come out, like a gargantuan striking cobra, and slam itself closed on the stern of one raft, before the second raft opened fire and severed the neck. But then another mouth hurtled out, then another . . . then a second incursion began to open.

'Bastard! It was local fauna – we got nothing!' Theldon's hands were now motionless on his console.

Goron called up an external view, while with one eye he continued watching the battle in the abutment chamber. His people were dying in there, all due to him. Outside he observed a macabre landscape of seared dinosaur fauna. The torbeast had driven these creatures ahead of it to take the brunt of Sauros's first defensive measures. Goron did not like the intelligence that revealed. Beyond the carnage he saw a line of incursions closing in.

'Hit them with everything we've got,' he instructed.

'All of them?' Silleck asked. 'They are all around us.'

More views, and Goron observed the ring as it closed.

'Do what you can,' he said, now operating controls that had been set in the control pillar ever since Sauros had been built, but had never been used. Now he watched missiles hammering out from the city, hitting the incursions – some of those nacreous whirlwinds collapsing, but always others moving into their place.

'We've lost it, we've fucking lost it!' Theldon protested, turning from his console and staring at Goron.

Goron gestured to the rear of the chamber. 'Get to the displacement generator. It's set to drop us ten kilometres away, which should put us outside the beast's immediate reach. I doubt it's much interested in us, anyway – there's a bigger prize at the other end of the tunnel.'

'OK,' said Theldon, turning back to his console.

In a flash Goron understood why Silleck had picked up on that first incursion before Theldon had. Quickly he shifted virtual controls and saw that somehow Theldon had gained access, through equipment made for external and internal monitoring and some adjustment of internal systems, to the abutment controls. Using yet another control protocol he had never revealed to anyone but Palleque, the Engineer shut off Theldon's console.

Theldon turned. 'Maybe, if we—'

'Nothing we can do,' Goron interrupted, his face expressionless. 'We blow the abutments and New London goes anyway. Get out of here.'

Theldon turned back to his console, stared at it for a moment, then slapping his hands against it, stood and, without meeting Goron's gaze, headed for the generator. Goron watched the displacement sphere flick the man away from Sauros. Blowing the abutments would certainly close the mouth of the wormhole and prevent the beast reaching New London, and just as certainly the feedback energy, and that projected from the sun tap, would fry the city. Goron returned his attention to more exigent concerns now the man was gone.

'This is Engineer Goron,' he said over the public address system. 'All personnel head for your nearest displacement generator and get out of here. We have lost Sauros.'

He saw that many were not responding to his order. Some were fighting feeding mouths that were shooting up like trains from the corridors leading into the abutment chamber. Others seemed to be doing nothing at all, perhaps preferring to die with their city.

'This is Engineer Goron. I am now leaving this city. You must all come with me.'

This finally motivated many to head for the generator points. But, just then, most of them were thrown off their feet as the city lurched.

'What the hell was that?'

'I can't keep them out!' from Silleck.

An outside view showed Goron a wide-open incursion in which atomic fires burned and were swamped by the roll of megatonnes of flesh. From this extended the neck of a giant feeding mouth that was now chewing on the city wall. Lasers burnt grooves in it, and missiles blew away chunks of it the size of houses. Its neck broke then separated, the mouth end attached to the city crashing down and by its sheer weight causing Sauros to tilt. But then another of the giants hammered in from the other side of the city.

'Put a tactical into it,' Goron suggested, knowing Silleck's answer even as he spoke.

'I can't – we've got nothing left.'

'This is Engineer Goron. Everybody get out – get out now! This order includes all technicians vorpally interfaced. You must abandon this place. It is not worth your lives!'

'Silleck,' he said in quieter tones, 'that means you too.'

A display on the control pillar informed him that at least this latest order was being generally obeyed. The other controls there, having gone through their detachment sequence some minutes before, had freed a section of the pillar. He pulled the section away and stepped back, holding a control sphere and viewing sphere with all the vorpal tech that connected them together. Tucking under his arm this item, which looked like the severed head of a huge praying mantis fashioned of glass, he turned towards where the displacement generator was located. Then he heard the crashing hiss of monstrous progress coming up the lift shaft. Looking to those still trying to separate from their vorpal interfaces, he knew there was just no time left.

'Silleck . . .' he said, but could not go on. Abruptly he turned towards the generator.

The sphere enclosed him instantly, flicked him out between nightmare incursions and deposited him on a denuded mountainside, along with many other citizens of the place he had ruled. He spotted Palleque walking towards him, the other escapees too shocked to even feel motivated to attack the man. When Palleque reached him, both he and Goron turned to look back at the city.

Now some incursions were expanding and mating up, while others were closing. As further citizens suddenly appeared around the two men, they watched more of the beast's mass flowing in towards the city, tearing out walls and boring through the superstructure. Those displacing from there were now arriving injured, sometimes dead, till their numbers dwindled and finally reached zero. Now they could see the beast like the forever-turning back of a sea giant, diving in between the abutments of the wormhole and attenuating – flowing away like sump oil draining into some huge invisible funnel. But this was a flow that seemed as if it would never end.

'Palleque! Palleque you bastard!' The heliothant who stumbled up the slope towards them was drawing a weapon from his belt.

Goron held up his hand. 'Palleque did his duty.' He gestured towards the beast and the remaining skeleton of Sauros. 'This is what we wanted to happen.'

This news was spread gradually as the endless transit of the beast continued. Hours passed and the surviving citizens gathered around Goron to hear his explanation.

'But that means we are trapped here now,' someone managed.

'It means the survival of all we hold dear, and that is all that should concern you,' Palleque replied.

That stilled them, while in shock, then growing horror, they saw the seemingly endless monster flowing through their temporary home towards what they truly called home: New London.

Goron leaned close to Palleque. 'Get some help and find Theldon.' Palleque raised an eyebrow. Goron nodded to the heliothant who had earlier been intent on killing Palleque. 'Take him with you, and any others like him.'

'So my position as arch-traitor has been superceded,' said Palleque. 'What should I do when I find him?'

Goron just stared at him.

Thirteen screens flicked on, one after another, as the tachyon feed from the abutment chamber of Sauros caused vorpal sensors – spaced all the way down the wormhole – to come into phase. Talk ceased immediately, and it occurred to Maxell you could pluck a dismal tune on the tension stringing the air of the New London Abutment Control Centre.

'It's in,' said one of the interface techs needlessly, for the first screen briefly displayed a giant feeding mouth flung out from an incursion in the abutment chamber of Sauros, before that particular sensor in the wormhole was knocked spinning through the air. All in the room now glimpsed the heaving roll of beast, its probing tentacles and glistening red caves, and one brief glimpse of a defence raft, with its back end sheered off, falling and burning, spilling screaming Heliothane into a tree on which every leaf was a mouth.

'Anything yet from Goron?' Maxell asked, walking over to

stand behind the sensor operator's chair and peering up at the view on his first screen.

'Nothing,' said Carloon, as he too gazed up at the chaotic image and tried to get his first sensor back under control. Abruptly the first screen blanked and the man swore, pushing his chair back from his console, then turning to Maxell.

'The attack hit them too quickly, so maybe he didn't get out,' he said. 'We'll know soon enough.'

On the second screen a tiny speck grew into a distant darkness, at the centre of the triangular tunnel.

Already?

Maxell made a rough calculation: ten thousand million kilometres, and no sign of closure from Sauros. Of course, inside the wormhole, the distance the torbeast extended itself through and its speed were a function of the energy it could expend, nevertheless . . .

'Any mass readings yet?'

The interface tech who had first spoken said, 'Nothing yet, we can't get that until it's all entirely in the wormhole, where we can calculate then subtract its energy level.'

'Mother of fuck,' said Carloon.

Now, in the second screen, the image had grown and was becoming clear. Maxell considered this view similar to what the prey of a piranha shoal might see in its last moments. The wormhole was filled with a great triangular plug of flesh that consisted almost entirely of mouths. This was the sharp end of the torbeast – that which was the essence of its ferocity and voracity. There was something wolfish about this mass, but with everything else but teeth and jaws stripped away. There could be no doubt, seeing this, that the torbeast's intentions were not benign.

'It's pressed right up against the walls. I'll not be able to get my sensor out of the way of that,' said Carloon.

'Can you take it out of phase?'

'I can, but how will I know when to bring it back in?'

'When I tell you.'

As the torbeast completely filled the screen, Carloon put that particular sensor a hundred and eighty degrees out of phase, folding the picture into black, speckled with the flashes of potential photons generated by the beast's energy front.

Maxell considered her options. If they left bringing the sensor back into phase until the last moment, and then saw that the beast was entirely inside the wormhole, this would indicate that Goron had failed. If it revealed, however briefly, that the beast was still pouring in, they could drop the structural energy feed and thus extend the tunnel by perhaps another third of a light-year. After that, without closure at Sauros, they must act. It meant catastrophic feedback to Sauros and the certain deaths of any survivors there, along with most of the life existing on that past Earth. It was still a matter for conjecture whether this might shove the Heliothane Dominion down the probability slope just as firmly as anything Cowl might achieve.

On the third screen the beast came into view, eventually filled the screen, then folded away as Carloon put that sensor out of phase too. Maxell felt her body growing damp with perspiration.

Damnation! Twenty thousand million kilometres?

At fifty thousand million kilometres the sweat was actually trickling from her armpits.

'How big is that damned thing?' asked Carloon.

Maxell didn't try to formulate a reply. There was a contention amongst Heliothane chronophysicists that the creature was potentially infinite – and it was a contention she didn't want to think about.

'I'll bring the third sensor back into phase,' said Carloon. 'It doesn't matter if we lose that one.'

The sensor operated for less than a second. Carloon froze the view, displaying a blurred image as of a torch shone through someone's cheek from inside.

'Coming up on number seven,' said Carloon.

Maxell noticed how the man's hand was shaking as he poised a finger over the virtual icon that would put this next sensor out of phase. Three more sensors went the same way and when Carloon got the same view from number four as he had from number three, she knew there was no point in saving any more of them for a hoped-for rear view of the beast.

'Cut the structural feed to minimum sustainable,' she instructed the interface techs.

The immediate energy surge caused the floor to vibrate, and she knew the Heliothane population would be feeling this all across the city's disc. Now microwave projectors and terajoule lasers were pumping the energy excess out into space, but this was an emission the city could not sustain. Eventually something would burn out, and then systems would begin to break down. If that happened the wormhole extension would have to be cut, else the microwave beam transmitted from the sun tap would create a molten sea in the centre of their fine city.

'Coming up on eleven,' said Carloon. 'It's taking longer.'

'When it hits twelve, we do it,' said Maxell. She looked around, seeing that most of the superfluous control-room staff were now standing in a semi-circle behind her. 'And then we see if we survive.'

Theldon gazed back for a second to where the survivors of Sauros were setting up camp on the mountainside, then turned and negotiated his way down what was once the course of a stream between stands of charred vegetation. He needed a deep pool to take the emergency manifold and there was none around here, the water having been evaporated literally in the heat of battle.

Even though the differences between heliothant and umbrathant were a few minor genetic ones, but mostly a question of loyalties, Theldon had found it difficult to infiltrate the upper echelons of the Heliothane Dominion. It had in fact taken him fifty of his one hundred and twenty-five years of life, and just when he was in a position to strike a blow that would obliterate New London, and the threat that it posed, Goron had shut down his console. He would have liked to have acted even earlier, but only during the chaos of the attack could his own penetration of abutment control have gone unnoticed. He damned himself for not sticking entirely to his job, and warning them of that first incursion because that error had certainly been what had roused Goron's suspicions. Now fifty years of sycophancy were wasted and ten years of being subordinate to Cowl's previously unknown primary agent.

Palleque.

They'd brought him back wounded for an interrogation. Theldon was unworried that his own presence might be revealed by Palleque, for the identities of Umbrathane agents or Cowl's agents were never revealed to each other, precisely for this reason. What had worried him then was just how long it was taking for that interrogation to start. And now . . . now Palleque was Goron's great friend and a hero to the Heliothane. Palleque had always been a double agent and this was something Cowl needed to know because that, and the fatalistic way Goron had reacted to the torbeast's attack, made Theldon feel this whole situation stank.

At last, out of sight of the vast flow of the torbeast pouring into the wormhole, Theldon saw the glimmer of water between some rocks. Heading down, he scanned desperately for a deep pool, but none was yet in evidence. Then, thankfully, it appeared before him: a deep pool right by a seared pile of vegetation that must have been washed down here in an earlier flood. He hurried towards it, having no doubt that Goron's people would be hunting for him even now. Perhaps Cowl could somehow divert an outgrowth of the torbeast into depositing one of its active scales – or maybe Cowl possessed some other method of retrieving his loyal agents.

At the pool Theldon went down on his knees and observed the floating bodies of blue-skinned newts amid the scum of burnt leaves and twigs. Plunging his hand into the water, he found it still warm and thought about the other kind of heat that would still be in this area. Certainly some of the citizens of Sauros would be excising tumours from themselves in the immediate future and having to run anti-cancer enzymes through their bodies for years to come. But whatever technology they had would now no longer be available to Theldon himself. Cowl would have something, though, and Theldon, with his tough genetic structure resulting from Umbrathane breeding programs and direct genetic manipulation, would be able to survive any melanomas for quite a few years yet. He sat back and shook water from his hand, then he pressed the finger and thumb of his right hand into his left forearm. The lump embedded in his muscle became visible through taut skin and, as he kept on the pressure, a fistula developed and began to ooze plasma. He pinched the flesh hard and a flattened white spheroid, a centimetre across, popped out of his arm. He inspected the thing for a second, then tossed it into the pool.

In the Jurassic he had established a permanent manifold set deep and out-of-phase in granite, just like the one Palleque had supposedly been caught using. That was all well and good, as the device extruded layers of vorpal crystal through the surrounding rock with which to blur the tachyon signal and thus hide itself from detection. The only problem was that once the egg had been placed, it took a number of days to develop and become usable. Growing one in water was quick but risky, as the chances of detection increased by an order of magnitude.

The spheroid sank about half a metre below the surface and

there, with one twitch, expanded to twice its previous size. It then frayed around the edges, and all movement in the water surrounding it ceased as it set itself in a fast-propagating jelly. It then began to grow the hard tentacular arms of the manifold, like sulphate crystals dumped in a solution of isinglass. In seconds it was ready and he pressed his palm against the pool's now rubbery surface: like an attacking squid the manifold rose to bind with his hand. After a moment Cowl's beetle face looked up at him from the depths.

'Sauros has been evacuated,' Theldon said without preamble. 'Was Palleque really your primary agent?'

'He was,' Cowl replied.

'Then know that he was a double agent. Goron gave him a displacement generator *before* the torbeast's attack and now it seems they are the greatest of friends.'

Pain shot up Theldon's arm from the manifold and he found he could not pull his hand away.

'It's true!' he protested. 'Something more is going on! I'm sure Goron *expected* things to happen as they have.' The pain eased and Theldon took an unsteady breath. He went on, 'I don't know what they think to achieve, but you have been out-manoeuvred.'

Cowl's head turned sideways, and for a moment Theldon got a hint of nightmarish shapes deep down in the pool.

'The beast will not stop,' said Cowl. He turned back. 'The killer . . . my sister . . .'

Abruptly the connection broke, and the manifold sank and slowly broke apart. Theldon withdrew his hand and looked disbelievingly at the still pool. No chance of rescue now. Cowl had given him nothing, not even a chance to ask for help. Theldon turned and looked back the way he had come. Maybe he could still salvage something. Maybe, during the chaos of the torbeast's attack, what he had tried to do could be put down to panic . . . inexperience.

Theldon was halfway back along the course of the stream when Palleque spotted him, and folded up the scope of the Heliothane rifle he was carrying. Theldon did not even see the source of the shot that punched a finger-width hole through his chest and blew his spine out of his back. There were never any maybes in this conflict, and very little room for doubt.

Above Cowl's citadel the weird shapes of incipient horror continued their hideous dance. Cowl stood utterly still before his vorpal controls, his hands hanging slack against his sides. When Makali and her compatriots entered the sphere, he still did not move until Makali's second, Scour, spoke – before she could stop him.

'Have we killed them? Have you done it?' he asked eagerly.

Cowl turned slowly, then stalked towards them. Eventually he came to stand still and silent before Scour. Makali herself did not move, knowing the danger of this moment. Those Umbrathane whom Cowl had brought back to his citadel were here on sufferance and under his absolute autocratic rule, being viewed by their ruler with the same contempt with which he viewed all humankind. Any who had been there for some time knew when to keep their heads down – for if Cowl suffered any kind of reversal he would take it out on those nearest to him.

Finally Cowl's voice issued, as if out of the air, 'The assassin escaped to the sea. Bring Aconite to me.'

'About time we dealt with that bitch,' said Scour.

Makali winced. As Cowl backhanded Scour and sent him sprawling, Makali willed her second to just stay on the floor and make no further move. But he was new to this part of citadel and still retained all his Umbrathane pride. He moved his hand to the butt of his handgun, his face twisting in a sneer as if about to say something.

None of the seven Umbrathane saw Cowl cross the intervening

space. He was just there, jerking Scour high into the air, ripping and tearing at him. Then Scour arced away, trailing his own intestines, and hit a lambent transformer before sliding, burning and screaming, to the floor. None of the other six moved or spoke while Scour's screams turned to groans as he cooked, unable to drag himself out of the thermal containment field around the machine. Cowl stood amongst them utterly still, as oily smoke drifted across the sphere's interior. This stillness went on interminably, until Makali relaxed the tension gripping her body and slid her hand down to her belt, just a short distance from her own hand weapon. Cowl immediately spun round towards her, and for a moment she thought she would now die like Scour had.

Sibilant hissing drew in to Cowl, from the shadows amid the machines, and expressed from that entity in words: 'I do not give orders twice.'

Catching the attention of her companions, Makali twitched her head towards the exit, and the five of them began backing out of the sphere. Makali followed them, pausing at the exit.

'The torbeast?' she asked, knowing she was now risking her life.

Cowl hissed again as his face covering began to open up.

Makali fled.

If asked who she trusted, Polly could only suggest Nandru with certainty, since his fortunes were now utterly tied to her own; and Ygrol, maybe, because he was utterly ingenuous. The word 'trust' did not apply to Tacitus because, though always honest and utterly straight with the others, he also coldly informed them that he was loyal unto death to Aconite, and cared not one whit if the rest of them lived or died. Cheng-yi she felt was the kind of dog you daren't turn your back on, and Lostboy she included in her general assessement of Aconite, for most of what rested inside his skull the troll woman had put there. The heliothant herself Polly considered too complex a being to either trust or distrust. Tack she trusted even less than the Chinaman, and when she spotted her erstwhile killer sneaking out into the damp night, she took up her taser, and the Heliothane handgun Aconite had provided for her, and followed him.

Rain was now steadily pouring from a dark sky, but it was a warm downpour and Polly relished it as she fixed her mask across and tied her hair back.

Now then, is there something Mr U-gov arsehole has neglected to tell us?

'Well, I don't think he's out here to smell the roses, Nandru,' Polly replied.

I wonder what it's to be: some sort of doublecross, or is he still going after Cowl?

'We'll find out soon enough.' Polly set off after the half-seen figure. The light robe Aconite had provided him with was much more easily visible than the black skin-tight clothing Polly herself wore, but nevertheless she found what concealment she could. However, Tack did not look round once as he plodded stolidly into the night.

Polly tracked him down the hill, then up one bank of the river. She ducked down behind a low boulder when at one point he halted, turning his masked face up into the rain. She noticed that his fists were clenched at his sides, then she watched him bow his head and bring the fists up and crush them against his temples. Still he did not turn round, but after a moment moved on.

Migraine? Nandru suggested.

Polly did not answer, for just then Tack abruptly turned aside and she lost sight of him. Hurrying up to the point she had last seen him, she spotted a narrow watercourse leading away from the river bed, cut down through stone. Following this, she kept catching glimpses of him ahead of her. For a second time he disappeared, but then a dim light ignited somewhere in the watercourse, and she finally came upon a tent lit up from the inside.

Perhaps he don't like company.

Much as she appreciated how much Nandru had helped her, she sometimes wished she had an antidote for his verbal diarrhoea. She studied the tent for long-drawn-out minutes, but no movement was apparent inside it. As she considered turning round and heading home, there came a muttered curse from the interior. Leading with the barrel of her handgun, Polly ducked down and pressed through the entrance.

Tack was sitting cross-legged at the rear of the tent behind a suspended chemical light. To his left lay an empty pack and on the ground to his right, rested a Heliothane carbine. He made no move for the weapon as she entered. When Polly moved to where she could more clearly see his face, she saw that his mask was off revealing a cold, blank expression. She removed her own mask to sample the air, and saw, down in one corner of the tent, some insectile oxygenating device.

'I'm sorry I tried to kill you,' Tack said emotionlessly.

He's sorry. Well, that cuts no mustard on my fucking beef.

'*Go away, Nandru.*'

Well, excuse me.

Polly felt the presence of Nandru fade as he took the other option now available to him: shifting his awareness into Wasp.

'Are you really?' she sneered at Tack.

He looked confused for a moment, pressed the palm of his hand against his forehead, then went on, 'I killed Minister LaFrange, Joyce and Jack Tennyson, Theobald Rice and Smythe. I cut off Lucian's fingers one by one until he told me the file-access code at Green Engine, and then I gutted the guard who tried to stop me breaking in there.' Then he looked up, staring past her as if at something beyond the wall of the tent and beyond this time. 'The bomb in the protest meeting against U-gov killed forty-eight people and maimed twelve.'

He fell silent, and she knew he was enumerating further killings and tortures in his mind.

'Why did you come out here?' she asked, uncomfortable with the ensuing silence.

His gaze tracked across to her. 'I needed to think.'

'Nice thoughts you have,' she observed.

He flinched. 'How could they be otherwise? I've led such a nice life.'

'But it wasn't exactly your fault,' Polly conceded.

His stare was blank. 'Yes, I accept that I had only as much control over my actions, before the moment Cowl took my mind apart, as any other machine. But that doesn't help. It was *me* who planted that bomb. It was *me* who raped the teenage daughter of a certain terrorist, to force him to come after *me*. It was *me* who led him into a trap and blew his kneecaps away, *me* who worked him over with scopolamine, a scalpel and pliers, until *I* had extracted the required information. And it was *me* who then tied a kerbstone to him and dumped him off the New Thames Barrier.'

'Did he deserve it?'

'She didn't.'

Polly was at a loss. She had followed him here expecting the man to be involved in something nefarious – and perhaps to have the satisfaction of putting a cluster of explosive bullets in his back in repayment for past intended hurts. But this was something else, though what she did not yet know. Maybe he truly felt remorse, or maybe that was just what he wanted her to think.

'So you have suddenly become such a moral human being?' she queried.

Tack snorted. 'It's not morality – it's empathy. I cringe when I remember the things I did. I can still hear the sound of the wirecutters going through Lucian's fingers and the sounds he made. I can remember the girl's fear, then disbelief, then pain, every word she said to me while she begged for mercy, and I can see how I destroyed something essential.'

Polly sat back and crossed her legs, wondering at her own reaction. She had never killed anyone, but she had caused pain because of her lack of empathy. As for morality, previously she had never known the meaning of the word.

'Aconite told me that's the true mark of a criminal,' she murmured.

'Cruelty?' Tack asked.

'No, lack of empathy. The true criminal cannot conceptualize the experiences of his victims. He cannot feel their pain, or in any way understand their trauma. The true criminal is not a social creature. We were discussing her brother at the time.'

Tack shook his head. 'In U-gov terms, I was not a criminal. I was merely their agent – the ungloved hand of their justice.'

'*They* were the criminals,' said Polly. 'What they did to you was in many ways as bad as the things you inflicted on others. They suppressed your humanity and made you their absolute slave.'

'Knowing who to blame doesn't make me feel any better. There's a grey area . . . Why didn't I kill that terrorist cleanly rather than let him drown?'

'Perhaps you felt his actions justified that punishment?'

'Perhaps.'

Polly gazed at him for a long moment as he stared at his hands. 'Tell me,' she said. 'Tell me all those things you did.'

He looked up at her, a faint smile twisting his features. 'Catharsis?'

'Maybe.'

And so, in terse, leaden sentences, Tack told her. When he had finished, Polly reached out and pressed her hand down on his.

'Where do we go from here?' Tack asked.

Confused by what she was feeling, Polly leaned forwards and kissed him on the lips. For a moment it appeared he did not know how to respond, then he reached out to press his hand against the back of her head, returning the kiss with a kind of desperation.

Sorry to break up this romantic moment, but a shitstorm just arrived.

Polly sometimes wished Nandru had a face she could slap.

20

Modification Status Report:
That pain again. Perhaps I should have removed him at the foetal stage and continued his growth in the tank as I did with Amanita, but in me there is the abiding instinct to nurture my creation. Perhaps it is only that I should have made some modification to my womb to withstand the abrasion of his hardening carapace. Blood tests have shown that, unlike his sister, he is not poisoning me. His prematurely developed immune system is so alien it does not seek to attack his mother, whereas hers was just human enough to recognize the vessel that contained it. But there's something . . . I am reluctant to run another scan, as that process in itself can be damaging to delicate tissues, and truthfully I do not want to find out if there is anything going wrong.

Damn . . . it's just not stopping . . . getting worse . . . must scan . . . must . . .

As he ran the whetstone along the edge of his gladius, Tacitus could see that Cheng-yi was angry. The man was angry at Polly's continual rejection of him, angry at the low regard in which Aconite held him, and now he was angry that all his hard work to teach mahjong to the Neanderthal was paying off – for Ygrol was beating him. But the Chinaman would not start getting openly offensive – he'd tried that once with Ygrol already and suffered concussion for the following three days. The Neanderthal tended to react either with smiling delight or with his club. There was no middle ground.

Living up to his name, Lostboy was sitting staring blankly into space, and Tacitus wondered if his own and Cheng-yi's addition to the boy's programming had been to the good. Aconite's Pedagogue had taught them enough to construct a program that would enable the boy to swim, and to load it, but their knowledge was certainly not anything like as extensive as the heliothant's. Tacitus was even considering wiping what they had installed and going to ask Aconite what had gone wrong, when the outer door whoomphed open and the Umbrathane intruders entered, discarding rain capes and removing their masks.

Holding her carbine in readiness across her stomach, Makali marched to the centre of the room, her five fellows spreading out behind her as she scanned the surrounding area.

'Where is the killer?' she demanded.

Tacitus merely continued sharpening his sword, while Cheng-yi and Ygrol quietly proceeded with their game.

'Very well, then tell me where that piece-of-shit heliothant is,' Makali spat into the silence.

Tacitus felt a familiar surge of anger, and the whetstone slipped. He put a bloody finger in his mouth and watched while the umbrathant marched over to the mahjong table and swept its pieces onto the floor.

'I asked a question!'

'I think you asked *two* questions,' Cheng-yi smart-mouthed.

Makali backhanded him and he went flying out of his chair to sprawl on the floor. Tacitus stood. This was bad, not because of Makali's violent behaviour, but because of the expression now on Ygrol's face – he had been about to win the game.

'Ygrol,' Tacitus murmured warningly, stepping forward.

'Far enough, Roman.'

Tacitus had not even seen the Umbrathane male move round the room to come up behind him. He froze, feeling a hand on his shoulder and the barrel of a handgun pressed against his cheek.

'Perhaps you don't think I'm serious.' Without even looking in the direction she was pointing her carbine, Makali pulled the trigger. Lostboy's head blew open, flowering around the blockish cerebral augmentation, which clattered onto the floor as he slid from his chair. 'I'm serious.'

Flinging the games table aside, Ygrol came up with a roar, his bone club raised. Tacitus felt his mouth go dry as he saw how fast two of Makali's fellows shot in front of her, one of them stamping on Cheng-yi's head in passing as the Chinaman tried to rise. The first to reach the Neanderthal knocked away his club, then both umbrathants dragged him to his chair and forced him down into it. No matter how Ygrol strained he could not get up, and bellowed as Makali strolled forward to pick up the bone club and inspect it. She turned to Tacitus.

'Where is the killer? And where is Aconite?'

Aconite almost certainly knew about the arrival of these intruders, Tacitus supposed, but perhaps she was taking needed time to prepare, so he kept his mouth firmly shut. Without taking her eyes off Tacitus, Makali brought the bone club up hard to smash into Ygrol's face. Still seeing no reaction from the Roman, she turned on the Neanderthal and began to lay into him. As blood spattered her face and prosthetic arms, Tacitus realized that any answer he might give would not alter the outcome of what was happening here. Cowl had let Makali off the leash.

It was over in a minute, Ygrol's broken head lolling to one side.

'Well now,' said Makali. 'I guess we'll have to see what I can do with that sword of yours.'

'I'm here,' spoke a new voice.

Aconite had entered the room from her research area. Tacitus could see her rage and he prepared himself to do whatever was required of him.

'I think you're a little late for this party,' said Makali, inspecting the blood runneling in the circuit patterns on the bone club she held.

Aconite clicked her fingers and a sudden deep droning filled the room, along with a blast of air. Wasp rose vertically into view, its wings a blur behind it, and a glistening sting extruded into view. It drove forwards as one of the umbrathants turned towards it. He bowed over as it slammed into him, the sting going in through his chest and out of his back. Then the sting flicked and discarded him. Tacitus reversed his sword, its blade alongside his ribcage, and thrust back into the umbrathant behind him, turning as he did so. There came a gagging crunch from the man, and muzzle fire skinned the Roman's cheekbone. The bone club became a blurred wheel in the air, before it was caught and shattered in Aconite's massive hand. Pulling his gladius free from his dying captor, Tacitus threw it underhand, spearing its way towards Makali's back. Then a shot smacked into his chest and he staggered back, stumbling over the umbrathant he had impaled. He saw Makali whip round, impossibly fast, catching the gladius by the handle, bringing it over her head and almost casually squatting down to drive it through Cheng-yi's back to pin him to the floor. With teeth bared she pulled some device from her belt and aimed it at Wasp. The room whited out for a second, then the robot dropped out of the air and crashed to the floor.

'You think we didn't know?' said Makali.

The same white-out again. Now Aconite falling like an oak tree.

Tacitus slid down, with his back to the wall. He stared down at his shattered body – he had done his best.

Silleck was one of the few interface technicians who had survived, and like all of them only because she had torn herself away from her vorpal controls. Now, with open wounds in her scalp and undetached nubs of vorpal glass embedded in her skull like little windows into her brain, she suffered a headache that just would not go away. Only time would cure that, as the damaged tissue of her meninges healed around the vorpal fibres entering her brain. But she would never be rid of the facility to slide into a perception that stepped one dimension above that of her fellow, un-interfaced Heliothane. Gazing across the mountainside, she observed the survivors setting up their camps for the coming night; while, sliding into further perception, she saw them preparing to do this, and their camps already made. Watching also the endless flow of the beast into the wormhole, she saw images that both repelled and fascinated her.

This ability, Goron reassured her, would prove essential in the coming years, as there were few dangers on this Earth that could slip past guards able to see into the future – if only for a few minutes. Because of this extended perception, and because her gaze kept straying back to the beast, she was the first to see it happen.

She stood and walked upslope to Goron, who sat Buddha-like on the mountainside, the section of control pillar resting on his lap. His eyes were closed, for he was either asleep or meditating. She eyed Palleque who, despite what Goron had told them all, she still distrusted as she did all fanatics.

'It's happening,' she told Goron at last.

The Engineer opened his eyes and gazed towards Sauros. 'There was always the possibility it would be endless, though not for us.'

Silleck and the rest of the survivors had been waiting for a feedback cataclysm that would have swept them away from this mountainside in an ashy wind. Now this was not to be.

Then it all ended as suddenly as it had begun. The flow of torbeast attenuated, the roar of its progress dropping away. It broke up into trailing tentacles of raw flesh and spills of putrid dead matter – and then it was gone.

'And there it is,' said Palleque, standing up.

Goron reached inside the control sphere and did what he had to do. Just inside the ravaged structure of the city, the three abutments began to slide towards a centre point, closing the wormhole entrance. As they drew closer, Goron shaded his eyes, though the light was not really so intense, being to the infrared end of the spectrum. Dull thunder echoed and what remained of the city deformed under an intense burst of heat.

Silleck felt the heat on her face – and in her dry eyes.

Relaying what Nandru was telling her, Polly said, 'Aconite and Wasp were in the tor chamber when Aconite went charging out. Wasp followed her into the residential room, when suddenly some system inside Wasp cut in and it threw Nandru out. But he had time to see that Ygrol was dead – that you don't display that amount of brain to the air without needing a body bag shortly after.'

'Tell Nandru to describe exactly what else he saw,' said Tack.

Polly tilted her head for a moment, and her eyes narrowed. 'One of them held a gun to Tacitus's head. Two were holding Ygrol down in a chair and it seems Makali had just beaten his brains out. He didn't see the other two, though.'

'They're probably all dead,' said Tack.

'But if they are not, we have to do something for them,' Polly replied.

Resting his carbine across his shoulder, Tack stared at her. He was sick of these Umbrathane and Heliothane eternally killing each other and dragging others into the conflict. He was his own man now and he wanted no more of it. He also did not want to be forced into a position where he himself would have to kill again. However, Aconite had arranged to have him dragged from the sea, and she had subsequently put him back together. He owed her. And, at the last, he now wanted to gain Polly's respect – and whatever else she might be prepared to give. In that moment he felt, with a lurch, his life beginning again, and knew he could not renege on his new responsibilities. *Fucking hero*, he thought.

'Whatever's happened there, we're too late to stop it. But let's see what we can find out,' he said, his stomach turning over at such a positive statement.

He led the way up from the river bed, circling round to come down on Aconite's house from the mountainside. As they climbed, the rain turned to drizzle, then a wind picked up and blew that away. The cloud began to break, opening on stars and the first hint of topaz dawn behind the mountains. When the house finally came into view below them, lemon sunlight was already bathing the coastline beyond and flecking the sea with gold. The citadel, to their left, looked no different. Still, around its high points, bestial distortions crowded the sky.

'Why does that happen?' Tack asked.

After a moment Polly replied, 'Aconite says Cowl's energy source comes from thermal taps penetrating down to a geological fault running out from here. From that power source he feeds energy to the torbeast when he wants it to do his bidding, and that same energy feed opens a rift through to the beast's alternate. The beast always attempts to come through here to access that source directly and what we are seeing is the result of that.'

'But Cowl won't let it through.'

'No. I don't understand the tech he uses, but he prevents the beast from coming totally into phase. It is only a few degrees out, but enough for it to produce no more effect than this.'

'And if it came through?'

'Cowl would end up as dead as us.'

Tack remembered those thick cables snaking out into the sea.

Judging from them, he supposed the energy being utilized must be immense. However, it did not even compare to that transmitted by the sun tap, as no cables could ever carry that load. Glancing down at the house again, he abruptly caught Polly's shoulder and dragged her down. They observed an umbrathant guard emerge and walk around the back of the house to urinate against the wall.

'Here's what we'll do,' Tack said.

Polly walked casually up from the river towards the house, as if she had just been out for a pleasant stroll. The Umbrathane woman by the door called inside, and a man quickly joined her. Polly kept her gaze level on them, not daring to look up any higher. She raised a hand in a friendly wave. When she was still five metres away, Tack, leaping down from the roof, brought his right foot down squarely on top of the Umbrathane woman's head and, as she crumpled, snapped out his left foot to catch the man under his ear. By then Polly was flat on the ground – as instructed.

Tack forward-flipped off the woman, hit the ground on his feet, and rolled aside as shots splintered rock where he had been a fraction of a second before. Coming upright, he spun round, his foot coming up in an arc accelerated by the weight of his strange surgical boot. Straightening his leg at the last, he slammed the boot up into the man's throat. To his horror, he glimpsed Polly bringing to bear her handgun in what to Tack seemed slow motion. The woman, having hit the ground on her shoulder, was coming upright again, her weapon swinging towards Polly. And then Tack realized he would not be able to do this without killing.

He swung his carbine round towards the woman, but shots from the man shattered the barrel of the weapon. The Umbrathane woman hesitated for a microsecond, assessing the greatest danger. She began to turn towards Tack just as he dropped his carbine and flung himself back. A hole opened up in the woman's forehead and she began to drop. The man began yelling and swung towards Polly. But why was he moving so slowly? Then Tack realized the man had probably just seen his lover die. That did not slow Tack as he hurled himself forward. Closing in, the carbine swung back towards him. He caught the barrel, turning as he did so, its fire scoring his stomach. He jerked the weapon towards him, out of the man's grip, spinning it up around his back and over his shoulder. Catching it in his other hand, he fired it, slinging the man backwards. It was over. It had taken less than six seconds. Not much time to extinguish two lives.

'Accurate shooting,' said Tack, as Polly walked over to him.

Coming to a halt, Polly holstered her handgun, then gazed down at the two dead umbrathants. She said, 'Mortuus est. Mortua est.'

Tack looked at her queryingly.

'They're both dead,' she said.

'Yeah, certainly that,' he replied.

Polly looked up, eyeing the carbine Tack held. 'I knew a juggler once, called Berthold, who would have been impressed by the way you moved there.'

Tack gazed down at the two corpses, and could not find it in himself to be so flippant. When they entered the house, they found more dead inside. First there was the Chinaman.

Tack stooped down by Cheng-yi, checked the pulse at his throat then attempted to remove the sword. The weapon was so deeply embedded in the composite floor, it would not have yielded without Tack's augmentations. Tossing the weapon aside, he turned the body over and studied it, before switching his attention to Ygrol. No need to check the Neanderthal's pulse – his thick skull was broken open and most of his brain mashed.

'They shot Lostboy, too,' said Polly.

Tack stood and walked over to stand beside her. Only half of

Lostboy's head remained, and on the floor nearby lay his cerebral augmentation. Polly picked it up and carefully placed it on a table. 'Perhaps Aconite can save something,' she said.

Tack looked at her askance.

She tapped a finger against the blood-smeared device. 'They killed the animal part of him, but most of what was human is in here,' she explained.

Then a sound spun them both round, and they saw Tacitus slumped against a wall in a pool of his own blood. Polly rushed over and pressed her finger against his throat.

'He's still alive, but we'll have to get him into the surgery,' she announced.

As Tack stepped over the dead umbrathant, he noted the wound in the man's upper chest. So Tacitus had not gone down without taking one of them with him. Passing the carbine to Polly, he stooped to pick Tacitus up and turned towards Aconite's surgery. Polly darted past him to inspect the fallen Wasp and the dead umbrathant beside it. Tack supposed the intruders had swaggered into this place as arrogantly as any of their kind, but encountered some nasty surprises.

'I don't feel safe about staying here,' he said. 'They must know we're still about, and those outside might have sent off some sort of call.'

'I'll not abandon him,' said Polly.

'Then I'll check things out,' said Tack, laying Tacitus on the surgical table. 'Do you know how to operate this stuff?' He gestured to the surrounding equipment.

'What I don't know Nandru can tell me – he uploaded a lot from Wasp's database.'

Taking the carbine, which Polly handed back to him, Tack watched for a moment while she cut open the Roman soldier's clothing, and placed a monitoring device against his neck. Then acknowledging that she seemed to know what she was doing, Tack went off to search the house.

Polly assumed that Aconite herself had been dragged off to the citadel, but Tack was not so sure. It seemed to him that the Umbrathane intruders had come here simply to eliminate a potential threat. The house was a big place, so it was likely that he would find Aconite dead in one of its many rooms. With methodical caution he began at the top of the house in the attic, wondering at the precise purpose of the exposed vorpal substructure of the building visible there, with all those linked-up machines and heavy power cables. On the next floor down he found mostly sealed rooms, but one door was open and in it he thoughtfully eyed the racked carbines, catalysers, grenades and some other weapons he did not recognize. On the ground floor he checked all the living quarters, but ignored the many rooms that were sealed. The laboratories and research areas showed no sign of damage, so he did not spend long in them – just checking that no more bodies were visible. It was in the cellar he found the tors, and now understood why there had been so few lying on the seabed along with the arm bones. Here he felt the subversive control emanating from these parasitic devices and noted how many of them lay on the floor. He realized that they were regrowing their thorns, and that this process had forced some of them out of the racks. But Aconite, or her body, was not here either, so he closed the door and returned to Polly.

'We must save her,' Tacitus groaned, as Tack came back into the room.

Tack observed that plumbing and wiring now linked the Roman to several surrounding machines. He raised an eyebrow.

'All I need is an affixed and internally linked carapace, then I'll be able to move . . .' the soldier croaked.

Tack turned to Polly, who shrugged, then reached out a finger to touch the device now attached to the Roman's neck. With a sigh Tacitus closed his eyes and slumped unconscious.

'What did he mean by "carapace"?' Tack asked.

Polly pointed at his surgical boot. 'It supports both internally and externally while accelerated repair takes place, but it can only be used for minor injuries. Tacitus could have one placed on his chest, but only if he was prepared to move around very slowly and I do not think that was his intention.'

'So Cowl has Aconite,' said Tack.

'Yes.'

'What do we do?'

'We have to get her back. We need her.'

Tack absorbed the thought. They did not know how the mechanisms of the house operated and so could not survive here. But he did not think they stood much chance up against more Umbrathane and the last thing he wanted to do was face Cowl again.

'We have to get her out of there,' Polly affirmed, staring at him.

Tack swallowed dryly. 'OK,' he said.

The mantisal clipped wavetops, the vapour of its ablation giving it the appearance of hot glassware just cast out of the furnace. It rolled across the sea's surface and broke apart, the three Heliothane ejecting as if thrown from a car wreck, but controlling their descent at the last and each entering the sea in a perfectly orchestrated flat dive. Pieces of the mantisal skittered across the water and settled, floating, on the surface, as the final glowing ember extinguished in them. One of the three Heliothane resurfaced, cast a package out before him and watched as it unfolded into an inflatable raft. By the time it was fully expanded, the other two had surfaced and all three scrambled aboard.

'Nothing yet,' said Meelan, collapsing on her back and spitting out sea water as she studied her detector.

Saphothere started up the small engine mounted inside the back of the inflatable and got them moving. Coptic folded up a scope on the hand-held missile launcher he clutched, and watched the skies.

As soon as the raft was moving, Saphothere asked, 'Where are we?'

'About ten kilometres from the citadel itself and about an hour from the Nodus,' Meelan replied.

'Look,' said Saphothere, nodding ahead. The three of them gazed at the torbeast distortion wavering in the sky like a heat haze. Below it they could just about discern the spiky peaks of the citadel. Saphothere went on, 'We probably won't get any missiles heading this way. No doubt the attack on Sauros is in progress, and I'd guess Cowl won't spare attention to such minor matters as a tor falling through his trap and going into the sea. Probably thinks another torbearer just drowned – if he noticed at all. Then, when we get closure at Sauros, Cowl will be in a world of shit – no short-jumping inside his citadel and no way to dodge the bullets.'

'Shame we can't send some missiles from here,' opined Coptic.

'They would be detected,' Saphothere replied, 'especially if they were likely to be in any way effective.'

'Like atomics, you mean,' said Meelan acidly.

'Yeah, like atomics. Cowl probably detected those two I handed to Tack when he was within a kilometre of his destination – and no doubt had a double displacement fixed on them all the time.'

'Poor idiot,' said Meelan. 'At least Tack would have died believing that his assassination attempt was to prevent Cowl destroying human history.'

'In a roundabout way he was, actually,' said Saphothere. 'And, anyway, many Heliothane have died believing the same – so he was not unique.'

'Umbrathane believe that's Cowl's intention, too, and they die just the same.'

'Yeah,' said Saphothere.

'Saphothere,' Coptic interrupted, 'we've got company.'

The three of them turned their attention to the sky and the object becoming visible there: distant still, but growing closer.

'Another reason for him not sending a missile against us,' Meelan observed.

'That's it, then,' said Saphothere. 'Let's go and kill the bastard before he can do anything about it.'

'Sounds reasonable to me,' said Meelan.

The sky was growing dark and the effect was something like silt boiling up from the bottom of a deep pool. Wave after wave threw dark bands of shadow across the landscape. Polly looked up, feeling her mouth grow dry. This simply did not happen here – after a downpour like last night's, the sky usually remained clear for many weeks, and Polly had yet to witness any true extremity of weather. But this had an immensity: the bands of cloud spreading out from that central boiling point seemed almost solid. And that there was no sound as yet made it all the more threatening.

'What now?' asked Tack, as he too stepped outside Aconite's house.

'The Nodus,' said Polly. 'We knew it was close.'

Makes a kind of insane sense for it to arrive now. Makes you wonder if the Heliothane haven't unified everything yet. Perhaps there's still much they don't know.

'Does this mean Cowl has failed – or is he about to succeed?' Tack asked.

Polly turned and stared at him. 'Succeed at what?'

Still gazing at the sky, Tack said, 'At shoving human history down the probability slope and creating his own time-line at the top of the slope.'

'You still believe that?' Tack returned his attention to her, as she went on. 'That's just the great Heliothane lie told to justify continuing their extermination of Umbrathane. Admittedly their attempts to get to Cowl are in themselves justified because of the many Heliothane lives he has taken. But that doesn't make it any less of a lie.'

'What?'

He looked confused, and Polly realized she was pulling another bulwark of belief from underneath him, but it had to be done.

'Cowl is working to prevent the omission paradox,' she explained.

'And I thought I was confused,' said Tack, rediscovering the sense of humour for which Saphothere had once beaten him.

Polly went on, 'Cowl escaped Heliothane persecution, and he gave the Umbrathane an escape route too. The energy he carried in the big jump took him back before the Nodus and do you know what he found?'

'Tell me.'

'He found life without DNA. He found life that bore no relation to anything he knew, with minimal probability that it would develop into the life we know in the few centuries he had before the Nodus arrived.'

'And that means?'

'You have to be as utterly arrogant as Cowl to believe that you are the source of such a critical omission paradox.'

'You said that before and I still don't get it.'

'Cowl believes he is the source of the Nodus – that if he doesn't start DNA-based life in this ocean, there will be no life as we know it later. That by omission he will destroy the time-line and become a unique, unreferenced being, perpetually trapped in his own alternate.'

'So he's a good guy?'

'If a good guy is also one who's regard for any life but his own is nil – and who would, given the opportunity, wipe out the entire Heliothane Dominion.'

'But surely he could do that by doing what the Heliothane claimed he was doing?'

'No. He only has geothermal taps here. The energy levels he would need require a sun tap at the very least. That's just another Heliothane lie.'

'So what the fuck is going on?'

'That,' said Polly, pointing at the sky.

Gathering in a wheel above them, thick black clouds turned and rolled, expressing spokes of lightning. A low, growling storm was reaching them now. And behind these strange cloud formations a shape was resolving.

'A ship?' Tack wondered.

'Maybe. Or some living being in itself. Or even a seed pod.'

A flattened sphere now filled a quarter of the sky, the lower edge of it lost beyond the horizon. Segmented like an orange, it was translucent, and higher cloud layers showed through it as through a distorting lens. Other clouds broke over it, like the waves of a sea splashing over a boulder. As they watched, it tilted and came fully into view. In consonance with the tilting, the ground began to vibrate. Then came immense flashes of lightning, cracks in the heavens revealing another reality, and the gunshot crashing of thunder.

'What's happening?' Tack yelled.

'Seeding,' said Polly, leaning close. 'As the Heliothane knew, because their first interstellar probe sent back evidence of it elsewhere after Cowl had gone. I don't know how Aconite found out, which is why we have to get to her – she must have some access to the future that is her own.'

'But why didn't she tell him?'

'Because as long as he struggled to solve his omission paradox, he would not turn his full fury on the Heliothane. She has spent her life blunting the edge of Cowl's rage.'

Nandru took that moment to add, *I'm so glad you explained all that, Polly. There was me thinking it was all a bit complicated.*

'Nandru,' said Polly out loud, glancing apologetically at Tack. 'It gets even simpler now. As we move into the Nodus, the chances of the Heliothane reaching Cowl increase dramatically. And when that happens we'll need to be on the other side of the planet, at least, if we want to survive. We need Aconite and we need her as soon as possible.'

I can help you, but it means I must leave you, and I won't be able to come back this time, as I must be both the program and the memory.

'What the fuck are you on about?'

Don't be so unfriendly.

'I'm sorry, but things just got a lot more urgent.'

Well, goodbye, Polly.

'Wait! What are you—?'

Polly felt him go, just as he did when he transferred his awareness to Wasp.

'What the hell?' said Polly, then shook her head in irritation. Reaching up, she brushed her fingers through her hair then brought her hand down for inspection. There were gritty white crystals on her palm. She blinked and looked up. It was snowing, only this was no snow that she recognized.

'We have to get to Aconite – she's the only one who can help. She has to have a way out of here.'

Just then there came a loud clattering and droning from inside the house, and they whirled round as something shot out of the door to loom over them.

'And hello!' bellowed Nandru-Wasp.

The tension in the New London Abutment Control Centre was palpable. Maxell watched the screens and wondered just how much longer she could wait in the hope of totally completing this herculean task. So much had been invested and so much would be lost, whether they succeed or failed, so justification of the latter was not something she wanted to contemplate. Then the tension notched up a level.

'We have closure!' shouted an interface technician.

Maxell was frozen for half a second. They had time – they still had time.

'Do you have a mass reading?' she asked.

'Not yet . . . still calculating . . . I'm putting it up on a subscreen,' the technician replied.

Maxell felt her mouth go dry as she saw the figure. The subscreen opened in a band across the bottom of the screen and filled with digits. Abruptly it contracted, the number being rounded off and displayed with an exponent, because it was simply too big to fit on the screen.

'*That* cannot be taken out of existence,' moaned Carloon.

'Nevertheless,' said Maxell, 'we will try.' To the interface tech she said, 'Send the signal.'

'Sent,' replied the tech.

Now it was a matter of waiting. The tachyon signal would arrive at the moment of transmission, but the transit of the microwave beam was nominally six minutes. They were now utterly committed and history would judge them – if any history there was to be.

'How long before the beast reaches our abutments?' she asked.

Carloon replied, 'It was looking like about ten minutes, but now it's accelerating.'

'How the hell can it know?' an interface technician asked.

Carloon now brought the most distant sensor back into phase, displaying the far section of the wormhole empty of torbeast. This brought them no comfort – the end of it with the most mouths was coming at them like an accelerating juggernaut.

'Any of you know how to pray?' Maxell asked. Then to the negatives she said, 'Well, now might be a good time to learn.'

21

Cowl:
I am the pinnacle of the Darwinian evolution of the human species, even though my superiority has been achieved by genetic manipulation. I was made to survive in an extrapolation of the most hostile of human environments, by the most ruthless means. As such I am all that Umbra and Heliothane dogma would have humans come to be. But when a being is measured by its ability to survive ruthless selection processes, isn't its superiority equated with its ability to destroy and murder? Doesn't such a measure discount all creativity, and so much else? The ability to survive and to dominate is not all. I am a dead end, but I am also human, and know that what I was made to be is not enough. I am what I am.

He had never done this to her before and foolishly she had believed he never would. Aconite was appalled at the ruthless power of her brother's mind. His linking tendrils were fully developed and he knew how to use them to best effect. Her own had been stunted and virtually unusable since birth, so she'd had an autosurgeon remove them and cover the evidence with cosmetic surgery. With anguine deadliness his tendrils speared through her eardrum and into her skull, dividing and ever dividing down into synaptic plugs, connecting to the various portions of her brain. Cowl had never mind-fucked her before, but now he was.

Immediately she was dropped into the world of memory – but with her brother present as a hostile spectre. He stood behind her as she looked with some amazement at the ersatz assassin, and wondered why Tack was still alive and if she should allow him to continue to be. A jump, and Cowl listened to his explanation, her brother knowing that she already knew the truth: Tack had been sent here to reveal a weakness in the defences of Sauros, which was the jaws of a trap. But Cowl wanted the root of it:

The four stood on a viewing balcony overlooking the Tertiary park, where six-metre tall paraceratheriums were browsing. Though these creatures possessed skin like that of elephants and a llama-like appearance, they were, like all the prehistoric fauna of the New London parks, distinct animals in themselves. Watching them tearing down palm fronds to get at the ripening dates, Aconite felt that, of all Heliothane projects, this was the most worthy, and even to be able to recover Earth's genetic heritage was a gift indeed. It was a shame that, on the whole, time travel was used for more bellicose purposes.

'How did you manage to get here?' asked Engineer Goron.

Aconite held up her arm to display the enclosing tor. 'My brother has yet to completely hard-wire the programming. I simply inverted it, and I will return it to normal to take me back.'

Maxell turned to Goron. 'Goron, don't make the mistake of seeing Aconite forever in her brother's shadow. Her abilities are at least equal to his, even if her intentions are not.'

Cowl hissed at this, his breath liquid against Aconite's cheek.

'Did you think I couldn't plumb your technology? Did you really believe I was the poisonous failure our mother named me?' asked Aconite.

The tendrils tightened in her head, shooting agony around her skull and down her spine. She knew he wanted her to resist, but she let him have it all:

'So what is it you have to say?' asked Goron, eyeing Aconite with suspicion.

'My brother is not trying to destroy you by altering the time-line – in doing that he might well destroy himself. He has discovered he is the cause of the Nodus. Human history begins with a circular paradox.

He has found no DNA-based life before that point, so it can only be caused by him. Now he applies all his energies to stop himself causing the omission paradox that could destroy the entire time-line, and thus his own ancestry.'

The laughter came from the fourth member of this group.

'Such arrogance,' said Palleque, shaking his head.

Maxell gave him a look. 'Something of which we are all guilty. Please continue, Aconite.'

After a moment of puzzlement Aconite went on, 'My brother is not the greatest danger to you, not in himself.'

'The torbeast,' said Palleque. He wasn't laughing now.

Aconite nodded, 'Already it is immense and reaches uptime to feed. Cowl cannot entirely prevent it doing this, and already the anomalies it is creating are forcing its uptime substance further down the slope generated from the Nodus.'

'Then that will be the end of the problem,' said Palleque.

Aconite stared at him. 'No. My brother needs the torbeast to drop active tors, so he can sample the future and thus find out how to avoid the omission paradox – to find out if his experiments with the protoseas are having any effect – so he feeds energy to it from his geothermal taps to sustain its position on the slope.'

'It also serves another purpose for him,' said Palleque through gritting teeth.

Aconite turned to stare at him. 'Then you know that, while it serves his purposes, it also feeds.'

Grimacing, Palleque turned away from her.

'I do not yet see how his pet is the greater problem,' said Goron.

'As it feeds, it grows,' said Aconite. 'Its structure is more complex than anything else that has ever lived. It can grow organic time machines on itself . . . do I need to draw you a diagram?'

'Oh,' said Goron.

'What does she mean?' asked Palleque, turning back.

Maxell offered an explanation. 'It generates its own vorpal field, and once it reaches sufficient mass that field will be strong enough to enable the beast to shift itself anywhere on the probability slope.'

'And to feed,' Aconite added.

'And what precisely are we talking about here?' Palleque asked.

'An eater of worlds – all life, every shift-generated time-line, nothing but torbeast left.'

From her brother, Aconite felt confirmation of this, and understood in an instant that his sending of the beast against the Heliothane served two purposes: to kill his enemy and also to weaken his dangerous pet. The time frame jumped:

'It is the only way to take it out, completely out,' said Goron.

This time Aconite and the Engineer walked out together across the floor of one of New London's construction bays, towards the skeleton of a giant sphere – only this time the shadow of Cowl walked beside them.

'This was created to extend Heliothane Dominion throughout time. As a base from which to kill every last umbrathant, and finally from which to finish your brother. But perhaps now it can serve a more honourable purpose. I would wish it so.'

'The bait seems . . . small.'

'The largest fish can be hooked with the smallest fly.'

'Will the Heliothane, as a whole, countenance the loss?'

'Of this?' Goron asked, gesturing to the nascent Sauros.

'Of it all. You've spent two centuries on this project, and used up half the wealth of the Dominion. And just to lose it all to destroy a threat most of its citizens have never seen and many could not even comprehend?'

'It has to be done.'

Cowl's anger was like hot wires burning inside her skull. He was going to kill her with this and, if he did not, he would kill her later.

The tor called to everyone in the Antarctic research facility, but only Aconite intended to respond to that call. Palleque glared at the thing, but then he had more reason to hate its source than anyone else.

'Here, I have a present,' he said, turning to her and holding out a small glass cylinder containing white crystals. 'We found it on Mars, in strata a billion years old, and after that on every other solid planet in the solar system, in rock of the same age.'

'What is it?'

'You wondered why I laughed when you said Cowl was the cause of the Nodus.' He gestured at the cylinder she now held. 'There were hundreds of theories on the source of that, until our interstellar probe discovered the same substance on a dead world orbiting the red dwarf, Proxima Centauri.'

'You still haven't told me what it is.'

'Crystalline DNA in a protein matrix. As soon as it hits liquid water, it becomes active. In about a million years you've got metazoan life – and the rest is history, as they say. In the end, only one theory fits the facts.'

'Seeding.'

Cowl released his hold and Aconite dropped to her knees, blood running from her ear and glistening over the abrasions around her throat. She glared up at her brother and tested the thick ceramal cuffs that bound her wrists and ankles.

'How many more do you think I'd let you kill?' she spat.

Cowl tilted his head, but said nothing. Abruptly he spun round and headed for his vorpal controls. After a moment he uttered a shriek of rage.

In the sky, the spectral display of the torbeast juddered and bled away as, unnoticed, a raft drew into the citadel's shadow. With the energy feed severed at Sauros, a backlash rippled downtime from the city, taking no time at all, and for ever. Cowl withdrew his sharp fingers from the vorpal ovoid, and stepped back, turning his head to see lightning flashing between temporal capacitors and transformers. The sea boiled as safety trips attempted to divert the surge into the water. It was like trying to hold together a broken dam with Sellotape. Under the sea flare after flare ignited then died to dull red, stepping out in tens then hundreds then thousands towards the horizon, as geothermal generators vaporized and melted surrounding rock. Shortly after, explosions, as from depth charges, followed the same course. Inside the citadel darkness was lit up by machinery fires, then dispelled when auxiliary generators cut in. Emergency lights came on all over the structure, and Umbrathane ventured from their places of safety.

Clinging to the ledge, in the shadow of the out-flowering walls of the citadel above, Tack gazed at the other occupants and saw how they had accumulated. The torbearer in armour had been the first, his weight dropping him directly down from the chute mouth and, with whatever strength had remained to him, he had driven his dagger into a crevice where the ledge joined the pillar. There he must have died, for Aconite had not rescued him, and over time the rust from his armour had stuck him to the ledge. After him had come others: someone wearing a long robe had fallen, the material of which had snagged on one of the knight's greaves; arm bones had accumulated around these two, and other skeletons had become stuck to the ledge with the adipocere of decay. Occasional ornaments gleamed and weapons rusted. Tack noted a burnt-out Heliothane carbine resting against a ribcage enclosed in parchment skin, the weapon's black metal and plastic partially melted and turned grey with salt, and wondered about the story behind that. Then, keeping his foot firm against the adhesive mine, he raised the harpoon launcher he had taken from Aconite's armoury and fired upwards.

With the usual chemical flash, the head of the harpoon bonded to the upper lip of the chute, and after detaching the adhesive mine Tack set the winder spinning to haul him up into the chute's mouth. Here he stuck the mine to the floor of the chute to give himself a foothold, before detaching the harpoon and winding it all the way back into its launcher. He then gazed up into darkness.

Having little clear memory of his own descent down this pipe, Tack had consulted Nandru and was told it ran in a hundred-metre arc down from Cowl's spherical control centre. Easy enough to climb, but not yet – he waited.

The sky was still dark with the presence of that *thing* and the storm it had induced. Beyond the sheltering loom of the citadel, Tack observed the dusty snowstorm of the crystalline substance hazing the surface of the sea and somehow making the waves sluggish. Within a few minutes he spotted Nandru-Wasp hurtling towards him from the direction of Aconite's home, the robot clutching Polly underneath it like a stolen grub. Finally Tack turned and fired up into darkness, observing the glow of chemical bonding twenty metres above him. Winding the line in taut, he detached the mine and hooked it onto the shoulder strap of the weapons harness he had also acquired. There were three of these devices which, on their contact surfaces, possessed a layer of microscopic hairs much like those found on a gecko's foot. Unfortunately, unlike the lizard's foot, the mines were not made for repeated use and after a time would lose their adhesive quality. Hence three of them were needed for this climb. Tack had no intention of using them to blow up anything.

Nandru-Wasp flew into the shadow of the citadel, then descended to hover by the mouth of the chute. Polly, clasped firmly underneath the robot by its four spiky legs, brushed white powder from her face and eyes, before reaching out a hand to Tack. Standing with his boot on the chute's rim, Tack used the winder's friction control to allow himself enough slack to lean out and grasp her forearm.

'Do you have her?' Nandru asked. 'I don't want to be premature in letting her go.'

'I have her,' Tack replied tightly.

Nandru-Wasp released his hold, then shot up into the air with the sudden lightening in weight. Polly leapt inwards, her feet coming down on the chute's lip, and her other hand clutching at Tack's weapons harness.

'OK?' he asked.

'OK,' she replied.

Tack started the winder hauling them up the slope. Because of the risks he would rather have done this alone, but he just did not have the will to push Polly away. The thought of being separated from her aroused in him a feeling he had not often experienced but easily recognized. But this was a fear of a different kind.

Reaching the attachment point of the harpoon, Tack located two of the adhesive mines to serve as footholds for both himself and Polly. Then he heard a scrabbling and droning noise in the chute's throat as Nandru-Wasp tried to find purchase there. He observed the robot finally gain a foothold, then with its four spiked legs begin to advance up the pipe. It covered four metres before, with a screeching of metal being peeled up by its foot spikes, it slid back down. This had been no part of any plan.

'Stay there, Nandru – the noise you're making might carry above,' he whispered urgently.

Nandru managed to drive his spikes into the metal and hold his position. Tack detached the harpoon and fired it further up the slope again.

Cowl returned from studying his vorpal controls, utterly unreadable. Aconite glanced across to where Makali stood, then scanned around the chamber to where the woman's pet killers were positioned. Having lost the source of his power to manipulate time inside this sphere, Cowl's paranoia was showing. Aconite then glanced over at the chute down which Cowl had been tossing human remains for the best part of a century. With the manacles around her wrists and ankles she stood no chance of reaching that escape route, but she was sure she had heard something . . .

Aconite now turned her attention fully on her brother. 'It has been a stupid and destructive conflict – Umbrathane and Heliothane killing each other over centuries in the solar system and now throughout time,' she said, pushing herself back so she rested on her knees. 'I don't know which side could be judged the more guilty, as now most of them have been born to this conflict and know no different. But I do know who is guilty of most killing – and that's you, Brother dear.'

'Our war has been defensive!' Makali objected, stepping forward.

'Yes,' Aconite hissed. 'I've witnessed some of your defensive moves. I saw exactly how you defended yourself by beating a prehuman to death. What threat to you was Ygrol?'

Cowl halted before Aconite and crossed his arms. His voice then issued, as it always seemed to, from the very air around him, 'Where are the other two?'

'What do you think you'll obtain from them? A way of retrieving your creature? A way of instantly rebuilding your power sources? Face it, Brother, your run is over and now it's time to take yourself to the only place that will remain safe for you.'

'Where *are* they?' Cowl snarled.

'What? Would you like Makali to do a bit more defending for you? Haven't you caused enough death already? In making you, our mother thought to create a human nonpareil. Instead she only made a killer of humans. I *know* you, Brother.'

Cowl's arms unfolded and dropped to his sides. It was coming now, Aconite felt – now he would kill her. Then suddenly the lights went out and the glow of a catalyser ignited high up in one side of the sphere. On the opposing side a hole blew in through it, hurling an umbrathant off the adjacent walkway, his clothing on fire. Then two more catalysers ignited, their fuse-paper glow spreading out from a central point, incandescent dust billowing in from the burning edges. Momentarily, a glimpse of a big man diving through, a stuttering of fire, and two Umbrathane, struggling to don their masks, were slammed backwards through glowing debris. Another explosion and one of the heavy tubular transformers danced out of its support framework and began to topple. Cowl moved fast, half in a dive, towards his vorpal controls, and Aconite felt sinking dread. Then in a single bright flare a fast-acting catalyser opened a hole in the floor, and high in the sphere the bonding glow of a climbing harpoon was briefly visible. Then, rising up out of the floor on the harpoon's wire, came Meelan and Saphothere, back to back, each of them brandishing two carbines and spraying the interior of the sphere with fire. Aconite stared in horror at the holes growing in the sphere, and realized that snowing in was not the outfall of catalysis, but a white powder she recognized. And she knew what her brother intended.

'Stop him!' Aconite bellowed. 'He'll take us all down!'

Several shots slammed into Cowl's leg, dropping him before he reached his controls. Saphothere and Meelan detached five metres above the floor, then dropped and rolled for cover as return fire tracked their progress. Saphothere dived behind the fallen transformer, spraying fire behind him without even looking, his shots spinning one of Makali's killers in a wheel of breaking flesh, then a shield generator he had dropped activated behind him a microsecond later to absorb other returned fire. Meelan paused to take out an umbrathant who was now targeting

Saphothere, and didn't see the source of the projectile that smacked into the back of her neck, blowing most of it away and dropping her bonelessly to the floor.

'Meelan!' came the anguished shout from Coptic.

Yet another explosion separated a walkway from the dissolving wall and it swung out, Coptic standing on the end of it, shooting at the Umbrathane with both a carbine and his missile launcher. Returned sniping cut away one of his legs, and he shattered the source of that on the floor below. Other shots slammed into his torso, but he absorbed them and kept on firing. Umbrathane died one after another, explosions tearing them away from walkways or blowing them in tatters from whatever concealment they had found. He kept up this barrage until both weapons were empty; then the two remaining Umbrathane came out of cover and concentrated a fusillade on him. Eventually he went down, then toppled from the walkway as it jerked to a halt at the end of its arc.

Aconite kept her head down and dragged herself towards the slope leading down to the disposal chute, but a hand grabbed the back of her jacket and hauled her upright, a prosthetic arm looping around her neck and the snout of a carbine now pressing against her cheek. Holding this human shield, Makali gazed over to where Saphothere had concealed himself.

'Saphothere, you're finished now!' she shouted.

Looking round, she saw her two comrades aiming their weapons down at the fallen transformer.

Aconite directed her attention to her brother, and saw the bullet holes through his carapace and that he was up by his vorpal controls, trailing his shattered leg. In one hand he held a small remote key, which he now pointed towards Aconite and activated. Then he discarded the key and plunged his hand into a glistening sphere.

'No!' Makali exclaimed, her attention swinging towards Cowl.

Aconite felt the magnetic lock snicking open. She looked up into the fall of white powder, then, as the manacles dropped away, drove her elbow back hard into Makali, and as the umbrathant bowed over, snatched away her weapon and sent it skittering across the floor. Now someone fired up from the chute, and one of the two Umbrathane went down on his knees, smoke pouring from his front. Saphothere stood up and tracked the second one in his flight across a walkway, blowing away pieces of him – so he never made it to cover. Aconite turned and drove her knee up into Makali's face, flinging her upright, her face a ruin. She turned back to her brother.

From the surrounding air his voice issued in a hissing whisper, as shields activated between him and Saphothere. 'Go.'

She could see his hand in the vorpal spheroid, manipulating, moving. Aconite turned to where Tack stood beside the chute with his back against the wall, his weapon directed towards Cowl, and Polly on the other side of the chute, her handgun pointed at Makali. Almost casually, using the back of her larger hand, Aconite struck Makali, sending her sprawling, then stepped down towards the slope. She slid down and caught the edge, her bigger hand closing vicelike on the lip.

'We have to get out of here, fast,' she said. 'How did you get here?'

'Wasp-Nandru,' Polly replied.

'Carries the weight of two, at a push,' muttered Aconite.

Tack observed the current scene: Makali crawling brokenly along the floor; Cowl at his vorpal controls, operating shield generators set in the floor; Saphothere walking around outside the shields as they were flung up, then moving closer as their generators burnt out. Their number had to be finite and Tack knew that Saphothere was a tenacious killer.

'You two first,' said Tack, nodding back at the chute.

Aconite did not give Polly time to protest: she reached out, grabbed the girl's ankle and tugged her yelling towards her, then sent her down the chute.

'We've got twenty minutes at most, then this place is gone,' said Aconite. 'I'll send the dead soldier back for you.' She dived into the chute after Polly.

'Saphothere!' Tack yelled. 'There's no time!'

The man who had hunted and killed Umbrathane most of his life and who, Tack realized, must have dreamed of this moment for much of that period, did not even look round.

'Damn,' said Tack, firing his harpoon into the floor at his feet, then himself dropping down the chute, a friction setting on the winder controlling his descent. When he reached the opening above the sea, it was just in time to see Nandru-Wasp carrying a heavy load to the shore, sometimes skimming the surface of the water, then rising up again.

Twenty minutes before what?

Tack supposed Cowl had placed some kind of destructive device inside the citadel, probably atomic, probably powerful enough to vaporize the citadel right down to the bedrock – lunatics always provided that kind of an out. Tack was now standing balanced on two adhesive mines with his harpoon wound back into its launcher, wondering if the wasp-robot would return for him – when Makali slid down the chute and slammed into him.

One mine gave way, spinning off out into the air, but this was enough to absorb Makali's momentum, so that when they both fell it was down to the ledge below rather than out past it. Scrabbling to gain traction, they sent stray bones spilling down into the sea. Tack dropped his harpoon launcher and tried to bring his carbine to bear, but Makali successfully knocked it aside and stabbed her fingers at his eyes. He ducked, sliding out a leg to drive his boot into her shin. She toppled, but forwards onto him, driving her forehead into his nose. He then hook-punched her in the gut, but she drove down with her prosthetic arms, demonstrating their mechanical strength. He felt his carbine ripped away from him, and through tear-filled eyes saw that his launcher had fallen to lodge itself next to a half-crushed skull. Makali now tried to turn the carbine on him, but her feet slid out from under her, her shoulder thumping against the pillar as she fell towards Tack, shots punching a line of holes through rusting armour beside him. Tack rolled, grabbing up the launcher and firing it in one move. This close, the harpoon punched straight through her, bonding with a flash to the pillar behind. Still she tried to bring the carbine to bear on him. Tack hit fast wind, and let go of the launcher, which wound itself up to her torso, its flat snout crushing into the open wound the harpoon had already made. She shrieked as she was dragged back against the wall, yet managed to fire the carbine again. Tack rolled off the ledge with her shots scoring the air above him. He had no time to turn his fall into a dive – as sharp metallic legs closed around him in mid air.

Running along the shore, Polly looked back up, but, unable to see either Nandru-Wasp or the citadel through the dustfall, she hurried to catch up with Aconite. The dust now fell so thickly it formed conglomerated flakes. Polly glanced over at the water, at the slow roll of the waves humping up the beach, and in the confusion of the moment it took her a second to understand that there was something strange about these waves: they seemed too sluggish and produced little foam; they had the appearance not of sea water waves but of ripples in a thickening soup. Along the strand there now accumulated a mound of gelatinous fragments.

'What is that?' She pointed, as she came up beside Aconite, who did not seem in good shape.

'Hydroscopic,' Aconite said, pausing to press one hand against her blood-leaking ear.

The meaning of the word flowed easily to Polly from the Muse 184 reference, access to it, she had soon discovered, now so much easier without Nandru in the way. She stooped, picked up a handful of the dust, raised her mask, and spat into the gritty substance. The dust quickly absorbed her saliva; single grains expanding into gelatinous blobs a hundred times their original size.

'What is it?' she asked.

'The basis of Metazoan life – of us, too, eventually,' Aconite replied, as she set out again.

Soon they reached the estuary and ran along the bank of the river to where the water was shallowest. There they waded across through a thixotropic flow of jelly till they reached the other shore, knocking away blobs of the gelatinous substance clinging to their clothing. As they laboured up the hill, Nandru-Wasp thrummed overhead, bearing its new load.

'What . . . what is Cowl going to do?' Polly gasped.

Aconite did not have the breath to reply. She turned to Polly, then stumbled down on one knee. After Polly helped her up, they struggled on. Then a figure loomed out of the dust storm. Tack didn't hesitate: he grabbed Aconite and slung her over his shoulder, then turned and ran up towards the house. Polly was struggling to catch up and, reaching the door behind them, she looked back and caught a brief view of the citadel, a glow igniting underneath it – and spreading.

Once inside, Tack put Aconite down on her feet and she staggered over to lean against a table.

'Shut the door,' she rasped.

Polly did as instructed, stripping her mask off as she returned. Tack and Aconite removed their masks too.

Aconite turned to Nandru-Wasp, who was squatting amid the detritus of her home. 'Can you find the generator start-up code?'

'I should think so,' Nandru replied.

'Then start the fucking generators!'

After a pause, a low humming vibration permeated the house.

'Now turn on the vorpal feed.'

The tone of the hum changed, its pitch climbing in degrees until it escalated beyond human hearing. Polly felt again something of what she had experienced when she had shifted – a reminder of the last horrible stages of her journey into this past, a hint of the tor webwork in her flesh and bones and in the very air around her.

'That's the best we can do,' said Aconite, moving to a sofa and slumping down, to rest her head back and close her eyes.

'What's your brother doing?' Tack asked

With eyes still closed, Aconite said, 'My brother wanted to start again with a clean slate when he tried to avoid the omission paradox. He wiped out all pre-Nodus life on Earth by distributing a network of molecular catalysing engines across the ocean bottom. They do not destroy themselves like the weapons version, so that network still exists.'

'Why does that affect us? I don't understand,' Polly asked, sure she could now see glowing lines showing through the outer walls of the house.

Aconite's eyes snapped open. 'Where can my brother go now? Outside the Nodus the Heliothane will hunt him down. They'll never give up, no matter how inaccurate their vorpal jumping may be – he's too dangerous. The only place for him is to get beyond reach down the slope. So he has started those engines and the reaction will kill all nascent life existing in every drop of water on Earth – which would have had no temporal effect *before* this time. It won't end that nascent life because the dust will blow from land to sea. But enough of it will be wiped out for long enough, to shove him down to the bottom of the probability slope, where it starts here in the Nodus.'

'But then what, for him . . . for Saphothere?' Tack asked.

'Maybe there his alternate will slide into oblivion, maybe a new and distinct time-line will develop and create its own slopes. The strength of the paradox he is creating would have dragged us down with him, but here, with the vorpal skeleton of this house carrying a huge temporal charge, we may yet hold.'

'He's shooting his father,' observed Tack.

'Precisely,' Aconite replied. She waved towards the window, from which Cowl's citadel was visible. Polly moved over to it and Tack came up behind her. Through waves of falling dust they saw the citadel shimmering, the glow in the sea underneath it blooming and spreading to the horizon, and felt the tension drawing the air taut, as a whole world tried to fold away. The house now began to quake and Tack wrapped an arm around Polly's waist. Then suddenly light speared down through the citadel and began turning it into ineffable interspace. The house lurched in response to the turning, then juddered as if hit with a missile; fragments of wall material clattering down. Another violent wrench threw Polly and Tack to the floor, and sent things crashing down throughout the interior of the house.

Then stillness.

Tack helped Polly stand and they moved to the window. Cowl's citadel was gone, the glowing in the sea was gone. The dust storm was now settling.

A billion years in the future, in one possible future, a tachyon signal instantly caused thousands of displacement generators to switch on, where they had been placed on the ceramic shielding of thousands of giant antigravity motors. A second was all that was required, as in that second *everything* moved: sun, solar system, galaxy . . . Displaced spheres of tightly packed ceramo-composite components, sheered-off pure metal coils and optics, and silicon-controlling matrices appeared outside the motors, where their temperature rose some thousands of degrees. Metals burnt in bright primary colours, silicon melted, components shattered and the spheres flew apart. Down ducts wide enough to swallow Earth's moon, walls of fire travelled from these gaseous explosions. From outside, the sun tap blinked with a million stars as flame vented into the chromosphere and joined *that* fire.

With its antigravity motors no longer focusing and transmitting the candent energies below, the vast device now suffered the true brunt of its proximity to this fusion inferno. The ceramic materials of its construction were created to take huge temperatures, but not this. The underneath of the tap began to melt and ablate. For long minutes, like a drop of water dripped onto a hot plate, it skated on the vapour of its own destruction. It now glowed with an intensity as impossible for a human eye to view directly as were its surroundings. Then it distorted, structural plates the size of continents buckling and springing free. Now firestorms raged out through the gaps as further unprotected components, planetary in scale, felt the savage bite of the solar furnace. Then, as if the fiery elementals had tired of toying with this example of human hubris, gravity closed its fist and dragged the sun tap down into harsher flame. The only sign it left was a smear of cooler red on the sun's surface, and that lasted minutes only. And by then the back end of the microwave beam the sun tap had been transmitting reached New London and that vast source of power was cut off.

In the Abutment Chamber of New London, Heliothane soldiers watched in horror from behind the heat shields of their attack rafts as the fore of the torbeast fountained from the interface and treed out over them and came down: thousands of open mouths eager to rend and feed. Then light died as the power that kept apart the mono-singularities in the abutments shut down. It took less than a second for the three huge devices to slam together at a central point, severing this fraction of the monster that had shown itself, and incinerating much of it in the subsequent heat flash. The tree fell, writhing and burning, yet containing life still, and the Heliothane rafts attacked, cutting apart necks and smashing mouths, killing any of it that still moved.

The last shield generator burnt out, so nothing remained between Saphothere and Cowl. The Heliothane killer casually pointed his weapon at Cowl's torso and half expected to feel a lack of satisfaction in this moment, but he could not feel better about what he was going to do.

'You saw and felt the shift,' Cowl told him. 'We are now so far down the probability slope you will never again travel in time unless I can do something.'

Saphothere shrugged. He had seen interspace through the gaps in this control sphere and of course he had felt the shift. He was not sure what Cowl had done, but it seemed unlikely he was lying or that it could be undone. Saphothere was fatalistic about such things and, in his heart, had never expected to return from this last mission. He glanced across at the corpse of Meelan and then to the shattered remains of Coptic.

'And how should I respond to that?' he asked.

'You can survive here. There will be Umbrathane still alive in this citadel. We can build something.'

Yeah, thought Saphothere – now he knew Cowl was lying.

'Thing is,' he said, 'I was always better at destroying things.'

With improbable speed for one so injured, Cowl leapt towards him. Saphothere triggered his carbine, hitting the black shape in mid air and stepping aside as it flailed past him, smoking and with pieces of its carapace splintering away. Cowl hit the ground then writhed round, coming up into a crouch. Hissing, he opened his face. Saphothere concentrated his next shots into that and killed him there.

Saphothere briefly relished the moment, then went to pick up his second carbine from behind the fallen transformer. Touching the transformer's surface, he found it only warm, and seated himself there with his carbines resting beside him. He took out a hip flask containing the last of his stash of nineteenth-century whisky, and sipped at it. Then he waited for the Umbrathane to come.

The wormhole collapsed from both Sauros and New London. It took one and two-thirds years, it took all time and none. Like a hair singed at both ends by lighter flames, it contracted – huge forces closing it down to non-existence. Inside this contracting tube the torbeast raged against impenetrable surfaces – utterly confined in a self-referencing universe – without alternates on which to feed, without even time – and, in that infinite moment, the vast forces of this collapsing universe closed down on the beast's leviathan mass. But the Heliothane plan to crush this monstrosity out of existence failed, in the end, as mass and force found balance.

To human perception, motionless in interspace, rested a perfect black sphere nearly a kilometre in diameter.

Inside this the torbeast howled.

Forever.

Epilogue

Sauros was a radioactive ruin and the surrounding area uninhabitable. Only three mantisals had survived the battle, sitting nearby, a hundred and eighty degrees out of phase. One of them was dying, much of its complex internal workings wrecked by the EM pulse from a tactical nuke directed against the torbeast. Six survivors were chosen to take the remaining two uptime, and with luck return to New London. Their journey would be long and dangerous as, without the energy feed from the wormhole, their jumps would be short and they and their mantisals would require long intervening rests. It would take them over twenty time-jumps. However, they were envied by the other survivors, which was why Goron had made their selection utterly random and why he and Palleque had discounted themselves from it. Those who remained then had to move to safety.

The march through the mountains to find a cleaner environment had cost the lives of eight survivors, but the Engineer felt certain they would have died anyway, so severe were their injuries. No lives were lost to the local fauna, with Silleck and the other interface technicians keeping an eye on the immediate future. There had, in fact, been only the one attack from a small pack of carnosaurs, most of which had ended up suffering the same fate they had intended for their human prey. The creatures had tasted of chicken.

As he fed a large worm onto his hook, Goron gazed across at the city of tents now occupying the river valley they had selected. He was glad to see that it was slowly transforming into something more permanent, which he hoped meant that most of the survivors had now accepted their fate – to live and die here – though some things he had recently overheard made him doubt that.

Palleque had managed to rig a catalyser to fuse sand dug from the river bottom, and by using wooden moulds was producing building blocks and slabs. He was even managing to produce sheets of rough glass, and claimed he would soon be able to do better. His industriousness had helped greatly to eliminate the distrust many heliothants felt for him. Others were prospecting for ores which could be catalysed into pure metals. Still others hunted, while some were clearing the level ground lower down for the planting of crops, once seed suitable for that purpose was gathered.

'Power generation within a month,' promised Palleque, not taking his gaze off the float he had cast out into the deep pool they were sitting by.

'You're optimistic,' Goron replied.

'As soon as we obtain the required rare metals, I'll be able to use the catalyser to produce photovoltaic cells – probably in sufficient number to tile the roofs of the houses we build.'

'I thought you meant real power,' said Goron.

Palleque turned to him. 'About a year still before we can build generators and they'll only be driven by steam, wind or water.'

'So by then we should have a nice viable mini-civilization going here.'

'You don't sound very enthusiastic.'

'I *am* enthusiastic about that, but not about some of the other things I've been hearing – about our building a base for vorpal technology and eventually managing to go home.'

'People need hope.'

'Hope I don't mind, but when that moves into the region of blind faith I start to get a little edgy. You know as well as I that, at the present rate of progress, it would probably take us a century to build the technological base for any useful form of time travel, by which time the building of such a base would have forced us so far down the probability slope we'd never possess the required power sources to travel anyway.'

'There are other reasons for hope,' said Silleck, who had just climbed up onto the same slab of rock.

'And they would be?' asked Goron, turning to regard her. He was worried about this woman, as he was about all the other interface technicians like her. All of them were turning quite strange, with their constant four-dimensional view of the world.

'To learn that,' said Silleck, 'I suggest the both of you get off this slab quickly before you get crushed to death.'

Goron peered past her and saw how the other interface technicians were gathering some distance back, and that other heliothants were filtering down from the tent city to join them. Both Palleque and he hit the winders on their rods, then quickly followed the technician from the slab. When Silleck suggested something, it was best to do it quickly because you knew she was looking at the consequences of you not doing so.

'What's happening, Silleck?' Goron asked.

'We are finding we can feel and see things . . . deeper, further . . . and we have sensed this coming for some time. At first we couldn't be sure, as there's a lot of echoes and aftershocks disturbing interspace. But now we are sure – this is solid.'

Goron felt this explanation turbid at best, but turned his attention to the vacated rock slab, on which all the technicians were now concentrating. Silleck suddenly grinned and some of her fellows laughed out loud. That was the thing about the lot of them – you could never tell a joke in their presence, as they would always know the punchline before you said it. A minute after, a line of light speared down into the centre of the slab's surface, and out of it folded a great domed house, its walls and roof cracked and flaking away to expose its vorpal superstructure. First, out of an arched entrance, emerged a large insectile robot that Goron instantly recognized, so he figured who was going to step out next. This second figure was closely guarded by a Roman soldier, who fingered the pommel of his gladius as he eyed the spectators.

'I've found you at last, Engineer,' said Aconite.

'So you have,' Goron replied.

Aconite looked around. 'I have the means to transport those who want to go, back to New London. But I also have an alternative proposal.'

'I'm listening,' said Engineer Goron.

While Polly gazed up at the aircars in the far distance over Maldon Island, Tack studied their surroundings.

The nettles were dead and dry in the cavity walls and the grass was brown and crunched underfoot. There had been a temporary over-flood, and crab carapaces were scattered like confetti on the grass. A U-gov clean-up team had been here to remove the corpses, and the carcass of the Ford Macrojet that Nandru had destroyed. The only evidence now of what had happened was the scorched vegetation and some shattered trees. Closing his eyes, Tack sensed the temporal web inside himself, located their position in time, and their position on the probability slope.

'This is a week after the moment of our departure,' he said. 'Are you sure this is where we want to be?'

'Aconite wanted us to establish a base in this time,' Polly replied, her expression distant.

Tack turned to her. 'Her idea of "this time" covers about a thousand years – she thinks on a different scale.'

'Now is good enough,' said Polly.

He watched her run her hand over her new tor. Their travel by tor was limited by dangers of which they were both now well aware. But still they *could* travel in time.

'I don't see what's so great about this . . . now,' Tack said.

'It's convenient,' said Polly. 'Nandru told me certain bank codes, and where to locate certain chipcards. And with fifty million euros available, establishing Aconite's base won't be so difficult.'

Tack nodded. When he first met her, she would have been ecstatic to be able to lay her hands on such a sum. Now she merely looked ruminative.

'What is it?' he asked.

She gestured at their surroundings. 'It's here. It'll always be here: layers and layers of it, millions upon millions of years. We're so small.'

'That's called perspective.' Tack then nodded towards Maldon Island. 'Let's go.'